Voice to the Voiceless
The Power of People's Theatre in India

Jacob Srampickal

HURST & COMPANY, LONDON

ST. MARTIN'S PRESS, NEW YORK

© Jacob Srampickal, 1994

First Published in the United Kingdom by
C. Hurst & Co. (Publishers) Ltd.,
38 King Street, London WC2E 8JT,
and in the United States of America by
St. Martin's Press, Inc.,
Scholarly and Reference Division,
175 Fifth Avenue, New York, NY 10010
by arrangement with
Manohar Publishers & Distributors
2/6 Ansari Road, Daryaganj
New Delhi 110002, India
All rights reserved.

ISBNs
1-85065-199-X (Hurst)
0-312-10359-X (St. Martin's)

Library of Congress Cataloging-in-Publication Data

Srampickal, Jacob.
    Voice to the Voiceless : the power of people's theatre in India /
by Jacob Srampickal.
        p. cm.
    Includes bibliographical references and index.
    ISBN 0-312-10359-X
    1. Theater–India, 2. Folk drama, Indic–History and criticism.
3. Street theater–India. 4. Theater and society–India.
5. Community development–India. I. Title
PN2884. S73 1994
792'. 0954–dc20   93–32576
                                                                          CIP

Printed in India

Contents

Contents

Acknowledgements

This book is a modified version of my thesis submitted to the University of Leeds for the degree of doctor of philosophy.

There are several people to whom I am deeply indebted in the writing of the dissertation. Prof. Martin Banham, my guide, in spite of his heavy schedule as the Head of the Department of Theatre at the University of Leeds, always found time to help me clarify my thoughts. Every hour spent with him enlightened me. I thank him for his guidance, and above all, for his faith in me.

At various times Michael Etherton and Dr. Robert White of the Centre for the Study of Communication and Culture (CSCC), London, enlightened me with their own expertise in the field of theatre and communication in developing countries. Michael and Mary were more than professional friends. The staff and visitors at CSCC inspired many a thought. Others like David Kerr of the University of Malawi, Anuradha Kapur of the National School of Drama, New Delhi and the late G. Shanakarapillai of the University of Calicut were very co-operative in listening to my thesis schema and in guiding me.

A special word of thanks is due to all the groups in India, the street theatre and action groups, who shared their vision with me and furnished me with the necessary data. Among others, I cannot forget the commitment and generosity of Rati Bartholomew, Tripurari Sharma, Badal Sircar, Poornachandra Rao and Felix Sugirtharaj. They saved me many hours that I would otherwise have spent in tracing unimportant pieces of information.

At the Workshop Theatre in the University a number of students helped me at various times. I remember Jumai, Oga, Ozie, Vayu and Yucef with gratitude. Brian helped me greatly in shaping my ideas and polishing the English. I thank them.

The Missiological Institute, Aachen, Germany supported me with the finances for undertaking the study; I thank them for their generosity.

There are several friends who made my lonely life in my 'step-motherland' memorable. Some showed keen interest in discussing theatre with me. All of them may consider themselves remembered, even in

anonymity. The small commune at the Catholic Chaplaincy consisting of
Sr. Jeanette and Frs. Brian and Frank offered an outlet. Cecilia and her
parents were a source of friendship and inspiration.

I remember with great joy and gratitude the Sisters of Our Lady of the
Mission at the Burley Road Convent who put up with my 'theotrics'. They
and their many friends gave me the spiritual strength to keep going during
my three years' stay with them.

I also remember with gratitude Felix Abraham, Anand P. Lal and
Joseph Surin who helped with the final editing.

Introduction

India is one of the few countries in the world where people are classified into castes,[1] some of which are regarded as inherently inferior or superior to others. Caste consciousness, sanctioned by Hinduism, permeates all aspects of life–social, economic, cultural and religious. Those at the lowest rung, about 15% of the population, are the downtrodden, the untouchables or Harijans, despised by all and devoid of any opportunity to rise up in society. In spite of several government Acts to abolish the caste system, the vast majority of untouchables continue to suffer discrimination in everyday life with some encountering physical violence from those who consider themselves inherently superior.

A bitter pill in the Indian cup of misery is the lack of education among a large portion of the people. In spite of the Indian Constitution acknowledging the right of all to education (Directive Principles, Article 41) and the government's attempts at compulsory elementary education and adult literacy, India now has a literacy rate of only 40%. Again the poorer people in the villages lag behind. In the government's planning for rural education, the reasons for the low school attendance have not been properly considered.

Another malaise that eats up the soul of independent India is communalism. Britain divided Bengal in 1905 and India in 1947 on religious grounds. Since then the Muslims and Hindus have not been fully at peace with each other. Communal conflicts have rocked the country time and again. Terrorism unleashed for the first time during the British regime has continued unabated. Along with communalism other discriminatory evils like provincialism, regionalism and religious fundamentalism have resulted in relentless guerilla warfare bordering on civil war.

Abject destitution has led to the dehumanization of the masses and has brought about a state of inertia. The level of public cynicism, particularly among the few enlightened rural masses is such that they overlook gross abuses of public law and order and turn a deaf ear to calls for unity. Psychologically, they are a brow-beaten group forced to acquiesce in their lower caste origins and impoverished upbringing, which they understand as self-inflicted agonies from which they can never recover.

Corruption has seeped into every level of activity in the country. The growth of an enormous number of intermediaries in every sphere has enhanced this phenomenon. Each year the government allots large amounts of money for development but hardly anything reaches the villages. The bulk of the people are caught in a grim battle for survival. They have been effectively stifled by injustice, oppression and exploitation of all kinds. Exploitative situations like bonded labour, child labour and low wages are widespread in the villages. Villagers live in fear of their oppressors, ever afraid of reprisals if they dare to raise their voices. They are too weak to protest and if they protest they are silenced, . They have been forced to internalize their oppressors' ideology and hence to accept a subservient passive role, "a culture of silence".[2] Poverty, illiteracy and ignorance have made them tools in the hands of bureaucracy that professes to work for their development. In a situation of such fear and suspicion they have neither the will nor the leadership to become organized. Can the creative use of drama be a method to organize, educate, strengthen and develop them?

Theatre

In India there is a lively performative tradition from time immemorial. The literary tradition dates back to the origins of classical Sanskrit drama in the early 4th century BC as early as the Greek tradition. In the towns and villages of India the yearly round of religious, agricultural or civic festivals are largely centred around performances of religious pageants, hired folk opera groups, local balladeers, song and dance teams and political plays. Each state or region proudly boasts of its varieties of folk theatre.

For over 3,000 years, however, India has absorbed the cultural life and performative influences of Greek, Persian, Turkish, and other invaders. When the British brought their own strong theatre tradition to Calcutta and other centres, the anglicised elite quickly took to Shakespearean and contemporary English drama. This influence may be seen even now in the use of Western conventional theatre forms even in the villages. While the West has tended to cast its communication in rhetorical, persuasive discourse and in more denotative written and print media, in India a much more connotative, symbolic, mythic and narrative discourse of performance has continued to be central. While Western theatre fragmented into opera, ballet and drama based on dialogue, Indian theatre maintains a composite form of singing, dancing, verse, prose dialogue, and rhetorical speech with elements of social criticism.

Theatre and Development

Even from the early Sanskrit tradition theatre has been used to analyse and examine social issues. Folk theatre excelled in publicly admonishing evil-doers in society. During the middle ages the *Bhakti*[3] cult used theatre to attack superstitious practices. In the early 19th century, theatre became an important tool for conscientizing the people against colonial rule. As the national independence movement developed after 1850, many of the plays written for the numerous theatres of Calcutta and other cities risked British censorship with vigorous themes of cultural and political nationalism. Gandhi himself emerged a master of dramatic symbolic action as he ventured to create a new Indian socio-political culture.

In 1941 the founding of Indian People's Theatre Association (IPTA) with the direct aim of developing rural audiences, gave an impetus to the development of theatre. The street theatre movement evolved directly from the explosion of radical political theatre in the late 1940s and went on to dramatize the injustices of capitalist and caste exploitation.

Today it is not surprising to find that social action groups, health and agricultural educationists, student activists, political parties, religious reform groups and many other movements have gravitated towards some form of dramatic, performative communication.

The government, too, has been active in using theatre for development work. However, as will be made clear later, most of the themes of these plays are reformative like birth control, use of fertilizers, health care and so on. More importantly, the forceful 'top-down' teaching of these messages through didactic plays completely undermine the people's ability to learn for themselves.

Chapter I analyses the concept of development, the meaning of developing awareness and conscientization and the parameters of theatre. Chapter II focuses on people's theatre and presents a brief outline of Popular Theatre for development worldwide. Chapter III studies the Popular Theatre of India–the folk theatre. It examines how the cultural affinities of the people surface in folk performances. Even while accepting that the forms maintained a reactionary temperament, some attempts at challenging them are highlighted along with their major characteristics. Later in Chapter IV it will be seen that this protest element and several of the characteristics are carried into street and social action theatre groups, which goes to show that they are in continuity with the folk tradition in a changed socio-political situation.

Chapters IV and V are descriptive studies of the street theatre movements and theatre as used by social action groups. Instead of studying a particular group or a performance the effort has been to highlight the movements, their various features and significance, as political media for raising the consciousness of the people.

Chapter VI tries to present a critique of these two forms of Popular Theatre and suggests ways and means to improve them. Assuming that social action groups' theatre is the ideal form for conscientization and development, a systematic way of implementing it as a tool is suggested. Other models of Popular Theatre are also examined.

It is suggested that theatre by the people about their own problems using sound theatre techniques and indigenous elements can in itself be a means for them to become involved in social awareness building activities

Notes

1. According to *Manusmriti* (an ancient Hindu law book) there are four castes: *Brahmins* (priests), *Kshatriyas* (warriors), *Vaishyas* (traders) and *Shudras* (lowly workers). Brahmins are to be worshipped as gods regardless of their worth, while Shudras are to accept their lowly status and not aspire to learning or to any function except that of serving their superiors.

2. A term used by Freire to denote the total non-involvement of the poorer classes in nation-building activities. This is studied at length later.

3. The *Bhakti* movement was a wave of devotional fervour that swept India in the 10th century. It protested against religious formalism and priestly domination, insisting on the accessibility of God to everyone. Stressing the importance of inner experience and attacking purely external practices and pious hypocrisy, it denounced the caste system and found saints among minorities, women and untouchables.

I

Development and the Parameters of Theatre

The concept of development has undergone radical changes in the past two decades. Today there are several theories of development. Each of them highlights a different aspect although all of them include vague features like commitment to the goals of economic growth, social justice and the creation of an egalitarian society.

I. The Concept of Development

Humankind has always developed in the sense of having evolved better ways of exploring the natural environment for their own benefit thus making life less hazardous. Each country developed in its own way, according to its own local ecological and environmental variables. During the 11th and 12th centuries these finely tuned social systems suffered disruptions when Christians waged Crusades against the 'pagan' Moslems in the Middle East, paving the way for less altruistic missions in search of gold, silver, spices, silk and other valuables. European sea-adventurers began 'voyages of discovery' to the Americas and the East. Looting brought wealth to Europe and fired mercantile trade which changed world economies between 1500-1770. Vast treasure troves of gold and silver from the Spanish Americas and slave trade from other parts of the world was the impetus behind the subsequent Industrial Revolution and the birth of capitalism. This led to rapid economic growth and accumulation of wealth in the West. The consolidation of economic imperialism in the 20th century permitted decolonization, although the newly independent countries remained undeveloped.

Concept of Development in the Colonial Structures

In the context of colonialism, economic development was determined by power and control over wealth and resources. Development of colonial powers depended on the efficiency of invasion, pillage or unequal barter. This system continued to evolve even after colonisation has ended. Colonial control and the hierarchy of privileges induced the local elite to accept European cultural values and also perpetuated the imbalance of power in society. In this way Western values were internalized and economic neo-colonialism flourished resulting in the oppression of the weaker sections of society. It is in this context that theorists like Fanon and Myrdal described the third world as the world which was discovered, invaded, subjugated, governed, deculturalized and educated by the foreigners. Fanon captures the essence of colonial strategies.

The effect commonly sought by colonialism was to drive into the native's heads the idea that if the settlers were to leave they would at once fall back into barbarism, degradation and brutality.... Cultural obliteration is made possible by the negation of national reality, by new legal relations introduced by the occupying power, by the banishment of the natives and their customs to outlying districts by expropriation and by the systematic enslaving of men and women.[1]

Again, colonial control did not stimulate industrial growth. Ward points this out in the case of India.

Nothing is more illustrative of the degree to which Western colonial policy did not stimulate local industry than the comparison between independent Japan and India which was under British control through-out the crucial 19th century and early 20the century. Japan was the only Asian country to be absolutely free of colonial intervention and was also the first Asian country to make a thorough industrial breakthrough.[2]

Thus it can be argued that colonialism overthrew the necessary conditions for a country's steady development. Cultural imperialism, as Goonatilake shows, has been the most destructive.

The European expansion of the last five hundred years with its different economic thrusts corresponding roughly to mercantilist, industrial and present neo-colonial ones resulted in the throwing of a near complete cultural blanket over almost all the world. The cultural blanket has suppressed local cultures, local arts, local systems of valid and relevant science and has resulted in a virtual cultural genetic wipe out. Diversity and originality, arts and ideas which are not of European origin are vanishing and culture is getting packaged, served in a plastic form as the hegemonic machine of European culture moves forward.[3]

This explains why it was one of the cherished dreams of the British Empire in India "to create a class of people who would be Indian in blood and colour but English in taste, opinions, values and intellect"[4] during her two centuries of domination of the subcontinent.

Today the developing world, still under the influence of neo-colonialism is confronted with a number of problems, the most serious of which is the ever widening gulf between a small minority of the rich who have all the amenities of a first world country and are mainly responsible for governing the country, and the vast majority who do not even have the basic necessities of life. Illiteracy, discrimination, exploitation, corruption have so debilitated the rural poor that they have lost their sense of dignity and worth.

It is against this background that various theories of development need to be considered.

Modernization Theory

The emphasis of this theory as propounded by Weber, Durkheim, Tonnies and Spencer is on economic growth and productivity. Underlying this idea is the way in which the Western world was transformed from a traditional to a modern society, that is, from an agrarian to an industrial civilization, with advances in science and technology and a rise in the standard of living of the people. So development implied the bridging of the gap between the rich and the poor nations by means of an imitative process, in which the less developed countries gradually assumed the qualities of the industrialised nations. In practice modernization envisages a gradual transition from tradition to modernity and considers the stage achieved by the industrialised countries as the ideal. In its more simplistic form the modernization paradigm served as a development ideology that rationalised cultural colonialism. Other proponents of the theory like Eisenstadt and McClelland saw underdevelopment ahistorically, in terms of a culture of poverty in which the deprived and disadvantaged were seen as inherently deficient in achievement and motivations and afflicted with characteristics such as conservatism, fatalism and traditionalism. They argued that through the infusion of Western values and attitudes and the imitation of Western patterns, institutions and paradigms, developing countries would emerge out of their stagnancy and inertia.[5]

According to this model, development will flow almost automatically from capital accumulation—i.e. saving and investment. Hence there was stress on foreign aid and foreign trade. After the second World War, the USA emerged politically and economically strong and initiated this kind of development through the Marshall Plan to reconstruct Europe and by establishing World Bank and International Monetary Fund to provide loans to the developing world. The creation of the UN and its agencies like FAO and UNCTAD, and well as humanitarian bodies like the Ford and Rockefeller Foundations, may also be seen as means to implement these policies. Through a variety of means, including loans and technical assistance and the diffusion of information and technology, these institutions propagated a Western vision of development based on increased productivity and the virtues of a consumer society.

Dependency Theory

Obviously modernization of this sort has not only failed to close the gap between the haves and have-nots, but has widened it and has spread Western culture and the values of a consumer society throughout the developing world. For example, the Green Revolution in India brought about by the use of high yielding seeds, fertilizers and pesticides led to the pauperization of the small peasant. Myrdal argued that since the attitudes towards life, work and institutions in developing countries are fundamentally different from those of the Western world, it is futile to analyse these societies using Western economic concepts.[6] There was dissatisfaction in many parts of the developing world that modernization perpetuated colonial values through the spread of multinational corporations and other ramifications of international capitalism. The formation of the OPEC oil cartel, the development models in China, Cuba and Tanzania, the emphasis on neutrality and non-alignment and the growing voice of developing countries in international bodies demonstrated the desire of developing countries to protect their interests and safeguard their sovereignty. The call for a New International Economic

Order (UNCTAD, 1974) reflected the mood of the times.

An important landmark in the development of dependency theory was the discovery of the concept of imperialism in the works of Lenin, Bukharin, Trotsky and others. Lenin argued that the phenomenon of imperialism was rooted in the very fabric of capitalism. It arose, he said, because of a declining rate of profit in the capitalistic countries and hence the need to invest in the untapped colonial regions of the world to maximise profits.

Andre Gunder Frank who first proposed the dependency theory pointed out the colonial and neo-colonial dimensions of underdevelopment and blamed the theorists of modernisation for being ahistorical and ethnocentric. He observed:

> Once a country or a people is converted into the satellite of an external capitalist metropole, the exploitative metropolitan satellite structure quickly comes to organize and dominate the economic, political and social life of that people.[7]

According to him, the concept of development as proposed by the modernisation theorists was an attempt to replicate Western institutions and ways of life at the expense of autonomous growth and indigenous solutions. He argued that developing countries were forced into an international capitalist framework of relationships which reinforced conditions of dependency and unequal development. He pointed out that the nature of aid and capitalist relationship in general was exploitative and involved a process by which surplus was siphoned off from the developing countries to the developed.

Explaining the concept of dependency, Raul Prebisch divided the world into two distinct spheres— the centre and the periphery. According to him the real reason for underdevelopment was the stranglehold exerted by the developed capitalist countries over the international commodity markets and the unequal terms of exchange offered to the periphery nations. In essence, Western capitalism had developed at the expense of the underdeveloped world.[8]

The impact of the dependency theory was strong. It undermined the idea of progress as a more or less automatic and linear process, replaced the idealized and mechanical vision of development by a more historical method and shifted the focus to the particular conditions and contradictions affecting the development process. Governments like Allende's Chile, Manley's Jamaica and Nyerere's Tanzania were deeply influenced by this perspective. However, there are some basic weaknesses in the approach. It is mainly negative and lacks a positive theory of development. Stress is laid on the external obstacles to development and the problem of how to initiate a development process is neglected. The self–reliant national path it proposed is too inward looking. For, whether only likes it or not, there are possibilities of development within the capitalist world economy.

Freire's Theory of Conscientization

The flaws in the paradigms of development discussed above have led to a number of alternative theories. The model that stands out and has influenced the developing world most is Freire's approach of conscientization. He used concepts like values and ethics, quality of life and fullness of life to define development, and pointed out that development is more than economic growth and productivity or class struggle. According to him human growth toward the fullness of life marks the essence of development. Freire believed that development implies liberation, namely a freeing from the mental and physical shackles of existence within a "culture of silence" to the humanization of self as part of the community. Authentic development is a process whereby through an intense process of learning, characterized by the twin elements of action and reflection, the oppressed as a class confront and overcome the culture of domination and create meaningful alternatives for their own future.[9]

It was in the mid-sixties that Freire's work among the marginalised in Brazil began to attract the attention of social activists in the developing countries. His methodology, variously called "education to critical consciousness", "consciousness raising" or "conscientization", is based on a philosophy that relies heavily on the capabilities of the people to understand, learn and act using indigenous resources in a way that can change the course of history.

Coming from a lower middle class family, Freire from his early days, had experienced the reality of oppression in its political, economic and cultural forms. His writings show a steady growth in his thinking–from a reformist and liberal democratic stance in *Education and the Practice of Freedom* (1967) to revolutionary Marxist humanism in the *Pedagogy of the Oppressed* (1978). His involvement in adult literacy programmes with villagers in Brazil, Chile and Guinea Bissau helped him to test his theories in practice. The development of Freire's thinking is not an isolated phenomenon. The influence of Marxist thinking and analysis of society based on haves and have-nots, the unequal relationship between the ownership of the means of production and the producer is self evident. Philosophies of personalism and existentialism as exemplified in the writings of Gandhi, Mao, Alinsky, Eric Fromm, Martin Buber, Jean Paul Sartre, Victor Frankl and social revolutionaries like Che Guevara, Amilcar Cabral are discernible in Freire's eclectic philosophy.

Faced with a situation of imperialism and socio-political oppression in Brazil in the early sixties, Freire and his colleagues began to organize discussions on nationalism, development, illiteracy and democracy in their literacy classes. The introduced these concepts with pictures from everyday life. Amazed with the participation of the people in the discussions, Freire realized that for adults, learning to read and write can also be a process of analysing reality and of becoming critically aware of their situation. He noticed that the people live in a 'culture of silence' or ape the dominant culture that is forced on them. They believed in fatalism and attributed their condition to God's will. To change this attitude Freire introduced the anthropological concept of culture and insisted that people are the makers of their own culture, that change is possible if people work for it. His literacy programme was ultimately aimed at what he called conscientization, a process that would enable the marginalised people to learn to perceive social, political, and economic contradictions, and to fight against oppression. Action and reflection were not separate activities but an organic whole. It is the dialectical interplay between action and reflection that constitutes the process of conscientization. There is a denunciation of the old order with its myths, dependencies, and false consciousness and an announcing of the new order based on equality, freedom, political and economic rights. Conscientization is clearly a step beyond consciousness raising. For Freire, it needs to lead to participation, solidarity and collective action for liberation.

Freire's philosophy is based on the axiom that a human being's historical vocation is to become free from psychological and material oppression. Liberation is the central goal, and revolutionary pedagogy is the means. The liberation of the individual and the community comes through self-sustaining efforts, growth in individual awareness and community consciousness that evolve out of a process of learning. For Freire, all individuals have the capacity for reflection, abstract thinking, conceptualising, taking decisions, choosing alternatives and for planning social change. The task of the revolutionary educator is to equip the oppressed with a heightened sense of consciousness of the different forces at work in society.

Freire is critical of traditional forms of education. For him education is either liberating or domesticating. That is, it either teaches people to be critical and be free of constraints or to accept life as it is. This theory, he claims, is not limited to problems of adult literacy alone. He calls the traditional academic education a 'banking system ' and proposes a problem posing method. In the banking system, he points out, the teacher student relationship involves a narrating subject (teacher) and patient, listening objects (students). The contents of such narration tend, in the process of narrating, to become lifeless and petrified, whether they are values or empirical dimensions of reality. Essentially the characteristic of this method is the non-participation of the recipients of knowledge. There is no critical examination of facts and opinions for there is no opportunity for dialogue. For Freire, dialogue is a sign of having faith in the capabilities of peoples.

> Dialogue becomes a horizontal relationship of which mutual trust between the participants is a logical consequence. Without dialogue there is no communication, and without communication there can be no true education.[10]

The one way system of education, aimed at depositing 'materials' in the students, is a method of reproducing and guaranteeing the continuity of the species. When teaching becomes the entire activity of the one who instructs, and learning the duty of the student, the teacher is viewed as possessing knowledge as one might possess private property. Teaching is reduced to an activity of depositing pieces of information and skills into an empty and passive mind. This type of education is domesticating as it emphasizes transfer of existing knowledge to passive objects who memorize, recite and become more docile to manipulation. Banking educational methods are erroneous because in dichotomizing teacher from taught they also dichotomize human beings from the world. As opposed to this type of education Freire proposes a humanizing education which is dialogical, a constant co-investigation carried out by students who realize that learning and knowing are never-ending perceptions, and by the educators who recognize that they themselves are learning at every stage of their lives:

> One must not think that learning to read and write precedes conscientization or vice versa. Conscientization occurs simultane-

ously with the literacy or post literacy proces the world is not something static or disconnected from man's existential experience but a dimension of their thought-language about the world.[11]

The supreme human goal, for Freire, is humanization through the process of liberation. It is not an individual goal but a social goal which demands fellowship and solidarity from every member of the community.

Obviously Freire's theory of development which involves self-reliance and the transformation of self and society is different from other development theories. For him development is an integrated process involving psychological and material development which is not imposed, but comes about through the involvement of the people in the process of collective reflection and action. The initiatives of people are given primary importance. Development can take place only in an atmosphere of mutual reciprocity within a context of communion and fellowship. Its success depends on the ability of the educators to transcend the limitations of their own class, caste, values and attitudes and to learn with people in the context of actual struggle. This process demands collective reflection and action in which the people are fully involved.

What is Development?

According to Freire's model, development is not only a matter of statistical indices or a mathematical computation of per capita income, or a geographic representation of ancillary structures (schools, medical centres, piped water, roads, bridge) but also a phenomenon which shows how well the quality of human life improves. The concept of development needs to be based on the human person. This is what the United Nations Secretary General's report on International Dimensions of the Right to Development affirms in its formulation of the principles of development:

1. The realization of the potentialities of the human person in harmony with the community should be seen as the central purpose of development.
2. The human person should be regarded as the subject and not the object of development.
3. The human person must be able to participate fully in shaping his own reality.[12]

Obviously there are two levels of development. *Material develop-ment* is aimed at the provision of basic amenities and infrastructures which makes existence possible and bearable. In many developing nations these basic amenities such as water, food, electricity and health care are not available. *Human development* is the ability to understand and change a particular situation according to the interests of the community by concerted community effort. The following description of authentic development by Goulet captures the essence of this concept:

> Authentic development aims at the full realization of human capabilities, men and women become makers of their own histories, personal and social. They free themselves from every servitude imposed by nature or by oppressive systems, they achieve wisdom in their mastery over nature and over their own wants, they *create new webs of solidarity based not on domination but on reciprocity among themselves,* they achieve a rich symbiosis between contem-plation and transforming action, between efficiency and free expression. This total concept of development can perhaps be expressed as the "human ascent"– the ascent of all men in their integral humanity, including the spiritual, economic, biological, psychological, mystical and transcendental dimensions.[13]

Nat Colletta summed up the idea more succinctly.

> Development can best be described as a process of positive socio-economic changes in the quality and level of human existence which is aimed at raising the standard of living, quality of life and human dignity.[14]

The following articulation of what authentic development means, made by the Dag Hammarskjold Project on Development and Interna-tional Co-operation and propagated by the International Foundation for Development Alternatives (Geneva), takes into consideration every aspect of development:

Need oriented: that is being geared to meeting human needs, both material and non-material. It begins with the satisfaction of the basic need of those dominated and exploited, who constitute the majority of the world's inhabitants, and ensures at the same time the humanization of all human beings by the satisfaction of their needs for expression, creativity, equality and convivality and to understand and master their own destiny.

Endogenous, that is, stemming from the heart of each society, which defines in sovereignty its values and the visions of its future. Since development is not a linear process, there could be no universal model, and only the plurality of development patterns can answer the specificity of each situation.

Self-reliant, that is, implying that each society relies *primarily on its own strength and resources* in terms of its members' energies and its natural and cultural environment. Self reliance clearly needs to be exercised at national and international (collective self-reliance) levels but it acquires its full meaning only if rooted at local level, in the praxis of each community.

Ecologically sound, that is, utilizing rationally the resources of the biosphere in full–awareness of the potential of local ecosystem as the global and local outer limits imposed on present and future generations. It implies the equitable access to resources by all as well as careful, socially relevant technologies.

Based on structural transformation: they are required, more often than not, in social relations, in economic activities and in their spatial distribution, as well as in the power structure, so as to realize the conditions of self management and participation in decision-making by all those affected by it, from the rural or urban community to the world as a whole, without which the above goals could not be achieved.

These five points are organically linked. Taken in isolation from each other, they would not bring about the desired result. For development is seen as a whole, as an integral cultural process, as the development of every man and woman and the whole of man and woman. Another development means liberation.[15]

Here, in the context of India, it will be assumed that development is a systematic effort to improve the quality of life of the vast majority of people who are marginalised and exploited. It aims at enabling them to become persons with full and free use of their ability to reflect, make decisions and participate in nation-building activities.

Development, Knowledge and Culture

It needs to be stressed that development is intrinsically related to knowledge and power. In fact only the one with knowledge has the power to develop himself. Development, an economic concept with humanistic overtones, is a function of power relations, both historically and contemporarily. The economically powerful nations also wield physical and cultural power over the poor nations with the collaboration of the elite at the top of the social pyramid. Power is exercised physically by threat of violence, economically by controlling the productive behaviour of the labour forces which is the basis of wealth, and culturally or ideologically by conditioning people's minds, beliefs and values to accept the physical and economic power structures. Therefore development should be primarily concerned with redistribution of power. The organizations that link up planned development for the third world–banks, govern-ments, non-government voluntary agencies, agricultural and research institutes–tend, by their own internal structures, to consolidate such power mechanisms and incorporate minimal participation from below. This means that power is not being re-distributed. In the words of Nyerere:

> Both political and economic powers have to be held by the people in the village, in the region, in the nation if development is to be in the people's interest. People are the best creators and defenders of their own human rights, including right to eat.[16]

In India one cannot speak of knowledge helping development. The country has suffered a massive erosion of traditional values and culture. In the modernizing and Westernizing which followed colonialism the Indian elite lost most of their cultural identity. Traditional Indian wisdom has been displaced. Anything Western is considered superior. Aided by the mass media, traditional cultural values–family life, co-operation, simplicity, integrity, warm human relationships, behaviour determined by moral imperatives–have been under–valued. Although the masses have a rich, indigenous way of life and cultural forms, they are considered worthless and inferior to the Western way of life. Indigenous knowledge, with regard to health, education, agriculture and appropriate technology are branded as superstitious and backward. The upper classes who have copied Western norms downplay the traditional cultures and the masses are made to feel inferior to the so-called 'civilized' elite groups. And this helps the elite to dominate and exploit the weaker sections. Understandably, this crisis of culture, together with regionalism and fundamentalism, is at the very root of the socio-political and economic inequality and instability in the country. Consequently, even as a section of society achieves socio-economic liberation it can restore the old system by exploiting the other.

In any developmental process, people need to be active participants. For this it is essential that they become masters of knowledge. For the Indian masses their traditional knowledge provides a vast reserve which needs to be used properly. On the strength of this alone they can build up themselves.

II. Mass Media and Development

In a study on the effectiveness of theatre as a medium for social development, one cannot ignore the issue of mass media and development. Much has been written on the philosophy and methodology of using the media for developmental purposes.

Media or the use of technology by professionals to disseminate information in a uniform way to larger numbers of people over widely dispersed areas have a marked influence on society. Theorists such as McLuhan and Lazarsfeld have shown that in a society they function as watchman, forum, teacher, entertainer and salesman. The media are used for news dissemination, education, propaganda, indoctrination, advertising—indeed the power of the media seems limitless.

The media open up new and highly effective avenues of communication for all kinds of information, ideas and directives. The press, radio, cinema and television are today shaping the destinies of humanity. Just as the printing press opened man's mind beyond his immediate environment, television opened his eyes to newer styles of life. The world has exploded into the consciousness of ordinary people with an impact never before encountered.

The media undoubtedly helped in the flow of information, political and technological knowledge and potentially modernizing know-how. Schramm, Lazarsfeld and Lerner have shown how, by providing information, media can create the right climate for social revolution and change.

Lerner believes that mass media can help create empathy by which societies are able to recognize the qualities of their own individuality and borrow the best of other societies. From following traditional values and behaviour people transform themselves into modern human beings, characterised as "cash customers, radio listeners and voters".[17] According to Rogers, media facilitate the spread of ideas that help to produce a higher per capita income and thus raise the level of living through improved social organizations. The role of communication is not only to diffuse information and knowledge, but also to mobilize people and to persuade them to adopt innovations and ideas consistent with the ideals of modernization. With its emphasis on the two-step flow and the role of the opinion leader,[18] the diffusion model of communication integrated many of the qualities of the earlier models of development communication and stressed the combined use of media and interpersonal communication.

In the wake of such researches attempts have been made to use radio and TV as a development strategy. Rural radio programmes have been used in Ghana, Costa Rica, India, Kenya and Malawi for community development programmes. In Nicaragua, Mexico and the Dominican Republic radio has been introduced in class rooms. India's SITE (Satellite Instructional Television Experiment) and other TV experiments like those in American Samoa, El Salvador, Niger and the Ivory Coast have demonstrated the power of media in development education.

The Constraints

One cannot deny that media, with their consumerist and upper class bias have contributed greatly to the formation of the modern individual and the modern consumer society. Urbanization and individualization inculcated by the media, as reflected in Western societies, have gradually crept into the developing countries and prevented other forms of indigenous development. Media imperialism ensures not only the one-way flow of information from the North to South but also encourages dependence on foreign financial aid. The professional standards of broadcasting exported from the West, force, developing countries to maintain and reinforce Western systems of organizations and ways of thinking. The use of Western programmes in schools creates cultural dependencies and thus indigenous values are at risk.

Anthony Smith has documented the complete cultural domination of the North through its control of the major news collecting resources of the world. This includes the unrestrained flow of its cultural products across the world, the financial power of its advertising agencies, international newspaper chains and newsprint companies, and its hold over the electro-magnetic spectrum on which broadcasting, navigation, meteorology, and much else depend. The four major wire services or news agencies (Reuters, Agence-France-Presse, United Press International and the Associated Press) belong to three nations and supply information to 90% of the world.[19] Studying the content of Latin American television programmes, Beltran has commented that the images on local television are not consonant with the ideal of indigenous development. Instead they impose 'individualism, elitism, racism, materialism, adventurism, conservatism, conformism, self-defeatism, aggressiveness, and romanticism"–all values associated with the US.[20] The 'facade' of the free flow of information instituted after World War II has only helped to perpetuate dependencies in the developing world by actually enforcing a one-way flow of information.

Media are very costly and expensive affairs, operated and controlled by power-holders. The combination of wealth and power determines not only the information flow but also development, finance and technology which do not in any way reach down to help the lower classes. This can easily be seen in any country that has used the mass media for development. The Nicaraguan Educational Television (ETV) financed by the US to educate children in the schools, had hardly any effect on the socio-political and economic system in the country, as the power of the oligarchy prevented any programmes that challenged their stand. Again in the case of India's SITE, the world's largest attempt at ETV which was conducted for a year from August 1975 to July 1976 in 2330 villages of India, it was centrally controlled and depended on foreign hardware and popularized the modernization theory of development with hardly any effect.

Media Manipulation

The impact of the values propounded by the media is considerable. People begin to rely less and less on their own judgment and more and more on what is presented by the media. Too long an exposure to the imaginary world of the media can cause regression in a person's capacity to face life realistically.

Any study of the ethics of mass media should consider primarily the relative autonomy within which the media operate. The media are controlled by the power-holders. They use the media to integrate the

poorer classes into their value systems. They have developed highly
sophisticated techniques to obtain people's consent, to manipulate their
desires. Even the subconscious has been controlled so that without their
knowing they get drawn into the system. In most countries, media are
organized and controlled as private corporate businesses. Government
and advertising agencies dominate the media output. Regulation is mild
and advertisers have a free hand in controlling the system. Those who
desire to promote cultural and educational programmes may often have
to compromise, due to the selfish interests of media controllers. The
values exalted by advertising such as youthfulness, sexual attraction,
romance, prestige, affluence, power and so on corrupt the young and
the gullible. It is almost impossible for modern society to use its media as
a means to transmit and inculcate any coherent or meaningful ideas for the
very nature and function of these media are to serve consumer majorities
rather than idealistic minorities.

Indian Attempts at Media for Development

Mass media are not as widespread in India as in the West. Only All
India Radio (AIR) reaches out to nearly 90% of the population, but its
major output is songs from Indian films. Television too is developing and
reaches up to 76% of the population, although not more than 20% of them
can afford to own TV. These media are developed, operated and
controlled by the Information and Broadcasting Ministry of the government. Obviously they uphold the government's views on every issue and
discourage the airing of other challenging opinion. Cinema has become
a huge industry, the largest of its kind in the world. Roughly 50% of the
people have access to cinema. It is an independent industry but the free-
wheeling state censorship acts as a bottleneck. Yet to the majority of film-
makers film is a medium to entertain the masses and thus make huge
profits. Hence there can be hardly any social education through this
medium. The press has advanced very much among the literate (40%).
Since it is less strictly controlled there is more scope for free and forthright
expression of opinions.

The government introduced rural radio broadcasting in 1936. It was
centrally controlled as that was essential for the survival of the colonial
government. However, even after independence and despite massive
developments in radio transmission it has remained centrally controlled.
Its aim in development communication has been

to educate the masses on agriculture and health practice and on the virtues of thrift ... and to prepare the ground for social and economic development, to educate the public in the broadest sense of the word and more especially to awaken a desire for better things.[21]

Traces of modernization theory of development so much criticized all over the developing world are apparent in this statement.

After independence a neo-colonial system continued to enforce the policies of the empire with a strong hand. Brahminical cultural superiority and ideology persisted. The government machinery began to be controlled by the upper classes for their own benefit. The heavy reliance on classical music for entertainment and a sizeable number of programmes designed according to Western standards have alienated the villagers from the broadcasting system. In the Five Year Plans the need for developing facilities was often stressed. Community radios were installed but the programmes were planned and controlled by the centre, providing a top-down perspective of the upper, urban class who hardly knew the intricacies of the rural problems. Programmes were churned out without ascertaining the needs of the audience. The emphasis was more on the quantity of information than on its quality. There were hardly any attempts to find out if the people had the resources to make use of the information provided. Since its inception in the early sixties TV has also followed the pattern of radio broadcasting. The SITE programme, as pointed out earlier, was a worthwhile venture. However, it was an experiment which terminated after one year.

A major spin-off of SITE, again a short-lived experiment, more in consonance with a community based, local specific and decentralized system of communication, was the Kheda Project in Gujarat, initiated in 1976. The role of development communication involved here was to help change the unjust human structures and belief systems. It proved beyond doubt that development communication with and by the poor had much more potential for bringing about real change than programmes imposed from above.

In fact it is not the lack of information or attributes like fatalism and conservatism but structural factors that have prevented proper planning of development communication in India. Kidd echoed the same sentiments when he said:

The key constraint to progressive social change is not lack of skills and information about farming, nutrition, family planning, health, etc. It is structural inequality : inequality of wealth of government services, of educational and employment opportunities, of wages, of power and of basic human rights. This inequality *undermines the capacity and the confidence of the poor to control their lives*, it conditions them to accommodate themselves to the norm of the dominant groups rather than to struggle against them.[22]

It is hardly useful to disseminate information on the use of varieties of seeds, fertilizer, pesticides and technology among landless peasants. As long as the major issues of landlessness, poverty, minimum wages, bonded labour and other basic problems, like inequalities, discrimination and exploitation of the weaker sections, are not countered development communication remains a weak link.

From what has been said it is clear that mass media are effective in the diffusion of a large mass of information. But merely banking modern information, skills and technologies will only help the people become the new oppressors. Development as a modernization process can only integrate the poor more successfully into the structures which are exploiting them. Due to the complex technology, powerful bureaucratic clout and a general tendency to hold on to existing opinions, the mass media are considered unsuitable for development communication. Decentralization, democratization, participation and dialogue are the central tenets in the practice of development communication. This means in reality an equal involvement by the majority of the people in all aspects of production, dissemination and control of the contents of communication as well as in effecting changes in society. Genuine participation cannot be imposed from above but can emerge only through the inclusion of the majority of the people who then find out by themselves ways and means of tackling issues. In chapter VI, in the proposed methodology for using Popular Theatre as a medium of development, it will be seen how this aspect of participation and societal equality becomes possible.

III. Theatre and Development

The possibilities of mass media in consciousness-raising cannot be totally ignored. The SITE and Kheda experiments have proved beyond doubt that, if the philosophy of development is clearly understood, media can be utilized in an appropriate manner.

In this study on the effectiveness of theatre as a medium for development a natural question is, "Why theatre when mass media hold all the possibilities?" It has also been asked whether theatre is preferred because it does not need as much technical know-how, facilities and finances as do the mass media. Although these are relevant, there are also some basic, inherent advantages in theatre that do no exist in the mass media.

1. Theatre is a Live Experience

One of the major drawbacks in mass media, especially where total government control persists, is the difficulty in responding back (feedback) to the opinions expressed. In Yoruba radio and television are rightly called *ero asoro maghese* which means the machine that speaks but accepts no reply.[23] It can be very frustrating if the opinions expressed over these media are badly researched and are unacceptable to the target audience. Theatre, with its potential for persuasive and face-to-face communication with the masses enjoys an instant and intimate feedback. The actual presence of the actors increases the reality of the experiences presented, making it more potent. Boal and other practioners of Popular Theatre have exploited the live nature of theatre to the full. The participation of the audience is possible in deciding the issues to be dramatized and in the,'scripting' and performing in theatre.

2. Theatre is Indigenous to the Rural Masses

Theatre originated and grew among the rural masses and so can be used to express their ideas, hopes and visions. It can express the villagers deeply-felt joys and sorrow, triumphs and defeats, as no other media can. It employs the idioms and symbols that are easily intelligible to the people. What Eapen says of folk media in general can easily be applied to theatre:

> they are comparatively cheap. They do not have to be imported and therefore involve no foreign exchange, a scarce commodity except for oil kingdoms. They belong to the community and not to individuals, state or private/public industry. Many of the development efforts, anyway have to be aimed at the community as a whole rather than at atomised individuals if behavioural change is to occur.... There is no threat of cultural colonialism and foreign ideological domination.

Also *local talent and local message would have more credibility* than those centralised ones emanating from state capitals.... . They may prove a better outlet for egalitarian messages than the present elite press, film or radio-TV. There is a commonality about them. Acceptability, cultural relevance, entertainment value, localised language, legitimacy, flexibility, message repetitionability, instant two-way communication, etc. are among their virtues.[24]

In the villages, due to the impact of oral tradition people normally think and feel in images and visuals. This is different from the more literate patterns of problem analysis, cause and effect study. Hence theatre, being an ideal purveyor of feelings and sensations, can translate thoughts and abstract concepts into easily identifiable experiences that can be shared.

3. As an indigenous form, theatre helps further cultural explorations into the psyche and value systems of a people. According to Dissanayake:

It is important to remind ourselves that folk media are not quaint relics of the past but vigorously active and highly functional cultural institutions performing functions vital to the well-being of society: they provide entertainment, disseminate information, inculcate socially accepted norms and values and perform a general socializing function.[25]

Analytical studies of lives of the people help them experience a sense of dignity and pride in their culture. Their creative potentials are challenged and sharpened. The collective activity of producing plays helps to build group solidarity and to strengthen the potential for thinking and action.

4. As an educational tool, theatre can help deepen the powers of comprehension and memory. If the people are involved in creating plays their understanding of the issues can be deepened. As improvised plays are not stored or preserved like other media, the message is recorded in its entirety and stored in memory. Hence it may by argued that the power of 'oracy' as in primitive cultures is much higher among 'theatre cultures' than 'mass media cultures' where the audience is in danger of losing even their sense of imagination.

Considering these specific characteristics the following possibilities may be attributed to theatre:

—It can help initiate an action-reflection-action process which can lead to change.

—It can illuminate issues in a simple, direct and challenging way.

—If it grows out of the community it can reflect the community with a high degree of accuracy. This helps the people to identify instantly with the issues presented.

—Since it relies on indigenous facilities it is cheap. Make-up, special costumes, technical facilities like electricity, special stages are unnecessary.

—Since its structure is simple it can be managed by one and all. Literacy and high technical skills are not necessary for this form of theatre.

Notes

1. Fanon, F., *The Wretched of the Earth,* Penguin Books Ltd., London, 1973, pp. 169 and 54.
2. Ward, Barbara, *Towards a World of Plenty,* Toronto University Press, 1964, p. 124.
3. Goonatilake, Sussanta, *Crippled Minds,* Vikas Publishers, New Delhi, 1982, p. 4.
4. This statement by Lord Macaulay, the Education Secretary in Lord Bentinck's (1828-1848) government is quoted from the *Report of the Delhi Rural Broadcasting Scheme 1944-45,* India Office, London, p. 3.
5. Bernstein, H., "Modernization Theory and the Sociological Study of Development', *Journal of Development Studies,* vol. 7, no. 2, 1971, p. 141.
6. Myrdal, Gunnar, *Asian Drama: An Inquiry into the Poverty of Nations,* vols. I, II, and III, Pantheon, New York, 1968.
7. Frank, A.G., "Capitalism and Underdevelopment in Latin America," *Monthly Review Press,* New York and London, 1974, p. 43.
8. Prebisch, R., "The Dynamics of Peripheral Capitalism," in LeFeber and North (eds.), *Democracy and Development in Latin America,* New York, 1974.
9. These ideas are drawn from several of Freire's books, notably:
   Pedagogy of the Oppressed, Penguin Books, London, 1972.
   Pedagogy in Process, The Letters to Guinea Bissau, The Seabury Press, New York, 1978.
   The Politics of Education, Culture, Power and Liberation, Macmillan Pubs. Ltd., U.K., 1985.
10. Freire, *Pedagogy of the Oppressed,* p. 64.
11. Ibid., p. 42.

12. As quoted by Dieng Adama, "Self-reliant Development in Senegal, Myth or Reality?, *Ideas and Action,* FAO, Rome, no. 160, 1985, pp. 4-5.

13. Goulet, D., "An Ethical Model for the Study of Values," *Harvard Education Review,* 41/2/ 1971, p. 206 ff.

14. Colletta, Nat, "Traditions for Change: Indigenous Socio-Cultural Forms as a Basis for Non-Formal Education and Development," in Kidd and Colletta, *Traditions for Development,* Berlin, 1982.

15. As quoted in Foubert, Charles, "Development Theory and the Third World, *IFDA Dossier,* Switzerland, 1982.

16. Nyrere, Julius, "Speech at the 1974 World Conference on Agricultural Reforms and Rural Development' quoted from *Times of India,* Bombay, September 1977.

17. Lerner, D., *The Passing of Traditional Society,* Free Press, New York, 1958.

18. These concepts originated in the context of media research in the US in the forties, and were proposed by Lazarsfeld (1944). Two-step flow proved the stimulus-response model of communication research and laid stress on the importance of personal influence (opinion leader).

19. Smith, Anthony D., *Geo-politics of Information,* Faber and Faber, 1978, p. 3.

20. Beltran, L.R., "TV Etchings in the Minds of Latin Americans; Conservatism, Materialism and Conformism, *Gazette,* Amsterdam, 24/1/ 1978.

21. Quoted from Sharp, H. (ed.), *Selections from Educational Records Part I, 1781-1839,* Calcutta, 1920.

22. Kidd, Ross, "Folk Theatre, One-way or Two-way Communication?", *Development Communication Report,* Oct. 1979, p. 28.

23. Fiofori, Fo, "Traditional Media, Modern Messages: A Nigerian Study", *Rural African,* Michigan State University, 1975, p. 45.

24. Eapen, K.E., "Specific Problems of Research and Research Training in Asian/African Countries," *Communication Research in the Third World: The Need for Training,* Lutheran World Federation, Geneva, 1976, pp. 18-19.

25. Dissanayake, Wimal, "New Wine in old Bottles: Can Folk Media Convey Modern Messages?, *Journal of Communication,* Spring 1977, pp. 12-24.

Chapter II

The Concept and Philosophy of Popular Theatre

In the first part of this chapter the origin and growth of Popular Theatre as a medium of development in the world at large are discussed. The second part focuses on its development in India.

It is a common experience that when theatre becomes the trivial fashion of a leisured class, new forms spring up around the fringes to revitalize its dramatic content and bring it back closer to the life of the community. Socially committed theatre practitioners all over the world have realized that proclaiming a social revolution conceived by arm-chair philosophers and dramatized by actors and producers with commercial interests on a decorated stage serves only to provide information and emotional satisfaction, but does not provoke thought or lead to mature education and creative action. Many theatre practitioners have argued that such conventional theatres have ceased to provide an authentic exploratory space. Consequently, all over the world, attempts have been made by committed theatre practitioners to uproot this condescending and highly class-bound theatre.

I. The Beginnings of a Revolt

It has already been mentioned that in many parts of the world the exploitation of the colonized not only impoverished native cultures, but increased class consciousness, landlessness and unemployment. This led to struggles by peasants and workers all over the colonized world at the turn of the 20th century. Theatre activists took to themes of protest in the twenties and thirties. The 'art for art's sake'[1] theory was strongly contested by the socialist and progressive writers all over the world. Marxist and socialist perspectives gained ground in theatre in many parts of the world. The movement began with massive propagandist overtones. In the Russian 'proletcult' (a collection of organizations for the cultural revival of the people) and the Blue Blouse (1923-28), theatre was used as a means to build up the images of socialism. The highly theatrical mass political meetings, demonstrations and parades as well as agit prop plays of the Red Army Theatre contributed to the ideology of the mass spectacles.[2] Various forms of protest theatres–animated posters, puppet shows, sloganeering based on proverbs, folk singing, and 'living newspaper shows–helped to spread the ideology of the new-found freedom. Similarly in China live theatre was used as an effective socialising agent for political indoctrination. Drama teams were set up to perform themes of revolutionary romanticism in work places, fields and villages in order to proclaim the triumph of the revolution. Story-telling forms and wall poster campaigns became the immediate means to spread the ideology of communism.[3]

It was Meyerhold and Mayakovsky who made major contributions to the development of a truly proletarian theatre. Mayakovsky's plays *Bedbug* (1929) and *Bathhouse* (1930) sharply criticised the values of the petty bourgeoisie and the communist bureaucracy. Meyerhold's *D.E.*, a mass spectacle climaxing in the clash of ideologies between two world powers–the bourgeoisie and the proletariat–was of high technical quality. In his plays he extolled revolutionary experimentalism and socialist realism which helped proletarian theatre to mature.

In France Romain Roland (1866-1944) too had similar concepts about working class theatre. He qualified his theatre

> as an art explicitly meant for people who worked with their hands and who normally did not attend big theatre. They would try to create an inexpensive, and easily accessible dramatic art form specifically designed for the labouring poor in the cities and for the artisanat and peasant communities in the provinces.[4]

The most important contribution was from Germany. Piscator and Brecht propagated the ideas of class struggle and founded a number of militant workers' theatres to serve the needs of the proletarian revolution. Piscator's 'living wall' and Brecht's 'verfremdungseffekt' were experiments with the potential of theatre for political education. Brecht noted:

> Piscator's auditions became public meetings. He saw theatre as a

parliament, the audience as a legislative body. To this parliament were submitted in plastic form all the great public questions that needed an answer. It was the stage's ambition to supply the images, statistics, slogans, which would enable its parliament– the audience– to reach political decisions. His theatre was not indifferent to applause, but it preferred a discussion. It did not want only to provide its spectators with an experience but also to squeeze from him a practical decision to intervene actively in life.[5]

Influenced by Hegel, Brecht went on to propose a poetics in which the spectator was made critically aware of the situations dealt with on the stage. He destroyed illusion and created the 'wide awake audience' who is made to reflect on the situations presented on the stage in a conscious way. In his polemics against Lukacs, Brecht wrote:

Our concept of what is popular theatre refers to a people who not only play a full part in historical development, but actively usurp it, force its pace and determine its direction. We have a people in mind *who make history, change the world, and make themselves.* We have in mind a fighting people and therefore an aggressive concept of what is popular. Popular means intelligible to the masses, adopting and enriching their forms of expression, assuming their standpoint, conforming and correcting it... relating to their traditions and developing them.[6]

Brecht's political theatre differed considerably from the conventional Aristotelian theatre where problems were solved on the stage by presenting cathartic solutions. Brecht introduced a didactic element in which the spectator would be left doubting and thinking about the social and political forces that produce tragedy, rather than accepting the programmed and scripted deliberations of the classical heroes.

After the performance, discussions were held in which the audience's responses were heard and alternatives suggested. There was no audience participation in the production.

In the late sixties, Augusto Boal, a theatre practitioner working with Freire's literacy campaigns gave a fresh lease of life to this approach. A key element in Freire's 'education for liberation' was to focus group dialogue on pictures, photographs, charts and slides which represented symbolically central problems of poverty and dependence. The pictures depicted everyday events, but careful observations would make the subtle distinction between culture and nature, man and animal. Boal noticed that this form of discussion enabled the group to look at themselves from a distance and to discuss what they really thought caused the situation. A new culture rose out of a very different reconstruction of the causes of their problems. He realised that a dramatic re-enactment of key issues by the community could be an even more striking representation of situations because it portrayed the social roles of power and dependence and was visually and emotionally more concrete. Theatre could also be a more flexible representation because the portrayal could be immediately changed and refined by the participating audience. The process of creating theatre could become itself a tool for social interaction and analysis of society. These were the considerations that led Boal to the use of drama in literacy activities.[7]

II. A Theatre of the Oppressed

Boal's most significant contribution is the series of essays which questions the whole of the Western theory of theatre. In his view Aristotle's catharsis theory is essentially a justification of a vicarious emotional release which fits well with the desire of Athenian and subsequent European socio-political orders to dominate and control a potentially volatile expression of social frustration in real political action. He assumed that theatre is the art of the ordinary masses which has been usurped by the aristocracy. According to him the principal medium of theatrical production is the human body. Thus the first step in giving the poor control over their theatre is to understand the expression of the body and how to control this expression. Factory workers, housewives and peasant farmers ordinarily develop only those bodily muscles that their work demands, and they need special exercises to develop the wide range of muscular routines for creative drama. He sums up his concept thus:

the object of the theatre of the oppressed is to change the people—spectators and passive beings in the theatrical tradition—into subjects, into actors and transformers of the dramatic action. This action however, has effects beyond the drama as it is used to try out solutions to real problems and to discuss plans for change. In this case theatre becomes a rehearsal for revolution...theatre is a weapon and it is the people who should wield it.[8]

Differentiating his methodology from that of Aristotle and Brecht, Boal says:

Aristotle proposes a poetics in which the spectator delegates power to the dramatic character so that the latter may act and think for him. Brecht proposes a poetics in which the spectator delegates power to the character who thus acts in his place but the spectator reserves the right to think for himself, often in opposition to the character. In the first case a catharsis occurs, in the second an awakening of critical consciousness.[9]

But in Boal's poetics, the focus is on the action itself; the spectator delegates no power to the character either to act or to think in his place. On the contrary the spectator becomes the protagonist, changes the dramatic action, tries out solutions, discusses plans for change–in short, trains himself for real action. Boal proposes three forms of active participatory theatre.

1. Simultaneous Dramaturgy

In this case, there is firstly a performance on a social issue. The actors develop it to a point at which the main problems raised reach a crisis and need a solution. The actors stop the performance and ask the audience to suggest solutions. The audience intervenes, writes the scenario on the spot which the actors then perform following the audience's suggestions. In this form of play, the spectator becomes the creator. The actions cease to be presented in a pre-determined manner, as something inevitable, as fate, but become the spectator's creation. The actors are no more the tools of an absent author, but the interpreters of the collective thoughts of the masses.

2. Image Theatre

In this form of theatre everyone involved is asked to express their views on a topic of common interest, without speaking, using only the bodies of other participants to sculpt groups of statues in such a way that opinions and feelings become self-evident. Corrections by others are accepted and then the final form is studied by all. After this the ideal form, or what it should be like, is presented using the same imagery. Then the new image is studied. The exact areas of change are observed. In other words it is an exercise in carrying out change or revolution in one's society. When the transitional process is carried out by all the members of the audience, this projects the image of a people involved in social transformation in their own society.

3. Forum Theatre

In this form the people have to enter decisively in the dramatic action and change it. A group of people present a play about a social problem. Others are asked if they agree with the solution presented. Various opinions are expressed. The play is presented again, but this time the people are invited to intervene and change the action of the play. Actors are replaced but can intervene again when they feel they can contribute to the issue. Often a person accustomed to giving ideological interpretations to problems will find, when the tries to work out his solution, that other problems arise. Forum theatre evokes in the people a desire to practise in reality the act they have rehearsed in theatre.

Boal suggests that the theatre of the bourgeoisie is a finished theatre in which images of a complete and perfect world are presented. But since the oppressed classes do not know what their world would be like, their theatre is unfinished. So their theatre is rightly called a rehearsal for revolution.

Boal's method of theatre found instant success. For those who had been experimenting with various forms of theatre to reach out to the landless labourers and peasants it was a gold-mine of inspiration. It found immediate recognition in the third world under the ambiguous name of "Popular Theatre".

In essence Popular Theatre speaks to the common people in their language and idiom and deals with problems directly relevant to their situation. The purpose of this form of theatre is to raise the consciousness of the poor and uneducated, who form the major part of the once colonized, now domesticated and exploited third world, to the various social, political and economic issues that continually keep them in a state of dehumanization. Through the help of theatre the audience is made to reflect critically on such issues in the hope that by becoming aware of the intricate nature of their situation, they may become 'masters' who can challenge and change their world for the better. It aims to be:

- a medium controlled by the people for expressing their ideas and
  concerns at a time when no other forms of expression and media

are available to them;
- a means of resisting the ideas propagated by the dominant class, institutions and media;
- a way of recovering, reviving, validating and advancing the people's own culture and history;
an experience of participation, interaction and self expression through which people overcome their fears and develop a sense of their own identity, self confidence and class consciousness;
- a process of popular education — which acts as an analytic tool for testing the limits and possibilities for action and unveils the contradictions and structures underlying everyday reality, and a means for organizing and preparing the people for struggle–clarifying the target, working out strategies and tactics and testing out forms of confrontation.[10]

III. A Worldwide Phenomenon

Efforts at building up a people's theatre that would enhance developmental efforts have been made all over the world. Popular Theatre has become largely a third world affair, chiefly

because of differences in existing educational institutions and communications media which stand for elitism of colonial education and its irrelevancy to the goals of national development.[11]

Sub-Saharan Africa and the Caribbeans

African cultures have a strong performative tradition which combines dance, orchestral use of drums, choral singing, mime, oral poetry, public story-telling and the elaborate use of masks. In the various ethnic cultures public communication–especially in the yearly round of religious ritual and community festival–has been expressed largely in terms of dramatic performance. Pre-colonial African cultures rarely developed a highly literate theatre, and a formal theatre emerged only in a few places such as the Yoruba kingdom of present-day Western Nigeria. In the colonial period classical and contemporary European theatres were introduced. It did not take too long for the development of all kinds of plays–traditional, ritual, folk, modern and literary. Africa now has a long list of distinguished playwrights, the Nobel-prize winner Wole Soyinka in Nigeria, Leopold Senghor in Senegal, Kabwe Kasoma in Zambia,

Amadu Maddy in Sierra Leone, Ngugi wa Thiongo in Kenya and Efua Southerland in Ghana. Kabwe Kasoma and Stephen Chifunyise in Zambia and Soyinka in Nigeria have tried street theatre. The travelling theatres of Hubert Ogunde and Baba Sala in Nigeria, the comedy shows of the Ghanian Concert Party and several others have continued the tradition of popular entertainments.

With so much theatre it is not surprising that in virtually every country there have been attempts 'to take theatre to the people'. Various kinds of Centres, government departments and university based projects have supported participatory people's theatre. Travelling theatres from the universities established a reputation for themselves in Uganda, Kenya and Nigeria. Governments have been particularly interested in using theatre as a medium of development in Malawi, Ghana, Uganda, Mali and Nigeria.

Popular Theatre as a process for educating the disadvantaged began in the African countries, probably in Zambia, in the early seventies with the founding of Michael Etherton's Chikwakwa (grassroots) Theatre. The idea, according to Etherton, was to develop a truly Zambian theatre for the people through existing cultural and social traditions. The group staged a number of classic plays adapted to make them socially and politically relevant to people in the villages. Local people were involved in the production. The integration of local music, songs and dances made these productions native as well as contemporary. As it was based in the University, it gradually took the form of a travelling theatre. A second stage emerged with the founding of Laedza Batanani ("the sun is already up, let us come together and work") by Martin Byram and Ross Kidd in Botswana and the Samaru projects initiated at the Ahmadu Bello University in Nigeria by Salihu Bappa and Ross Kidd. Both groups performed plays about rural problems with the people in the villages and conducted post-performance discussions. The Zimbabawe, Benue (Nigeria) and Kumba (Cameroon) workshops initiated theatre performed by the villagers themselves, drawing elements from their traditional performing arts. A notable achievement was the involvement of Kenya''s foremost writer wa 'Thiongo with the Kamiriithu Community Educational and Cultural Centre. In sessions with the people a play on the history of Kenya, *I will Marry When I Want* was devised and staged many times. It was hailed as truly a people's play for it talked about the people of Kamiriithu, their lives, history, struggles, experiences, hopes and concerns. Through satire it exposed the manipulation of religion, the greed and corruption of the ruling classes, the treachery of colonial collaborators and the exploitative practices of the multinationals.

In the West Indies the university's extra-mural department initiated the development of a national theatre in order to promote social integration. A popular Caribbean theatre which took inspiration from carnival, calypso and dialect was the result. The emergence of Sistren, a rural women's theatre collective in 1975 and Graduate theatre company in 1978 in Jamaica stand out as landmarks in the spread of Popular Theatre.

Latin America

Most rural communities and urban *barrios* (neighbourhoods) in Latin America continue a long tradition of patron-saint festivals with processions, carnival-like fairs and forms of folk drama mixed with local civic celebration. However, in contrast to Asia and Africa, Popular Theatre has less roots in the religious cult and mythic history of Latin America. The popular performative tradition is related more to the high-hearted, joyful sociableness of family and community fiesta, carnival and amateur community entertainment than to religious ritual. Alberto Leis observes:

> the violent and systematic destruction of the civilization of the Americas which accompanied the Spanish conquests from 1492 onwards has made it impossible to retrieve and reconstruct all the forms of indigenous theatre that existed in the region.[12]

However, he provides three examples with a semblance of traditional drama–the *Inca* civilization with the *Ollantay* historical dramas, the *Maya* civilization's *Rabinal Achi* dramas and the *Nahuatl* culture with its *Gueguense* dramas. But none of these had any serious impact on later development of a powerful Popular Theatre.

In the 19th and early 20th centuries Latin America was sufficiently isolated geographically so that it developed its own tradition of local festivals, travelling theatre troupes, popular poetry and literature. But the impact of North American cultural imperialism in the thirties found strong opponents especially among the Catholic Church. The repressive military regimes forced several creative talents to work with popular movements. People such as Freire and Boal developed new methods of education, popular arts and theatre which would articulate the socio-political and cultural aspirations of the masses.

Ochsenius describes three major styles of grassroots theatre that have developed in Latin American countries:

1. Groups of non-commercial theatre students, amateur players or professional actors who tour urban neighbourhoods with semi-improvised street theatre with local people. Their objectives vary from purely didactic to the cultural groups such as Theatro Escambray and La Yaya in Cuba, Cuatrotablas in Peru, Theatro Popular in Bogota, the Cali Teatro Experimental, La Candelaria and La Mama in Puerto Rico, the Ollantay in Equator, the Libre Teator Libre in Argentina and CLETA in Mexico who stage highly entertaining cultural *tours de force*.

2. Groups of amateurs usually monitored by local leaders with some experience in theatre which create and perform for the local community. The performers may be drawn from trade unions, co-operatives and other people's organizations. Organizations like the Centre of Popular Communication and the Social Development Centre in Panama, Ayni Ruway in Bolivia, the Minimum Housing Foundation in El Salvador, the Educational Community in Guatemala and the Community Development Institute in Mexico have experimented with this form of theatre.

3. Theatre for education, community animation and organization of the poor. These follow the example of Boal's theatre without spectators. Here theatre is used by the marginalized people as a means to explore their social conditions. The Los Alpes in Nicaragua, working under the general umbrella of Mecate and supporting the Sandanista government, is a group formed by the workers and farmers themselves, with animateurs of guide them.[13]

Asia

In Bangladesh the Drama Circle was founded in 1956 in Dacca to communicate relevant social messages to the people. After the war of independence, Aranyak was founded in 1971 to use theatre for educating the peasants and workers. Later social action groups, like Proshika and Nijera Kori, have taken to theatre for the same reasons. In Pakistan traditional performers have been employed at festivals in order to educate the people. In Malaysia, the Federal Land Authority, a project for establishing new settlements in rural areas has employed traditional theatre troupes to visit these new communities.

The Philippine Educational Theatre Association (PETA) began in 1967 as a response to Spanish and US imperialism in the islands. Supported by the Catholic Church, PETA grew up to be a major force and popularized theatres as a national cultural activity. A number of offshoots of PETA like Kulturang Tabonon and the Mindanao Theatre Union continue PETA's vision. The LEKRA, Teater Arena and Teater Dinasti of Indonesia and the Open Street Theatre of Sri Lanka are other examples of the fledgling Popular Theatre.[14]

In the First World

Popular Theatre is not entirely confined to the developing world. It flourishes in repressive regimes like the apartheid world of South Africa and the West Bank of Palestine. Although there may be great variations of theatre as one moves from the experimental theatre of New York or among black, feminist and Hispanic minorities in the USA, to the street theatres of India and to the community theatres of Sierra Leone, the same drive to represent the concerns of the minorities and the oppressed is evident. There are also important common denominators and a great deal of interchange of ideas across national and cultural boundaries. Boal, though now settled in Paris, tours Europe and the USA conducting workshops in his form of theatre. Ross Kidd who has documented practically the whole of development based theatre in the world has an active group in his native Ontario.[15] Other Westerners like Michael Etherton, David Kerr, Frank Dall have initiated Popular Theatre schemes in Africa. Schechner's Performance Group, the San Francisco Mime Troupe, France's Theatre du Soleil, Dario Fo and Franca Rame's Colletivo Teatrale La Commune in Italy, Karagoz in Turkey, and Welfare State and the Colway Theatre of Anne Jellicoe in England contain elements of Popular Theatre in them. Doctoral students from Africa and Asia study Popular Theatre at theatre schools in Europe, Canada and the US. Institutions in Germany, Canada, Switzerland and the Netherlands organize international workshops on Popular Theatre.

Why "Popular Theatre"–a crisis of terminology?

Several theatre practitioners have expressed dissatisfaction with the term 'popular' and there have been attempts at renaming. Groups like Mecate (Nicaragua), Ayni Ruway (Bolivia), PETA (Philippines), Proshika (Bangladesh) have shown preference for the term 'people's theatre'.

However, in India and several Asian countries 'people's theatre' denotes theatre outside the temple, palace structures and classical traditions. The IPTA in India meant precisely that. The African Popular Theatre practitioners too have come up with various names. Theatre for Development (TFD) in Nigeria, Theatre of Integral Development (TIDE) in Botswana, and Theatre for Integrated Rural Development (THIRD) in Cameroon are some of the suggested names. However, none of these have gained universal acceptance. In England 'community theatre' is used to indicate theatre in the form of carnivals and pageantry by the Welfare State and the Colway theatre. People's participation, local cultural flavours and contents that largely analyse local issues have made these true community plays.

The truth of the matter, some third world practitioners argue, is that the term "popular theatre" means different things to different people. Generally, there are three levels, of 'popular'.

1. Intellectual and elitist popularity is the first level. This is made up of well-known works of authors following cherished traditions. Plays by Ibsen, Chekhov, Shakespeare, Moliere are examples. They reflect the values of their times and have become classics. They are the authors studied in Universities and performed in traditional theatres. Playwrights like Eugene O'Neil, Genet, Tennesse Williams, Wilder, Albee, Ionesco, Beckett, Pinter and Miller have continued in this tradition. They have popularised newer forms of theatrical expressions—theatre of the absurd, surrealism, stream of consciousness and so on.

2. The second level of popularity is determined by commercial success. West End and Broadway hits like *Phantom of the Opera*, *Cats*, *Mouse Trap*, and *Les Miserable*, which play for several consecutive years, are in this category. In the third world a number of touring companies that portray the dreams of the people as does the commercial cinema, like several Calcutta theatres, Kerala People's Arts Club (KPAC) and Nigeria's Hubert Ogunde Theatre are in the same category. These may be better termed 'commercial' theatre.

Finally there is Popular Theatre in the sense used in this book.

Why is this the appropriate term?

The word *popular* means 'of the people, by the people, for the people.' The word *people* has undergone subtle semantic changes in the last two decades. It started in South America where the nouns *pueblo* or *povo* and the adjective 'popular' began to denote a movement of liberation. The ordinary people were determined to free themselves from the political and socio-cultural constraints of the power structures. This group was called 'the people'. The people's movement signifies the action of this type of people who are gradually waking up to the reality of oppression and exploitation. They intend to challenge fatalistic ideas and to make their own history.[16] 'People' in this sense is different from the *masses* of the mass media or the readers of the *popular* press or the *pop* music fans. Here people means workers, peasants, the oppressed, the minorities, women, children, unemployed, the old–all victims of the dominant mass media including the much loved commercial films that make them forget real issues.

In this form of Popular Theatre the people's own ideals and visions find expression in their own cultural forms. The people themselves in a democratic process decide the themes to be tackled and how they are to be presented. The ultimate goal is not the performance, but the process of devising the play in a dialogical way. The aim of this theatre is for people to build up their communities by discovering their own cultural identity and analysing ways and means of countering their basic problems. It encompasses a great variety of theatre–based forms including mime, puppetry, story-telling and political protest theatre–all of which are specifically employed to advance and validate a people–based counter culture. Needless to say this form of theatre can be, and probably is, practised by people in all cultures. For example, in India unlike 'popular' films like *Mother India* and *Sholay*,[17] which may not reach more than 50 per cent of the people and sell canned dreams manufactured by the industrialists in Bombay to exploit the poor, Popular Theatre as practised by the social action groups can truly be by the people and for the people. It can analyse the crucial issues that face them using indigenous cultural forms, touching their hearts and heads at the same time. For this reason the much misused term Popular Theatre is appropriate.

IV. Characteristics of Popular Theatre

In this section the characteristics of Popular Theatre are discussed.

1. An Expression of Cultural Identity

For Schechner good theatre is always entertaining. There is colourful impersonation, wit and humour, satire and dialogue which says what we think better than we can say it, a poetic language with heightened emotion that captures moods, and a suspenseful plot. There is always an element of festival, leisure, emotional release, celebration and dreaming.[18] However, Popular Theatre emerges most strongly in contexts where there is a combination of awakening cultural identity among the people and a degree of cultural and political repression. In politically repressive regimes, where modern media are owned and controlled by government or wealthy landowners or industrialists, live performance is one of the few outlets open for political expression, the assertion of group identity and a source of alternative information. In many cases Popular Theatre is the first articulation of a new cultural awareness that strikes a sympathetic chord in an ever-widening circle of people. The dramatisation of repressed feelings of exploitation or other intolerable conditions may at first cause a cultural shock, but cultural honesty eventually becomes the source for revitalising the traditions of theatre and the performative arts in general.

Consider a few examples: Popular Theatre became an important expression of the growing Palestinian national and cultural identity in the West Bank especially after the 1967 war. Some of the first community theatre activities were begun by Bethlehem-born Francois Abu-Salem, who returned to his native Palestine in the late 1960s , after theatre education in Paris. Under his initiative theatre became not only a vehicle for Palestinian nation-building but also played a cathartic role as an agent of social integration, mobilization, cultural innovation and artistic animation. When he helped to form the El-Hakawati (The Storyteller) Theatre group, he found that they were operating in a society without a theatrical tradition. Thus the group sought to shape its own stories and style, drawing inspiration from Palestinian folklore. They developed a new symbolic language that served as a code between the theatre and the people of the West Bank. In a 1978-79 production, *In the Name of the Father, the Mother and the Son*, Palestinians are symbolically portrayed as animals in cages with a symbolic tamer (whose Israeli identity few missed) sneaking into the cages to educate and reform the hapless animals. Another play *Mahjoob Mahjoob* features an anti-hero, accidentally dropped on his head at birth by his father in a moment of excitement. Mahjoob, in his befuddled way, outwits Israeli occupying forces in a series of hilarious adventures as a prospective member of the Israeli worker's Union, but also draws caustic criticism of the sterile security rituals of his Palestinian neighbours.[19]

In Poland theatre groups emerged as early as the 1950s among young people's movements following the relaxation of Stalinism. There were as many as 200 theatre groups in the late 1960s and early 1970s and they have continued in new forms through the Solidarity period. It began as a reaction against the boredom and constraint of the official professional theatre. Over the years, the plays have dramatised protest against repression, the hypocrisy of officialdom, the hollowness of propaganda, the constant indoctrination, the passive conformity of the Polish people. A constant theme is the remembrance of Polish cultural history. At times it is more lyrical, trying to catch the visual images of circus, carnival, street fairs and music halls. At other times it is more political satire, inviting the spectators into a discussion and debate. In the seventies, the groups went in for more spectacular sets and elaborate lighting. In the eighties, they have been touring the rural towns and villages, celebrating the memory of Polish folk history with songs, legends and folk tales. Some groups have taken advantage of the patronage of the Church, itself a network of alternative communication in Poland and deeply aware of dramatic symbolic actions. In general, Popular Theatre in Poland is wedded to a fine arts tradition for it is an integral part of both literate and popular culture in Polish history.[20]

In Chile between 100-150 theatre groups operate at any given time. This has been not only a form of political awareness but an articulation of the humour, pathos, human tenderness, and neighbourly solidarity among the poor in an otherwise brutalising military police state. In the USA alternative, experimental theatre reached its peak in the late sixties and through the seventies when the groundswell of public disagreement with the government's insistence on pursuing the disastrous Vietnam war often could not find expression in the more public media.

A common denominator in Popular Theatre in various parts of the world is a protest against 'modernization' for it tries to maintain 'free space' against the total mobilisation of human life towards rationalised progress and economic productivity. Modernity is a human achievement, but modernization tends to obliterate distinctive subcultures and traditions under one overall consumer culture. Those who cannot enter the competitive race of productivity–the handicapped, the elderly, the poor, those who have less technical education or access to technical resources for productivity–fall to the bottom of the heap and are crushed. Worse yet are the cases of those whose traditional cultures are wiped out and find themselves rootless. Blacks in America, peasant farmers in Latin America or India, Palestinians caught in the wake of Israeli cultural and economic aggressiveness, the Poles trying to maintain their cultural freedom in the shadow of the Russian giant, villagers in Nigeria–all share in this decimation of values. Popular Theatre is an attempt to restore the values of community and personal dignity in societies where technical progress and productivity threaten to become the only values.

Keeping these developments in mind, Popular Theatre tries to recapture the essence of the indigenous folk forms. Not that folk forms are to be adapted *per se*. Those forms existed at a particular time in history. Popular theatre does not and should not try to perpetuate those forms. It needs a new form while continuing to draw from the older forms. In today's rootlessness and crisis of identity Popular Theatre needs to look back to the ancient traditional cultures and examine how particular forms represented the expression of those people. There is a tendency among development workers to adapt folk forms to present-day themes. Utpal Dutt condemns this attitude:

> By knocking out content and using only the score is to replace a vision with a slogan, to misuse folklore, to descend to formalism. Form and content are thoroughly integrated in folklore, to divide them is to kill them. The score by itself is so simplistic, repetitive and even crude, it is probably boring.[21]

Hence Popular Theatre need not attempt to resurrect old folk forms or adapt them to modern themes and situations. But it must seek to adapt elements from existing forms which have indigenous cultural traits.

2. Consciousness Raising

It has been mentioned (chapter I) how Freire and others found that the poor had learned to repress their real thoughts for fear of antagonizing powerful figures who could deprive them of jobs and other basic necessities. The heart of the educational process was to create within a small group a space of freedom and mutual respect—especially the respect of the animateur for the group–so that the group's real perceptions of the causes of their problems could come to a conscious cultural expression. Thus they could gain the confidence necessary to reject the false explanations of poverty (ignorance, helplessness, fatalism) that kept them down. Within this group and within the network of hundreds of other similar groups and community organizations, a new socio-political culture gradually emerged. The network of Popular Theatre operating in Brazil in the seventies and eighties was an important factor in bringing Brazil back to a democratic government and making labour unions and other people's organization independent forces in Brazilian society.

Essentially, consciousness raising reaches its full extent only when people are enabled to analyse and find out the relations between various issues, how an event happening in their village falls in line with the national and worldwide system of oppression.

3. Community Building and Social Change

Schechner sees theatre essentially as a dramatic performance, a cultural space separated from everyday life in which human and social issues are symbolically and fictionally re-enacted. To explain more clearly the nature of theatre he distinguishes two basic elements of theatre: entertainment and efficaciousness. All theatres have something of both elements but if placed on a continuum, contemporary conventional theatre tends much more towards entertainment, while Popular Theatre tends to emphasize socio-cultural and political change. That is, efficacious theatre not only symbolizes change but the participants actually begin to deeply internalise the symbolization and to live within the symbolic world. In the performance, people actually strengthen bonds of community. Social status is redefined so that people act differently toward each other and there is a commitment to change society.

In Schechner's view, the purest form of efficacious theatre is socio-religious ritual. In religious ritual, the mythic harmony established by divinity or the history of salvation is symbolically re-enacted. Through this re-enactment the community of participants affirm an alliance both with the divinity and among themselves. In social ritual, there is more emphasis on a strong sense of community, the resolution of conflict and the definition of the community's role responsibility for the harmonious welfare of the whole group.

In entertainment theatre participants are more concerned with the aesthetic and emotional aspects of the performance: the techniques of artistic combination of poetic expression, music, dance, the suspense of plot, the impersonation, elaborate costuming, stage setting and cathartic relaxation. There is an increasing separation of the audience and the professional performers who possess a high degree of technical performative skills. Efficacious theatre is concerned that all members of the community participate in the play and that all, the audience and actors, deeply identify with and intend to carry out the symbolic action of the play in their own lives. While efficacious theatre is considered to be a central locus of symbolic actualisation which is essential for the maintenance of the community and requires participation by all, entertainment theatre is an optional choice. When entertainment dominates, the performance tends to be class-oriented, individualistic, a matter of show business, constantly adjusting to suit the tastes of a fickle audience. This is why Schechner thinks, as do many others, that today the most vital forms of theatre are experimental, community involving and popular which have many of the elements of social ritual. On the other hand, when theatre becomes too ritualised and philosophical, it can also become tied to an established order.[22]

4. Performance not the Ultimate Aim

Popular Theatre consciously avoids a cathartic satisfaction and emotional release by seeing the problems fictionally resolved on the stage. The script must be completed in the real drama of community action. Hence there are two important areas to be considered: a. the process of making theatre more crucial than performance and b. action orientation.
a.   The process of making theatre is more important than the completed performance.

Leaders of Popular Theatre often mistakenly think that it is the performance that helps raise the consciousness of the people. The tradition of literary theatre is so strong that many well intentioned Popular Theatre groups think it their role to find or to write scripts that are incisive and powerful. They forget that the raising of consciousness comes from the *process* of creating drama rather than from the dramatic product. This means that discussion, performance and changes move in circles, all the while allowing the problem deeper and deeper analysis. Among professional theatre people there is almost a compulsion to present a completed and well rounded solution that plays upon the audience 's desire to see the question harmoniously 'wrapped up' at least in fictional presentation. For Kidd, posing the right sort of question is more important :

> Problem posing makes one question the deeper structures; it is a process of challenging commonly accepted ideas; of posing more and more questions to dig beneath the conventional explanations of reality, of raising and analysing contradictions; its object is understanding. Problem solving on the other hand is a more

pragmatic concern with immediate relief, with symptomatic treatment and therefore easily falls into the conventional extension exercise of looking for technically appropriate solutions.[23]

For Aristotle the best structured plays restored social harmony by re-affirming the existing power relations within the state. This is based on continuing the status quo and not on change. For the permanence of such a society completed plays were important. In Popular Theatre it is not fair to present a solution, for it there was one single solution to the problems that are presented it would be so unlike life. According to Etherton,

> the desire for completeness in dramatic art is the basis of an aesthetic which is highly effective in abstracting social problems. The 'completeness' is created by concluding narratives. A satisfying conclusion—either tragic or comic—to an enacted fictional depiction of reality actually removes the audience from that reality.[24]

In Aristotle's times although the slaves were never happy, they had to accept the philosophy of the completed plays which justified oppression when staged in theatre halls.[25] This pattern continues in today's conventional theatre. However, when the play is prepared by the people they analyse every bit of the issues involved. This is how they come to know that the real causes of poverty and underdevelopment are not their ignorance and weakness but the structural relationships which keep them powerless and exploited. They realize that the real problems are not lack of proper drinking water, illiteracy, superstition, large families and malnutrition, but exploitation, victimization, corruption and injustice.

b. Action Orientation

Following Boal's dictum 'theatre is a rehearsal for revolution,'[26] it is important that the issues presented in the plays are realistic. Von der Weid observes:

Conscientization is not simply a process of making conscious. The permanent liberation of man and his full humanization are not worked out in the interior of his consciousness, but in the area of history.[27]

Theatre activists need to give the necessary leadership in organizing protest marches and sit-ins, deliberating with government officials and leading the group into other forms of revolutionary action. Gradually the people gain confidence. Then it is time for the activists to withdraw. This explains why post-performance discussions and follow-up are crucial to the development of Popular Theatre.

5. People Participation

In this section also there are two levels of participation: a. in the real sense of the term where the audience can take control of the production and b. performing in a space where audience participation in play-acting becomes inevitable.

a. The essence of Popular Theatre is the full participation of the people. They need to be fully in charge—from deciding the themes to be drama-tized, the scripting, improvisations, acting, performance plans, follow up—everything needs to be handed over to the people. For, as Kidd observes, the key question is:

> *who controls the process?* Popular theatre may be participatory in the sense that local people are involved in producing it, in acting out the dramas and singing the songs, but unless they control the selection of content and the whole educational process they may become willing accomplices in their own domestication. Participation as mere performance is no guarantee of progressive change; unless rural villagers control the popular theatre process they may be used as mere mouthpieces for ideas produced by others which mystify their reality and condition them to accept a passive, dependent, uncritical role in an inequitable social structure.[28]

In Boal's methodology (simultaneous dramaturgy), the players invite the members of the community to discuss whether the drama did capture the real human and social problems of the community and incorporate their suggestions in subsequent staging of the play. In some cases (forum theatre) the action of the play may be stopped for the audience to discuss how the play should proceed. In a sense there is no definitive script or resolution. The community is encouraged to continue the exploration, and to move towards a solution in real action. Linking the aspect of audience participation in play production with the incomplete nature of the final production Etherton comments:

Enabling the actors-cum-audience to determine the content and direction of the drama means that *they discover the social contradictions for themselves*, in their own language, and so have the knowledge and understanding appropriate for political action. It is this praxis which 'completes' the 'incomplete' play. The play which is complete even before its first performance, on the other hand, communicates through a precise structure those social contradictions which have already been articulated into a wider strategy for change.[29]

b. Audience Participation in Performance

Most Popular Theatre groups attempt to take the performance off the stage and out of the architecture of proscenium into a space where the public habitually congregates. The purpose is to enable the audience to become an active part of the performance. Schechner has experimented with and written extensively on the environment of theatre. He suggests that space, movement and the architecture of performative environments are as communicative as the spoken text itself.[30] Proscenium theatre is a language which separates performance and audience; the stage gives the text an absolute, mystical authority. The audience is placed in a darkened house, relating individually, passively to the distant actors. Popular Theatre brings the performance into the midst of the audience where members of the audience can become aware of each other.

In Popular Theatre, actors not only speak to each other in a story close to the life of the audience, but they speak to the audience and in some cases, allow. the audience to enter into a dialogue. The performative action may move around a large room or a village square; at times diverse imagined scenes may suddenly pop up in the middle of the audience. The audience may move around with the action or suddenly find themselves part of a scene.

It should not be assumed from the above that Popular Theatre is a unified discipline. It is used by different groups with different interests– varying from domestication theatre and propaganda at one end of the spectrum to a process of consciousness raising, organization building and struggle at the other end.

V. Development of a Socially Conscious Theatre in India

We have no account of any early religio-civic ritual or community theatre which is critical of social orders or attempts political education. Some traces, however, may be noticed in the early Sanskrit literary tradition, although these are minimal. Two plays from this period need to be mentioned here for their attempts at tackling socio-political issues. *Mrichchakatika*, popularly ascribed to the legendary King Shudraka, deals with the love story of a poor cultured Brahmin and a rich courtesan. The play ends with a benediction justifying the doings of the Brahmins and the aristocracy: "May the people rejoice and the Brahmins be honoured, may the virtuous kings tame their foes and rule the earth".[31] Can there be a better eulogy for the aristocracy? In Vishakadatta's *Mudrarakshasa*, his only historical play, Chanakya, modelled on the historical character of Chandra Gupta Maurya's (322 - 298 BC) political adviser of the same name, plots to overthrow a king so as to replace him with another. Chanakya does not dare question the authority of the autocratic king and, as in the former play, mildly submits himself to the aristocracy.

Though a number of Sanskrit plays have references to wars and palace intrigues, these never become a challenge to the power of the aristocracy. As the playwrights were sponsored by kings, ministers and their social equals, they were secluded from real life situation, and their plays were a form of aesthetic entertainment meant for the aristocracy. But by the 11th century the tradition declined due to repression of the arts by the Muslim rulers and lack of support from the masses.

Colonial Legacy

Under the British, who drastically changed the educational system and literally uprooted the cultural fibres of the country, Indian theatre underwent considerable changes. In Calcutta, where the British first established themselves, the legend of the superiority of the British in everything began to show its ugly face. Before the battle of Plassey (1757), there was an English theatre in Calcutta and Warren Hastings is mentioned as one of its patrons. Apart from the English, only the rich native landlords or *bhadraloks* were allowed through the portals of this holy of holies. Playwright and producers were sent from England to produce English classics in India. Shakespeare, Marlowe, Sheridan and other English dramatists were presented as in Shaftesbury Avenue. Under the influence of these theatres the rich English-educated Indians began to produce English plays, taking their cue from English stagecraft and inventions. The first play was staged by a Russian adventurer, Herashim Lebedeff with the help of Goloknath Doss, on 7th November, 1795. No one knows if it was the Russian's love for Indian theatre or his dislike for the British which led him to translate two English comedies into Bengali. In spite of his success hardly anything happened for the next 40 to 50 years. An anaemic imitation of British theatre was produced by Prasannakumar Tagore in 1831 in English. Two years later, a Bengali theatre was founded in the house of Nabin Chandra Basu.

Meanwhile in 1842, in Sangli in Maharastra, the local king was fascinated by the *yakshagana* form. Whether through love of art or a sense of patriotism or to have an indirect dig at the British, he decided to patronize this form of theatre. A year later a mythological play *Sitaswayamvara* containing many of the elements of folk and English theatre was staged before a select audience. Back in Bengal, more socially conscious plays began to be staged. Ramnarain Tarakratna's *Kulin Kulasarvaswa* and *Naba Natak* were acclaimed social plays, directed against the practice of polygamy and the unquestioned supremacy of the Brahmins. A number of Sanskrit plays were translated into Bengali during this period. In 1853 Amanat's *Indersabha*, a play full of music, fantasy and hardly any content, was produced in Lucknow. It was so popular that it spawned a number of 'Indersabhas'. Indeed it was the time when the Sepoy Mutiny was in the air, but theatre had hardly grown sufficiently to venture into anything political. Nearly ten years later Michael Madhusoodan Dutt's *Sharmista*, although mythological in theme, explored the contemporary political situation. Vinayak Janardan Keertane's *Thorle Madhavrao Peshwe* analysed very briefly one of the reasons for the defeat in the Sepoy Mutiny. In Hindi, Bharatendu Harischandra's contribution in giving Indian theatre a specific form and social content was remarkable at this time. His plays *Satya Harischandra, Bharat Durdasha* and *Andher Nagari Chaupat Raja* were not only rich in social criticism but blended folk, Sanskrit, European and Bengali elements to form a refreshing theatre. Girish Chandra Ghosh launched, in 1872, a regular National Theatre with a professional company in Calcutta. This became a model for a number of other companies like 'The Star' and 'The Minerva'. The repertory of these theatres included tales from the Indian epics adapted to an English style of production.

A major reaction to this sort of cultural dominance, by the British was imminent from the Indians who took pride in their cultural heritage. The quest for a more realistic theatre mirroring the socio-political realities and the struggles of the people found its first expression in Dinabandhu Mitra's *Nildarpan* in 1872. It was a protest play intended to attack the tyranny of the British indigo planters in the rural areas. The play proved such a threat to the imperialists that the Dramatic Control Act was passed soon after. As a result for a while the plays emphasized social themes like alcoholism, superstition and casteism. However, in a number of mythological plays characters such as Keechaka, Kamsa and other evil giants from the Hindu mythology symbolized the evils of colonialism. In Khadilkar's *Keechakavadha* (1906) people immediately recognized in Bhima the person of Lokmanya Tilak, the national leader and in Keechaka, the character of Lord Curzon, the Viceroy of India. A stock character, the anglicized Indian who aped British customs and manners became the butt of jokes in several plays. Girish Ghosh exposed the corruption, bribery and blackmail that enabled the British to establish their supremacy in Bengal in his play, *Mir Kasim*, in 1907, much to the chagrin of the British. Similar efforts were seen in the works of D.L. Roy, Sisir Bhaduri, Manmanath Ray and others.

In the twenties, Mama Warerkar's socio-political plays *Satte Che Gulam, Sonya Cha Kalas* and *Bhomi Kanya Sita* were realistic and sober, but more or less couched in romantic notions of class struggle. Around the same time in Gujerat, Chandravadan Mehta was a considerable force. His *Aga Gari* and *Pinjara Pole* were successful attempts at exposing the evil practices in society. Around this time on the South India stage, Bellary Raghavachari and Adya Rangacharya were also concerned with theatre as a social force. In the thirties, in Tamil Nadu, Dravidian leaders, such as Periyar and Annadurai wrote *Velaikari* and *Chandrodayam* which not only denounced Brahminic superiority but also emphasized the need for legal reforms and the abolition of the *zamindari* (landlord) system.

The Development of Political Theatre

The political theatre movement did not emerge from folk theatre forms but from the tradition of Indian adaptations of Western proscenium theatre in urban centres such as Calcutta. The major inspiration was not the national independence movement or the Congress Party, but from Marxist-inspired currents of thought. Theatre became a nationwide movement with the founding of the IPTA in 1942 by the cultural wing of the Communist Party of India. The immediate cause for this was the

Bengal famine, when 3 million people starved to death, allegedly, due to the negligence of the ruling class. In 1944, Bijon Bhattacharya, one of the founders of the IPTA in Calcutta, wrote the play *Nabanna* which dramatized the exploitation of peasants by landowners, their gradual pauperisation and their death by starvation. The play was conventional in style, but was a conscious break with the artificial literary style of Bengali middle class theatre and eliminated the romantic sets and histrionic pyrotechnics of urban theatre. With its vivid portrayal of events, its genuineness of emotion and its use of the rustic language of the poor the play proved enormously successful.

This was just the beginning of the success of IPTA. Drawing heavily from the folk theatre forms of each region, IPTA became a powerful tool to spread nationalist and socialist ideals. The IPTA troupes, well established in every region took theatre to the masses and encouraged working class and peasant artists to join the movement and perform important roles. A number of IPTA plays agitated against national evils like black-marketeering, casteism and exploitation of the weaker sections. Plays like Bijon Bhattacharya's *Anthim Abhilasha*, K.A. Abbas' *Zubeida* and *Mai Kaun Hun*, Pritwiraj Kapoor's *Deewar* and *Pathan*, Thoppil Bhasi's *Ningalenne Commyunistaki*, Ghatak's *Dolil, India Immortal Ballet* and the Telugu *MaaBhoomi* exposed the ugly side of communalism and capitalist exploitation of the poorer classes.[32]

Sadly, after the Congress victory and independence, IPTA disintegrated—chiefly due to the problems within the Communist Party. But it spawned smaller units all over the country. Notable among these were: The Indian National Theatre (INT, Kamaladevi Chattopadhaya), the Little Theatre Group (LTG, Utpal Dutt), Kerala People's Arts Club (KPAC, Thoppil Bhasi) and several other state units of IPTA existing independently, but carrying on the crusade begun by IPTA. A number of playwrights like Habib Tanvir, Lakshmi Narain Lal, Badal Sircar, P.L. Deshpande, Sarveswar Dayal Saksena, Tripurari Sharma and others have faithfully continued the unique tradition of IPTA.

VI. Theatre and Education

It is important here to look at the dynamics of the educational process involved in Popular Theatre. Time and again critics have pointed out that Popular Theatre fails to steer clear of the dividing line between theatre and propaganda. If Popular Theatre is educational theatre, with a strong emphasis on enlightening the masses and providing incentives to reflect about their own lives, it has to be extremely cautious not to sound didactic and patronising. If Popular Theatre is accepted as the people's own art form, it is the people who should decide how the message is to be presented. The effectiveness of Popular Theatre depends on the four stages of information, education, motivation and action. All these can be attained without forced or pedantic communication. Here it may be useful to look at the way Theatre-In-Education functions.

Theatre-In-Education (TIE)

TIE creates opportunities for students to discover for themselves how to deal with their own social environment in all its complexity. This happens by 'stage-managing' contemporary or historical situations in which the young people are called upon to play roles, take sides, deal with confrontation, and make decisions on issues like racism, trade unions, colonialism, ecology, local problems, etcetera. Pammeter differentiates the method of TIE from indoctrination:

TIE seeks literate understanding and not imposed order...to make sense of the chaos of the real world...and so allow children to perceive and understand the changes and contradictions going on around them and of which they are a part.[33]

Evidently TIE is influenced by Freire's theory of conscientization. The rich theatrical content in TIE productions attracts the students. Creative demands are made on their imagination and vocal expression which they enjoy considerably. The process of play-making helps them develop an acute sense of character observation and understanding of other people, leading to a broader social sense. It also acts as an important therapeutic effect, the value of which can be realised when emotions like hate, fear or suspicion are discussed, evaluated and then channelled into creative drama.

Theatre for Propaganda

Given the potential of theatre as a powerful political art, it is no wonder that a number of newly independent governments of the third world have used it to consolidate themselves. Theatre has often been used to inculcate a sense of national identity and unity, to legitimize the ways of the ruling party and to disseminate national policies and ideologies. Being the most public of arts it offers a powerful opportunity for persuasion, motivation and mobilization. Following the example of countries like France, Russia and many other independent countries, the Indian government and a number of government-supported private organizations began to use theatre as a tool for propaganda.

It was in this context that during the turbulent years after independence, the government of India, under the auspices of the Song and Drama Division (SDD), set out to awaken the rural and urban poor through the creative use of theatre. The major task of the department was to promote national unity and to persuade the rural poor to accept reformist and government controlled ways for dealing with problems like population explosion, poverty, casteism, bonded labour, lack of housing and illiteracy. SDD grew into a massive programme with subunits in each state, 40 full-time troupes and about 500 registered part-time troupes. During the war against China (1962) and Pakistan (1965 and 1971) SDD was active in the villages, playing on the patriotic sentiments of the people. Taking a leaf out of the experiences of IPTA, INT and other community theatres before and after independence, SDD went all out to exploit the rich treasures of the folk forms–dance drama, poetry, ballads, puppetry. Looking back at the activities of SDD one may say that the performing arts were not used as strategy for raising the awareness of the people, or for making the people challenge their oppressive situation, but for mass information and for legitimizing the policies and practices of the government. The messages of all the SDD plays had been decided and worked out in advance by the 'experts' and not in consultation with the people. Most of the scripts present a neat technical solution of a single problem. They were unrealistic and often presented in the form of a service provided by the government without any reference to socio-political content or implications of the solution prescribed. For example, it was not enough to persuade the traditional farmer to apply fertilizer to his crops without discussing the problem of its availability and the financial implication connected with it. In the same way it was unfair to advocate family planning without tackling the popular belief that a large family provides extra labour and security in one's old age. As a result the plays did not help the people to reflect on the basic structural incongruities in society.[34]

Another voluntary agency Jagran (awakening) was founded in 1968 by the independent mime artist Aloke Roy at the suggestion of a government family planning official. The success of mime in cutting across language barriers in India impressed everyone and Roy launched

a nationwide campaign propagating the government ideology. Funds
flowed in from national as well as foreign sources. During the emergency
(1975-77) imposed by Indira Gandhi, Jagran settled down to a
motivational campaign in the slums of north Delhi at the request of the
Delhi Development Authority. Briefly Jagran's job was to make the
people conscious of a) obstacles to their development, b) the services
provided by the government, c) their responsibilities to their community,
and d) their rights as citizens. In other words Jagran became an unproclaimed
offshoot of SDD.[35]

VII. Types of Popular Theatre in Present-Day India

After the decline of IPTA the interest in theatre as a tool for mass
education, politicization and mobilization continued, but in a less
organized way. A new generation of playwrights began to experiment
with three major types of socially committed theatre: 1) professional
drama with literarily crafted scripts staged in conventional theatres; 2)
fairly radical adaptations of folk opera traditions, but orienting them more
to peasant folk rituals, religious observances and dialects than to the
classical Sanskrit and Brahminic forms; 3) non-professional street theatre
which at times adapted styles of village folk performances such as
narrative ballads, but more generally were direct educational and political
dramatisations. Here we are concerned with the latter two forms, both
of which come under the title of Popular Theatre.

Three forms of Popular Theatre with distinct, yet overlapping
approaches emerged from these two forms.

1. Street theatre

Here theatre is taken by middle class artists to peasants, workers and
slum dwellers in order to conscientize and politicize them. Its main
strength lies in it being the work of people outside the generally accepted
theatre boundary. Examples of this category are Jan Natay Manch,
Samudaya and some IPTA branches in Kerala, Andhra Pradesh, Bihar
and West Bengal who concentrate on current problems like dowry deaths,
price hikes and caste atrocities. This form of theatre is studied in chapter
IV.

2. Community theatre

Another form of theatre may be called workshop or community theatre. In this, a cultural activist with sufficient knowledge of the theatre runs a workshop with a group of people who belong to an organization or institute. The activist devises plays with them on problems crucial to their work. Habib Tanvir began in this way in Chattisgarh. The trend was carried on by Badal Sircar, Tripurari Sharma and Rati Bartholomew. Community theatre, however, has been amalgamated into a third form–the SAG theatre.

3. Social Action Group (SAG) theatre

Activists have realised that workshops are too short and have inadequate follow-up. Although theatre animateurs may work for sometime in the villages, enthusiasm soon runs dry and conscientization remains only skin-deep. Hence, action groups that follow Freirian methods have formed their own theatre groups which regularly stage plays in the villages and with the help of the villagers. From the early seventies, theatre has become for many action groups a means to build up confidence to analyse social issues. At a recent conference on Community Development in Delhi this work was described as "the new panacea":

> More and more agencies are using these methods where conventional strategies have failed, or have not been quick enough.... We are either entering a new renaissance with this work or we are watching the last desperate, attempt to have some impact on these global problems.[33]

This phenomenon is studied in chapter V.

Understandably there is a common factor in all these forms; they accept theatre not as an end in itself but as a part of a larger organizational process of development for people. They address and involve the community directly and simply. They are not merely linked with the poor and the oppressed communities but exist only for them; outside of that context they are meaningless.

Notes

1. Art for art's sake theory connotes the idea that a work of art has an intrinsic value without didactic or moral purpose. It was first forwarded by Lessing in 1766. It became something of an artistic battle cry or slogan following the publication of Gautier's *Preface to Mademoiselle de Maup* (1835). Oscar Wilde was one of its strong advocates.

2. Deak, F., "Russian Mass Spectacles," *TDR* 66, June 1975, p. 22.

3. Howard, Roger, "Agitation and Anaesthesia: Aspects of Chinese Drama Today,"*Theatre Research International*, no. 11, p. 53.

4. Fisher, DJ., "Romain Rolland and the French People's Theatre", *TDR*, T., 73, March 1977, p. 76.

5. Brecht, Bertolt, "Brecht on Experimental Theatre" in *Brecht On Theatre*, trans. John Willet, Methuen, London, 1964, p. 130.

6. Ibid., p. 108.

7. Boal's ideas on theatre are collated from his work, *Theatre of the Oppressed*, Pluto Press, London, 1979.

8. Ibid., p. 122.

9. Ibid.

10. The statement was issued at an International Conference on Popular Theatre held at Koitta, Bangladesh, 1982.

11. Kerr, David, "Didactic Theatre in Africa," *Harward Educational Review*, February 1981, pp. 145-55.

12. Leis, Raul Alberto, "Popular Theatre and Development in Latin America," *Educational Broadcasting International*, London, March 1979.

13. These ideas are from Srampickal, Jacob and White, Robert A. (eds.), *Trends in Communication Research*, CSCC, London, March 1988.

14. Erven, Eugene Van, "Beyond the Shadows of Wayang: Liberation Theatre in Indonesia" *National Theatre Quarterly*, vol.V no. 17, 1989.

15. Kidd, Ross, *The Popular Performing Act, Non-formal Education and Social Change in the Third World: a Bibliography and Review Essay* (bibliography no. 7), The Hague (CESO), Netherlands, 1982. This excellent bibliography contains 1799 entries and is the most comprehensive listing of publications on the performing arts, Third World development and political action.

16. This explanation of *povo* is adapted from *Media Development*, 1/88, p. 1.

17. *Mother India* and *Sholay* were the biggest box-office hits in Indian cinema and have been widely shown in the country.

18. These ideas are taken from Schechner, Richard, *Performative Circumstances from the Avant Garde to Ramlila*, Seagull Books, Calcutta, 1983, p. 140ff.

19. Shehadeh, Radi D., " El-Hakawati Theatre Company: Thorn in the Flesh of Oppression" *Media Development*, vol. 5 no. 3, p. 8.

20. Semil, Malgorzata, "Young People's Theatre in Poland Reaches for Truth" *Media Development*, 35/3, p. 12.

21. Dutt, Utpal, *Towards a Revolutionary Theatre*, p. 142.
22. Schechner, op. cit., (no. 18).
23. Kidd, Ross and Byram, Martin, "De-mystifying Pseudo-Freirian Non-Formal Education: A case description and analaysis of Laedza Batanani," *Canadian Journal of Development Studies*, 3/2/1983, p. 284.
24. Etherton, Michael, "Popular Theatre for Change from Literacy to Oracy", in *Media Development*, 35/3, WACC, London, 1988. All references to Etherton in this section are from this article.
25. Ibid.
26. Boal, op. cit. (no. 7), p. 122.
27. Quoted by Kidd, Ross in "Domestication Theatre and Conscientization Drama in India" in Colletta Nat and Kidd, Ross, *Traditions for Development*, German Foundation for International Development, Berlin, 1983, p. 493.
28. Kidd, Ross, op. cit. (no. 23).
29. Etherton, Michael, "African Theatre and Political Action," manuscript, p. 8.
30. Schechner's ideas are taken from various places, notably, op. cit . (no. 18) above.
31. This quote from the play *The Clay Cart* is my own translation from the Sanskrit text.
32. Pradhan, Sudhi, *Marxist Cultural Movements: Chronicles and Documents*. Vols. 1 and 2 have a lot of material on IPTA. National Book Agency Pvt. Ltd., Calcutta, 1979.
33. Pammeter, S., in Jackson, Tony, *Learning Through Theatre*, Manchester University Press, 1980, p. 3.
34. Kidd, Ross, op. cit., (no. 27), p. 487.
35. Personal conversations and op. cit. (no. 27.), p. 490.
36. As quoted by Burns, Kevin, "Theatre for Development,"*Media in Education and Development*, London, June 1985, p. 87.

Chapter III

Folk Theatre:
The Root of Popular Theatre

Two distinct conclusions emerge from an analysis of folk theatre: a. despite its support and legitimation of the Brahminic principles and status quo, folk theatre has espoused the vision of a just and egalitarian society and has been a vehicle of protest; b. folk theatre has a form that is highly colourful and vibrant and helps effective communication. Modern street theatre (chapter IV) adapts these forms and continues in the same tradition.

I. Folk Tradition—An Introduction

The word 'tradition' connotes the act of handing down and what is handed down from one generation to another. It is generally understood as the cumulative heritage of a society including customs, habits and ways of life which become embodied in institutions, and then tend to become frozen because of stability and autonomous existence of these institutions. Tradition, therefore, implies age and a long period of continuity. It can be transmitted through written scriptures or through word of mouth. The tradition transmitted through word of mouth is termed 'oral'. A group of nomadic, primitive people sharing a common cultural heritage based on oral traditions is generally said to have a folk culture. Cultural forms that follow codified and strict rules may be called classical. 'folk' implies community participation and spontaneity whereas 'classical' implies the use of highly technical forms.

Anthropologically, India is divided into tribal (12%), rural (75%) and urban (13%) levels. Due to vast geographic disparities, rural settlements and lack of modern education folk cultures abound in India. Folk forms may arbitrarily be said to belong to the tribal and rural belts and classical to the urban. But a closer examination will show that such assumptions are not fully true. Kapila Vatsyayan explains:

> An analysis of the music, dance and drama of the tribals make little or no distinction between verbal and non-verbal communication systems and techniques. Expression is total. Individually the expressions may be free, but in groups, life-functions and experiences condition movements and sounds. Song and dance may be a participative activity but never spontaneous. Like the tribal society artistic forms too are highly structured.[1]

In the same way it may be noticed that urban centres like Calcutta and Bombay were the seats of folk culture before they came under western influence.

Folk culture in a society is seen in four different forms:

1. *Oral tradition.* These are mostly verbal arts or expressive literature consisting of spoken, sung, and voiced forms of traditional utterances like songs, tales, poetry, ballads, anecdotes, rhymes, proverbs and elaborate epics.

2. *Material culture.* These are visible aspects of folk behaviour such as skills, recipes and formulae as displayed in rural arts and crafts, traditional motifs, architectural designs, clothes, fashions, farming, fishing and various other types of tools and machinery.

3. *Social folk customs.* These are areas of traditional life which emphasize the group rather than the individual skills and performances. They include large family and community observances and relate to rites of passages such as birth, initiation, marriage and death or annual celebrations, festivals, fairs, ritual and ceremonial gatherings, market occasions and rural meets.

4. *Performing arts.* These include traditional music, masquerades, dance and drama. This form is discussed at length later.[2]

Some authors describe the concept of folk as being smaller, isolated, homogeneous, simple, less systematic and less specialized in comparison with the up-market classical forms.[3] Others emphasise its tightly knit kinship structures, common sentiments and shared values. There are others who hold that folk arts are unsophisticated and localized. In fact all these are true and each partially reveal the concept of folk art. But basically what is unacceptable is to regard folk culture as static remnants of the past. For then the concept may appear pejorative whereas it needs to be seen as syncretic, flexible and able to adapt to the changing situations. As folk cultures evolve and change over the years they come into contact with other communities.

Folk Forms as Communication Media

Among the four forms listed, oral tradition and the performing arts appear to be the main media of communication. Story-tellers, singers, jesters, minstrels and other kinds of folk entertainers, have acted for centuries as sources for the transmission and dissemination of news and information through face to face live communication. Families, social groups, organization and community gatherings serve as the main fora of communication and sources for feedback for the folk performers. It is through these forms that values, attitudes, beliefs and culture of the people are propagated, reinforced and perpetuated. Very often they have been used to fortify the feudal servility of the masses, the myths of the powerful and the superstitions that control much of their lives. The folk artists have also tried to make comments on particular members of the community or issues in the form of satires in order to correct societal ills.

Studies done by Shyam Parmar and H.K. Ranganath underline areas where folk media scores over mass media.

- they are local, intimate and establish immediate rapport with the masses in all the regions of the country;
- their primary appeal is to the emotions rather than to the intellect and they have greater potential for persuasive communication and instant feedback;
- they belong to the community and not to any individual, state, or public industry. There are no organized institutions or persons to control either the quality or quantity of these media. There are no authors, or copyrights, but they remain anonymous and can be adapted at will by anyone to suit a particular need;
- they use the language, idiom and symbols of the people. Because of this they can be highly participatory and form part of communal celebrations wherein everyone takes an active part ;

- they command an immense variety of forms and themes to suit the communication requirements of the masses. Themes ranging from myths to current issues can easily find expression through these forms. The use of these media to disseminate development messages in newly independent countries is a case in point.[4]

Folk media are relatively inexpensive and do not require specialized skills that the ordinary people cannot learn. This adds to the popularity of the folk media in rural areas. Above all, their highly spontaneous, participatory and involving quality make them the media par excellence for any powerful and effective communication.

II. Folk Theatre

It is against this background that folk theatre emerges as a powerful means of social communication in traditional societies. Folk theatre, vibrant, rugged and unsophisticated in form and rich in variety and colour is an expression of the cultural heritage of a region. As practised in folk societies it has evolved from oral literature like songs, folk tales, proverbs, ballads, chants, riddles, jokes, anecdotes and all sorts of verbal utterances. It is assumed that these forms were accompanied by visual representations like facial expressions, mimicry, gestures, and other histrionic effects that made them more than mere oral utterances. Dorson rightly notices that the folk communicators in their performances while facing a live audience employed gestures, eye contact, intonation, panto-mime and histrionics, and probed as the authors of written words never did.[5] In the same vein Ruth Finnegan suggests,

the expression of tone, gestures, facial expressions, dramatic use of pause and rhythm, the interplay of passion, dignity or humour and receptivity to the reactions of the audience are integral as well as flexible parts of its full realization as a work of art.[6]

All these show that folk theatre was the most powerful medium of communication in folk cultures. Gradually as folk theatre took shape, it pooled together the communicative powers of all the myriad forms of folk literature. Mathur observes:

Folk theatre freely uses songs, dances, and instrumental music, blends dialogue and acting. This multiple approach results in a form that is self-contained and a complete entertainment for the audience at whom it is directed. It is more than entertainment, it is a complete emotional experience and aims at creating an environment of receptivity in which communication of ideas is an effortless process.[7]

While the spectacle of classical theatre and the naturalistic details of a conventional modern play tend to divert the attention from the central idea of the play, folk theatre simplifies realism and suggestivity to rural symbols to which the mass audience can easily relate.

The Origin of Folk Theatre

It was pointed out in chapter I how theatre may have evolved from natural needs like hunting and religious worship. It was also mentioned that folk cultures engage in celebrations which include singing, dancing and playing. These cultures celebrate events such as birth, initiation, marriage, death, burial, thanksgiving for special favours received, traditional year cycles and occupational pursuits like hunting and fishing. Folk theatre performances are closely associated to such celebrations. There are a number of fertility rites linked to food gathering, the earth, the sun and the moon. In these the immediacy of life experiences is recalled in sound, rhythm and movement. Dramatic action, too, in the form of spoken words and gestures makes its appearance.

In the villages music, dance, and drama have been woven into agricultural functions, seemingly integral to the daily routine of the peasants. The traces of tribal practices are clearly seen in the agricultural rites connected with sowing, reaping and harvesting. Similarly, studying the various forms of folk theatre prevalent in rural England from the 16th and 17th centuries, Harrop suggests that these were primarily meant for maintaining traditions and upholding the values of community life through celebrations.[8]

It is important here to note that within the context of folk performances there are traditional demands for ritual observances before, during and after the celebrations. Conversely, in some of the ceremonies associated with these festivals there is a great deal of dialogue or interaction between the celebrants and members of the family, community or social groups. In some cases, as in a festival, the whole community is involved.

Since Indian society was nurtured in the oral tradition where the bulk of learning was transferred through the narration of stories, myths, hymns and songs, it is only natural that one of the ways through which they expressed their feelings about social problems was the theatre. This may have provided them with a forum of rebelling against feudal landlords and oppressive regimes. But, sadly, we have no written documents to prove this.

There are good reasons to believe that a clearly defined form of folk theatre may have emerged even before the ornate Sanskrit tradition. Apart from the standard classical drama, *bhana* and *prahasana* are two rustic forms of drama mentioned in the Sanskrit tradition. In both these forms several elements of the now popular folk theatre are present. In a *bhana*, the performer narrates dramatically a variety of events. Love, war, fraud and intrigue are narrated, interspersed with music and singing. The *prahasana* is a farcical satire levelled at ascetics, Brahmins and men of wealth and rank. Such plays are marked by extreme indelicacy and sensuality. Their main object is to provoke laughter.

A number of characteristics of the Sanskrit classical tradition is seen in the more refined folk theatre that developed from the 11th century and is still extant in the rural areas. This poses another problem about the origin of folk theatres. The intentional denial of the unities of space and time, the conventional *purvaranga* or stage preliminaries, the division of the play into plots and sub-plots, the presence of the hero and the heroine, anti-heroes and villains and the all-important use of *vidhushaka* (jester) and *sutradhar* (stage manager) are some of the common elements found both in Sanskrit and folk theatre. This intermingling of *margi* (Sanskrit) and *desi* (local) forms presents us with another dilemma about the beginning of folk theatre.

It may be assumed that folk tradition existed well before Sanskrit tradition, but it was not developed as we know it today. However, with the decline of the Sanskrit tradition in the 11th century its various elements splintered into regional vernacular forms. Folk theatre assimilated all these and survived, unopposed by the Muslim rulers, in the villages of India. The style and content of Sanskrit plays underwent drastic changes in folk theatre. The wide kaleidoscopic variety of Indian culture may have given rise to multiple varieties of folk theatre rich in content, heritage and form. The tremendous lucidity these forms enjoyed, compared to the stringent and esoteric nature of Sanskrit theatre, allowed them to flourish and find expression in a number of genres, forms, styles and techniques.

From the 9th century onwards, there was political chaos and disintegration all over India.[9] Besides, a moral reaction against the ritualistic excesses propagated by the decadent Buddhism had set in. The *bhanas* and *prahasana* of the period reflected the general immoral and unethical outlook. It was against all these excesses that powerful and popular religious movements emerged. Religious leaders like Vallabhacharya (11th), Shankaradeva (12th), Narain Bhatt (12th), Surdas (13th), Chaitanya (15th), Purandaradas (15th) and others made use of theatre for this purpose. The drama that followed turned to mythology for characters, moral content, and devotional inspiration. The *Bhagavata* cult managed effectively to use all the available audio-visual media like folk theatre, music and puppetry with effortless ease for nearly 400 years.[10] Since this coincided with Muslim conquests[11] when theatre was denied any royal patronage, only folk theatre forms, supported by petty kings and temple priests, could flourish.

Mention must also be made of the rise of a professional hereditary class of theatre artists called *charanas* around the 11th century. They were partonized by the local kings and nobles. Specializing in one-man shows that sang the praises of the kings and their exploits, they developed a theatre. Following the Sanskrit tradition the *nati* (actress) and other stock characters were introduced. Later associating themselves with saints and religious leaders they contributed enormously to make the theatre popular among the people.

Origin of Some of the Popular Folk Forms

According to Gargi,[12] *yatra* grew out of the musical enactment of an episode from Lord Krishna's life. Krishna leaves his foster parents and milk-maids in the woods of Vrindavan and goes to Mathura to kill King Kamsa. His march or *yatra* has been celebrated in the *palas* (plays) and the heart-rending separation became the favourite theme of singers and players. Later any play about Krishan or any mythological character was called a *yatra*. Consolidation of this form of performance came from the Vaishnava saint, Chaitanya Deb. In his discourses on the equality of man and the fraternity of all castes, he would go into ecstasies as he sang and danced in the streets with his followers.

Nautanki, the popular folk form of north India evolved out of ballads and the recitals of poets. The ballad singers, as they narrated their stories, dramatized the emotions of the characters. Gradually more singers joined in, explanations were added in prose, and each actor began to specialise

3. Narrative Ballads

The most widespread forms of folk theatre are the long narrative songs performed more often by local villagers who have handed down the stories and musical skills for generations. In these forms there is one principal performer assisted by singers and musicians. The *burrakatha* of Andhra Pradesh or the *Veedhinatakam* or Tamil Nadu are examples.

4. Puppetry

Puppet troupes, varying from a one-man team to seven or eight family members, are engaged for village festivals or travel about to market fairs. Performances are usually accompanied by singing, interspersed with stylized prose dialogue. In India string (marionettes), rod shadow and glove puppets are popular.

III. The Content Of Folk Theatre

The first thing that strikes anyone about the content of folk theatre is the clear demarcation between the religious and the secular with an undercurrent of the romantic. However, the two do not continue in isolation; whenever possible, they have been synthesized into one whole. In a study on the feasibility of adapting folk media for nation-building purposes by the Government of India, H.K. Ranganath made the following categorical divisions:

1. Ritual forms: These are inappropriate for the development of communication because of their insistence on religious decorum and inbuilt resistance to the insertion of foreign contents. Examples of this form are religious arts masquerades, *theyyam*, *yellamma* songs, tribal dances, etc.
2. Semi-flexible forms: These are traditional forms on mythological or historical theme whose overall structure is rigid, but permit didactic contents to be communicated through the jester or narrator during the interludes between episodes. For instance in *yakshagana*, the jester enjoys the freedom to pass comments on issues of contemporary relevance and the stage manager intervenes to carry on a dialogue with the audience.
3. Flexible forms: These can be fully modernized and a thoroughly new

storyline followed. Termed "syncretic" or "transitional" these include story telling forms like *harikatha, pad, kavi gaan,* ballad singing, pupperty.[16]

Ranganath's analysis, too, boils down to the three basic themes: religious, romantic and social.

1. Religious Themes

The two Hindu epics—the *Ramayana* and the *Mahabharata*—are crowded with gods and demons, kings and holy men, nymphs and fairies, heroes and heroines. The *Mahabharata* is the story of the long feud between the five Pandava brothers and their hundred cousins, the Kauravas. The Pandavas represent good and the Kauravas evil. Krishna, an incarnation of God, is on the side of the Pandavas. The philosophical idea at the root of this story is the operation of *Dharma*, the principle of right conduct which each person must find for himself, which, when rightly understood, is discipline and order, yet also freedom. What inspires one are the stories of courage, idealism, rectitude, salvation, sincerity etc., as typified through characters, both good and evil. The *Ramayana* is the story of Ram and Sita, his wife; the ideal man and woman. Laxman and Bharat, the brothers of Ram are models of selfless brotherly love.

Both these epics are long, rambling, adventure stories dealing with morality and maxims, differentiating between noble and base behaviour. As gods and human beings mix freely in heaven and earth through the aeons of time, a plethora of philosophies, arguments, logic and a highly spiritual drama of passion and sentiments emerge. All these explain the profound effect the epics have on the lives, attitudes, ethos, morals and aspirations of the ordinary people. Characters like Ram, Krishna, Sita, Arjun, Ravana, Hanuman, Radha and others appear in folk theatre in gorgeous costumes to inspire the teeming millions. *Ramlila* and *Krishnalila,* literally meaning the play of Rama and Krishna, use the word 'play' *(lila)* to denote acts of the gods.

Stories that have rich religious content gain acceptance all over India even if these are not about the central characters of the epics. Stories with moral instruction, that show the triumph of the spirit of devotion and the fall of pride and pomp are favourites in religious folk theatre. Stories like *Parashurama Vijaya, Ravana Vadha, Rukmini Haran* and *Prahlad Vijay* have become popular among the people.

Mythological themes were also treated in a lighter vein in the folk plays. Krishna is often presented as a prankster who could love, deceive, laugh and tease exactly as an ordinary human being would. One of his popular images in the *Raslila* of Mathura and Vrindavan near Delhi, and the *ankiya naat* of Assam has been as a young cow-herd, full of pranks, among the maidens of Braj. In *Parijat Haran* he is shown as an ordinary husband out to please both his wives. In *Danlila* he is a Romeo stopping all the maidens who refuse to pay so as to be allowed to sell curds and milk. In all these plays the human and attractive aspects of Krishna are brought out, the aim being to arouse deep affection among the devotees for him and to fill their hearts with joy in an otherwise joyless existence. In terms of form, such presentations have enriched the folk theatre with pastoral songs and group dances.

Besides the Hindu epics, the many *Jatakas* and *Puranas* of Buddhist and Jain origins are also a reservoir of stories and legends for the folk theatre practitioner. Add to these other local legends of a religious nature and we have a complete picture of the religious content of folk theatre. From these emerge a number of forms like *jhaanki, koodiyattom, ramanattom, yakshagana* and *therukoothu.*

The Romantic Element

Romantic tales were used by sundry schools of mystics for spreading their ideas. This was particularly suitable at a time when the Muslim rulers shunned any reference to figures from Hindu mythology. Secular heroes and heroines were fashioned as spokesmen of morality and mysticism. The *Kathasaritasagar,* for instance, is a collection of short stories of this nature, but extolling virtues of family love, dedication, generosity and sacrifice. *Nautanki,* the chivalrous story of the romance between Bhup Singh and the princess Nautanki became so popular that the word 'nautanki' began to be associated with any story of similar romantic style. Other romantic stories like *Siya Posh, Padmavati, Khuda Dost* and *Chandra Kiran* were built around the romances of the princely classes with a number of stock characters like faithful friend, servant, gardener, executioner and other situations like mistaken identity and disguise. In later years the romantic tales shifted from the princely classes to the middle and lower classes. In *Rangila Rashma* and *Lilo Chaman* there are characters of lower castes in leading roles. In the *khyals* of Rajasthan, similarly, the romantic tales of humble and ordinary folk are presented as having become legendary figures due to their strength of character and virtuous behaviour. The legend of *Tejaji* in Rajasthan or *Jasma Odan* in Gujarat come under this category. Analysing these romantic tales Mathur notes that a number of them end in tragedy. There are characters eternally separated from their loved ones, offering up their lives for noble causes, men sacrificing their lives for others. However, this is not a tragedy of waste and annihilation for there is reconciliation in every tear, a chastening experience in suffering for higher ends. Again in these stories love is coupled with passion and eroticism, which to some may seem crude and obscene.[17] Didactic passages are only too common in these stories. In the play *Siya Posh,* when the hero Gabru is about to be hanged, he exhorts his wife to conduct herself worthily as a widow and stresses the values of a simple life and high thinking for women in such situations. In sum it may be noticed that in spite of dabbling in romantic stories the major concerns of these folk theatres are the basic values upon which the faith of the common people depends.

Social Themes

The 18th century brought along with it rapid social and political changes. Folk theatre joined forces with the changing times by including numerous socio-political themes. It is in this period that the more secular forms like *nautanki, khyals, bhavai* and *chhau* flourished. These were replete with the social situations of the time but, as times changed, their contents became irrelevant and were forgotten.

Nautanki, an operatic form, concentrated on historical characters, famous warriors and legendary lovers like Laila-Majnu, Shirin-Farhad, Seth-Sethani, Amar Singh Rathod and others. Even within the context of such romantic stories *nautanki* commented upon the existing situations in society. The buffoon, speaking in prose, caricatured persons in authority making satirical comments on local worthies, denouncing social evils and injustices and extemporizing on matters that directly concerned the villagers. Political leaders, landlords and police officers came up against sharp criticism.

Bhavai dealt mostly with medieval tales of chivalry. It is said that this form was begun by Asahita Takur, a 14th century poet singer and actor of a high caste Brahmin family, who was boycotted by his community for the crime of eating with a low caste woman. He resorted to music and acting to earn his livelihood. Gradually under this tutelage, the *bhavai* form developed. In this he narrated the stories of heroes, knights, cavaliers and gallant lords. With a cast of about 14 people long narrative stories were enacted in song, dance and drama. Needless to say his stories were full of social content. Similarly Phatte Bapu Rao, one of the prominent *tamasha* writers who gave up everything including his place in society to marry a poor lower caste woman has also written a number of plays about the evils of the caste system and the disparity between the rich and the poor.

The *swaang* is a light farce enacted by two *bhanda* or village buffoons. Their acerbic comments belie a shrewdness and intelligence almost masked by stupidity yet provide an analysis of topical events with pungent humour. Holding a triangular folder to slap his partner, the *bhaiaya,* or the elder brother, lets loose a barrage of questions on what is happening in and around the villages, to which the younger brother gives thought-provoking and sarcastic answers.

The *Kharyala* of Himachal Pradesh are crude 'acts' built around character types. The acts of various village powerholders like the revenue officer and policeman expose corrupt practices. The acts of the village witch are meant to expose superstitious beliefs. Similarly the acts of other people in the village also uncover other evils, and thus the people are enlightened. In one play some holy men visit a village and exhort the people, but their acts are shown to be hypocritical.

Bidesia is a very popular form of play in Bihar originating from the late 19th century. An illiterate barber Bhikari Thakur performed a play *Bidesia* with a roving group of actors about a current problem of labourers from Bihar going away to Calcutta, leaving their young wives at home and becoming attached to city women. They play was so popular that a new form of *Bidesia* plays began to be staged about the problems of unequal marriage, young brides and older men, poor men and rich wives.[18]

Yatra, the folk form of Bengal began as a religious celebration. Gradually it incorporated secular themes and characters. The improvisations of the singers and actors were replete with comments on contemporary life and political realities. During the reign of the British, in the period of nationalism and independence movements, *Yatra* became a potent political form.

The *bhands*, the wandering minstrels of the Punjab and Kashmir entertained the audience with satirical commentaries on matters of contemporary interest. The audience was shown their faults and indirectly advised to lead a better life. This is a typical style of folk education. Another example of this is *Ramadhanaya natak* by Kanaka-dasa, a Kannada verse play. It is about *ragi* , a cereal popular in the state. As *ragi* is black, other cereals began to ridicule it. An argument follows as to which is the greatest. Lord Rama is invited down as the judge. He asks all the seeds to go underground. After two years when they were all dug out, only the *ragi* seed is found to be sprouting. The moral is obvious.[19] In this way folk theatre forms show a gradual progression from mythological to socio-political themes. Current-event subjects like co-operative agricultural farming, national integration, religious unity, the evils of corruption, dowry and the standards of modern morality have been scrutinized through these plays well before they were used in a propagandist way. Drawing on well-known classics as well as proverbs and parables with popular appeal, and laced with humour and satire, these plays comment subtly on contemporary life. In all these the denunciation of evil and the triumph of good over evil and of right over wrong are emphatically proclaimed, echoing 'the victory of the gods over the demons' syndrome.

IV. Protest Themes in Folk Theatre

There have been occasions when the treatment of social themes in theatres have gone beyond just a study of a social situation, and have taken a more aggressive form of protest against current social practices. One of the earliest forms of protest was against the practice of the caste system.

Caste Consciousness in Folk Theatre

The traditional account preserved in the *Natyasastra* indicates that drama was composed to provide relaxation to all castes, and especially for those who had no access to the *vedas* or holy books. Although Bharata has mentioned that theatre needs to challenge the barriers of caste and creed, in actual practice each caste was allotted a specific function in folk theatre, thus legitimating the discrimination. He prescribes that the four main pillars of a theatre hall and the four colours used to paint the walls are representative of the four castes: *Brahmins, Kshatriyas, Vaishyas* and *Sudras*. No doubt following this concern theatre began to maintain the role and position of all castes.[20]

It is true that all over India most of the folk theatre forms are commonly practised by professional classes of lower castes known as *Bhadas, Nats, Ghandarvas, Vairagis, Bhavayas, Bauls, Gaajis, Binkaras.* However, in many of the major forms like *Ramlila, Raslila, ankiya naat, bhaona, yakshagana and koodiyattom* there are specific roles allotted to the different castes.

In *Ramlila,* the chief roles are always played by young Brahmin boys under the age of fourteen. Panicker records the case of *patayani,* a Kerala ritual theatre where each caste has a special role. The *parayan* provides the leather for the drum, the *tandan* must bring the areca nut fronds required for the mask and head gear, the *ganakan* paints the mask and sings, the *kuruvan* keeps the country torches burning, the *patiyan* washes the clothes to be used for deity's dress and the *maran* gets the torches ready and keeps them supplied with oil. Similarly the *nambudiri,* the *konkan* and even the Christian, the Muslim and the foreigner have their specific roles to perform.[21]

It is important here to examine why folk theatre preserves the traditional allocation of caste separation, before any attempt at protest theatre is mentioned.

According to Srinivas[22] from the beginning of the Aryan invasion of India around 1500 BC from the Middle East, two traditions, Great and Little have flourished. Both have their roots in the Hindu scriptures and these are mediated and appropriated through participation in festivals and traditional media of communications. The accent of the Great tradition is on the worship of pure deities like Brahma and Vishnu, but the little tradition, surviving in the rural and tribal areas, worship local gods and goddesses. The major points of difference between the Great and Little traditions lie in a literate versus an oral culture and a classical as against a folk and the worship of the female principle dominating the little tradition. However, all these gods are connected through myths and tradition to the larger framework of Sanskrit Hinduism. This leads to: 1) Sanskritization, or the desire of the lower castes to gradually move up the ladder and become part of the Great tradition, and 2) the higher caste patronage of lower caste festivals and dramatic performances. It is the latter issue which causes the legitimization and preservation of the caste status quo. For traditionally, only the higher castes of the Great tradition could use the ritual language of religion. This indeed is an expression of power which was totally denied to the lower classes. Sharma notes the importance of the role of a Brahmin priest during a *katha* (story-telling) ceremony.

The services of a Brahmin priest are essential to the villager for this kind of ritual, not merely becasue only the priest has the required training to understand the directions for worship contained in the text but also because a Brahmin is considered to be fit by virtue of his special ritual status to utter and expound the holy verses in question.[23]

Ashley also notes the power of the Brahmin priests to bring the gods down to earth in the *teyyam* ritual of Kerala.

The Brahmin community plays a significant role in the event. Although they rarely take part in or are present at the festival of the other communities, their position is evident. According to one informant no *teyyam* shrine is considered sacred/operative until a *tantri* Brahmin consecrates it, thus bringing it into existence. The *tantri* is the sole possessor of highly charged *mantras* and rituals which transfer *shakti* (power) to the idol of the shrine endowing it with its power. Without such a ceremony, the idol is impotent and in the eyes of the community the shrine does not exist.[24]

Through such exercise of power Brahmins play a decisive role in the legitimation of the existing forces. Their patronage can be observed in the way folk theatre is sponsored and subsidized by the local landlords in the villages. The landlords are generally from the higher castes and wish to keep the lower castes in their place, where they own no land and often are at the mercy of the landlords. Arden found, in the *Chhau* dances of Purulia, that this system fosters economic dependence on the upper castes.[25]

Another major device by which the system of caste-based inequalities is maintained, is by the allotment of roles to a particular caste in the production of a play. Lower caste people are given the roles of gods and goddesses to whom they are normally denied access. For example, when in *teyyam*, a lower caste man assumes the role of a god and is worshipped by the Brahmins and landlords, the repressed sentiments of the lower caste are given an outlet and this ensures the continuance of the system. Similarly, there are role reversals. During the festival of *holi*, for instance, in many places the lower castes sling mud and dirt on the higer castes in a playful way and so feel the satisfaction of having beaten up their traditional enemy. Thus the lower castes, who are totally outside the purview of the Great tradition, are actively involved in propagating it.

Some of the most popular stories of folk theatre also conform to this analysis. A traditional play very popular among the lower castes is *Satya Harish Chandra*, the story of a truth-loving young man. The plot revolves around the outcome of a wager between two celestial beings, Vasista and Vishwamitra, on the importance of truth in the lives of earthly beings. In the process, the truth loving Harish Chandra is tested and he confirms that the defilement of caste laws is an explicit sin. Other social evils and beliefs like *sati* (the self-immolation of a wife in the funeral pyre of her husband) and re-incarnation are taken for granted.[26] In the same way the *Ramilia* of Ramnagar, as Kapur observed, is an opportunity for the local *Maharajah* to ally himself with the timeless realm of the gods. The *lila* helps him bring the extraordinary presence of god into the ordinary history of Benares, into its every day structure and rub shoulders with the king of the immortal world. Thus he relives his past glory as an emperor and legitimizes his kinghsip.[27]

Protest in Ritual Theatre

In has been mentioned, quoting Ranganath's findings, that ritual theatre does not allow the introduction of modern messages. But there have been exceptions, especially in Tamil Nadu. There the non-Brahmin movement is based on the larger movement of Dravidian cultural renaissance. The Aryans had complete control in north India. But in the south, Dravidian elements persisted. This can be observed in the south Indian languages, customs and the ethnic characteristics of the people. Once they crossed over to the south, the Aryan Brahmins, in Tamil Nadu, though few in number, dominated every sphere of life. They Aryan kings of the Pallava and Pandya dynasties (300-910 AD) levied heavy taxes on the local people. They insisted that the kings were of divine origin and hence they needed to be paid in kind. To protest against this the *kabaliga* movement arose among the rural peasantry. There was a ritual drama called *masana kollai* among these peasants, the climax of which was the killing of a buffalo. The *pujari*, a low caste priest assumes the role of Kali, Siva's wife, kills the buffalo, smears the blood on himself, tears open its abdomen and wearing the intestines around his neck like a garland, runs towards the burial ground with a blood-curdling cry.

This ritual drama is symbolic and representative of a story which militates against the concept of the divine origin of kingship. The story, as Appavoo narrates it, is about a king called Vallala Magarasan. He has no children and prays fervently to the god Siva. The god appears before him, and the king requests that the god himself be born as his child. Siva grants the request and allows himself to be conceived by the queen. But Kali, on hearing this, becomes furious. She does not approve of god coming out of a human womb. When the queen is about to deliver the child, Kali kills her, tears open her womb, takes the child out and runs to the burial ground. The king follows her and begs for mercy. Both Siva and Kali appear before him, give life to the queen and bless them with a human child.

The purpose behind this story is to demonstrate that the kings are not born of gods and hence divine tax need not be paid to kings who are only human.[28]

Protest in Folklore

Studying the various forms of folklore–songs, stories and sayings–one notices that several of them have elements that protest against the low position of women, disrespect to folk gods, the caste system, land and labour appropriation by the richer classes. Especially notable are those that protest vehemently against the caste system. For example there is a story which says that the toddy- tappers once belonged a higher caste. Once six Brahmin brothers were asked to render unpaid service to the temple. They refused and the king ordered that they be killed. But since the youngest was only eight years old, he was not killed but banished. The boy went south and worked hard as a toddy-tapper and became the ancestor of his caste.

Similarly among the *parayas* (low caste) of Kerala there is a story which says that they were originally Brahmins. Once they were compelled to eat beef and lost their caste.

In Bihar, among the *chamars* (outcastes), there is a story that in the beginning there was but one family of people, all belonging to the same caste. It happened that a cow died and that there was no one to remove it. The older brothers forced their youngest brother to remove the cow on condition that he would be accepted back after a bath. However, they did not keep their word and forced him to become an outcaste.

Attempts at reinterpreting the epics are also common all over India. For instance, in the early part of this century the Tamil poet Subramanya Bharati (1881-1956) reinterpreted the *Mahabharata* in his fight against British imperialism. In one of his poems, he criticises the elder Pandava sharply for pawning his country, the people and Panchali, their wife. Bharati questions the right of ruler to treat his subject as slaves. He compares the incident to that of a temple-priest selling the idol for personal gain.[29]

These stories show how through folklore, the oppressed have tried to assert themselves and retain their self-esteem. We can hazard a generalization that most of these stories were expressed in the form of community plays at festivals and ritual gatherings.

Folk Theatre against the Great Tradition

It has been mentioned that the *Bhakti* (devotion) movements (9th to 16th century) led by saints and popular religious leaders from the lower classes mark the beginning of cultural movements against the Great tradition. The Brahmo Samaj (1891) and the Arya Samaj (1898) in recent years also tried to renew Hinduism from within, but with very little success. Other major movements sprung up among different sections of people, but did not gain national importance. Unlike earlier movements, they were not religious, but linked to political and economic issues. They made good use of folk theatre to reach out to the masses. Some examples are examined below.

1. The Upsurge in Maharastra

Under the auspices of the Sathya Shodhak Samaj (Truth Seeking Society) established in 1873 Jyotirao Phule in Pune, the Marathas, a major caste group, lower in status than the Brahmins, tried to project the lower castes like Kunbis and Malis against the superiority of the Brahmins.

The Brahmins, 4.5% of the population, were the educated class and so had complete control over the print medium, the only existing mass medium. The British had groomed the Brahmins to take over as village leaders after the land settlements. This again angered the Marathas. The Sathya Shodhak Samaj resurrected the 17th century Maratha warrior Chhatrapathi Shivaji as the symbol of both Indian nationalism and Maratha pride and inspired the people to long for a land without caste discrimination. Every form of media available at the time was utilized in fighting the superiority of the Brahmins. Considering the widespread illiteracy of the people it may be assumed that the traditional media especially the *tamasha* and *powada*, contributed more to the cause than newspapers, magazines, journals and pamphlets put together.

Traditionaly, the *powada* is a ballad form of theatre which celebrated the heroic feats of Maratha warriors. Several of these had concentrated on events from the life of the Maratha hero Shivaji. Since it emphasized Shivaji's close contacts with the land and agriculture, this form was loved by the cultivators and their protectors, the landlords. Like any other true folk media it succeeded in integrating the village communities with the higher classes. But in Jyotirao Phule's hands the form underwent drastic changes. Shivaji was represented as the leader of

Maharastra's lower castes. As O'Hanlon observes.

> This new version of the *powada* presented Shivaji as the leader of
> Maharastra's *sudra* and ascribed his achievements to the strength
> and skill of his *sudra* armies, rather than to his Brahmin ministers.
> The lower castes of Maharastra, the tillers of the land and its protectors
> in times of war, were presented as the architects of the Maratha
> state.[30]

Phule went on to blame the Great tradition o. Sanskrit Hinduism and
its champions, the Brahmins, for perverting the society of the Marathas,
originally castelss and egalitarian into one in which inequalities, both in
the religious and material spheres of life, were introduced and perpetuated by misinterpretations of the Hindu scriptures.

In his *powada*, Phule spoke of a pre-Aryan golden age in India in
which the cultivators prospered under the benign rule of Bali. In this
idyllic kingdom, all the people were called *kshatriya*, because they owned
and worked on the *kshetra*, the land. Jealous of their prosperity, the
Aryan kings of the North Parashuram and Brahma invaded and defeated
the *kshatriyas*. It may be mentioned here that in the mythology of epics
and *puranas*, Bali was the Daitya king who was deprived of his kingdom
by Vishnu, incarnated as the Brahmin dwarf, Vaman. Thus in his *powada*,
strongly identifying with the tillers of the soil, the land, labour and the
puranas, Phule captured the imagination of the agriculturists and farm-
hands.

It may be useful to look at some important details in Phule's *powada*
on Shivaji. While Shivaji is still very young his mother Jijabai seats him
in the garden and tells him the story of their ancestors, the *kshatriyas* of
pre-Aryan India. Throughout the account of the Muslim invasions, the
Brahmin's helplesness and the *kshatriya's* valour are depicted. "As his
mother's teaching was impressed upon his tender mind, his rage against
the outsiders grew and he made his plans to fight them," comments Phule.
In another place, Phule describes the exploits of Shivaji while fighting
against the Mughals. In this description of the exploits and successes of
their leader, it is as though Phule is inviting his lower caste audience to
experience the same sense of power vicariously and to assert themselves
in a Brahmin dominated land despite their lowly rank. Phule dismisses any
potential source of Brahmin influence on Shivaji.

Who should be the guru of the fish that plays
In the water? Shivaji made Ramdev his guru only
In order to win the love of the people.[31]

At Shivaji's death bed, Phule has this comment to make:

He gave life to the peasants
He does not deprive the *rayats* of their happiness
He passes new regulations,
Both great and small have redress,
No one suffers oppression.[32]

This statement, in more than one sense is a cry from the heart of the leaderless low castes of the present, in protest against the contrast between their original greatness and their present position. Towards the end of the same *powada* Phule comments on the tyranny of the Brahmins and appeals to the colonial powers:

Oh Queen you have the power, Hindustan is asleep
Everywhere there is the rule of the Brahmans
Open your eyes and see
In the small villages, the *kulkarnis* are the masters
of the pen, in the *mahals* they hold great offices, they
alone have high authority, like *yama*, the *mamledar* gives the sudras
ceaseless punishment
the poor, foolish collector stands before the cunning *Chitnis*; how
great is the authority of the *Brahmanas* in the revenue departments;
the Bhats are everywhere, the *kunbis* have no redress; Jyoti says we
run for help, release us from these evils...[33]

It may be argued that in spite of their overtly one-sided nature Phule's *powada* helped to question the Brahmin superiority, to delegitimize the commonly held mythology of the Great tradition and replace it with the mythology of the pre-vedic, non-Brahminic Maratha past i.e., the kingdom of Bali. He thus provided the *sudra* with a history with which they could identify. Phule also highlighted the need to worship a 'divine being' who was unconcerned with the rites and rituals of the Great tradition but insisted on justice and equality for all. In sum, Phule succeeded through his *powada* to provide the lower castes with a culture of their own.

Tamasha

One of the pioneers of Sathya Shodhak *tamasha* was a Maratha peasant, Ramachandrarao Ghadge of Kale, in 1915. He was a poor man with some education. By 1925 he had 29 troupes under his name spread around the length and breadth of Maharastra. People from various lower castes were given roles and responsibilities in his *tamasha*.

Sathya Shodhak *tamasha* followed the traditional form, but it had a new content. The traditional *tamasha* opened with an invocation to Ganpati, the Brahmin deity. It was followed by a great deal of byplay in a dialogue centering around the Krishna theme, clowning with a man dressed as a woman. The third part was the *wag* or the real play in which the Brahmins were glorifed as the saviours of the peasantry. However, in the Sathya Shodhak *tamasha* a new interpretation was introduced. The word *Ganpati* was re-interpreted to mean *gan* or people and *pati* or leader; and so the initial invocation was to the leader of the people. The second part of Krishna's dalliance with the village milk-maids was replaced by the encounter of the hero, Sathyaji, with the village Brahim women using insulting and challenging language and ridiculing Brahmin superiority. In the third section, a farce was introduced in which Brahmins and moneylenders were shown cheating the poor, and innocent peasants. A number of songs invoking opposition to caste and religious superstitions followed. The nature of the attack on Brahmins in the *tamasha* varied from the farcical to the subtle.

In one of Jyotirao Phule's *tamasha*, they mocked almost all the sacred religious books and traditional stories of the origin of gods and castes and attacked popular religious traditions such as the Pandharpur cult, and the fast-growing Sathyanarain *puja*. One song in a *tamasha* narrated the story of a peasant pilgrim to Pandharpur who lost his health in the diseases of the rainy season and his money to the cunning Brahmin priests. The Brahmins were shown as oppressing holy men and murdering Sant Thukaram, the saint of Pandharpur.

In another *tamasha*, *Kulkarnilia*, a heroic weaver whose generosity and service win him accolades in the village, becomes the object of a Brahmin's jealousy. Winning over the village headman to his side, the Brahmin brings a law suit against the weaver for building a section of his house on government land. The humiliated weaver finds a government official (a Christian, who had earlier been converted from Mahar, a lower caste) to support him. And together they manage to have the court decision reversed. At this point the Brahmin appeals to the headman and urges him to assist him. When the headman next encounters the Christian, he throws him off his horse in a fit of anger. The result is disastrous for the headman, who has to take the blame while the Brahmin forsakes him and escapes scot-free.[34] Among other things this *tamasha* outlined the need for the lower classes to stick together to counteract the machinations of the Brahmins.

Some non-Brahmins used *tamasha* for election propaganda. One urged that peasants vote for men of their own caste as opposed to sweet-talking Brahmin candidates.

Another *tamasha* by Tatobha Yadav representing a more conservative approach praised the Hindu religion but tried to separate the religion from *Brahminism* and included a long history of Marathas, who as *kshatriyas* were said to have played the role of protectors of religion. At the same time it included songs asserting basic human equality and attacking the hypocrisy of the Brahmins who practised intercaste marriages in the cities.

It is important to mention here that the Sathya Shodhak *tamasha* was not merely interested in tarnishing the image of the Brahmins. There were some with very strong progressive themes. Several of the *tamasha* songs emphasized the value of education and modern technology.

> Let us go to school young and old
> and get acquainted with education
> It is the experience of so many people
> that education brings happiness
> in the world and removes calamities.
> railroads, bicycles, cars, airplanes,
> like birds, steam boats, merchant
> and passenger ships go on the sea...
> This is all the work of knowledge
> It is man's greatness, but if he misses,
> the opportunity it is time of destruction.
> Tatobha says, hold this in your mind.[35]

In general the *tamasha* played a prominent part in spreading a popular Maharastrian culture and gave an impetus to the movements of the untouchables.

3. Folk Theatre in IPTA

During the golden years of IPTA (1942-52) it was customary to use all forms of folk expressisons to enhance rural concerns in theatre. Conscious attempts were made at rooting theatre in the lives of the people, using their own modes of expression in music, dance, puppets and mime.[36]

The *tamasha* was often used to mobilize public opinion when nationalistic sentiments were riding high, Playwrights like D.N. Gowankar, Madgulkar, P.L. Deshpande, Vasant Sabnis and Vasant Bapat combined topical subjects and the traditional forms like *tamasha* and *powada* in a bid to reach the masses. One of Gowankar's *tamasha* was about how a grain hoarder of a starving village was cornered by the villagers. A *powada* based on a well known Russian heroine Tanya, who faced all sorts of odds, concluded with a call to the peasants to unite and to overthrow oppression and injustice. Gowankar had with him two talented youngsters: an untouchable writer, Anna Bhau Sathe and Omar Shaik, a landless Muslim peasant, both of whom went on to become noted popular cultural leaders in the state. Together they staged numerous *tamasha* and *powada* all over Maharastra before massive crowds.

In Kerala, traditional forms like *kathakali* and *ottamthullal* were taken out of their temple surroundings and staged before larger audiences with new themes portraying the struggles of the masses. During the elections a *kathakali* based on *kuchela vrittam* depicted Krishna as a power drunk minister and his impoverished childhood colleague, Sudama, as a poor honest school teacher.

In Andhra Pradesh *burrakatha* and *Harikatha* were often used for social education. Leaving aside the mythological content, *burrakatha* was used to educate the public about the significance of contemporary events and to invoke solidarity and patriotism in the people. One of the most popular *burrakatha* was *Ahuti* (sacrifice) dealing with the Bengal famine. Gopal Krishnayya's "medicine man" was another feat of folk entertainment. Posing as a doctor he claimed that he could eradicate social diseases and national evils and prescribed the methodologies of Lenin, Stalin and Gandhi as remedies to dislodge the Nazis, Fascists and Imperialists.

Social consciousness also began to seep into the folk structure of *raslila*. An essential religious theatre, it also projected secular values. For example Mansukh, a companion of Krishna who normally plays the role of the *Vidhushak*, would break out from the staid, religious themes to comment on issues like the independence struggle and the Bengal famine.

In Bengal, the use of the folk form was much less compared to the other states. However, in 1944, the IPTA unit staged a *kabi ladai*. It was a potent form of folk art where a band of village poets waged a poetic duel with another group. They composed verses impromptu. In this programme organized by IPTA, burning problems of the day were avidly discussed, providing usefull information and instruction to those who attended. In 1954, the Badartala unit staged a *jatra* entitled *Sangat* written by Gurudas Paul on the problems of the working class. Later IPTA stalwarts like Mukunda Das and Utpal Dutt took to *jatra* in a more creative way. In Das's *jatra* gods and goddesses were transformed to freedom fighters and patriots, the devils and villains became members of the ruling class. In several, Marx, Lenin, and Mao appeared in the coveted roles of heroes.

For Dutt, even after leaving IPTA, *jatra* offered a golden vehicle for communicating with the masses. Fascinated by the robust and overwhelmingly magical nature of *jatra* he took to it right from his early days in the Little Theatre Group. The language of his productions was transformed into a bold, declamatory form to reach the working class. He shortened the form to three hours, cutting down the number of songs and gave it a more vibrant form—fast moving, tempestuous and hard hitting. Most of his productions were allegorical—taking events from the distant past, he gave them contemporary relevance. In plays like *Sanyasir Tarabiri* (1968), *Leniner Dak* (1968), Rifle (1969), *Surya Shikar* (1971), *Tiner Talwar* (1971), and *Jallianwallah Bag* (1971) he presented overtly political statements about such diverse issues as Marxism, the fall of Berlin, Vietnam, the Indigo revolt of 1856-60, the Indian guerillas of 1944, the Punjabi revolt of 1919. Commenting on Dutt's use of *jatra* techniques and dialogues for the propagation of political idea, Bharucha notes:

> He is not interested in reviving *jatra*. That would be appallingly antiquarian to him. Nor should he be criticized for catering to a new movement in the Bengali theatre—the urban *jatra*. His use of *jatra* is more pragmatic and intellectually sound than the purists of the Bengali theatre care to admit.[37]

4. Habib Tanvir

Joining the IPTA in 1945, Tanvir experimented with the folk forms of the Chhattisgarh area of Madhya Pradesh with the help of local tribal performers. Trained at the Royal Academy of Dramatic Arts and the Bristol Old Vic Theatre, Tanvir returned to India convinced that urban theatre forms borrowed from the West were totally inadequate for effectively projecting the social aspirations, ways of life, cultural patterns and fundamental problems of contemporary India. Determined to use the folk forms in a creative way, he returned to his roots and blended the *nachha* (Chhattisgarhi folk) form with contemporary ideas to turn his Naya Theatre into an explosively energetic and original theatre group. He found the illiterate folk actors articulate, creative, receptive and brimming over with gusto and virtuosity, and gave them prominent roles in his plays. In *Charandas Chor* (1963) he took the first step towards a combination of modern content and folk form. The story of *Charandas Chor*, borrowed from Rajasthani folklore and improvised by the performers, is about a Robin Hood type character who sacrifices his life in order to be true to the three promises he made to his *guru*. Tanvir not only found contemporary relevance in this and other plays like *Jamadarin* (1965), *Sadhu Nakkal* (1967) and *Gaaon Ka Naam Sasural Mor Naam Daamad* (1968) but also explored the myths and the subconscious of the rural people. In *Bhadur Kalarin* (1975) he made subtle references to the patronizing ways of Indira Gandhi and her attempts to groom her younger son Sanjay to political ascendancy.

The new trends set by Dutt and Tanvir have had wide repercussions in India. For instance, a number of plays like *Aala Afsar* (1973) and *Ek Sathya Harischandra* (1975) in *nautanki* form, *Amar Singh Rathod* (1968) and *Jasma Odan* (1968) in *bhavai* form, and *Bakari* (1974) in several north Indian forms have continued the tradition. Studying some of these new plays Hansen observed:

> In the feudal value system of traditional *nautanki* the rich are the virtuous and they generally triumph. In these urban plays, however, the poor people are the heroes and whether they storm the politician's bungalow *(Bakari)* or simply sing Urdu poems in praise of vegetables *(Agra Bazaar)* their victory is desired, foreshadowed and proclaimed in each of these plays. Their purpose is to communicate a social and political perspective on contemporary society and *to convince the audience of the injustices committed against the*

ordinary man. Their fondness for traditional techniques represents a political alliance as much as an aesthetic preference. It also provides them with a persuasive rhetoric–for it is through the art forms of the rural people that their cause is being exposed.[38]

P.L . Deshpande in Maharastra, B.V. Karanth and C. Kambar in Karnataka, K.N. Panicker and G. Shankarapillai in Kerala, Kanhaiya Lal and Ratan Thiyam in Manipur offer some good examples of blending local folk idioms with socio-political issues.

5. The Song and Drama Division

The SDD have used a number of folk theatre forms like ballads, story-telling, dance and drama to persuade the rural poor to accept government controlled ways to deal with the problems in the country. There have been instances when the overtly propagandist nature of the programmes have strangled the folk elements and the people have revolted against the manipulation. For example in Karnataka, when family planning themes were included in the *yellamma* songs popular with the rural masses who have large families, the people protested, stating that the messages were incongruous and sacrilegious. Studying the use of *tamasha* to disseminate the message of familiy planing in Maharastra Abrams suggests,

much improvement could have been made by sharpening scripting and staging techniques. To maintain artistic worth and to gain greater effectivness of the social use of the form a delicate balance must be struck between good, recognized artistry, the new and traditional conventions of the form and modern message content.[39]

According to Kidd, the performers were used as mercenaries. Analysing a number of cliche-ridden formats of the scripts he contends that in SDD there was no special interest in encouraging or developing any folk media: the empahsis was mainly on mass information and legitimizing the policies and practices of the government.[40]

V. The Formal Characteristics of Folk Theatre

One examining the vast area of folk theatre in India, one is struck by the fact that each state or culture has its own form of theatre. A closer examination will show that despite the different names, languages and styles they have much in common. As Vatsyayan notes:

A mention of the performing arts of India brings to one's mind the single-bodied and many-armed image of Durga or of Shiva in his form as Nataraja, ever destroying, ever creating newer forms of the dance *Tandawa*. These symbols in plastic forms suggest at one level the unified equilibrium, the still centre and at the other, the continual display of energy and rhythm in plural forms. The varied art forms like the multiple arms and hands though distinct and separate are all limbs of the same body, the seeming heterogeneity and multiplicity are different modes of the *Tandawa*.[41]

Hence, despite a multiplicity of genres, forms, styles and techniques there are a number of common characteristics.

Community-based, Spontaneous and Vibrant

As is well-known, folk performance is normally part of a community celebration. Everyone in the community, from a child in arms to the great grandfather trudging along supported by a stick, takes part in these night-long performances. They have items in them that appeal to everyone in the audience: poor and rich, literate and illiterate, rural and urban, young and old, men and women. Most of the folk performances are held in village squares around which the community lives. Therefore performances can take on an informal and festival note where families, neighbours, relatives and friends gather together in the evening. As the performances run through the whole night as in a religious worship, it is not surprising that at times some take a nap and wake up to continue watching in rapt attention.

Participating in a folk theatre performance is like attending a fair in one of the busiest streets of India where a person's body acquires an automatic mobility. For in the vast crowd the individual becomes part of a mass of bodies and moves with the crowd to where the action is. In the same way in a folk theatre performance, no one responds to the performance as an individual, but as part of a mass of people.

Folk theatre has evolved in step with the pattern of people's lives and is conncected with seasonal changes, the harvests and festival seasons. In these performances there is hardly any distinction between the audience and the actors. Everyone participates spontaneously. Speaking of the participation of the audience in *Ramlila,* Gargi comments:

> If an important dialogue or a message or a decisive sentence is spoken by a principal character, it is preceded by a loud ejaculation by the *vyasa* (stage manager) *bol sia pathi Ram Chandra ki jai* (shout Ramchandra's victory) and the audience roars in a chorus the last word 'jai' of the *vyasa.*[42]

Sometimes enthusiastic spectators shout slogans in praise of Ram and the rest of the crowd joins in, stopping all other action on the stage. This flow of audience intervention breaks the monotony, enlivens the spectators and acts as a brake on the speech dialogues. In almost all cases the accompanying cheers, laughter, sobbing, wailing and rapt silence of the audience are clear signs of intense participation. It is a common practice for members of the audience to walk onto the stage to offer a prize or a medallion to an actor. At times the audience may be invited onstage and some of them walk up and perform bit parts spontaneously.

The setting of the *Ramlila* of Ramnagar with different acting areas for the performers allows for audience participation. The scenes are performed on multiple stages, each like an island amidst a sea of people. Dialogues, chants and sound–effects come from different location offering a magnificent vision–easy, intimate, and multi-dimensional. In *yakshagana,* the characters make their entry, not from the green room, but from among the audience. With the accompaniment of drums and torches, the performers proceed through the midst of the audience inviting them to join in. Here is a description of a *Rashdhari Khyal* from Rajastan in the words of Samar, which could broadly be substitued for any other form:

> The actors keep on moving all the time in order to be visible to the audience from all sides. Since the acting area is circular and the audience is seated all round, the actors have no particular place for entry. It has to be done at any convenient point by breaking the cordon of spectators. The musical accompaniment does not sit in a conspicuous place. Their usual seat is among the audience. This intermingling of the accompanists with the audience is perhaps

necessary for public participation... .

A narrow and compact place for its performance is necessary for public participation. Stage decor is deliberately avoided in order to keep the visibility of the play intact and the stage arena comparatively free from physical and visual obstacles. For example, if a throne is required for a king, any person from the audience can be picked up and the actor can use his back as a throne. Any encroachment or forcible participation by the audience is invariably taken in a sporting spirit.[45]

Clearly folk theatre allows spontaneity and improvisation as against the stringent rules of classical theatre. Often the reactions of the audience are as important as the performers' whims in determining the length and intensity of the performance. Certain forms like the *bhand pather* and *khariyala* of Kashmir are entirely improvised. These have a few traditional themes, but an adept artist improvises the whole show on the spot. In *yakshagana*, there is no pre-meditated prose dialogue. While the *bhagavatha* (stage manager) sings a stanza, the actors dance and when he stops singing they interpret the stanza in the form of a dialogue with the audience. As a result, according to the extent of audience participation, each stanza is elaborated by extempore dialogue. In the *bhavai* froms the relevant songs and verses are selected from traditional stock, but the dramatic dialogue in prose is provided by the actors. Such allowances have made these forms extremely flexible enabling a smooth transition from heaven to earth, from the sublime to the absurd. Actors can comment on a contemporary event even while playing a historical or a mythological role without appearing incongruous. If the village audience grows restless, while watching a long, serious scene, a smart actor turns up in a comic role and justifies his presence by clever dialogues. It is an accepted custom that a folk performance varies from day to day depending on the mood of the actors and more so on the demands made by the discerning audience. Thus it takes full advantage of the live nature of theatre.

Although acting in folk theatre incorporates the suggestions of Bharata in the *Natyasastra*, there is a certain amount of non-theatricality associated with these forms. For example, in *Ramlila* the *vyasa* (stage manager) stands close to the actors and openly prompts them. The actors speak in mono-syllabic or even split mono-syllabic speech drawling the words so that they are stretched and made clear. In a *nautanki* performance, when a member of the audience passes a remark at a character, the actor picks it up and makes it a part of his dialogue. All these are taken well by the audience, even while they maintain a spirit of identity with the characters on the stage. Considering the many possibilities offered by folk theatre in audience participation and spontaneity, Habib Tanvir has observed that it is no wonder that Western theatre experimentalists involved in establishing closer interaction between the actors and audience found a goldmine in the Indian folk theatre.[44]

Mime

It has already been mentioned that folk theatre absorbed several characteristics of the Sanskrit tradition. According to this tradition, *natya* (words and gestures), *nritya* (mime or meaningful gestures) and *nritta* (dance or meaningful and beautiful movements) are the three cognates of drama. Mime was accepted as one of the most powerful tools of folk expression, as it cuts across language barriers and has a tremendous capacity to hold the attention of the audience.

The early treatises on theatre had divided drama into *lokdharmi* (popular or realistic) and *natyadharmi* (theatrical or conventional). A *lokdharmi* play is said to be one which reproduced human behaviour and natural objects as they are, without flourish or exaggeration. Ordinary people acted out ordinary situations in an ordinary way. Obviously such enactments became boring in the course of time. Hence *natyadharmi* forms were introduced, where a play was presented through stylized gestures and symbolism. It was indeed artificial, but the poetic fancy and lyrical expressions were highly imaginative. Consequently richly painted scenery and ornate sets were done away with and emphasis was laid on descriptive poetry. Mime was a major aspect in the symbolic form of acting. The *Natyasastra* says:

> Tall mountains and trees may be suggested by out–stretched hands and hands lifted over the head, a sea or an expansive lake, etc., may be shown by hands thrown out in an open gesture.[45]

In folk theatre it is not unusual to see an actor lift the latch of a non-existent door and enter the room by taking a high step. In a bare stage two men can row a boat, guiding it through troubled waters. The pitch and toss of the boat can be conveyed through gestures and mime. It was common to show in the Sanskrit dramas an actor swim, ride an elephant, or fly across space through mimetic action. Darkness was conveyed not by blotting out stage-lights but by groping with the hands in bright light.

Similarly all forms of actions were shown on the stage by miming. Once this convention was accepted by the audience, theatre was able to forge ahead without the restraints of visual narration.

Sanskrit tradition did not accept the unity of time and place. Hence, within the act itself locations could be changed. If the change was from one outdoor scene to another, the characters would make a circular movement on the stage and the location was understood to have changed. If, however, the change was from an outdoor to an indoor scene then the whole group would go through the backstage created by holding a small curtain. No other changes were made on the scene. Similarly shifts to other locations are established through conventional movement of this type which are easily accepted by the audience.

Scenography: theatres, stages, sets, props

Performances are normally held in the open air in large fields, temple courtyards or village quadrangles. The idea of dramatic performance being an open air street show is so basic that the very name of some of these presentation like *therukoothu* and *veedhinatakam* literally means "street" plays. Closed theatres are almost unknown to the masses although Bharata spoke about *natyasala* or theatre hall in his treatise. On the large field the plays are staged sometimes on a raised podium, but mostly at ground level resulting in a great deal of intimacy between the actors and the audience. The traditional forms had arena stagings with round, parabolical, horizontal, square or multiple-set stages with different type of gangways and environments. The technique of arranging various scenes at the same time in different spots, and the people seated all around and above as in *Ramlila* is seen to be very effective. Schechner, in devising his Perfromance Theory, was inspired by some elements from the spatial structures and environmental designs of the *Ramlila* of Ramnagar. According to him the environments, movements and processions of vastly spread out performance in time and space have greatly enhanced the participation of the audience in the 31-day ritual theatre.

In no other theatre does the audience as such emerge so clearly as part of the performance. Neither else is there time/space allotted for the audiende to so clearly, easily, and fully play their various roles. . . .

More than half of the *lilas* include (journeys), processions or pilgrimages. Movement from place to place is the most salient theatrical action of *Ramlila*. The permanent environments of the various places in the story are linked by processions that trace the outline of the story. Instead of ending one day's show in place A and beginning the next day in place B often the move from A to B is the start of an event in most of the performance.[46]

In these processions many spectators join in weeping and rejoicing as the situations in the play demand. Schechner was particularly impressed by the position of the audience in the *Ramlila*. As the performance area is not restricted to a particular proscenium, everyone chooses seats around the scattered performance area at will; some on the side of the main characters, others on the floor adjacent to the characters, some on the side-walls, or on the branches of tree and others standing and moving around the action as in a promenade. Awasthy points out that similar settings enliven *raslila* performances:

> ramparts, balconies, terraces, and groves are used for the presentation of the action of the story, and the action keeps flowing freely in all directions at various levels. The spectators move along with the action; they are seldom immobile. Actors often appear in the midst of the audience, sometimes passing through them to the main acting area.[47]

Kapur notes the dramatic changes that come over an audience that participates in such an intimate way:

> The spectators cease to exist as spectators as soon as they join the processions, because the very act of walking becomes invested with special significance. They are walking as pilgrims, to sites sanctified by god, on routes they believe to be sacred, on journies, inspired because they are in the footsteps of the deity. They are not, then, a diverse band of onlookers following itinerant players, they are a single-minded body of devotees witnessing the deeds of god as he acts out his history on their ground.[48]

In folk theatre, when surrounded by ordinary village folk, there are hardly any rules as to where the actors perform and where the audience sits. Everything is arranged according to convenience, which in the final analysis is geared towards the full participation of the audience.

The use of sophisticated curtains, lighting techniques and micro-phones is unheard of in this form of theatre. The stage is often bare. This demands the use of imagination from the audience to understand the settings. The absence of any form of curtains makes the stage a vibrant centre of action, where dramatic episodes move with speed. It is the same spot, but it is always a different place. Like the image in the shining crystal of a conjurer's ring, the stage keeps assuming as many forms as the actor desires. From this it may not be assumed that folk theatre strives to create an illusion of reality. Rather it break the illusion and creates in turn a world of its own. Thus the barrenness of the stage is an advantage. The actor cannot take shelter behind the wings or seek help from sets, but depends solely on his art, learned with care from his elders. The lack of a conventional stage lends power to the drama and makes for directness of action and a close emotional accord between the audience and the actors.

In most traditional theatres the main characters are introduced from behind a hand-held curtain. In *yakshagana, kuchipudi, raslila, therukoothu, ankiya naat, kathakali* and *bahagavatamela* the first entry of the main characters are thus made suspenseful. This coloured curtain held by two stage-hands is used as a stage property for the actors who peer and grimace over it, clutch it and dance behind it. The demons and titans are very effective as they grunt and stomp behind this mask and give occasional partial glimpses to the audience.

Decorations and properties, too, are non-existent in most of the folk theatre forms. No property seems to have been used since the *Natyasastra* says that trying to represent trees or mountains as realistically as possible is not only a fatiguing job, but a needless one! A bench, a chair or a stool can be suggestively placed to indicate a throne, a bed or something similar.[49] A king can hold court without the architectural trappings of a historical play. When he rides a horse, he mimics the action much as a *kathakali* actor would do in a more refined, stylized way. Eulogizing this aspect in the folk form, Tagore said:

> No one comes to see a play after locking his sensibility and imagination back at home. Some things are to be suggested by the actor and some things the audience has to receive with his imagina-tion. A gardener has not to create a whole garden around himself to suggest the act of plucking and selecting beautiful flowers.[50]

Acting style, Dialogue delivery

Acting in general is loud and exaggerated, aimed more at clarity rather than naturalness. The folk actors make tremendous use of the human body with wild gestures, elaborate facial expressions and other suggestive gyrations. Normally they stand for the most part. There is a tendency to move around in irregular patterns, irrespective of the content of the dialogues. At times, the responses of the audience dictate these movements to a great extent. They force their bodies, gestures and speeches in the direction of the audience. Focusing on the stage is mostly for dramatic conflicts, otherwise the play is acted out to the audience addressing them directly. The actors adapt to various story-telling patterns with extended pictorial gestures, pointing fingers at the audience and answering their queries. They are ready to break out into song and dance any moment, accompanied by the musicians.

The dialogues are hardly naturalistic. They are improvised, but well rehearsed poetical recitations. Plenty of local imageries make the dialogues rich, but what is more appealing to the audience is the poetical, rhythmic way of reciting. The style of dialogue delivery is rapid and strident. There is continual variation in the vocal range climaxing at times in shouts and loud peals. Music, dance, rhyming words, verbal innuendoes, poetical phrases and *double entendres* make a fine mosaic of words.

Costumes, Make-up, Masks

Bharata has laid down an elaborate set of instructions on these aspects in the section on *aharya abhinaya*. The choice of colours, costumes and the combination of make-up, maintains Bharata, is determined according to the quality and nature of the particular type of characters. According to him the heroic sentiment is to be represented by orange, the marvellous by yellow, the terrible by black, the odious by blue, the erotic by light green, the comic by white, the pathetic by ash and the fierce by red.[51]

The characters in folk theatre, being gods, demi-gods, godmen, demons and other supernatural beings lend themselves to colourful and imaginative costuming and make-up. These can be at once beautiful, bizzare and frightening. Vatsyayan observes:

Costuming is of a vast variety: highly stylized as in *yakshagana* or *raslila*, thus eternal and timeless; period costumes even if anachronistic or incongruous as in *yatra* and *nautanki* or purely naturalistic as in *bhavai* and *tamasha*.[52]

The costumes have been intuitively designed to suit the gods, demons and heroes. The most essential feature of costumes and ornaments is colour and glitter. The mere sight of these is thrilling to the audience who is transported to the world of gods, heroes, giants and ogresses. As already mentioned *nautanki* and *yatra* use haphazard costumes, sometimes not belonging to any defintie period. King Harishchandra appears wearing a 17th century gilded tunic, while Queen Taramati appears in a 20th century saree. The romantic hero may put on a Western cowboy suit while the heroine may adorn herself in a colourful Benarasi saree. The ultimate aim is to capture the attention of the audience who take all these 'inadequacies' in their stride.

The principle of using make-up to transform a face to a character-type is common to many forms of Asian theatre like the Japanese Kabuki and Chinese opera. In India, besides the traditional classical forms like *kathakali*, *koodiyattom* and *yakshagana* a number of other folk theatres use masks and headgear to achieve dissimilitude with life. Different characters have different schemes of make-up. They can be highly elaborate, full of colour and symbolism and ritualistic significance as in *koodiyattom*, *yakshagana* and *kathakali*–or grotesque as in *Ramlila* and *raslila*, and realistic as in *nautanki* and *tamasha*. The exaggerated artificiality of the eye-brows and the moustache is peculiar to a number of folk theatre forms.

In a number of forms ready-made masks are worn by the characters. No doubt wearing a mask frees an actor from inhibitions and allows him total freedom. They also make the characters stand out and be readily noticed. The wearing of masks means that perfomers must act more with their bodies since no facial expressions are possible. Besides, in *kathakali*, *chhau* and *yakshagana* masks are essential ingredients as most of these deal with demons and supernatural beings. These masks produce a startling effect of terror and ugliness. The *Seraikella chhau* uses exquisite masks which avoid any exaggeration and adapt a static expression. The symbolic curl of a lip, a little drunkenness in the eye or an almost imperceptible scowl sums up the whole individual. The body movements of the actor express everything else. Speaking of the use of masks, Rajkumar Sudhendra of Seraikella commented:

When I put on the mask I become impersonal. It is easier to step into the body of another character. The face is not required to express, it passes its function to the body.[53]

Music, Musical Instruments, Singing

High pitched singing is a characteristic feature of folk theatre. The words of the songs are clearly pronounced and the meaning vividly visualised. There are classical as well as folk tunes, devotional and folk songs in these plays. The main feature of the songs is their emotional appeal. There are different *ragas* to express the emotions of anger, heroism, pity, horror and fear. A fast *raga* accompanied by frenzied beating of drums and an appropriate dance can evoke the feeling of roar of a lion in a burst of fury, and can have a blood-curdling effect on the audience. At times the instrumentalists vie with each other with a competitive gusto offering an electrifying feeling of entertainment to the audience.

In the *lavani*, a poetical composition of Maharastra, the prinicipal singer sings the first line on a high note and gradually keeps going higher. The lines that follow are spoken quickly in a sing-song fashion giving details that make the story move. At a dramatic line, the drummer thumps the drums and the chorus repeats the line in a shrill summing up of the preceding lines, their voices rising higher and higher reaching a delirious groan of "hai...hai...hai...", and then suddenly there is silence. This kind of frenzied singing adds to the vibrant character of folk theatre.[54]

Similarly *therukoothu* of Tamil Nadu is made up entirely of songs. It evolved from earlier ballads, *villupattu* (musical narration of a story) and *nondinatakam* (morality plays). The music dramatizes the entrance and exit of the main characters and heightens the emotional response of the audience to the usually well known plot and characters.

The Ramayanis of *Ramilia*, sitting away from the scene of the action, sing the entire story in verses while it is being enacted on the stage. They sing in high pitched voices what the actors say in speech. At times they produce an unpleasant metallic musical note from tiny bronze cymbals. This helps them keep the rhythm.

There are musical instruments characteristic to folk theatre. The drum is a common instrument in almost all the forms. It has a vast repertoire of rhythmic beats. Cymbals and stringed and wind instruments of various kinds are used, but they are homemade and unsophisticated. Generally the singers and instumentalists sit on the sides or at the back of the stage clearly visible to the audience. They provide the necessary support and accompaniment to the actors on stage, especially to those who do not have good voice.

What is striking about the music in these plays is its indigenous nature. Culled from the people's own native cultures, the music evokes daily work, agricultural festivals and ritual celebrations. This enables the people to hum the tunes along with the singers, thus enabling immediate participation.

Dance and Rhythmic Movements

Dance is an integral part of any Indian ritual. Farmers, hunters and fishermen danced to express their happiness. Worshippers and temple belles (*devadasi*) dance, losing themselves in dithyrambic music. The world itself, the Hinuds believe, is created from the cosmic dance of Shiva. His *nataraja* form is preserved in almost all the temples devoted to him. As against Shiva's violent *tandava* dance, which is at the same time creative and destructive, Parvati's *lasya* dance represents the tender, lyrical and graceful side. Together these form the basis of all Indian dance.

The *angika abhinaya* mentioned in *Natyasastra* refers to various forms of dances and rhythmic movements of the actors. With such elaborate religious and cultural background in dance it is only natural that folk theatre has an inexhaustible fund of dance forms and rhythms. Folk dances vary according to the regions, occupations and castes of the people. Tribals, farmers, gypsies, hill tribes and labourers have their particular forms of dance. In each of the folk theatre forms examined, the indigenous dance of the area finds a place, for people know dance is expressive and capable of involving the whole community. It is a common belief among folk theatre practitioners that some emotions are better expressed in dance and so, at appropriate moments, the chorus or the actor breaks into a dance to the accompaniment of several musical instruments. It is an involving experience, as in the *bhangra* (Punjabi dance) when the drums pound heavily and the dancers whirl around violently wriggling their shoulders, eyes sparkling and arms flung in abandon. The audience simply cannot be content watching all this, they join in.

In some forms like the *raslila*, the whole performance is in dance. Based on Krishna's love-play with the milk-maids of Vrindavan, it describes the meeting of the lovers, the pangs of separation and reunion in delicate dance steps. More stringent forms like *kathakali, koodiyattom* and *chhau* depend on classical dance steps to narrate a story.

Purvaranga or Stage Preliminaries

No folk theatre ever begins without a preparatory session. This helps to bring the audience together, calm them down and prepare them for the programme. According to Bharata, *purvaranga* or stage preliminaries are essential features of every play. The plays open with a prayer and a reverential address to the audience. These are indeed only the remnants of the elaborate preliminaries Bharata suggested before the start of the play and resemble the numerous 'rubrics' or rules to be followed before the start of a ritual.[55] The preliminaries made sure that a play was staged in the most becoming manner. In folk theatre these range from the detailed preliminaries in the *chhau* forms, which go on for as many as 27 days, to the simple *Ganesha vandana* of the *tamasha*.

On the first day of the *Seraikella chhau*, the priests hoist the *jarjara* (a banner tied with mango leaves) and carry it ceremoniously from the temple to the bathing *ghat* at the rivulet close by. Thirteen devout men chosen from different communities accompany him. Music follows. In a nearby temple the *jarjara* is worshipped for some time. Then a series of processions follow carrying the *jarjara* to Siva's temple, to the palace courtyard, and back again to the temple. This ritual is repeated every evening for nine days until the main part of the performance begins. After the first nine days, another series of rituals precede the remaining days of the perfromance. In all these processions the people actively participate.

In *chhau*, *ankiya naat* and *yatra* the erection of a pole marks the beginning of play. This kind of beginning has a magical significance dating back to the Vedic ages. In the *bhavai* after putting on the make-up, the players sing a devotional song invoking the goddess, Ambamata. On the stage they sing as many as five devotional songs and invoke the goddess to bless them and the audience. In *nautanki*, *tamasha* and *yakshagana*, *Ganesha vandana* is a requirement. The action begins with the entry of Ganesh, the elephant headed god. The actor wearing the mask dances for a few minutes swirling his head and then sits on a chair. The *sutradhar* (stage manager) offers a ceremonial *aarti* (blessing with a light in a round plate, decked in flowers) to worship him. The argument of the play to be followed is sometimes given at this moment in the form of a song. After this another hymn in honour of Ganesh is sung. It is also customary to sing a song of thanksgiving at the end of the play.

It is obvious that folk theatre follows the traditions of *Natyasastra* which stresses that drama is a gift of the gods who must therefore be venerated before the beginning of any theatrical activity. The Sanskrit plays continued this tradition. It is believed that the invocation of the gods at the beginning of any performance alerts the audience about the presence of the gods at the performance and so enhances their rapt participation. But in folk theatre in the villages, it acts in effect as a starter, to prepare the audience to receive the message of the play.

Sutradhar and Vidhushak

The *sutradhar* (stage manager) and the *vidhushak* (jester) appear in almost all the folk theatre forms under various names. The *sutradhar* is the *bhagavathar* in *yakshagana*, *bhagavathalu* in *bhagavathamela*, *vyasa* in *Ramlila*, *sami* or *gosai* in *raslila*, *sutradhikari* in *ankiya naat*, *phadkari* in *tamasha*, *kattiankaran* in *therukoothu*, *adhikari* in *yatra* and *naik* in *bhavai*. In short he is the playwright, director and producer combined and is present at every performance as co-ordinator, narrator, singer, actor and controller of almost everything. *Sutradhar*, literally one who holds the strings, is a term drawn from puppet theatre widespread in India. According to the Sanskrit tradition he is supposed to be a perfect master of many arts and sciences especially music, dance and mime. It is he who starts the singing and it is on his appreciation of the subtleties and conflicts in the play that the success of the show depends.

The folk entertainers find the direct intervention of the *sutradhar* convenient because he is able to bridge the gap in the stories and explain matters to the mostly illiterate audience in a friendly manner. He often distances himself from the dramatic action on the stage in order to have a rapport with the audience and to stimulate their thinking.

The *vidhushak* or buffoon is another traditional character emerging from the Sanskrit plays. He is not merely an entertainer, but the link between the past and the present and the purposive breaker of the conventions of unities of time and space. Like the *sutradhar*, he too is known by various names. He continues to be *vidhushak* in *koodiyattom*, but is the *kodangi* in *yakshagana*, *vivek* in *yatra*, *munshi* in *nautanki*, *udhawa* in *raslila*, and *komali* in *therukoothu*. Normally he enters into comical dialogues with the *sutradhar* and the audience, eliciting sarcastic comments on contemporary situations. Generally he speaks in rustic prose dialect. In a drama about the gods and goddesses he freely brings in current affairs much to the amazement and laughter of the audience. He thus becomes the liaison between the audience and the players.

According to Varadpande,

a *vidhushak* is dear to the audience not only because he evokes laughter and relieves them of the tensions of day to day life which is full of difficulties and hard work, but they feel that he is one of them, going through the same experiences of life. He establishes rapport with the audience crossing all psychological barriers between him and them. He has always shown concern about their problems and never spared the persons in authority responsible for the same.... While indulging with the audience he keeps his rustic audience under control and happy by sharp repartee and a keen sense of humour.[56]

A typical *vidhushak* is the *jootha mian* of *bhavai*. He is a rib-tickling burlesque, a chracter created by Thakur himself, wears a conical turban with coloured tassels. His chalky, clownish face is dotted with red and black and he wear bells around his shins. Gargi quotes his style of greeting the audience which alone is sufficient to show his brand of humour:

To the squatting people I offer a squatting salaam; to the standing spectators a standing salaam; to the fat ones a fat salaam; to the slim ones a slim salaam, to the tall ones a tall salaam; to the pigmy ones a pigmy salaam...[57]

After this he sticks out his tongue, dances, brags and barks.

A *vidhushak* can easily mimic a woman, a king, a thief, a wrestler as he narrates the exploits in between the main story. In fact it is this talent for mimicry that makes him the favourite of the audience. He appears at any moment as an all-knowing character, breaking the serious mood when appropriate with incongrous remarks. He can easily join the flow of the main story or stop the action and comment on what is happening, either by himself or with the help of the *sutradhar* or one of the actors. He even picks on members of the audience to comment on what is happening on the stage. Through his improvisations and interpolations as well as wide deviations and departures the stories become more relevant to the audience. Through his irreverent humour he makes fun of the local leaders exposes social evils and injustices and extemporizes on topics of concern to the villagers.

In this way the instituion of the *vidhushak* and *sutradhar*, with their incessant contact with the audience, make folk theatre an occasion for the audience to become invloved in the play. According to Parmar, these are

the lively humorous techniques that have enlivened folk theatre throughout the centuries.[58]

What Dutt says about the power of *yatra* typifies the richness of
theatre for communication:

> Its instinctive feature is its mimetic element, its robust and
> unashamed use of every emotion, every passion, every violence to
> subdue the audience to its will. This is theatre as magic.....It is theatre
> at its primitive best. It relies on nothig but declamation in heavy
> poetic prose and must capture the attention of a more or less unruly
> proletarian audience by intensity of action, by royal assassination
> and retribution, by Machiavellian villainy and the clash of arms.[59]

Notes

1. Vatsyayan, Kapila, *Traditional Indian Theatre Multiple Streams,* National
   Boook Trust, New Delhi, 1983, p. 3.
2. This information is gathered from various sources, notably the Encyclope-
   dia Brittanica, 1982.
3. Ibid.
4. Parmar, Shyam, *Traditional Folk Media in India,* Geka Books, New Delhi,
   p. 14 ff. See also Ranganath, H.K., *Using Folk Enterainment to Promote
   National Development,* UNESCO, 1980.
5. Dorson, Richard M., *Folklore to Folklife: An Introduction,* University of
   Chicago, 1972, p. 22.
6. Finnegan, Ruth, *Oral Tradition in Africa,* Oxford Library of African
   Literature, 1970, p. 76.
7. Mathur, J.C., *Drama in Rural India,* Asia Publishing House, London, 1982,
   p. 3.
8. Harrop, J.K., *Folk Plays: A Study in Dramatic Form and Social Structure,*
   University of Leeds, 1980, p. 378.
9. It is difficult to get exact dates for these events. The religious movements
   came to the fore in the early 9th century and went on till the 16th century.
10. Rangacharya, A., *Indian Theatre,* National Book Trust, New Delhi, 1971, p.
    32.
11. The Muslims conquered and ruled over various parts of India from 711-753
    (Muhammed-bin Kasim), 1028-1191 (Muhammed Ghazni and his
    followers) and from 1192-1757) (Muhammed Gori, Khiljis and the
    Mughals). Britain took control from 1757.
12. Gargi, Balwant, *Folk Theatre in India,* University of Washington Press,
    Seattle and London, 1965, p. 14. This is also the claim of seasoned actor-

director-writer Phani Bhushan Bidyabinod.

13. Ibid., p. 167.

14. Researchers have pointed out that the classification of several forms like *yakshagana* and *therukoothu* as classical is controversial, as they have both folk and classical elements in them. This is one of the arguments to show that folk theatre has borrowed heavily from classical theatre or vice versa. Merging of various elements is commonplace in classical as well as folk theatre.

15. Parmar, op.cit., p. 35 ff.

16. Ranganath, op.cit, p. 23.

17. Hawley, J.S., *At Play With Krishna*, Princeton University Press. Several examples of *raslila* are provided in this study.

18. Mathur, op.cit., p. 82.

19. Rangacharya, op.cit., p. 84.

20. *Natyasastra*, ch. 2.

21. Panicker, A., in *Theatre of the Earth is Never Dead*, ed. Shankarapillai G., University of Calicut, 1986, p. 6.

22. Srinivas, M.N., *Caste in Modern India and Other Essays*, Asia Publishig House, Bombay, 1962.

23. Sharma, U.M., "The Problem of Village Hinduism: Fragmentation and Integration" in *Indian Contribution to Sociology*, 1970, p. 14.

24. Ashley, W., 'Teyyame Kettu of North Kerala', *TDR*, 23/2, 1979, p. 101.

25. Arden, J., "Chhau Dancers of Purulia, *TDR* 15/2/, 1971.

26. Tapper, B.E., " An Enactment of Perfect Morality: The Meaning and Social Context of a South Indian Ritual Drama", in Mayer, A.C. (ed.), *Culture and Morality*, OUP, New Delhi, 1981. Although Tapper studies this play he does not make the critical note that is made here.

27. Kapur, Anuradha, "Ramilia at Ramnagar", unpublished Ph.D . diss., University of Leeds, 1982, p. 306.

28. Appavoo, T.J., *Folklore for Change*, T.T.S, Madurai, 1986, p. 55

29. Amaldoss, P.J., "Protest Themes in Therukoothu," paper presented at a seminar, Kottayam, 1987.

30. O'Hanlon, R., "Maratha History as Polemic: Low Caste Ideology and Political Debate in Late Nineteenth Century Western India, *Modern Asian Studies*, 17/1, 1987, p. 3.

31. Ibid., p. 4.

32. Ibid., p. 6.

33. Ibid., p. 8.

34. Omvedt, G., "The Satya Shodhak Samaj and Peasant Agitation," in *Economic and Politcal Weekly*, Bombay, vol. 44, p. 1971 ff.

35. Ibid., p. 1974.

36. Information on this section is from Pradhan Sudhi (ed.), *Marxist Cultural Movements* , Parts I and II.

37. Bharucha, Rustom, *Towards a Revolutionary Theatre*, University of Hawaii

Press, 1983, p. 97.

38. Hansen Kathryn, " Indian Folk Tradition and Modern Theatre," *Asian Folklore Studies*, Nagoya, (Japan) XLII, 1983, p. 88.

39. Abram, Tevia, "Tamasha, The People's Theatre of Maharastra State", Michigan State University Press, 1974, unpublished Ph.D. diss., p. 234.

40. Kidd, Ross, "Domestication Theatre and Conscientization Drama" in Colletta, N. and Kidd, R., (eds), *Traditions for Developmet*, Berlin, 1982. pp. 480-88.

41. Vatsyayan, op. cit., p. 1.

42. Gargi, op. cit., p. 97 ff.

43. Samar, D.L., *Sangeet Natak*, New Delhi, vol. 20, p. 53.

44. Ahmed, Tanvir, "Theatre is in the Villages," *Asian Action*, Bangkok, 1977, p. 16.

45. *Natyasastra*, ch. 25, 76-77.

46. Schechner, R., *Performative Circumstances from the Avant Garde to Ramlila*, Seagull Books, Calcutta, 1983, pp. 262, 271.

47. Awasthy, S., "Scenography of Traditional Theatre in India, *TDR*, T. 64. p. 41.

48. Kapur, Anuradha, op. cit., p. 380.

49. Tarlekar, G.H., *Studies in Natyasastra*, Motilal Banarsidas, N. Delhi, 1975, p. 142. This is an explanation of the facts presented in the *Natyasastra*, ch. 25.

50. Quoted by Machwe, Prabhakar in *Indian Drama* (ed.), Gowda, Anniah, seminar papers, University of Mysore, 1971, p. 2.

51. *Natyasastra*, nos. 107-108.

52. Vatsyayan, op.cit., p. 12.

53. Gargi, op. cit., p. 176.

54. Ibid., p. 177.

55. Natyasastra, ch. 29.

56. Varadpande, *Traditions of Indian Theatre*, Abhinav Publishers, N. Delhi, 1979, p. 85.

57. Gargi, op. cit., p. 57.

58. Parmar, op.cit., p. 18.

59. Dutt, Utpal, *Towards a Revolutionary Theatre*, Calcutta, 1984, p. 145.

Chapter IV

Street Theatre: Protest all The Way

I. The Nature of Street Theatre

Basically, street theatre is a short sketch performed on the roadside or street corner in order to give a quick, encapsulated statement about a socio-political problem, or to motivate spectators to take swift action on a particular issue, through the use of highly imaginative allegory. Obviously, the circle is the natural shape when a group of people assemble to watch an event taking place in the open. This is probably why Richard Southern argues that the original and natural shape of theatre is the circle.[1] In such a situation, the audience and the performers are on the same level emphasizing the fact that the performers are no different from the audience. themselves.

From the analysis of folk theatre in chapter II it is obvious that in India waysides, streets, village-markets, open air grounds, fair-sites, court-yards and other crowded areas have remained the ideal venues to present plays. However, street theatre, as a phenomenon with pronounced political overtones, made its way only in the nineteen twenties. A statement issued in 1984 said:

> Street theatre, an ancient tradition of performance in India, has been kept alive for centuries by the creativity of well versed actors. In recent years it has emerged as a living and dynamic force in the socio-cultural milieu of present day society. Comprising of a popular expression of the people it absorbs different languages, performing styles and methods of appeal.[2]

Unlike its Western counterpart where there are giant puppets, stilt walkers, masquerades, large banners, placards and posters, in these street plays the emphasis is more on the performance of the actors. A number of elements of the folk theatre help invite even a totally uninterested audience to these performances. Equipped with song and dance, mime and mask, the performers do not wait for an audience, but go out in search of one. Street theatre dispenses with stage and lights, minimizes props, simplifies costumes and adapts a flexible format without being restricted by the unities of time and space. Critical as a whole of the status quo and the ruling party's policies of development, and militant in character, it is a tool for social activists to hone in on the public's concern about social and political happenings, not only as individuals but also as members of society. According to Reynold,

> theatre in the streets in India is an artistic expression of left wing politics. Born out of the need for a social change it is essentially a people's theatre embracing the daily life of the common man.[3]

Today in almost every city groups of committed youngsters have taken to street plays on topical issues. On any one day there are nearly 7,000[4] active groups in the country. All kinds of people from factory workers to college students, professors to professional theatre activists and political agitators are involved. Normally such plays are performed outside offices during lunch intervals or after office hours. In the evenings, and during holidays, festivals and fairs, the roadsides, street corners and open grounds are ideal places. The audience varies from a handful to hundreds. The performers can easily reach out to nearly 400-500 people in the open air and crowded streets without the help of amplifying systems. Padamsee, a connoisseur of street theatre observes:

> Incorporating elements of ritual song and dance they have woven spectacles that are colourful and representative of popular beliefs. Whether it is the immediacy of the content, novelty of form or the spontaneous warmth that it generates, one thing is certain—that it seems to have caught the imagination of the people.[6]

From the days of IPTA, techniques have become more subtle, and the contents more boisterous and challenging to the establishment. In essence it is a theatre that dispenses with formality, illusion and inequality and concentrates on the establishment of a rapport between the performers and the audience. It resembles graffiti'—short, hard hitting and provocative. It is a form in which the performers invite the audience to participate in a game of "how would you behave if you were in a situation like this?"

What Sue Fox says about English street theatre is true of Indian street theatre;

> With street theatre you are as good as the moment and no more. You have no reputation in the places you will normally work. Yours is not a theatre audience. They have never heard of you, and usually they were not intending to see a show. They have chanced upon you while they were out, as a rule, and if they don't like the show they can walk away. But if they love it, they forget the shopping.....They get lost in your dreams and share them for a few moments. There's an honesty in the contract between street theatre performer and audience.... . As performers you know when it is working—you never get a bored, indulgent audience.[6]

In street theatre, there is direct reflection of values and social relevance, which begin to serve the purpose of social communication. When fully imagined, felt, and skilfully presented, it widens the perception and consciousness, enabling the audience to participate more fully in the lives of their fellow human beings. It serves to develop empathy with them, understand their motivation and comprehend the realities of social and personal existence.

It is also a vibrant, mobile and flexible form, constantly experimenting with new concepts and techniques and surviving on contemporary issues. Its resistance to any attempt to restrict it within a rigid framework makes it different from any other media. Ultimately, what emerges as street theatre is a mobile, didactic theatre, more often than not infused with political implications, in which there has been a simultaneous evolution of form and content—each necessitating the other. In the past three decades the movement has evolved more as an effective form of social protest than as purely dramatic form. In moments of desperation during political upheavals, amidst feelings of helplessness, such staged protests bring hope. It is a way of keeping up one's morale. Its ability for direct communication unlike any other form of art enables it to be a powerful tool in political propaganda. In India where there is a high degree of illiteracy and diversity of language and dialects, a theatre form of this sort, versatile and adaptable, cheap and mobile has indeed a tremendous potential.

II. The Origin

Street theatre is in fact the continuation of folk theatre. The protest element, dormant in folk theatre, finds expression in a changed socio-political situation where educated youngsters are increasingly becoming disenchanted with the lack of opportunities in the country.

The traditional folk theatres owe their origin to the streets, fields or temple courtyards. India is an 'open air society' with a warm climate most of the year. It is reasonable to suppose that open air performances, being cheaper and more participative, were encouraged even from the earliest of times.

Towards the turn of the century popular leaders like Tilak and Gandhi had begun to attract the masses to their struggle against the British regime with the help of powerful symbols. Tilak's re-interpretation of the Ganesh festival [7] and Gandhi's prayer meetings, marches and the use of Swadeshi (home-spun cloths) are instances in point. One of the first examples of street theatre is perhaps Gandhi's Salt March at Dandi (1930). It contained elements normally associated with street theatre. The march and the picking up of the salt was a staging. It was a community activity involving actors and audience and asserting the public's rights against the threats of an oppressor.

Street theatre took to direct socio-political protest themes during the days of IPTA, which had absorbed the best of Sanskrit and Western tradition and was considered part of the mainstream theatre. It had some of the best artists in the country. However, IPTA's main focus was political. It was backed by the Communist Party of India and concerned with the struggles of the ordinary masses. All over India, prompted by the belief that a 'revolutionary content' necessitates a 'revolutionary form' IPTA sought to modify conventional proscenium theatre in order to reach the people. Aided by the Progressive Writers' Association,[8] it was fired with anger against the imperialists and came out of the closed halls to perform under open skies, on street corners and city centres. For the first time, as Gargi observes, 'people and players, the two pillars of theatre kept apart for so long, joined and became one whole.'[9] The Punjab unit of IPTA had already taken to street theatre in 1943:

> at a very short notice some men who had just conducted a strike were called upon to produce a play; within two hours, they were able to put up an extempore play on the strike more or less exactly as it had

happened. The play when produced was coherent and the whole thing gave the impression that it was carefully written up and laboriously rehearsed. The play was good because:

    (i)   it came straight from life;

    (ii) it was collectively produced; and

    (iii) it was performed by men who had personal experience of the incidents depicted on the stage.

Let it not be understood that such plays are good propaganda and bad art; all who saw the play felt that it was good art, first and foremost.[10]

In Andhra Pradesh following the example of the folk form *veedhinatakam* (street theatre) a play called *Hitler Parajayam* (1944) did the rounds of the villages, denouncing the rise of Hitler and its aftermath in the world at large. A local critic wrote:

The street play on Hitler was heartily enjoyed by all. Hitler bragged and bragged. His entourage of yes-men, two typical prosperous peasants and their wives made him sound ridiculous by repeating his words. The best fun came when Mussolini and Jajo spoke of their plight and putting their heads on Hitler's shoulders began crying. Roars of laughter rent the air.[11]

Around the same time, in Agra too, the IPTA unit experimented with improvised plays. The plays were composed in such a manner that the incidents were made quite clear and each character was drawn very neatly. The actors rehearsed a few times improvising the dialogues, each one remaining within the framework of their characters. Some of the plays staged this way under the guidance of Rajendra Raghuvanshi about contemporary problems were *Aaj Ka Sawaal*, (The Problems of Today), *Swathantra Sangram* (Independence Struggle) and *Bhook Ki Jwaala* (The Flames of Hunger).

In the early fifties, in Calcutta it was Utpal Dutt and Panu Pal who ventured into this form. They began experimenting with the form in 1950 in a play called *Charge Sheet* about the Communist leaders held in prison without trial. It was improvised overnight and hastily rehearsed for a couple of hours. Dutt notes:

The play lasting about half an hour was taken to working class slums

and remote villages...analysing the absurd charges levelled against
the Communist detenues and finally exploding into a slogan for their
release.[12]

Within a week, the General Secretary and the President of the Bengal
unit of IPTA were arrested for allowing IPTA to be used for direct party
propaganda. Dutt was soon asked to leave IPTA because of political
differences. However, Dutt continued with street theatre which many
thought was too daring especially at a time when the police were looking
for any excuse to swoop down on communist party workers. For him street
theatre seemed the ideal means to take theatre to the masses. He realised
that street theatre forms ensured maximum mobility by doing away with
sets and lights and cutting down the number of actors. Learning from
the experiences of Living Newspaper Theatre, guerilla theatre and other
forms from abroad, he created plays in which a group of actors would go
to a street corner or a village market and begin to improvise. Extempora-
neous dialogues and local subjects came up from the audience automatically.

For Dutt this form of theatre seemed an effective method of
propaganda. Later he became aware of its specific strategies, for
example, the importance of matters of immediate relevance and the need
to entertain in a big way. In 1953 he launched a street play in
Maheshtolla, a suburb of Calcutta. The occasion was a by-election. An
unknown Communist Party worker, a tailor by profession, had beaten up
a big boss of the Congress Party. On the latter's appeal the elections had
been postponed and now a by-election was ordered. Dutt's group of street
players stayed there with the people for two months, playing five to six
times a day at every corner of the constituency, canvassing with the
people to vote for the Community Party. The effort was successful.

Other issues like the enhancement of second class fare in tram cars
and the lives and struggles of the peasants of Kakdwip were also acted out
in later street plays. Plays like *Passport* (1950), *Saurin Master* (1950),
Naya Tughlaq (1953) helped spread Dutt's reputation as a playwright.
His *Special Train* (1954) about the striking workers of Hindustan
Automobile Factory, exposing the alliance between the Birlas, the
owners of the Company and the Congress government, which attempted
to break the strike by sending a special train full of thugs and scabs,
remains a classic example of protest theatre.[13]

In the mid-fifties Habib Tanvir who worked for the IPTA devised
a number of agit-prop plays in the Chhattisgarh area of Madhya Pradesh.

He not only blended the folk forms but began to train local artists, villagers and tribals in his plays. His 'theatre on wheels' also known as 'street corner shows' or 'living newspaper', was a novel concept–a mobile theatre going out in lorries. Tanvir remembers:

> In one play we did, *Shantidoot Kaamgaar* (1955), we used to go from place to place. One man would put up a poster and another would come up dressed as a policeman and a quarrel would start, a crowd would collect and a short play would be staged.[14]

In general Tanvir took a non-party political stance in his street plays. However, his *Indra Loksabha* (1961), staged on a truck, while helping the audience to analyse the differences between the major political parties vindicated the Congress Party.

The efforts of Dutt and Tanvir gave the necessary fillip to street theatre all over India in the fifties and sixties until Badal Sircar emerged on the Indian scene.

Badal Sircar

Although there had been sporadic attempts at street theatre all over India, it was with the emergence of Sircar's 'third theatre' that street theatre became a force to reckon with. All over India, 'third theatre' is recognised as the epitome of conscientious and experimental theatre.

Sircar, though trained as a town planner, had already made a name for himself as one of the most promising playwrights of the mid-sixties. His psychological absurd plays like *Evam Indrajt, Baki Ithihas, Shesh Nei, Tringsha Shatabdi, Pagla Ghora* rank among the best Indian plays. In these plays he had perfected a style of writing where his words resonated with ideas rather than feelings. He also tried docu-drama, and several other experimental forms, performed in the West on the conventional stage. By the mid-sixties, he opted out of the comfort and security of the picture frame stage and large auditoria to experiment with open theatre forms. After a few years he developed a theatre of conscience and concern, involved more with live social and political issues and reaching out to people and communities in both urban and rural areas. He called his form of theatre 'third theatre' to differentiate in from Westernized proscenium theatre and traditional folk theatre, but drawing from both. He insisted that his theatre be free and not bought like a commodity with tickets.

Sircar was fully aware of the dichotomy between urban proscenium theatre and traditional rural theatre. He tried to create a theatre of synthesis. Making good use of a Jawaharlal Nehru scholarship which enabled him to tour around the world, he participated in and studied various forms of experimental theatre workshops. On his return, he experimented with his group, Shatabdi, on a trial and error basis. Initially, as Sircar recalls, he went through a period of introspection. The popularity of cinema and television and the attempt of theatre to match that popularity baffled him. Like Grotowski, he resorted to the elimination process and asked: "Without the presence of what, can theatre cease to exist?[15] This helped him to reach the very core of theatre, avoiding all incidentals like make-up, music, costumes, lights, sets and props. He realized that the distinctive nature of theatre is that it is a 'live' show which offers scope for a direct person-to-person communication, involving four distinct forms—performer and performer performer and spectator, spectator and performer and spectator and spectator. Commenting on the third and fourth forms of communication Sircar said:

> When we speak of the latter two ways of communication we get panicky. We think that the spectator communicating to the perform-ers or to other spectators would mean chaos. And so it would be if we assume that communication is limited to language. The attention of the spectator, concentration, the reaction to the performance reflected in his facial expression or the tension in his body—all these can be feed-backs to the performer or to another spectator.... This is an intimate theatre...the language of this theatre involves being within and in experiencing, not viewing and hearing from a separate sanctum at a distance...[16]

His convictions led him to minimize and even eliminate the barriers between performers and the spectators. He broke down the proscenium and experimented with circular staging, without props, sets or stage lights. It was becoming clearer to him that ultimately theatre depended on the performer's body and the spectators' imagination. Techniques like the elaborate use of mime, body language, symbols and imageries, stylized movements, human props and chorus singing were tried to enlighten the imagination of the audience. An important means of partici-pation was by urging the audience to concentrate intently on the actions of play, most of which were done in highly imaginative mimes. Direct eye contact with the audience was also encouraged in order to heighten participation.

Sircar also experimented with themes, archetypes and stereo-types instead of plots and characters. In plays like *Sagina Mahato* (1970), *Spartacus* (1972), *Michil* (1973) and *Bhoma* (1974) there was no one protagonist with whom the audience could identify, nor was there a clear story line with a beginning, middle, climax and denoument. The plays evoked deep concern through short, compact scenes. *Bhoma* was about tribals from the Sunderban jungles of south Bengal where, in the early 20th century, the tribals cleared the forest to make cultivable land for settlement. The civil authorities had deforested it, thus endangering the tribals. In the play there was no protagonist as such, nor a story about Bhoma's life and death, but through concrete short and swift dialogues and images and symbols of oppression Sircar made an attempt to find out "if the blood of the tribals is still hot or has it grown cold in their fight for survival both against nature and the onslaught of the civilized world"[17] In Michil as in most of his other plays, the performers played different roles in different scenes. The method worked efficiently in conveying to the viewer the thoughts and feelings of the play, without identifying them with any character in particular. Here is an example which illustrates some techniques.

[TWO, FOUR, FIVE, SIX, put their hands on each other's shoulders, form a close circle, and begin to go round like a planet. ONE kneels on one side. THREE lies in a corner for some time before suddenly jumping up]

THREE: If the blood of man is cold, then how can he love? Tell me, answer! Don't human beings love? Is love dead? Come on, come on, answer! Do you want to kill love? Can you kill it? Can you?

[The planet does not answer; it goes, round and round. ONE gradually becomes a deformed human being, with a clown's grin fixed on his face]

No, you can't. The earth will die before that.

TWO, FOUR, FIVE SIX: This earth.

THREE: Yes, yes, the earth will...

[ONE comes closer, THREE is terribly shocked.]

What's this? Who are you?

ONE: I'm one of the two million.

THREE: What two million? Which two million?

ONE: All the experiments with atom bombs that have been conducted up to 1962 on this earth...

TWO, FOUR, FIVE, SIX: This earth...

ONE: Have released enough radio activity to cause the birth of
                two million maimed and deformed children. I'm one of the
                first lot.

TWO, FOUR, FIVE, SIX: This earth.

ONE: They are still being born. Being born often. After a while
                they'll be born every day.

THREE: That–that's not this country's doing.

ONE: Not yet. Now it will be.
                [They walk in procession]

TWO, FOUR, SIX: Rejoice! Rejoice!

FIVE: 18th May 1974.

TWO, FOUR, SIX: Rejoice! Rejoice!

FIVE: India becomes a nuclear power!

TWO, FOUR, SIX: Rejoice! Rejoice!

FIVE: Number six in the world! (Bhoma, pp. 71-72)

As Sircar experimented with and was exposed to the works of
Schechner, Julian Beck, Judith Malina, Andre Gregory and others he went
on to make his theatre increasingly subtle and at times incomprehensible.
Into a fragmented script he introduced techniques like physical acting,
stylized movements, chorus of voice, non-verbal sounds, alternative
music, rhetorical techniques of dialogue delivery sounding more like the
phrases and *non-sequiturs* of Pinter and Beckett, juxtaposing comments
which the actors mouthed mechanically, collages of images and words and
the repetition of words to create an effect of incantation. He also adapted
the spatial, environmental seating of the audience as propounded by
Schechner. Techniques like magical sculpting in space, simultaneous
action, lack of time-space barrier, slow motion and freeze created the
magic of the third theatre. These techniques were closely related to the
fragmented and episodic format of the script. For example in *Bhoma* in
the relentless chants of the slogan, "The blood of fish is cold, the blood
of men is cold, cold, cold, cold...", Sircar not only created rhythms and
choreography but also challenged the inaction and irresponsibility of his
audience in a subtle way. All these innovations appealed greatly to the
aesthetic canons of his audience who were mostly theatre-crazy, urban,
lower middle class dilettanti.

As with the form, it may be observed that Sircar changed the content
of his plays drastically. Although there were political undertones in the
earlier proscenium plays, his third theatre plays like *Spartacus, Prastab,*

Bhoma, Michil and Tringsha Shatabdi were powerful responses to the various socio-political realities he encountered. These plays show Sircar's deeper understanding of the problems of nuclear age and of poverty, corruption, greed, and the industrial and agricultural exploitation of the poor. Through his novel style of production he asked his audience to face these problems as personal issues and to try to do something about them. The plays were not overtly political, but showed the individuals caught in the web of politics. Instead of advocating strikes, lock-outs and the overthrow of the government, he was content to disturb the conscience of his spectators, urging them to contribute their mite to reconstructing the state of chaos. Bharucha observes:

> One leaves a play by Sircar acutely aware of the exploitation and injustices that pervade life in Calcutta and rural Bengal. Sircar makes his audience confront their indifference to the chaos and corruption that characterize urban life. He never fails to emphasize that his spectators are responsible for the world they live in. Instead of exaggerating the threat of the exploiters and the callousness of the political leaders (as Dutt tends to do) Sircar focuses on the callousness of the middle class and their capacity to watch the suffering of the people without doing anything about it.[18]

For example in *Bhoma*, the story of the persecuted tribals, Sircar tells the audience in a matter of fact way: "We drink the blood of Bhoma and live in the city" (p. 84). There is no indictment, anger or call for revenge, but a discerning audience finds their complacency assaulted. In *Michil*, the chorus represents the mass of people in India who accept every form of corruption unleashed by the ruling class and those in power. The chorus seeks the help of these 'mentors' to help them when misfortune befalls them. The mentors only help them get drunk!

Third Theatre and After

With his group Satabdi, Sircar established Angamancha (courtyard) in a room of 850 square feet in central Calcutta. From then on his repertory of plays grew. Regular performances in parks and roadsides continued. The audience varied from a handful in the halls to thousands in the open air grounds. Over the years Sircar and his group have developed a workshop format of functioning. Their theatre was instantly recognized all over India as it was inexpensive, flexible, portable, yet imaginative, challenging the aesthetic notions and social sense of the audience.

Sircar was much in demand for conducting workshops for a number of alternative theatre groups that dabbled in street theatre from the early seventies. His approach was soon the talking point among street theatre activists. They borrowed so heavily from his techniques that in some places street theatre became identified with third theatre. Following the example of street theatre groups, action groups involved in consciousness raising work in rural areas also sought Sircar's help when they became aware of the power of theatre. This aspect is dealt with in chapter V.

Sircar has had unparalleled influence in the resurgence of street theatre in the seventies. However, his techniques are first and foremost designed for small groups, arranged spatially in small halls. Large masses of people carelessly moving around in the streets may not find these techniques suitable. Although several of his techniques such as mime, choreographed movements, incantations and choral singing may be found in folk theatre he seems to have discovered them in the works of Grotowski, Schechner and Barba! Some of his techniques are too subtle, especially those borrowing from the psycho-physical actor training methods of Grotowski and the 'cosmic trance' of Artaud, and may not make much sense to the ordinary people in the street. The lack of a well plotted story or sequential narratives may make comprehension difficult for some. However, it is heartening to see Sircar's many followers turning to folk theatre for inspiration.

III. Emergence of Street Theatre

Theatre has always felt at home on the streets of India. The explosion of street theatre activities however, with definite socio-political motivations was indeed the result of certain specific factors.

1. A Response to the Needs of the Time

After independence, street theatre got a shot in the arm as India decided to follow a democratic form of government where freedom of speech and public expression were guaranteed by the Fundamental Rights of the Constitution. The IPTA activists, who were all in the opposition, found theatre a potent weapon for contacting the people and voicing their opinions. However, this freedom was short-lived. The government made sporadic attempts to enforce repressive measures to throttle the growth of theatre that challenged its policies. For example, the West Bengal unit of IPTA received this notice from the Commissioner of Police, Calcutta, early in 1953:

In accordance with the provision laid down under Section 7 of the Dramatic Performance Act of 1876, you are hearby requested to furnish this office by 18th February, 1953 at the latest with the printed or manuscript copy of the dramas mentioned in the statement enclosed herewith and which the IPTA have already staged in public places. The dramas are requested by the office for review so as to ascertain the character of each of the same.[19]

Almost every play of the Bengal unit of IPTA from 1942 was on this list. In other parts of India too maximum powers were given to the police to resort to punitive measures against authors, artists and theatre proprietors. Several of the plays that served to raise the consciousness of the people during the British regime, for example, *Navanna, Keechakavadha* and *Nildarpan* were shut down.

The entertainment tax introduced by the British government continued to be misused by the Congress party, which forced several of the activists to leave the proscenium theatre. Sathyu, one of the earlier directors of IPTA relates how they used street plays to circumvent the strict censorship laws:

Players dressed as ordinary workers would go and stand in front of factory gates in between shifts. They would start arguing about some political issue among themselves. Attracted, the real workers would listen, some would even join in. But before the real police could come and round up the IPTA activists an actor dressed as policeman would come rushing in and disrupt the mock fight and the players and the workers would disperse. The real police would arrive to find that the whole thing was over. But the questions posed by the players would remain with the workers, thus raising their consciousness.[20]

All over India the fifties and sixties were times of political unrest and social upheaval. Theatre activists were becoming disillusioned with the British conventional theatre. Calcutta led the way in the quest for newer forms of theatre. Revolting against the conservatism and elitism of the proscenium stage, several radical groups started staging plays at street corners and in public parks. There were times when as many as six groups would be performing plays in different parts of a park at the same time. These plays, though theatrically not of a very high quality, helped to create political awareness among the common people.

As a counter measure the government took to hiring artists to eulogize its policies and programmes through its Song and Drama Division. This inevitably spurred the leftist minded artists to resort to street theatre in a more committed way. There were other contributory factors. The growing discontent among the educated unemployed youth of the lower middle class (who attributed their misery and negligence to those in power), as well ass their sense of adventure and exuberance found expression in Street Theatre. Also, the masses were becoming increasingly aware of the vast corruption in public life. In their frustration, they turned to Street Theatre more and more.

2. Breaching the Cultural Barrier

In the past popular culture was created by the people. Today with the emergence of the mass media, especially cinema, it is sold to the people by the powerful and the rich as a commodity. Radio, cinema, and the press have become fortresses of stagnation against change and social transformation. Controlled entirely by the government and the industrialists they have deprived a vast majority of the people of their traditional value systems. The cinema has provided escapist entertainment for a gullible audience. Much of conventional theatre is but a poor imitation of films. As a result, traditional values–family relationships, religion and respect for elders– are being destroyed. But at the same time, in the rural areas and among reactionary groups, these traditional values survive intact. Consequently, a cultural gap is developing in the country. Das echoes similar sentiments:

> To compensate for the lapses of the cultural gap and to dilute the influence of the sophisticated media, a broad-based mode of communication closer to all the people is necessary. Street theatre with its contemporary relevance to daily life, probably meets these specifications, which other traditional folk forms are incapable of meeting due to their codified structures and mythological overtones.[21]

In fact most of the groups behind street theatre were once active in proscenium theatre. Sensing the futility of their effort to reach out to the masses they went in search of a cheap and mobile medium that would help them work towards an egalitarian society. This search resulted in street theatre. Thus street theatre may be seen as an invention precipitated by a necessity or a crisis. It is a modern, urbanized version of the numerous folk forms. For as more people moved to the urban centres they brought along their own cultural expressions with them while borrowing from their new urban culture. The possibilities of dynamic improvisations in folk theatre have made street theatre a popular medium.

3. Priorities of Concern

It is important to note here that a large section of the practitioners of street theatre are lower middle class urban activists. The question may be posed as to the priorities in their concern: is it purely love of theatre, an expression of responsible citizenship in developing the consciousness of uneducated masses, or is it to demonstrate a left-wing stance in support of party interests? Although priorities vary, any one of these is a sufficient reason for the emergence of a group.

Jan Natya Manch (Janam) of Delhi is lively group of professionals who were earlier involved in proscenium theatre. They believe that the enormous popularity of cinema and television, which are basically theatre presented in highly technical and miniscule forms, have all but annihilated the role of proscenium theatre in the auditoria. There is hardly an audience that realizes the value of 'live' theatre rather than filmed theatre. Hence for Janam street theatre is a means to take live theatre to where the people are, that is, to the streets.

In the same way environmentalists and ecologists, those fighting for women's rights and other concerns like child and bonded labour and civil rights strongly believe that street theatre is the ideal platform for them. They argue that they have a role to play as citizens, as privileged people with education, to enlighten the masses on issues that are important. A plethora of social, political, religious and economic issues like communalism, caste disparities, terrorism, nuclear disasters, corruption in high places and police terrorism find a place in their repertory of plays.

There are also street theatre groups with seemingly extreme leftist tendencies. These are more or less concentrated in the Marxist and Naxalite-dominated[22] states of Bengal, Kerala, Andhra Pradesh and Bihar. Their theatre is aesthetically and ideologically forcible and ruthless in inciting violence and mindless annihilation of corrupt forces. Although their theatre may project their concerns with the growing problems in the country, their primary aim is apparently to oppose the ruling government without offering an alternative.

4. Love of Experimental Theatre

Street theatre provides an outlet for those involved in experimental theatre as it encourages participatory performances of small groups. Initially Sircar began experimenting with theatre forms. Today there are a number of groups who perform in halls for small audiences. Their contribution to street theatre can not be underestimated. Probir Guha's work in the Living Theatre of Kharadah is one that comes readily to mind. Experimenting with the expressive skills and techniques of traditional forms like *chhau, jatra, baul* singing, *kalari payattu* and other forms of martial arts he has developed a skilful form of the theatre that builds on Sircar's experiments. Guha explains:

> The basic principles of the body in a whole spectrum of forms across the Asian scene are the same be it *kalari, kabuki, chhau, noh, bharatnatyam, kathakali,* or *legong.* The basic body frame, body positions, breathing, movements, steps, energy points, tension points, the streets on the vertebral column are the same in all these forms. Which means these forms have something valuable for us which we must consciously rediscover for our own needs.[23]

The group had been trying to learn more about theatre by looking at traditional peoples, dancers, martial arts and rituals while analysing and integrating these with modern theatre. The group's theory, as Guha puts it, is philosophical:

> It you want to communicate you must penetrate yourself; if you can penetrate yourself you can sacrifice yourself before the audience. When you sacrifice, your whole self becomes ego-less and you achieve the quality of a baby; only at that moment can you really communicate.[24]

Commenting on Guha's theatre Padamsee notes:

> As they huddle, whisper, dance in slow motion secretly creating terror in the audience, they scream for a violent revolution. It is almost therapeutic to watch them. The imagery is strong, direct, using force which seems beyond the natural boundaries of man. Pictorial images

of greed, struggle, drought, famine, sweat and toil clamour for a cathartic ending.[25]

IV. Theme Analysis

1. Socio-political Issues

The majority of street plays in the repretory of the groups in India is undoubtedly on socio-political issues. Some of these are based on topical events, others are on perennial issues like communalism, terrorism, police brutality, bride-burning, dowry system, caste inequalities, industrial and agricultural exploitation, alcoholism, health care and elections.

4. Topical Events

Contemporaneity is primarily what makes a street play succeed. Given the structure of a street play, it is not difficult to improvise a play on an event that happened only a few hours before. Topicality is one of the major qualities of the plays improvised by Janam, the Delhi based group. For instance, in 1978, the workers in a factory in north Delhi went on strike over two small demands—a cycle stand and a tea-shop in the factory premises. It was the time when the Industrial Relations Bill, which was stealthily put into practice during the emergency (1975-77), was about to be legalized. Its provisions were harsh and consequently the striking workers were treated badly. Eventually the strike ended in the death of six workers. This incident triggered off Janam's play, *Machine*, which was performed numerous times in front of the very same factory. The play, enacted in mime, underlines the tensions present when work stops in a factory and employers use force and other means to break the strikers.

Another play by the same group *Hatyara* (1981) drew inspiration from the Babli Nagpal Report (1981) on communal violence in Aligarh.[26]

The Samudaya (Bangalore) play, *Struggle* (1977), very much like *Machine*, depicted the struggle of a group of striking workers of the Metal Lamp Cap Factory. The strike had been going on for seven months with the workers being refused the right to form a union. They were paid a daily wage of Rs. 2.50. The struggle was dramatized by using some of the striking workers themselves as actors. Performing almost everyday outside the factory gates, the workers enlightened the public about the sordid conditions in the factory. At the same time they were gaining the necessary confidence to counter the management.[27]

Another example, though on a smaller scale, was the effort of Aahvaan Natya Manch, a university based theatre group. In 1980, the Bombay University decided to pass an ordinance on the Codes of Conduct and Rules of Discipline for the students of the university. Although passed surreptitiously by the executive committee and kept top secret, it leaked out, and was seen to contain clauses giving the principal and vice-principal enormous powers over all the actions of the students. Thirteen disciplinary measures ranging from a fine of Rs.300 to expulsion from the university for up to five years were suggested if a student was found guilty of unbecoming conduct. Aahvaan rose to the occasion and satirized the ordinance in various colleges of the university for a month, preparing the students to oppose the ordinance unanimously.[28]

In 1982 India hosted the Asian Games in New Delhi. A street theatre group from Baroda, Jangbash, staged a play *Safed Appu* (white elephant: the emblem of the Asian Games was a baby elephant) questioning the enormous expense in building fly-overs when 80% of the country slept on empty stomach. The play concerned the sordid living conditions of the construction workers involved in building the fly-overs. The organizers went ahead with the Games, but it helped raise the issue of unequal distribution of wealth and sensitized the audiences to the dangerous and hazardous living conditions of construction workers as they struggle to feed their family.[29]

Street theatre has played a major role in election campaigns all over India. Samudaya's role in spreading the anti-Congress wave in the Chickmagalur by election (1977) revealed in no uncertain terms the power of street theatre. Focusing on the killing of a bonded labourer in Bhadravati, the play *Pathre Sangapana Kole* became a major talking point during the elections. Although Congress won, it did so with a smaller majority.[30]

The proliferation of street plays on particular themes has undoubtedly been due to events of the recent years. The communal riots after the murder (1984) of Indira Gandhi by her Sikh bodyguards[31] gave rise to a series of plays all over India on communalism, patriotism and terrorism.

In the same way the Bhopal gas tragedy (1984)[32] spurred groups like KSSP and others to produce plays on the evils of multinationals, nuclear armaments and scientific developments. Numerous cases of bride burning in recent years and the Deorala Sati case (1987) where a young Rajput girl Roop Kanwar was thrown into the funeral pyre of her husband, have given rise to many plays on issues like dowry, women's education and equal status for women.

B. Perennial Issues

There are two categories of plays that deal with problems of a permanent nature: those that try to popularize the government's methods and policies and others that call for a total re-structuring of society. Plays dealing with issues like communalism, superstition, alcoholism, health care, nutrition, use of fertilizers, improving the educational system and government inspired methods of family planning are in the former. Plays on caste system, rich-poor disparity, and others that challenge government's ways of running the country come in the latter.

It was pointed out in chapter III that the government under the umbrella of SDD is involved in this type of propaganda. There are also numerous street theatre groups that pick up these themes and present them in a low-key way for fear of the police or to win the favour and support of the local officials. But all these very same problems can be treated in ways that challenge the government and its policies. For example, communalism is a major problem in the country. The government would be only too happy if street theatre groups took up the issue and spread the ideas of religious brotherhood and harmony. But Theatre Union's *Toba Tegh Singh* (1978) points an accusing finger at the government for encouraging communal rivalry in the country. The play, based on a short story by Sadat Hassan Manto and set in the days of partition (1947) is a spoof dramatizing the effect of the division of the country on the basis of religion on a group of mental patients living on the border. The order comes that the inmates, too, would be divided on communal grounds and sent either to Pakistan or India. Finally, one man who calls himself Toba Tegh Singh because of the name of the border town where he hails from, refuses to leave the asylum and dies in a no-man's land. Each country tries to push the responsibility of the corpse onto the other. The play is an indictment of the uncaring attitude of fanatical authorities.[33]

Several groups argue that over the years, religions have been institutionalised and are used today as weapons by the ruling class. Religious passion is effectively whipped up time and again to divert the attention from economic and political issues and thus to break the unity of the working class. Such issues are powerfully dealt with by Gurcharan Singh and his Amritsar School of Drama. Amidst the chaos of Hindu-Sikh animosity, Singh has risen Phoenix-like in the strife-torn state of Punjab to preach a message of understanding, patience and tolerance. Starting with the IPTA, he took to the streets to use plays as a means of awakening the people to their fundamental and political rights. He has been a crusader against communalism, factionalism, terrorism and political manipulation. In the early eighties when the Punjab was swept by the Bhindranwale wave, Singh went out into the streets performing *Sadharan Log* (1981), a play about two communities, one Sikh and the other Hindu both living in peace and harmony. A certain anti-social element enters the scene and destroys their peace and they quarrel. But before long they realize the truth and join hands in friendship once again.

In another play a young religious minded Sikh has to choose between his religious conviction and proletarian solidarity. He opts for his Hindu fellow workers, making a resounding statement: "I respect the Scriptures and the saffron flag, but when, I sit with my fellow workers it will be under the red flag. Singhs' work was recognised and financially aided by the government. But Singh, a confirmed member of CPI (ML) continued to expose the hypocrisy of the ruling class. His plays against the excesses of the emergency landed him in jail. With Akali unity in the air, Singh staged a play *Dharam Mamla Nij Da* (1982). In this play he accused the Sikh high priests of dishonesty, the Barnala ministry of selfishness in adopting foul means to hold on to power, and the dissident Akalis of irresponsible behaviour and greed for power.

Similarly *Baba Bolda Hai* (1985) is a scathing attack on the Congress(I)'s opportunistic policies and the medieval fundamentalism of the Akalis. The central character is an old man (baba) played by Singh himself. In one scene he rebukes the Congress politician who shows hypocritical concern for the suffering Sikhs during the riots after Mrs. Gandhi's murder. He also chides a Sikh militant who holds that the Sikhs cannot live in India with honour. The Baba goes on to ask the militant if the Sikh section of the Punjab were to be given the status of a state, who among the Sikhs—the landlords, the capitalists or the poor on the pavement—will rule that state?[34]

Besides Singh's group there are others that deal with the theme of communalism. In a festival of street plays organized by the Nav Nirman Sanskritik Manch of Bombay in 1987, Arunodaya from Andhra Pradesh staged a play showing how political parties use the weapon of communalism for electoral purposes. More striking was Vartaman's (Dehra Doon) *Subse Sasta Gost* (1983). The play directly attacks the religious leaders for aligning themselves with politicians and anti-social elements in creating riots by throwing beef and pork[35] at the temple and mosques respectively, and thus inciting riots. When the truth is revealed that it was actually human flesh the riot stops as that does not defile any place of worship![36]

Observing the treatment of this theme in these plays it may be noticed that communalism is a theme that can be dealt with either way—to please the government in power or to challenge their hidden motives.

2. Challenging the Social Structures

A major section of street theatre is inspired by leftist ideologies and the need to restructure society. They go all out to expose corruption in government and challenge the established and accepted values and institutions. In this category come plays on the caste system, all forms of exploitation by the powerful, rural poverty, exploitation of women and children, class hierarchies and bonded labour.

Saksena's satirical play *Bakari* (1974) has often been cited as the first major street play in Hindi that tried to expose exploitation and religious bigotry. In the play three decoits seek to enrich themselves. They ally themselves with a policeman and snatch a poor woman's only sheep. They install the sheep in the village square, announcing that it is Gandhi's sheep and that it would be venerated as a god. The illiterate villagers, intimidated by the policeman, worship the sheep and donate everything they have to erect a shrine. News spreads all over and an enormous amount of money pours into the shrine. The dacoits soon become politicians and capture power. The sheep is killed and cooked and its skin given to the gardener who has unwittingly provided them with the original idea. The play suggests in the end that only through the awakening of the rural masses can India confront the country's ills. This play has spawned a generation of street plays that has tried to understand and make clear to the masses some of India's most striking problems.[37]

Gadda (1978), loosely based on a short story by Kishan Chander, is performed by different groups adapted to suit topical issues and local conditions. In the play a man falls into a pit on a public road and is unable to get out. Passers-by who include two municipal workers, a policeman on the beat, a religious man, a foreign tourist and a politician (changed at will by different groups), are unable or unwilling to help this man out of the pit. The political leader flatly refuses, saying that it is not his job to rescue those who fall in pits. Others offer interesting insights:

A Municipality worker: Oh! Don't bother! You have been down there
   only for a short while. The people of this country are in a pit for
   the last forty one years. And nothing has happened to them. You
   will survive.
Holy man: you foolish man! Don't you realize, the whole world is like
   a pit. Everyone is lying in a pit, some in small pits, some in big
   pits. Only he, the one who lives up there can pull us out. A good
   opportunity for you to turn to him.
The tourist: *(after taking a couple of snaps)* You say you fell into this
   pit. I sense sabotage. Tell me who are you for, pro-American, pro-
   Russian"?
The victim: For whoever gets me out...

   In the end the pit is covered up even while the victim is in it, to make
a platform for a visiting MP who comes to give a speech on rural
electrification. Thus the play shows that the poor struggling masses cannot
expect anyone to support them. It may be hailed as a typical parable on
the Indian situation.[38]
   In a similar play *Chapa Para Manush* (1980), Calcutta Progressive
Theatre explores gvernmental red-tape and the average man's inertia. A
man gets caught under a tree uprooted by storm. This comes to the notice
of a gardener who tells the local authorities that he should be rescued.
The matter keeps circulating to different offices where everyone
concerned tries to exploit the situation for personal gain. The gardener
goes from pillar to post even as the man under the tree is breathing his last.
The play ends suggesting that people need to pool their resources to fight
bureaucracy and redtape.[39]
   Tripurai Sharma's (Alarippu, Delhi) *Uplabdiyan* (1982), is a biting
satire on the achievements in the country since independence.
Constantly updated to include current events, the play focuses on the
miseries of the common man even as the upper classes become richer. The
play opens with a group of blind-folded people moving around in circles
shouting "Quit India". The *sutradhar* stops them, announcing that the
British have left the country forty-one years ago and helps remove their
blind-folds. The irony is obvious–for the common man independence has
made no difference. In a classroom situation, an analysis of the various
colours of the tricolour follows which hints at the dreams promised at the
time of independence. In brief scenes the play goes on to analyse the fact
that all the achievements have benefited the richer classes, while the poor
are left behind. For instance, the use of farmland to produce for export

has impoverished the countryside. An excerpt:

[A lean impoverished man appears before the political leader who is boasting of all the achievements of the country.]
Leader: Who are you?
Man: A symbol of independent India.
Leader: How sad! *(to his aides)* Fatten him up. *(The aides wrap him up with shawls and mufflers borrowed from the audience.)*
Leader: Well it is something. But his face... not enough... Give him a *paan* or a sweet...
Aides: *(going closer to him fill scraps of paper into his mouth.)* Now this is the Five Year Plan, and this is the 20-point programme, eat up and fatten up, and don't complain.

In another scene the *sutradhar* produces a tiny box and announces that it contains all the achievements of the country. When all huddle together to see the contents, he takes out a moth-eaten book and a piece of red cloth and announces that these are the copies of the Constitution and the Five Year Plans which, due to non-use, have been eaten up by moths. A small balance with one plate missing and the other with a large hole is declared the symbol of justice. A number of other objects are pulled out from the Pandora's box, each signifying a calamity that has befallen the poor people in the past forty-one years of independence.[40]

Arena's (Calcutta) *Ha Ha Anahar* (1981), in a similar way hits out at the government's complacency and the elite classes' alienation from rural realities. It is about a man who has died of starvation in village. A journalist, ignorant of such happenings, comes to this village, finds this to be true and publishes his findings. This creates confusion in political circles and much concern to the ruling party which claims to have eradicated poverty completely.[41]

In another play *Raja Ka Baaja Bajaa* (1980) by Vartaman, the education system as well as the corrupt practices in the country are under attack.

Student: I come walking from a far away place... why is that no one cares to teach me?
Lecturer: Don't grumble, you brat! If you find your house far away, get one closer to the college.
Now, get out.

After graduation, the student finally manages to get an interview for a job. Nearly 4000 applications have been received. In the end the Chairman's niece's mother-in-law's sister's husband, an incompetent person gets the job. "Get-out", the authorities shriek at the student. "Where to?" he hits back spontaneously. They kick him till he is reduced to silence–an angry indictment of the state of stagnation in the country.[42]

Another play that challenges religious bigotry is *Miya ki Joothi Miya ka Sar* (1979) by Chetna, a troup consisting of mine-workers from Madhya Pradesh. The play, based on Shanta Mukherjea's skit for the IPTA in the forties, is about a Pundit (brahmin) who tries to beguile the villagers. The pundit is sent by the government to a village starved of grain and other essentials. The farmers listen to him intently as he quotes devoutly from the scriptures– how the immortal soul outlives the mortal body, how all actions are pre-determined by the gods and nothing can be changed by the efforts of human beings; how water is divine and can sustain lives. After listening to the pundit the farmers turn the tables on him by strangling him with a towel and drowning him in water.[43]

The oppression of the common people by the police and landlords in alliance with the politicians has become the theme of scores of plays. One of the earlier plays in this category is Chandresh's *Janata Pagal Ho Gayee* (1981). This hour-long controlled piece of work is packed with every form of atrocity inflicted on the poorer sections of the people, who in the end are shown to be going mad. Similar echoes were found in Wynadu Baby's *Nattugaddika* (1983), a street play popularized by the Kerala Sanskarika Vedi, about the exploitation of the tribals of Wynadu by vested interests.

V. The Impact of Movements

Street theatre has been carefully cultivated by various movements. Following, the success of IPTA, political parties have associated themselves with street theatre. Some movements, other than political parties, are examined here.

Women's Movements

In the wake of the feminist movements worldwide, a number of women's organizations have blossomed in the urban areas in the last two decades. Women activists have condemned the deplorable conditions of women in a male-dominated society. They have not only fought for their rights but have tried to raise the consciousness of their fellow-women against all sorts of atrocities like rape, dowry, bride-burning, *sati* and the treatment of women as sex objects and commodities in advertisements. National and regional conferences have raised these issues for critical study and analysis. The International Women's Day (8th March) is observed with public demonstration of women-power in the cities. Street theatre is one of the most common forms used to protest as well as enlighten others about their rights. One reason why such plays receive enthusiastic response is that most urban women seem to find it easier to express themselves through songs or skits than by speaking at formal gatherings. Moreover, in a country where the performative tradition has such deep roots, acting comes more naturally than delivering speeches.

One of the finest plays staged about atrocities on women is Anarya's (Jadhavpur) *Bandarkhela* (1986) which has been adapted by several groups. *Bandarkhel* itself is a traditional form of folk play wherein monkeys perform to the delight of the crowds. In this play two people wearing monkey-masks have a dialogue with a talkative woman. The monkeys do not speak at all, their actions are interpreted by the woman. Incidentally they are called Rajesh Khanna and Hema Malini both popular stars of the cinema in the seventies and early eighties. Rajesh Khanna wants to marry Hema Malini. As usual the dowry is decided, paid, and they are happily married. Hema Malini, as expected, is somewhat servile and the trouble starts there. Rajesh Khanna is bored and suggests that she bring in more dowry or else he will divorce her. At the end of series of arguments which get nowhere, a woman persuades Rajesh Khanna to kill Hema Malini in the kitchen by burning her in the usual manner of dowry-deaths. He refuses: "What, you won't kill her? asks the woman, "then you will remain a monkey all your life". Rajesh Khanna calmly retorts: what do you think? I want to be like you human beings? Like you heartless humans?" The play effectively shows the audience what they really are by comparing them to what they think they are not.[44]

In 1979, Stree Sangharsh, Delhi produced a play *Om Swahha* which was much acclaimed for its simplicity, subtlety and audience participation. The play begins with a woman *madari* showing matrimonial advertisements to the audience and taunting them. She chants a *sloka* asking, "What is the meaning of marriage for an Indian woman? Self-denial, subjugation, humiliation, drudgery, victimization?" When the central character of the play is married off, she is taunted, beaten and harassed by her in-laws who ultimately murder her. The police, as usual, registers a case of suicide.

After this theatre is a break and the actors address the audience and pose a series of questions like: should all women meet the same fate? Why should women tolerate such degradation? Why can't their fate be different? The audience is invited to create the dead girl's story as in a fantasy, with her playing a different character. She resists the haggling for dowry with confidence as well as family pressures and revolts against her greedy husband and in-laws. She dreams of becoming independent, of studying and leading a dignified life.

At this stage one of the actors who plays the part of the *sutradhar* says, "Look, her struggle has made a difference to her life." And the performers invite the audience to express solidarity with this struggling girl. For some, the play served a cathartic function and helped build up confidence in facing the dilemmas of life.[45]

The anti-rape movement in 1980 gave rise to a large member of plays on the theme. The Forum Against Oppression of Women (FAOW) based in Bombay staged and encouraged a number of women's groups to get involved in street demonstrations. One of their popular plays, *Abala* (1981), depicts the trauma of a middle-aged woman who has been raped by a policeman and the antipathy of her neighbours against her. She wages a lone battle against them all, aided by her teenage daughter.

Bombay's Sthree Mukti Sangatna, one of the pioneers in women's movement, has performed the play *Mulghi Zhali Ho* (1976) about 500 times and it has been seen by nearly 100 thousand people. It vividly portrays the problems of working class women such as poor working conditions, wage discrimination, harassment by the boss and job insecurity. The play was based on real life experiences of working women, maid servants and housewives.[46]

For most of the women's groups street theatre is a staged demonstration against a male dominated society in which the women are victimized. Some groups believe that it is not enough to stage plays before an all female audience. There have been occasions when the male section in the audience have tried to quietly take the seriousness out of the message through heckling and mild hand-claps. However, groups like Bangalore's Vimochana have succeeded in persuading enlightened male audiences to support them in their ventures.

Other socially conscious groups have involved themselves in plays on women's problems as for example, Janam's *Aurat* (1981), one of the most staged plays. It presents a woman in four roles—daughter, wife, student and worker. In the first scene the school-going daughter is seen doing house-work and being told by her invalid father that she can't go to school anymore because he cant' afford to buy her books. It is more important that her brother gets the necessary education. The father is not presented as a male chauvinist, but a man caught in the system that enforces such beliefs. In the second scene when she goes to the shop, the shopkeeper's son tells her if she comes alone late in the evening she can get things on credit. In the following scene where she is a student and a wife, again she is discriminated against and looked down on. In the last scene, she is an old woman working in a factory. One day she is made redundant and told to leave. The other workers strike in protest, and she hesitatingly joins them.[47] The play is full of realism and tries to dissect the social systems that have endangered women's position.

In this way a number of other groups like Living Theatre of Khardah (*Ahalya*), Anarya (*Meye Dile Sajiye*), Asha Kendra (*Sthree Yathra*) have given a more concrete shape to women's movements.

Children's Issues

India has numerous slum children, who are illiterate and poor. Their only means of entertainment and education is an occasional visit to the cinemas. Some groups have shown concern for their plight. An attempt to provide them with wholesome entertainment was made by Bal Varsh Pratistan of Bombay in their *Rang Yatra* in 1982. Performances were given on decorated trucks, in the open. Bereft of the trappings of curtains and lights, valuebased entertainment was provided through children themselves singing, acting, miming and operating puppets.

More commendable is the work of Ravi Varma of Vikas Lok Manch who, with the help of slum children, has been creatively interpreting social realities in a way that makes sense to the children. His theatre workshop for the slum children of Bombay normally begins with discussion on topics like the Punjab, alcoholism, pollution, religion, inequalities of caste and class, communalism. In the second stage there is improvisation, body movements and mime. One of the group's plays *Hame Jawab Chahiya* (1985) on the Bhopal gas tragedy began with the children piecing together information and suggestions. The play reminds the audience, who are mostly children, that the Bhopal incident is not a dead issue, and that its aftermath still haunts the lives of many. The play concentrates on a gas-affected boy wondering how to use the Rs. 40,000 that he will get as compensation for losing his entire family. It makes the issues real for the children as it is interwoven into the fabric of folk dances, choral singing and humour.[48]

Environmental Groups

One of the more established groups that has been working towards saving the environment using theatre is Kerala Shastra Sahithya Parishad (KSSP), now known all over India for its science *jatha* (rallies). Started as a science movement in 1962, it has gradually spread its reach to every aspect of human life in the country. Their concern is to popularize scientific attitudes among the people, for they believe that through this they can raise questions about whatever is unscientific and unreasonable. They have also concentrated on storming the citadels of superstition and anti-social concepts. Their street plays cover themes from education to health care, drugs, pollution, conservation, multinationals, oppression, participatory development and nuclear destruction. One of their early successes was an adaptation of Brecht's *Galileo* (1974) for street performance. In another play, *Vijayam* (1984), a group of villagers waiting to catch a bus taking them to the 21st century are left behind on the wayside as the bus is already full with industrialists, religious leaders, dacoits and politicians. In the end a literate elderly villager with the help of others in the village forces the bus conductor to reverse the decision. The powerful use of village idioms and folk media endear their theatre to the masses.[49]

Drought and floods have been perennial problems in India. Environmentalists have observed that these are often caused by those in power and by industrialists who are anxious to get more foreign money in the form of famine relief. In 1988, a group based in Tilonia (Rajasthan) organized a month-long rally through the villages performing plays under the guidance of Tripurari Sharma. The plays emphasized the impoverished state of village agronomy due to floods and drought. One play depicted how animals die when fodder is not available, while it is sold at throw-away prices in the markets of Delhi. Another play examined famine relief works and the middlemen who profit from them.

Other groups like the Chipko and Apilko movements which say 'ecology is wealth' and create an awareness about the fragile ecological balance among the villagers, have also been instrumental in creating a quiet revolution through the medium of street plays. In the south, the "Save the Western Ghats" (1985) campaign headed by Seva Sangh and supported by a number of other activist groups also found environmentalists resorting to street theatre.

VI. Formal Characteristics of Street Theatre

A. General Characteristics

The general characteristics are examined here prior to looking at the formal similarities with the folk theatre tradition.

1. Collective Authorship

Although playwrights like Badal Sircar, Gurcharan Singh and C.G. Krishnaswami are proficient writers of street plays in their own right, they have realized that the performers can contribute to make the play richer. In his later plays, Sircar introduced the workshop system and created plays with his group. Delhi's Janam does not even have a director. In most of the groups there are democratic discussions during practice sessions. The members sit in a circle symbolizing their unity and equality and each one is encouraged to express his or her opinion. There are times when the responses of the audience, too, have contributed to the final shape of the play.

One of the popular plays in the women's genre is *Ehsaas*, which grew out of a group of students from Miranda House College, Delhi, sharing their experiences during their afternoon breaks in 1979. Collating experiences of their fathers, brothers, sons and husbands they devised a play which challenges present social values. What is remarkable in this form of play production is that communication does not remain one-sided, with the playwright or director imposing his or her views on the rest, but it succeeds in presenting a collective opinion.[50]

2. Living Newspaper Theatre Techniques

This form of theatre popular in the West and Indianized by Sircar has become a distinctive feature of street plays. In Sircar's *Basi Khabar* (1976) he used this format to full effect. Reciting facts and figures in tandem the performers create a mosaic of the current Indian situation:

TWO: According to a survey on bonded labour, or men who have been forced to sign bonds enslvaing themselves for life, there are 555,000 of these in UP, 467,000 in MP...

THREE: 70% of the population of W. Bengal live below the poverty

	line, and 95% below the basic nutrition line...
FOUR:	In the third devastating flood in a row 152,55,000 people have been affected in W. Bengal...
FIVE:	92% of India children live below the poverty line... (p. 120ff).

This format, accepted in almost all plays, helps to prepare the background for the theme about to be analysed in the play. Janam's *Aurat* is a case in point:

ACTOR I:	A mother, a sister, a woman, who doesn't know from whence, has been running barefoot along the burning sands of the desert.
ACTRESS:	I have come from far away villages in the north.
ACTOR II:	A woman who doesn't know from whence she has been toiling in the rice fields and tea estates, more than her body can take.
ACTRESS:	I have come from the ruins of the East where I wandered the fields with my dying cow.

There have also been cases where the actors together narrate a story as if being read from a newspaper.

3. Flexibility

The mobile form of street theatre helps it to reach people who normally do not go to the theatre. It may be performed anytime, anywhere, even without rehearsals. In a way this suits the type of audience it tries to reach–mostly the poorer sections for whom theatre is a luxury. It is also economical in that hardly any money is needed to set up a performance. The total absence of stage, lights, props and make-up make it even more flexible.

The newspaper format enables flexibility in the matter of themes. In a college play in Bangalore, *Watch Out We Are Heading Nowhere* (1982) which lasted for about 30 miniutes, a broad range of current events like the Meenakshipuram conversions (1982, when Harijans turned to Islam), a national liquor tragedy, a scandal in a major watch company and more general matters like the dowry system and the ills of Bangalore University were juxtaposed.[51]

B. Continuity With Folk Tradition

It is a common mistake to believe that street theatre is basically urban and has no folk elements. A closer understanding of the lives of the people, so essential in street theatre, demands that it adapt elements of folk theatre. Moreover, it is only natural that in its effort to be truly a people's theatre it should draw heavily from the elements of the real people's theatre, i.e., folk theatre.

Following the example of Habib Tanvir in the fifties, several street theatre groups have found the use of folk idioms powerful even in the urban settings. The Sutradhar Theatre Institute headed by Ratnakar Matkari in Maharastra has used various elements of the *tamasha* and *powada* in street plays. His *Lok katha* (1983) effectively used the *sutradhar* to maintain continuity and focus the attention of the audience on the central theme. Ravi Varma's experiments with children's theatre in Bombay draw their inspiration from folk traditions. The folk-style opening of the play with stage preliminaries, the *sutradhar* and folk dances make this theatre popular with the children. In *Nari Jagaran* (1982), by Vimochana, a Bangalore Women's group, which depicts dowry death, the victim, in a nostalgic flashback scene portraying her childhood, is shown playing the *kolata*, a traditional dance form, with her friends. Gaddar, a popular folk singer and revolutionary artist of rural Andhra Pradesh has contributed immensely to the street theatre scene in the state by way of songs, poetry and *burrakatha*. Similarly Arunodaya has carried out a considerable number of studies in the folk forms of Andhra Pradesh before deciding to incorporate the *burrakatha* and *vogguktha* formats in their street plays. Aahvaan, in Maharastra, often uses the *powada* style of singing in their plays. The Bangalore branch of Akhila Bharatiya Vidhyarti Parishad (All India Student Committee or ABVP) make extensive use of the *lavani* form of singing in their plays. The role played by folksongs and traditional dances like *ottamthullal*, *mappilapattu*, *chavittunatakam* cannot be underestimated in the enormous popularity of KSSP all over Kerala.

Similarities with Folk Theatre

Similarities with folk theatre can be seen in some specific area:

1. Audience Participation

In its format, street theatre performances resemble folk theatre very closely in the matter of audience participation. Everything—action, movement, dialogue–songs in a street play is geared to audience participation. Be it the imaginative use of mime by the actors to capture the intense concentration of the audience or the audience dropping a few coins in the hat that is passed around at the end of a performance, it is an act that points to the involvement and participation of the audience in the play. It is useful to ask how participation through physical inclusion draws freely from folk tradition.

Street theatre has accepted the free-flowing spatial relationship of the audience and the performers as seen in folk theatre. There are no stages and auditoria, and therefore the question of a divide between actors and audience does not arise. The audience normally stands or squats comfortably around the action of the play; there is hardly any place designated for them. They are only asked not to block the free movement of the performers in and around the acting area. Sometimes the performers are even planted among the audience. This sort of free spatial arrangement invites physical inclusion.

There is considerable research by both Schechner and Sircar on the effect of environment and space in the production of a play. In his Performance Theory Schechner states that the theatrical space or area in and around which the action of a play takes place, including the auditorium or the hall, is as important as the action and dialogue in the play. He allowed the characters in some of his experiments to develop not through the constraints of a previously prepared script but through contact with the audience. He has credited the *Ramlila* of Ramnagar with having confirmed his concepts.[52]

Sircar, following the example of Schechner, had arranged seats in such a way that the play took place in and around the audience. For example, in *Michil* the acting area resembled the lanes and by-lanes of Calcutta so that when his actors performed they seemed to be actually participating in a procession winding its way through the Calcutta streets. Similarly in his play *Spartacus*, the 'island' arrangement of seats helped brings the spectators into the action of the play.

Close eye-contact with the audience is another element in street theatre which helps the audience remain glued to the action of the play. The performers too are under the eagle eye of the audience who surround them on all sides. The sincerity of the players more than their acting ability is under scrutiny. Besides, together they feel a sense of belonging and responsibility to each other. It is hard not to be sincere when two people are confronting each other eye to eye. As Bharucha observes:

> When the actors confront the audience, look them in the eye and tell them that in such and such a village a man is dying because he has no means of subsistence and no one to help him, it is difficult to be indifferent to the fact. There is nothing to interfere with it.[53]

The audience is often invited to play bit parts or lend small pieces of properties like a shawl or a coin to the players. In Probir Guha's (Living Theatre, Calcutta) production of *Samvad* (1983), the autobiography of a political reporter, four aspects of his consciousness come forward and tie him up with ropes, the ends of which are given to the audience to hold. The actor tries hard to free himself. But the audience holds on to the ropes so tight that normally he cannot move. In this way the audience is given the responsibility of pinning down a socially evil character. In another play of the same group, *Gramer Panchali* (1983), a market scene takes place amidst the audience. The actors meet the audience, begin a conversation about the price of vegetables in the market and gradually, without any one actually noticing, they use the facts gleaned from the audience to start off the play. These experiments, as in Sircar's case are done behind closed doors with refined spectators who come specifically to watch a play. However, street theatre groups have found these experiments inspiring.[54]

Sometimes the audience is invited to join in the chanting of slogans or act as chorus for the singing, and hold aloft banners, posters and placards. Often in scenes depicting mass uprisings the audience help to swell the crowds.

Talking with the audience is common feature in street theatre. Some players give the impression that but for the responses of the audience the play cannot proceed. Even unexpected occurrences during the play are used to the advantage of the players. Such ebullient improvisatory techniques came in handy in one of Chitra's performances in Bangalore in 1983. While performing in Kanakapura, during a scene dramatizing the issue of shortage of kerosene, a drunken man from the audience came and joined the queue of the actors who were lining up for kerosene at the shop and proceeded to launch a tirade against a kerosene distributor who had cheated him of his quota. Little did he realize that it was not an actual situation but a play. The *sutradhar* turning the situation to his advantage engaged the individual in a lively dialogue much to the entertainment of the audience who knew the distributor in question. Care was taken, however, to ensure that the play did not deviate too far from the main story line.[55]

Post-performance discussions have been one of the controversial issues in street theatre. According to some groups the audience are in no mood to have a discussion, as they had their entertainment directly from the play. Issues have been clear and they are now ready to leave. However, others maintain that a few questions need to be asked to make sure that the message has got through. A remarkable form of post-performance discussion was carried out by the Sthree Sangharsh of Delhi when the performers asked the audience, in the manner of Boal, to reconstruct the play *Om Swaha* on the dowry system, as they would like to see the events happen.

There are other groups who insist that some literature explaining the problems presented in the play needs to be supplied to the audience which they can take back with them. Living Theatre of Kharadah does not agree:

> Primarily we used to have discussions, but later we felt it might not be the right thing. Because the change we create through our production needs some silence afterwards. So we stopped the discussion sessions. But if any one starts a discussion we join in.[56]

After the group's production of *Rat Din* (1984) the audience did not want either to talk or move. They set still for about 15-20 minutes. Then they slowly got up, said good-bye and went away quietly.

Such reactions are possible in a closed hall with an audience of 40-60. Several groups find it practical to ask the audience a few questions to make sure that the message has had some impact on them. The situation at the end of a play in India, they argue, is often one of waiting, asking for more and hence this is the right time to ask questions and get the audience involved.

Pani relates the efforts of Samudaya to facilitate audience participation and identification by having in its plays not only its own actors but also members of the audience, for example the slum dwellers, factory workers or villagers. This way Samudaya hopes to foster, encourage and incorporate local talent "which can depict the spirit of that reality far more convincingly than their more talented counterparts from other sections of society."[57]

Politicians are often the butt of the satire in street plays. Here Patna City's Gathividhi poke pun at aspiring politicians. in Yeh Natak Nahin.

The women too are waking up. The women's section of Chetna Natya Manch Bettiah, Bihar perform a play on minimum wages.

Mime is an important element in street plays. Minimum properties are sometimes used to enhance effect.

Mime can be as or more effective than vocal drama.

Janam (Delhi) India's premier street theatre group has tackled every issue. Here corruption is the central issue.

Action songs are an important element of street plays. Bettiah's (Bihar) READ sing in unision.

Plays on the oppression of women have been quite popular. Patna's IPTA stage Janam's (Delhi) Aurat.

Simultaneous staging is part of street theatre. Here Tripurari Sharma's Alarippu, discuss a social issue.

Action scenes can be more powerful in slow motion.

Any formations are possible in street theatre. Here Arrah's (Bihar) Yuvanithi row a boat.

2. *Mime in Street Theatre*

The flexibility and the low cost nature of street theatre require mime as one of its major tools. Following the trend of folk theatre here too, the actors not only mime their actions but most of the stage, sets and props also are imagined. The powerful use of rich mimetic action in theatre led Sircar to observe:

> The spectators always come to the theatre ready to use their imagination to fill in the gaps. They are prepared to accept the stage as a stage and the attempt of the theatre realist to delude them to believing that it is not a stage is vain and unnecessary. Instead if a few packing boxes are stacked together to indicate a mountain the spectators will not only accept it, but will get an extra kick in the process of using their imagination.[58]

In other words mime is a device which helps the audience gain fuller participation in the play by a more intense use of their imagination. Sircar went on to suggest ways of imagining, sculpting in space and creating images through postures and situations through movements. For example in the opening scenes of Sircar's *Spartacus* on the slave revolt in 71 B.C. based on a novel by Howard Fast,

> there are no words but a steady crescendo of rhythmic pants that become deafening in the small room. The relentless movements of the actors as they raise their hands and thump them down in unison convey the sheer agony of slave labour.[59]

Delhi's Jagran relies heavily on mime and a commentator to tell a story. The massive multiplicity of languages in the country and the facility of mime to include numerous local nuances are what give an extra fillip to their kind of mime. The use of white face-masks with the lips coloured red, stylized movements and a commentator who tries to repeat all that the mimes express may seem trivial, but it does carry the message powerfully. Although Modi suggests that "at the risk of deserting classical mime the troupe should perhaps tailor its gestures to the local audience in order to avoid ambiguous interpretations"[60] it needs to be emphasised that Jagran's form of mime is an original contribution which has a clientele in the slums of Delhi.

3. Costumes, Make-up and Masks

Street theatre also resembles folk theatre in the use of costumes. Costumes are normally distinctive and dependent on the extent of the group's budget. At times, if necessary, they are exaggerated to attract attention. Some groups stick to uniform–blue jeans and black T-shirts, or *kurthas*, or all-white with a black or red belt, are the basic outfits. However, they also use minor representative costumes or props to typify the role they play–a *topi* or a hat for a businessman, a hat and a *lathi* (baton) for a policeman and a shawl to signify a rich man.

Make-up is rarely used except maybe simple touch-ups that can be done out of one's personal kits. The enormous popularity of a mask to arrest the attention of the audience has encouraged some groups to wear it, but its use as an interpretative symbol is stereotyped. For example, antisocial characters are shown wearing masks, as in real life they pretend to be do-gooders. Some groups use masks when one person has to play several roles, or has to play animals or objects.

4. Stage Preliminaries

These are not as elaborate as in a folk theatre. A number of groups move around the streets playing the drum or other loud instruments announcing to the audience that the play is about to begin. KSSP uses a *chenda*, a special type of drum which makes a loud resounding noise. Some groups begin by marching around the performance area singing the theme song of the group. Normally the play begins with all the actors engaging in another action song which has a direct relevance to the theme of the play, or with a rhythmic clapping in which theatre audience joins. Several groups use harmonium, tabla (a set of two drums) and bells as musical instruments.

More sophisticated preliminaries have been tried by some groups following the example of folk theatre. Ravi Sharma's *Hame Jawab Chahiya* (1985), opens with a *sutradhar* and his wife trying to do a traditional play. The actors led by another *sutradhar* insist that they should do a play about human issues like the Bhopal gas tragedy. As the conflict rages, the director enters and instantly agrees with the actors. After an apologetic request to the audience to excuse them for their lapses in the impromptu production, the play moves on.

The preliminaries do not stop there. A *vandana* (praise) song follows as in the Satya Shodhak *tamasha* of the 19th century. Here the good Lord is accused instead of praised. He is charged with class bias:

> It is difficult to sing of your glory Lord
> Who has called you a preserver
> Who said you are the beloved of all
> You are ensconced on the side of the rich
> Who comes to the succour of poor.[61]

This type of re-interpreted folk form has been quite popular in other parts of the country.

5. Sutradhar and Vidhushak

Inevitably these two characters from folk theatre have found ready acceptance in the street theatre for their informality and immediate rapport with the audience and complete control over any situation. At times they even stand out of the play and directly interact with the audience.

As these characters serve to explain and simplify matters to the illiterate masses they fit in well in a street play. It is their function to carry the action forward, to narrate, to comment, to question, to relate the situation to contemporary reality, to introduce new characters or even to take the place of other characters in the play. All these functions can be translated ebulliently into the scheme of a street play. The *vidhushak*, seemingly a joker, has been developed as a philosopher and a Chaplinesque character in some of the recent folk adaptations of Bansi Kaul.[62] Following the tradition of Narad, the humorous sage and heavenly message bearer of Hindu mythology, he has taken on the role of an erudite wisecrack and philosopher who with pointed remarks not only arouses peels of laughter but makes the audience think about their own daily situations in a critical way. Small wonder that a character of such dimensions finds easy acceptance in street plays.[63]

In some street plays both these characters are not as clearly delineated as in folk theatre. However, elements of their way of performing is an integral part of every street play.

6. Songs, Slogans, and other Histrionics

Songs can restate and summarize the major themes with catchy, easily remembered tunes and slogans. These help enormously in audience participation in street theatre. Hence songs accompanied by dance movements are essential items. The contribution of *Dalit* [64] poets like Puttappa and Siddalingaiah in Bangalore, Garedkar in Maharastra, Gaddar in Andhra and several others all over the rural belt cannot be underestimated. Their revolutionary compositions have indeed enriched street theatre. A number of poets like Dinkar, Rajgopal Dixit, Gopal Das Neeraj, S.D. Saksena, Dharmvir Bharati, and activists such as Vibhuti Patel, Joyti Mhapsekar and Kamla Bhasin have contributed to the composition of protest songs. These are normally sung in film, folk or other popular tunes, but the contents are always charged with revolutionary vigour. A popular *quwwali* song from Chetan's collection is worded like this:

> You have oppressed us for many days
> like a devil you have cruelly exploited us. [65]

It is also customary for these groups to sing some of the most popular patriotic songs in a sarcastic manner. For example in Sircar's play *Michil* one of the most popular patriotic songs—*Saare jahan se acha Hinudustan humara* (of all the places in the world India is the most beautiful), has been used to underline the decay in the country. This very song has been repeatedly used in similar situations by other groups. Similarly, in *Bakari*, the tune of *Jan gan man adhi nayaka jai he*, the national anthem is sung to verses that glorify corruption. Studying the creative use of revolutionary songs in consciousness raising, Mies observed:

> If one looks at these revolutionary songs one cannot but be astonished at their clear analysis of the new type of agrarian capitalism, of the class structure in the area, and of the role of government and foreign aid which come to them in the form of grain 'meant for animals only'. In the songs the landlords are attacked as having cheated them of their lands, their bullocks, even their ploughs, and of having monopolized the rural co-operative societies, thus appropriating all government funds for development. The refrain of many of these songs is that now the poor are fed up with empty promises and will take things in their own hands. 'The lion in the cage has woken up and now the day of revolution has come.' [66]

Street theatre is noted for its highly imaginative use of skills. Its practitioners produce sound effects by using simple things like a piece of rock, coconut shells or simply by the inventive use of their fingers and mouth. It is amazing how they can create the atmosphere of an exploding earthquake or the calm of a seaside with no instruments at all.

Although the economics of street theatre do not allow the luxury of giant puppets or stilt walkers, nonetheless, placards, flags, banners and other visual effects are used. Slogan recitals accompanied by processional movements, holding placards and banners as in a demonstration, is a common sight. This is probably why street plays are nicknamed "staged demonstrations". Slogans like *"Hindu Muslim Sikh Isai Sab Mazdooren Bhai Bhai"* (all workers irrespective of their religion are brothers) and *Pandit neta seth maulvi lute apne desh ko, Kaum vaad ne gher liya hai apne sare deh ko* (religious and political leaders and capitalists exploit the country; communalism has surrounded our people) have often reverberated in street theatre scenes.

7. Dance

The term "body theatre" has often been used by those working in street theatre to emphasize the value of body movements in their performance. These movements have given birth to simple, rhythmic dances–representing a running train, trees swaying in the winds, or birds in the air. Others who use dances take to very simple steps that can be learned with a little practice. Normally all the characters join in as some of the songs require accompanying action. It is fascinating to observe how actors playing different roles fall into a dance formation, breaking off the build-up of the story they are telling. Often the story is told through fragmented pieces and these dance steps cement them together. Theatre Union's production of *Marz ka Munafa* (1985), about drugs and multinationals is replete with beautifully choreographed movements. Gurcharan Singh's plays, too depend heavily on local dance steps for their popularity.

8. Use of Imagery and Symbols

Powerful images are more important in street plays than in any other form. Because of its short duration it is important to compel the attention of the audience by using visually evocative images and symbols. In Sircar's *Michil* there is a powerful multiple image of a young man killed on the streets of Calcutta and an old man who has lost his way. Juxtaposed with these images are the cries of the chorus, "someone has been murdered". Their speculations about the murderer create a montage of impressions. A policeman keeps on appearing in between to announce. "No one is murdered. No one is lost. Everything is all right. Continue working."

Stree Jagruthi Kalapathak of Rajastan staged a play, *Pyramid* (1979), about the increasing labours of a housewife without love, let alone any material benefits. The play demonstrates vividly that although the woman is the central figure in the family, she is totally exploited. She occupies the lowest rung in the family pyramid. The play ends with the breaking down of this pyramid and with men and women forming a circle which grows larger and larger as the audience too join in.[67]

In Janghosh's *Safed Appu* (1982), the play on the construction workers involved in building fly-overs in preparation for the Asiad in Delhi, the fly-over is beautifully and effectively constructed not with cement and frames but with bodies arranged and packed close. As a cheering crowd walks over it, the workers sink until it is completely flat and their pained cries are "muffled in the enthusiastic din of the crowd praising the progress and achievement."[68]

In Stree Sangharsh's *Om Swaha* (1979), in order to depict bride-burning they used strips of red cloth which were swished up and down swiftly to create the illusion of fire. Another feminist group showed the forces of revolt and exploitation tugging at opposite ends of a rope, while a woman tries desperately to strike a balance by jumping repeatedly on the rope from side to side.[69]

9. Satire

It is clear from the various examples quoted so far that satire and irony are elements that help street theatre make powerful indictments against society. At one point *Bandarkhela* (1986), the play about bride burning after the additional dowry has been demanded and refused, the loquacious woman asks theatre audience, "What do you think will happen? One woman answers, "Now they will burn the bride". The woman answers with a wry smile, "Oh you feminists are all the same everywhere."

The IPTA branch of Sahranpur in UP has a play in their repertoire entitled *Cricket Match* (1981). The contending teams are easily identifiable as the Congress (I) and the Janata Party, the two major parties in the country. Through satire the absurdities in both the parties are exposed.

10. Humour

What holds the audience together in a very busy street is the side-splitting humour of the street players. Without humour, the documentary aspect in the play can look colourless. One of the finest examples of humour may be observed in Janam's *Samarath Ko Nahin Dosh Gosain* (1979) about malpractices like black-marketing and hoarding. In a variety of magical feats, the street magician and his assistant locate the hoarded cereal in the godown of a black-marketeer with the right kind of connections. With his magic wand, the magician brings one of the sacks to life and the sack tells its story in song. On the scene arrives the black-marketeer and, with the help of the police, captures the sack once again. To liven up the issues, meanwhile the assistant seeks the help of a minister and thereby hangs another tale! In the end a delightful caricature of the unholy alliance between the establishment and the black-marketeers emerges. In the 45 minutes of the play, there is not a dull moment.

VII. Dissemination Methodologies

1. The Jatha (rallies)

Taking theatre to the people does not stop with performing on the streets alone. A number of well established groups like Samudaya of Karnataka and KSSP of Kerala have successfully organized month-long rallies throughout the length and breadth of the country.

Rallies began in Gandhi's time, when he toured the villages, learning from the rural poor. But rallies taking the theatre around to observe and learn from the people began with Samudaya. As a socio-cultural movement, founded in 1974 by theatre activists, professors and other interested people it provided meaningful progressive theatre for the masses. In course of time the movement spread all over Karnataka with over 20 units and 3000 members. Initially it was confined mainly to the urban middle class, then it moved to the urban working class. The rallies were attempts to

reach the rural peasantry, to make contact with them at grassroot level, to know and experience rural realities; and then to use theatre as a means of education to attack feudal and semi-feudal values: evils of caste, communalism, superstition, exploitation and inequalities in society.[70]

In 1974 equipped with a few selected plays, songs and slogans, two groups traversed different routes to cover the whole of Karnataka state on cycles, performing on the way for nearly a month. At the end of the month they met at a central place for a grand celebration of people power. A similar rally was organized in 1981.

KSSP had grown sufficiently to organize rallies from 1981. Its efforts to popularize science and develop scientific attitudes among the masses seemed so effective that in the last seven years it has organized regional rallies every year. In 1987, encouraged by the support it received from all over India, a massive all India rally was organized. It lasted forty days with five zonal groups traversing the north, west, south, east and north-east regions, each halting at over 500 places, covering about 25,000 kilometres and finally converging at Bhopal for a grand finale. Among the participants were over 1000 scientists and 5000 teachers. The map on page 141 shows the all-India coverage of the rally.

The success of this form of dissemination of ideas has resulted in a number of groups organizing similar rallies on a smaller scale. The Save the Western Ghats rally in the south (1986) the Tilonia group's environmental rally in Rajastan (1988), the IPTA unit rallies (1988) in north India are some of the recent theatre rallies.

These rallies have served two very important purposes:

1. They have taken a number of urban street theatre practitioners to interior areas and helped them see rural realities for themselves. They have also come to realize that scores of activist groups are working in these areas struggling to bring about an egalitarian society.
2. A number of groups who have worked in isolation in the past have come to know of the efforts of other groups in their own towns and have initiated joint programmes.

2. Workshops, Seminars, Festivals

Street theatre groups and others interested in forming new groups normally organize workshops. Several street theatre groups attended the workshops of Sircar, Tripurai Sharma, Shamshul Islam and others. These workshops last for a week or so and include a number of exercises to help utilize the full potential of the human body for dramatic expression. Several of Sircar's techniques are considered standard street theatre techniques. Workshop procedures are described in detail in chapter V.

As an opportunity for like-minded groups to meet and exchange

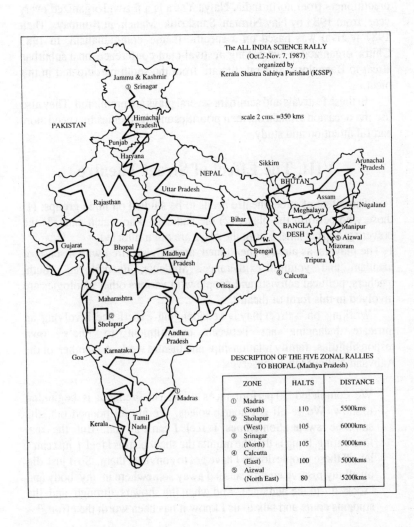

The ALL INDIA SCIENCE RALLY
(Oct.2-Nov. 7, 1987)
organized by
Kerala Shastra Sahitya Parishad (KSSP)

scale 2 cms. =350 kms

Jammu & Kashmir
③ Srinagar

Himachal
Pradesh

PAKISTAN

Punjab

Haryana

Sikkim

Arunachal
Pradesh

NEPAL

BHUTAN

Uttar Pradesh

Assam

Nagaland

Rajasthan

Meghalaya

Bihar

BANGLA
DESH

Manipur

⑤ Aizwal
Mizoram

Gujarat

Bhopal

Madhya
Pradesh

W.
Bengal

Tripura

④ Calcutta

Orissa

Maharashtra

①②
Sholapur

Andhra
Pradesh

Goa

Karnataka

① Madras

Kerala

Tamil
Nadu

DESCRIPTION OF THE FIVE ZONAL RALLIES
TO BHOPAL (Madhya Pradesh)

ZONE	HALTS	DISTANCE
① Madras (South)	110	5500kms
② Sholapur (West)	105	6000kms
③ Srinagar (North)	105	5000kms
④ Calcutta (East)	100	5000kms
⑤ Aizwal (North East)	80	5200kms

ideas, seminars and festivals have come in handy. The first major festival-cum-seminar held at Bhopal in 1983 brought together numerous practitioners from north India. Natya Yatra is a festival organized every year from 1983 by Nav Nirman Sanskritik Manch in Bombay. Their 1987 festival was based on a specific theme—communalism. In 1983 Chitra organized a week-long festival-cum-conference on a suburban street in Bangalore. Several literati from the south participated in this meet.

In these festivals and seminars several plays are premiered. They also use the occasion to chalk out their priorities and the themes that need more careful attention and study.

VIII. The Effect of Street Theatre

The effect of street theatre needs to be studied on three groups: (1) those who perform the plays; (2) the audience who watch and; (3) the powers groups against whom the plays are often directed.

1. The players, as already mentioned, are activists fired with a sense of idealism and youthful exuberance. Students, unemployed youth, teachers, political activists and people with various other ideologies are involved in this form of theatre.

Working on a street play is a challenging experience involving an intricate balancing act between commitment to one's own responsibilities, family relationships and theatre work. A member of the Aahvaan Natya Manch, observes:

> We completed 30 performances today. The tiredness is beginning to show. We've all got hoarse voices. We are all pooped out...the sun...the sweat...Sometimes I feel I can't go on. But the real fascinating thing is that the minute the show begins I feel I just can't let all these people down. I have got to convince them. So I just dig up all my reserve energy stashed away somewhere in my body and "sock it' to the audience. And when the show is through and the students come and talk to us I know it has been worth the effort.[71]

"Working in a street play has opened up new avenues for observing and understanding people," remarks a student from Delhi university who has been working with a group for several years. "I know that this has helped me relate to people, enlarge my world. Also, I find it exciting as a form of intervention in the social process. My chances in the a academic field have certainly been influenced by experiences gained here."[72]

The effect on the students of the Religious Department of St. Xavier's College, Bombay, who came together in 1987 to participate in a theatrical activity based on communalism, was nothing less than therapeutic.

We will never allow us to react to another communal riot with indifference or cynicism. . . when we began practising for the play we were acting without feeling... .By the end of it, we didn't need to act any more. It was as if we had lived the experience of riot...[73]

Another participant in the same workshop commented: The play has set me thinking. Why do we have religions? Why are there so many religions? Why is there so much violence within us? Why can't we live and let live?[74]

For Pani, a lecturer at Jyotiniwas College, Bangalore and the initiator of street theatre in the campus (1983) for rural education, street theatre is an attempt at developing definite social attitude, in the absence of which it becomes difficult to operate as a responsible person.

To counter the forces of illiteracy one has to look for non-literate approaches. Faced with the task of conveying messages of heterogeneous range covering as wide an area as hygiene and family planning, leadership and improved agriculture, politics and religion, one had to resort to a short-cut in communication. No amount of door-to-door talks, amusement games or fireside chats with women could help us make a dent. Then street theatre did the trick.[75]

Josantony Joseph who heads the Department of Religious Studies at St. Xavier's College, Bombay, strongly believes that real education does not work through courses at the University. For him and the students street theatre is a means to think, learn, react and thus be exposed to the realities that affect millions of people in the country.[76]

As for other political activists it may be assumed that every performance is a reassertion of the values they stand for.

2. Effect on the Audience

The effect on the audience who watch street plays can be immediate and delayed.

A. Immediate Effect

An incident related by a member of Arunodaya (Andhra Pradesh) speaks volumes for the immediate impact had potential of the medium.

In one village we were performing a play in which a landlord rapes a Harijan's wife soon after such an event had actually happened. The people got so aroused that they were about to beat up the actor playing the landlord, and the actor playing the Harijan had to intervene and save him.[77]

Similarly a member of the Aahvaan Natya Manch observes about their play against a Bombay University ordinance on the examination system.

There was laughter at the right places. Someone even raised a jeer at the Executive Committee. Another threw a banana peel at Devu who was playing the Vice Chancellor.... At the end of the play we urged them to join in raising slogans–some turned away embarrassed, but most joined in lustily, drowning our own voices.... The play was over. For a few seconds there was an uneasy silence. And then we were mobbed. "Come down to the canteen–we will treat you all to tea...? "We must do something against the ordinance", "Could I join Aahvaan?", I would love to act in this play... ."[78]

After watching Theatre Union's *Toba Tegh Singh* on the partition issues, at a street corner in Ahmedabad where the victims still live and communal riots still flare up, an old, frail man hugged an actor and sobbed, "Where were you all these years? All that you say is so real and close to our experience and reality."[79]

B. Delayed Effect

The following remarks are based on interviews with and observations of people attending street performances at various places in India.

The majority of the people attending these plays are unemployed and probably have time to while away. The plays performed outside offices are short, and have a very small floating audience who are mostly office-goers. They peer in for a few minutes and move away. Those at the evening performances are poor and cannot afford costly entertainments. There people seem to be capable of identifying with the problems dealt with in the plays. For, street theatre focuses on the dreary side of life and tries to lend a voice against all forms of injustice.

Here a question needs to be posed: if there were no unemployed and disgruntled people would street theatre have a *raison d'etre* for its existence? In fact, there are a number of groups run by employed people. It is not so much their love of experimental theatre as their commitment to the large section of Indian society who are uneducated and do not share any responsibility in the running of the country, that spurs them to take to theatre.

There are more young people than old at these plays. This is probably because the elderly do not find it easy to grasp the content of the plays, as they are not fully aware of the issues outside their immediate experience. Besides, it is the young who seek entertainment. Women are hardly found at these plays except in big cities and when the plays are about women. The social system in India restricts women from going out to such functions.

Several among the audience expressed displeasure at the plays not being as entertaining and versatile as the films. A college student complained that every other play is on corruption. He demanded more dances, fights and songs. This is a clear indication that more often than not street plays are seen as entertainment. The Indian folk tradition has conditioned them to look at any performance as a means of community gathering, celebration and entertainment.

As against this, where the audiences are used to the plays of particular groups—as in Delhi where Janam has made a sizeable audience for itself— the reaction of the audience has been very positive. They are aware that they have come to watch a play where a topical issue of a serious nature will be analysed. "Their plays give us a new perspective on current issues", said one. In many places the performances become an event—people talk about it for days. Men debate the pros and cons in the play at tea-sessions, in their evening jaunts, children re-enact their favourite scenes, recite the dialogues and hum the tunes. This can add up to an on-going education.

There is no doubt that street theatre has had some effect on people's lives but due to several restrictions and limitation it has not produced quantifiable results.

C. Effect on Mainstream Media

The urban proscenium theatre practitioners and other media merchants look down on street theatre practitioners. For them they are 'gutter theatre' people, resorting to street theatre for lack of finances, talent, managerial skills and opportunities. However, it may be observed that street theatre has had some positive effect on mainstream media. A number of playwrights like Lakshmi Narain Lal, S.D. Saksena, Mudrarakshasa and Chandresh, who normally write for the stage, have turned to the street theatre format. Plays like *Bakari, Ala Afsar* and *Ek Tha Gadha* may be staged easily on the street. The techniques of street theatre as popularized by Sircar have been adapted in several stage plays. With European experimentalists like Brook, Barba, Schechner and others supporting newer formats, even conventional theatre practitioners have turned to street theatre for creative challenges. Directors such as Feizel Alkazi and Rati Bartholomew have taken to street theatre.

In the field of cinema, mainstream commercial film has accepted the emergence of a parallel cinema[80] that deals with social problems in a challenging way. The success of films like *Garam Hawa* (1975) *Akrosh* (1983), *Paar* (1985) and *Damul* (1986) are indications that the concerns of street theatre are being widely accepted. Even the government sponsors television serials like *Shakti, Adhikar, Sthree* and *Nukkad* which concern women's issues and the rights of the oppressed classes.

3. Effect on the Power Groups

Generally street plays are not aimed at the policy makers, opinion leaders or power holders, although in most of the plays these persons are caricatured. Rather, these plays reach out to the ordinary citizens, to raise their awareness about the situation in the country.

There have been occasions however, when the power groups have been shaken. One instance that Chitra recalls is worth mentioning. Their play *Bandaro Bander* (1975) is based on a real event wherein MLAs and MPs misused large sums of money drawn from the public coffers to build a temple. When the truth was revealed in the play, it sent shock waves through the state government headed by K. Hanumanthayya. It was staged more than five hundred times in a number of towns in the state, rousing the people to be more alert to corrupt practices by the rulers.[81]

Local governments and others in power at times categorize theatre activities as 'subversive activity'. Instances of police intervention to disrupt performances date back to the early days of the IPTA. All over India political plays were banned and scripts destroyed. There have been several instances when players have been murdered in police encounters in Bhopal, Andhra Pradesh and Kerala. In April 1989, theatre activists all over India were shocked at the murder of Safdar Hashmi, a prominent writer of Janam, and two others by their opponents. Dutt's political theatre has been subjected to stone-throwing and the actors chased around the streets of Calcutta. Dutt observes:

> A revolutionary theatre is noted by the number of attacks it has faced from the agents of the ruling class. No amount of sophistry can obscure the truth that if a play is genuinely revolutionary, the ruling class cannot possibly tolerate its performance and in the long run will seek to wipe it out.[82]

In recent years street theatre performers have become the target of suppression. *Lathi* (baton) charges and arrests are routinely used for dispersing the players and the audience. In 1984 a street theatre group, Hiraval from Lucknow, Uttar Pradesh performing in a suburban street close to Patan was arrested and kept in prison for over three months at the insistence of the landlords. The performers of the Amritsar School of Drama including Gurcharan Singh were arrested in 1984 in Bombay when they came to the city to participate in a street theatre festival. The police have repeatedly insisted that Living Theatre of Kharadah submit their scripts for approval, even though the group depends heavily on improvisational techniques.

The constitutional provision about staging of plays is so vague that it can be interpreted at will. The act says that the government can prohibit the performance of plays which they think are likely to defame, scandalize, corrupt or deprave the people and which can create disloyalty against the government. But nothing can be banned only because it is against the policies of the ruling party.[83]

In 1982, Kerala's Janakiya Sanskarika Vedi, which staged two controversial political plays, *Nattugaddika* and *Chennay Chennay*, took the police to court for disrupting the performances. The verdict went in favour of Vedi. The judgment read:

> A citizen cannot be denied his freedom of expression simply because what is said is not palatable to those in power. Often we witness political demonstrators shouting slogans that the government in

power should be dumped in the Arabian sea. In the political musical chairs that is going on in this state from more than a quarter of a century, those who are in the opposition and in the government get in turn an opportunity to shout such slogans on the streets.[84]

This sort of suppression is only one side of the coin, for according to Lenin,

Ruling classes always try at first to destroy any revolutionary call by brutishness, anger, hate and force, and when they are unsuccessful in their effort to do so, then they try to blunt the edge of this revolutionary campaign by ideological attacks.[85]

Shamshul Islam of Nishant Natya Mandali based at Delhi University, holds that physical force and suppression are only a minor aspect of state oppression. The real attack is at the level of principles and ideologies:

The dramas of change that are being presented by cultural activists in the street plays are clear to the people as they reflect their own aspirations. Hence in the last few years, the government has tried to mislead and co-opt people's theatre. They have financed workshops on street theatre. International conferences have been arranged.[86]

Examples of such attempts to tame the street theatre practitioners are many. The Andhra Pradesh police resorted to training in street theatre to combat the 'venomous preaching' of the revolutionary groups. In 1985 the Ford Foundation organized a street theatre workshop at the Sri Ram Centre, Delhi, the headquarters of the Indian National Theatre which once tried to counter the influence of IPTA. In this workshop, Dutt was invited as one of the chief speakers. Activists believe that the object of this strategy of co-option by the government is to create the feeling among street theatre practitioners that they are incapable of the task undertaken, that they are ignorant of art and culture. The culture activists are thus coaxed into accepting government direction and guidance.

In fact various forms of repression by the government are what spur the groups to seek protection under the umbrella of established political parties. The ruling party hesitates to directly smother a group supported by an opposition party for fear of a counter attack. Hence these groups feel free to perform in public places, although at time they may be ambushed. S.D. Saksena, one of the promoters of street theatre, believed strongly that the movement cannot survive unless it associates itself with one or other left political parties. Gurcharan Singh's group has been under threat several times, but whenever they performed under the banner of their political group CPI (ML) they were left alone.

Speaking of political party support, it may be mentioned that some parties have floated their own theatre groups to proclaim their ideologies. These groups are well funded and have a thorough professional profile like Janam of Delhi and the many revived branches of the IPTA.[87]

Is Street Theatre Propaganda?

Often street theatre activists have been accused of being propagandists and peddlers of leftist ideologies. This may appear true, considering the enormous influence political parties and others have over certain groups. In some of their plays monologues are close to political speeches. Such plays have always been in the forefront of election campaigns. It is not surprising that these plays have been accused of indoctrination, brain washing and initiating ideologies, systems and cults by the supporters of the ruling party and the powerful.

If theatre is indeed one of the liveliest of all media there should be no hesitation in acknowledging it as an instrument of propaganda, to put across ideas, messages, emotions and sentiments. The theatre of social awareness has always emphasised education. However, theatre is primarily an art form. Thematic integrity, emotional depth and portrayal of reality and verisimilitude are some of the requisites which make social awareness theatre a piece of art. When the centre of focus shifts from these to pure ideological perspectives, the propaganda elements creep in.

The mode of expression accepted in street theatre is geared to exploring newer ways of artistic presentation. The short street plays come across as brilliant nuggets of art to the connoisseur. The various technical devices to make the communicative aspects powerful are rarely direct, but subtle and thought-provoking. The humour, satire, sarcasm and irony make the plays artistically rich. All in all, it is a very remarkable work of art exploding in the minds of the audience.

In sum it may be stated that street theatre activists are basically propgandists, but their contribution to the art of theatre is undeniable. Sircar, Tanvir, Gurcharan and Guha have made the form rich through their innovative expressions. However, in the hands of incompetent activists and artists it can be reduced to mere propaganda. If there is no mass mobilization and active participation of the people and ideas are imposed from above, it slides back to propaganda. Educating the people by anaesthetizing their subconscious is also propaganda. What is important is to make the people aware of situations without forcing them to follow a particular course of action.

Notes

1. Southern, R., *Seven Ages of Theatre*, Faber and Faber, London and Boston, 1965, pp. 21-34.
2. News release from the Bhopal Rang Yatra, 1984.
3. As quoted by Laud Rahul in "All the Street is a Stage," *Free Press Journal*, Bombay, 20/9/1987.
4. This is the considered opinion of street theatre activists and others involved in spreading the movement.
5. Padamsee, Pearl, "Theatre of the Street" in *Sunday Observer*, Bombay, 27/3/84.
6. Fox, Sue in Coult, Tony and Kershaw, Baz, *Engineers of the Imagination*, Eyre Methuen, 1983, p. 31.
7. Ganesh festival, a popular event in Maharastra was given political significance by Bal Gangadhar Tilak early in this century, when he used the occasion to urge the people to unite together against British imperialism.
8. The Progressive Writers Association was a popular socialist writers' union among Indian writers such as Mulkraj Anand, K.A. Abbas, Sarojini Naidu and others.
9. Gargi, Balwant, *Theatre in India*, Theatre Arts Books, New York, 1962, p. 173.
10. Pradhan, Sudhi, *Marxist Cultural Movements in India*, vol. I, National Book Agency, Calcutta, 1879, p. 158.
11. Ibid., p. 275.
12. Dutt, Utpal, *Towards a Revolutionary Theatre*, M.C. Sircar and Sons Calcutta, 1982. Also "Interview with Dutt," *The Drama Review*, 15 (3), 1971.
13. Ibid.
14. Tanvir, Habib, interview by Sonalkar, Sudhir, *Onlooker*, 16/9/1976.
15. Personal interview.
16. The ideas are from Sircar's book, *Third Theatre*, published by the author, Calcutta, 1978.
17. Sircar, Badal, *Three Plays: Bhoma, Stale News, Michil*, Seagull Press, Calcutta, 1983, p. 71.
18. Bharucha, R., *Rehearsals for Revolution, The Political Theatre of Bengal*,

Seagull Books, Calcutta, 1983, p. 132.

19. Sen, Niranjan, in Pradhan Sudhi, *Marxist Cultural Movements*, vol. II, Navanna, Calcutta, 1982, p. 187.

20. Sathyu, M.S., in Menon, Meen and Mathur, Anjali, "Bringing Theatre to the People," *Indian Express*, Bombay, 28/10/84.

21. Das, Rathin, "Street Theatre, the Modern Folk Form," in *Vidura*, 18/5, Press Institute of India, Delhi, 1981, p. 309.

22. The Communist Party of India (CPI) broke up in 1964 into three factions: the relatively less radical group retained the name CPI and is committed to national democratic revolution; the leftist faction is CPI Marxist, committed to people's democratic revolution and the third faction CPI (Marxist - Leninist) also known as Naxalites has no faith in parliamentary democracy and believes in guerilla warfare.

23. Guha, Probir, as quoted by Menon, Sadanand, "Towards a People's Theatre," *Sunday Observer*, Bombay, 30/9/84.

24. Ibid.

25. Padamsee, op. cit.

26. Interview on 20/11/87.

27. Interview with the members on 10/1/88.

28. Aahvaan Natya Manch, "Bombay, Playing in the Streets," *Sunday Standard*, Bombay, 30/11/1980.

29. Pani, Rajni, "A Maiden on the Street," personal experiences of participating in street theatre. Jyoti Niwas College, Bangalore, 1983 p. 20.

30. Interview on 10/1/88.

31. The Punjab problem (demand for a separate state by the Sikhs) began in early 1970s. The Sikhs of Punjab set up a Sikh regional party, Akali Dal, in order to press their demands. Sant Bhindranwale established a militant relationship with the Congress in order to restore peace in 1980. The growing crisis resulted in the storming of the Golden Temple (the most sacred Sikh shrine) in 1983 as that was used by Sikh terrorists as their base. This led to the subsequent murder of Mrs. Gandhi in 1984 by her Sikh bodyguards. The problem still simmers on.

32. The Bhopal gas tragedy occurred on the night of 3rd December 1984 when poisonous gas leaked from the US owned Union Carbide Plant killing 5000 and handicapping thousands for life.

33. Tanushree, "Natya Yatra 87", in *Padgham* an occasional news magazine of Nav Nirman Sanskritik Samiti, Bombay, 2/2/1987.

34. Interview on 14/11/87.

35. Pork is abhorrent to Muslims for religious reasons, while the cow is sacred to the Hindus.

36. Pani, op. cit.

37. *Bakari* was written by Sarveswar Dayal Saksena in 1974 and is probably the most staged play in the country.

38. Nevatia, Smriti, "Taking Theatre to the People", *Sunday Observer*, Bombay,

        11/11//84.
39. Mukerjea, Ananya, "Theatre as True as Hunger," *Telegraph* Calcutta, 5/1/
        84.
40. The excerpt from the play *Uplabdiyan* is my own translation.
41. Mukerjea, op. cit.
42. Padamsee, op. cit.
43. Nevatia, S., op. cit.
44. Sahane, Charu, "All the Street is a Stage," *Indian Express,* Bombay, 12/
        2/86.
45. Interview with the group Saheli, Delhi, on 11/11/87.
46. Interview with the group, Sthree Mukti Sanghatana, Bombay, on 13/4/88.
47. Interview with the group Janam on 22/11/87.
48. Javed Anand, "Real Life Dramas", *Sunday Observer*, Bombay, 11/8/85.
49. Interview with KSSP on 5/1/88.
50. *Nukkad-nukkad Aangan-aangan*, Jagori, N. Delhi, 1988.
51. Pani, Rajni, op. cit.
52. Schechner, op. cit.
53. Bharucha, op. cit., p. 130.
54. Guha, op. cit.
55. Pani, op. cit.
56. Guha, op. cit.
57. Pani, op. cit.
58. Sircar, op. cit., p. 19. (no. 16 above).
59. Bharucha, op. cit., p. 149.
60. Mody, Bella, as quoted by Krishnan Prabha in "Catalyst Theatre," a study of
        street theatre groups in Delhi, 1980.
61. Javed, Anand, op. cit.
62. Interview with Bansi Kaul by N.K. Sharma, *Dinman*, Delhi, 12/1/86.
63. Kees, P. Epscamp's paper, "Fools For Development" provides a useful
        analysis on how the buffoon character helps disseminate development
        themes in various cultures. The paper was presented on April Fools's day
        Conference on Linguistic Humour, Arizona State University, 1982.
64. The word 'dalit' literally means the oppressed. It was often used to denote
        the lower castes in western India. Today it is replacing 'Harijan' (people of
        God), the word used by Gandhi to denote the untouchables.
65. Nevatia, op. cit.
66. Mies, Maria, "Indian Women and Leadership," *Bulletin of Concerned Asian
        Scholars*, 7/1, 1975, pp. 56-66.
67. Patel, Vibhuti, "The Street is the Thing," *Indian Post* , Bombay, 20/8/87.
68. Pani, op. cit.
69. Pani, op. cit.
70. Bartholomew, Rati, "Samudaya's Jatha: Karnataka," in *How*, N. Delhi, Jan-
        Feb 1983.
71. Ahvaan Natya Manch, op. cit.

72. Quoted by Mahrotra Deepa, "Drama of the Streets," *Surya India,* N. Delhi, 1-15, 1982.
73. Quoted by Mehra, Preeti, "The Theatre of No Return," *Times of India,* Bombay, 1/11/87.
74. Ibid.
75. Pani, op. cit.
76. Quoted by James, Teresa Viju, "A Time for Exta," *Indian Post,* Bombay, 29/11/87.
77. Prestonji, Meher, "All the Street is a Stage," *Indian Express,* Bombay, 19/4/87.
78. Ahvaan Natya Manch, op. cit.
79. Tanushree, op. cit.
80. The "Parallel cinema", or films with more aesthetic sense and social purpose as against the run of the mill commercial films began to be sponsored both by the government and trained artists from the late sixties. However, this has had very little effect on the film industry.
81. Interview with the group on 14.1.88.
82. Dutt, op. cit., p. 37.
83. CPDR, *Know Your Rights,* Bombay, 12.3.1983.
84. Editorial, *The Hindu,* Madras, 24th April 1982, p. 9.
85. Quoted by Islam, Shamshul, in "Theatre v/s the State," in *Padgham,* Bombay, 2/2, 1987.
86. Ibid.
87. From January 1986 attempts are being made by the CPI (M) to revive the IPTA. Various activities are going on in Bihar, Kerala, Delhi, and Uttar Pradesh.

Chapter V

Theatre in Action Groups: Developing Social Awareness

Part I

I. Theatre in Present-Day Indian Villages

Despite a throbbing, vibrant folk theatre which has flourished in villages of India from time immemorial, today these villages present a different picture altogether. Be it the literate villages of Kerala, or politically conscious Bengalees or the illiterate rural folk of Bihar, theatre among all has been deeply influenced by the Western conventional style. The degree of refinement or polish may vary according to the level of educational standards of the performers and the audience, but basically they all show some common Western traits.

As a common practice plays are staged during festivals and other special occasions in the villages. Annual festival like Durga Pooja, Saraswati Pooja, Diwali, Id, Muharram, Christmas, birthdays of Gandhi, Nehru, Amebdkar, Patron Saint's Day and other anniversaries and jubilees are considered ideal occasions for staging plays. These often run for the whole night, extending the festivities. Occasionally city-based travelling troupes are invited, if the village can afford the money. The purpose of all these performances is basically to add entertainment to the community celebrations.

The village theatres in Bihar may be taken as typical examples of the pattern of village theatre in India. With regard to themes in these plays, three types may be easily identified. First there are the religious plays. These draw inspiration from the scriptures and *puranas*. Mythological characters like Ram, Sita, Ravan and Krishna—from the classics and epics like the *Mahabharatha* and the *Ramayana*—come alive in colourful costumes, rickety sets and gaudy make-up. The Muslims and Christians retell the events from the Koran, the Bible and the lives of holy men and women. Then there are plays that expose social evils like the *zamindari* (landlords) system, the practice of dowry, and the ever increasing menace of dacoity. Other problems like exploitation in the name of caste and social status, bonded labour, low wages, poverty, illiteracy, health issues, unemployment and the struggle for an equitable social order have been examined from ramshackle village stages to the accompaniment of thundering applause from the audience. The third type of plays are historical, based on the lives of figures such as Laxmi Bai, Maharana Pratap, Amarsingh Rathod, Vir Kunwar Singh, Shivaji, Chandrasekhar Azad, Khudiram Bose and so on. These plays are meant to evoke patriotic sentiments.

The contents of these plays reflect the religiosity, vulnerability and the dreams and aspirations of a peasant class that seeks justice from the powerful groups who control their destiny. After a whole day's hard work in the fields, rehearsals can be boring and tiresome especially when most of the actors are illiterate and the only method is improvisation. Most of the villagers have no training at all; they have only seen touring troupes perform.

Is it the entertainment associated with theatre, or love for culture, or the sense of social responsibility to enlighten the masses, that attract the villagers to theatre even in the most trying conditions? Probably all these reasons are present, but what predominates, is the spirit of celebration, the community aspect of bringing everyone together. Raja Ram'[1] a Harijan leader and the manager of the Durga Pooja Festival Committee in a Bihar village, is convinced of the need for having a play at a festival. "We cannot afford a film. Hence we need plays. A play makes all the difference. Otherwise the feast ends by the evening. When we stage a play by ourselves, we feel our strength. We are able to entertain and teach our people as the troupes from the cities do." This is a typical response to play acting in the village. There are also those who enjoy plays just for the fun of it. "I like it for the fun it gives me and to the audience who watch me", says Ramdev, a 28-year old, who often plays humorous roles. "I feel very happy when the audience laughs at the funny things I say and do. Films are far away and dear, so we like our plays." In fact, theatre plays an important role in helping them forget their every day blues and just have a good laugh. And that is an important need. However there are exceptions.

Bhola Master, a 35-year-old elementary school teacher and a Harijan from Pakpar, Bihar, plays the tabla and sings rather well. He has been associated with plays in his village from childhood. "In our village people are very poor and illiterate," he says, " their only concern is to find food for their family. I think drama can be used to teach those who do not go to school at all. We may not succeed in teaching them to read and write but we can give them motivation. We can help them think about themselves. We can help them raise questions. In our plays we raise simple questions like, "Why are we what we are? Can we ever change our situation? Why are the higher caste people richer and more powerful than us? Why the Caste system? What are the obstacles to changing our situation? These are problems our people face everyday, but no one bothers about them. However, when we raise these issues from the stage they look at them in a new way. Not that they produce any drastic changes. Some social plays present these problems in newer forms. Some people get the message. But the results are not worth mentioning...." Bhola Master is known to discuss every play that is staged in the village with his students in the school. But teachers of Bhola's type are very rare.

Nand Kishore, an undergraduate Harijan, now teaching in a Middle School in Bihar has been involved with theatre ever since he could read and write. His concern with theatre is more articulate: "What fascinates me about plays in the villages is the acting potential of the people. Once they understand the character, they play elegantly. They do not even need written scripts. If our people are such good communicators drama can surely be used as a means for enlightenment". He points out the case of Ramprakash, a 52-year old labourer, who though illiterate, is fully in control of the character he plays. "He has learned his lines well after some practice. On stage he becomes dynamite. No one can stop him. The realism with which he communicates is beyond description, you need to see it to believe. Acting is not about learning lines, it is a lot about doing, in the right way. He has it all in him in the right measure".

The plays staged in the villages are often based on cheap scripts written and published locally by villagers most of whom belong to the higher castes. The influence of melodramatic films and soap operas is immediately noticeable in these plays. There are plays written like a film script with scenes set in numerous locations, complete with dream and song sequences, flashes back and forward, stereo-typed characters. The Indian cinema has unarguably made a mockery of social themes by 'treating' them with the general formula of escapist entertainment. For example, in a typical film dealing with a real problem like the unemployment of educated youth, the hero is a handsome, good-natured young man who suffers at the hand of fate. As luck would have it, one day he is knocked down by a car driven by the heroine, the beautiful daughter of the richest businessman in town. Love at first sight inspires her to take him to her home to nurse. As they fall in love, he is employed in a high post at her father's office. Soon he discovers the father's smuggling contacts abroad. Meanwhile the heroine's suitor who operates the smuggling connections abroad—the archetypal villain—arrives. Now the hero has two issues on hand, to win his lady love and to fight smuggling and corruption. The Indian hero, always righteous, ultimately conquers all hazards. The initial, real problem of unemployment has disappeared and a magical solution has been found.

Such films are the inspiration for most social plays. They contain the magic formulae of success. Plays like *Mujhe Insaaf Chahiya* (I Need Justice), *Zulm Ki Pukaar* (The Call of Violence) and *Kraanti* (Revolution) are not only imitations of film titles; the stories too are drawn from films.

Consequently the plays staged in villages often repeat similar themes and styles. Oppression and exploitation of all sorts recur in almost every play. But the performers and the audience are incapable of analysing them.

Plays by better known playwrights are not staged for several reasons. Generally the villagers are not literate enough to fathom the richness of a well written play. These plays treat themes in an abstract or deeply philosophical way. Nand Kishore, who is familiar with the plays of Mohan Rakesh, Badal Sircar, Lakshmi Narain Lal, Shankar Shesh and others, believes that the villagers would find it hard not only to learn the lines but also to comprehend the inner meaning, although the plays speak about problems familiar to the villagers.

Village theatre today has an archaic flavour with a mixture of folk theatre, some elements of the classical and a dash of the Western. Western theatre has supplied the concept of the proscenium, lighting designs and written texts which have to be memorized. These have facilitated a systematized play production, but have eliminated some of the more intimate communication channels with the audience, so much a part of folk theatre. Only a few elements of folk and classical theatre like the *sutradhar*, *vidhushak* and the song and dance tradition have been retained. Cinema has cast its shadow over the village theatre, not merely as a formidable rival, but as a polluting agent. The springs of good taste have dried up and plays are often marred by crude imported techniques and styles.

Theatre as practised in the villages today presents feudal and pre-feudal themes, primarily mythological and historical, glorifying gods and superhuman beings. The values they reinforce are totally divorced from reality. This theatre, needless to say, is controlled by the ruling class and only the themes that are of direct interest to them are presented. However entertaining this theatre may be, it does not relate to the day to day lives of the rural masses. The emphasis is on the formulae of entertainment — dances, fiery dialogues, songs, conflicts and fights. All these can easily be contained in the context of the oppressor-oppressed syndrome. It does not provide a vehicle for a confrontation between the ruling class and the masses which is vital to the development of social awareness. This is basically because the social problems are studied and analysed from the bourgeois point of view, that is, the way the ruling class and the power holders see them. However, there are a few people like Bhola Master and Nand Kishore who realize the value of theatre for developing the social consciousness of the villagers.

Given the innate interest of the villagers in theatre it was not surprising that social activists would begin using theatre as a tool for developing the consciousness of the illiterate villagers. The emergence of IPTA in the forties and the street theatre movement accentuated this process. There are basically three groups that take theatre to the people:

1. Conventional city-based theatre groups that have powerful social themes in their repertory. They often tour the smaller towns and villages with sets and props in their vehicles. The Little Theatre Group (Utpal Dutt) in West Bengal and the Kerala People's Arts Club are good examples of such groups. Since they do not directly aim at social education or awareness building, they fall outside the purview of this chapter.
2. Street theatre groups that use the medium for social education in cities as well as in villages.
3. Action groups that use theatre as part of their strategy of social awareness raising in the villages.

II. Village oriented Street Theatre Groups

These groups which are active in the cities, have been discussed in chapter IV. Those that reach out to the villages are briefly touched upon here.

It is difficult to pinpoint where a city ends and the village begins in India. A number of active street theatre groups tour the villages (*jatha*) or have their own units in the villages. Groups like Gurcharan Singh's Amritsar School of Drama, Samudaya, Chitra, groups animated by Delhi's Alarippu, and units of IPTA, though based in urban centres, perform regularly in the villages. These groups, used to performing for slum dwellers in the city, find it easy to adjust to the villages.

The success of Samudaya's *jatha* in the villages bears testimony to the popularity of urban street theatre groups in the villages. As observed earlier, Samudaya's shift from urban middle class to rural peasantry was quite smooth. Without abandoning any one sector the group succeeded in creating some integration between the urban and rural sector. In the 1979 *jatha* the group had six plays in their repertory. Five of these were based on real life incidents. *Belchi* dealt with the burning of Harijan and agricultural labourers in south Bihar in May 1977, *Chasnala* with the tragic death of mine workers in the Dhanabad coal mines in 1975, *Pathre Sangappe* with the brutal murder of a bonded Harijan labourer by his master in Shimoga District, *Bale Davru* with the hypocrisy of "godmen" and *Bharata Darshana* was based on the Tarkunde Commission's Report on the police killings in Andhra (1978). In the 1980 *jatha* the group also included *Naraguuda Bandaya*, based on the peasant movement in Dharwar (1977). All these incidents, which hit the national news headlines were about different aspects of the lives of the poorer sections in the country. Their contemporary relevance helped to make a mark on the audience whether staged in the villages or in the city. In the villages some came forward to report on similar incidents known to them. Some gave written statements of the injustices committed against them. High caste Hindus reacted violently against the depiction of bonded labour and religious superstitions. Bartholomew observes:

> Tangibly the participants got knowledge of real problems. Intangibly, the people— the exploited, the bonded labourers, the untouchables— realized that they are not totally isolated. That there are forces with them in their struggle.[2]

A whole cross-section of society participated in the plays. Several villagers showed interest in starting units of the group. The Samudaya members themselves felt that the venture provided a cultural platform for interaction between progressive democratic individuals and organization and the common man in the village. The *jatha* was indeed a step in the right direction, a step that reached towards the foot of the mountain.

From 1948 onwards, Gurcharan Singh's group also toured the villages of Punjab, enacting plays on communal harmony, national unity and corruption among government officials. Plays like *Takht Lahore Da* (1957) about the legendary figure Dulla Bhatt who had rebelled against Akbar (16th century) to protest against dictatorship, *Mashall* (1978) a protest against the excesses of the emergency (1975-77), *Ek Kursi, Ek Morcha aur Hawa mein Latalk Rahe Log* about factionalism in Punjab (1972), *Har Ek Ko Jeene Ka Hak Hai* (1983) and *Main Ugravadi Nahin* (1984), both direct attacks on terrorism and *Chandigarh Pavadi Di Jad* (1984), on the uncertain future of Chandigarh were as suited to urban as to rural audience. Singh summed up his achievements:

> All through my tours in the villages people have come in thousands to watch my plays. Of course the use of Punjabi folk idioms in my plays, as also situations which confront the farmer in his day to day life help me reach out to them. I have found the rural audience more receptive and appreciative. The people come to see my plays mainly because the plays talk for them. The folk hero of Punjab today is not the legendary Ranjha or Majnu, but an alive, thinking individuals who plans to continue his crusade for peace in Punjab and for the common man.[3]

Singh's haunting tunes and dance steps are so much part of his Punjabi tradition that they succeed in both the urban and rural centres. His use of puppets also endears his plays to the rural audience.

Patna's IPTA unit has a play *Sawa Ser Gehun* (1983) based on a Premchand[4] story about the legitimation of bonded labour by religious chiefs. This play was well received in the interior villages of West Champaran District and on the vast Gandhi Maiden in the heart of Patna city. Similarly, other plays like *Janata Pagal Ho Gayee* (1984) and *Raja Ka Baaja Bajaa* (1985) can easily be staged anywhere in the state. This is because in states like Bihar and Uttar Pradesh there is hardly any difference between city and village audience. Even the language used in the city can be a strange mixture of many village dialects.

Although KSSP is not a theatre group all their plays are well accepted in the cities as well as in the villages. Similarly Bombay's Stree Mukti Sanghatna, Calcutta's Chorus and Centre for Communication and Cultural Action perform equally well in the city and in the villages.

Sircar's first workshop in a village (1972) with tribals of the Sunderbans was an eye-opener for him. Though he was apprehensive in the beginning, he claimed that the villagers in rural Bengal adapted to his styles more easily than the urban intelligentsia. In the workshop, he was able to establish a close communion with the villagers. The play *Bhoma* devised with the villagers, spoke about the way the villagers overcome man eating tigers, dacoits, poachers, police brutality and the exploitation by money-lenders. He was so successful that he termed his third theatre 'urban-rural link' theatre. From 1973, he has conducted workshops in rural Bengal, Manipur, Uttar Pradesh, Andhra Pradesh, Tamil Nadu, Karnataka and Maharastra. His style has been accepted and widely used by the villagers. Sircar explains:

I am invited to diverse kinds of groups like students, youth, villagers, etc. I particularly like being with rural people involved in grassroot level consciousness raising work. I have always noticed that within two or three days of my workshop, the participants use my technique. It has been my experience all over.[5]

Similarly, the Delhi based Alarippu, a voluntary agency that specializes in using theatre to enlighten rural masses, headed by Tripurari Sharma and Laksmi Krishnamoorthy has conducted numerous workshops and seminars to enlighten rural masses to the use of theatre. From 1979, their work has taken them to village-groups like Gram Vikas (Orissa‾ 1981, 83, 87), Antoyday (Bihar‾ 1984, 87), Action India (slums of Delhi‾ 1984, 85, 86, 87,), Sabla Sangh (outskirts of Delhi‾1982, 83, 84,) Pidith (Madhya Pradesh‾1983, 85, 87), Lok Samiti Bihar‾1986-88) and Vanvasi Sevashram (Rajastan‾1986-88). They have found working with the rural masses exceedingly enriching. According to Sharma:

Most of the techniques of street theatre are already familiar to the villagers. If we do not make them more crude, they will easily assimilate the content of the plays. If we use the dialects, music, idioms and thus catch the temper of the village in our plays, we can be successful. We do this by getting the villagers to improvise the plays.[6]

Rao, who has organized street theatre workshops with Sircar (1975) and Sharma (1976) for rural activists and villagers working in the interior of Andhra Pradesh and Tamil Nadu observes:

Contrary to the popular notion that the street play is essentially an

urban middle class phenomenon even our little experience proves
that the street play with all its peculiar technical devices is acceptable
to the rural masses. The circular structure without any stage, make-
up, costumes bridging devices like the screen and fade-out and in
addition to this, actors switching roles in the same play, human
props, mime, symbolic props, oral sound-effects all have been accepted by the rural uneducated masses in the villages.[7]

Rao's experience shows that the ready acceptance of street theatre by
the masses is due to the use of several folklore devices in street theatre.
The circular structure of the stage, distancing ('alienation') devices
like *sutradhar* and *vidhushak* and asides to speak directly to the audience,
stylized acting, dialogue delivery and mime are all part of the folk
tradition. Oral sound effects, symbolic and illusionary props and people
playing animals and trees are common in folk theatre. The villagers'
uncanny talent for improvisation was noticed in the creation of characters
and dialogues. The constant exposure to harsh realities provides them
with insights into characters and situations. Uninfluenced by commercial
cinema, they are realistic and intense in their presentations. In one village
a fifty year old lady performed as many as ten roles with ease in an
improvisation session. It was the first time she ever 'performed' in front
of an audience. In another place a group of young villagers performed
the extraordinary feat of sacrificing a buffalo on the stage in mime. Again
their exposure to plays or films was minimal. It is no wonder that such
groups take to mime easily.

The villagers also seemed familiar with scene transitions—from the
landlord's house, to the field, to the labourers' house, to the next village,
to the headman's meeting, to the town, to the market, to the village and
back to the landlord's house. The transitions were smooth and easily
comprehensible to the villagers.

It is appropriate here to examine the development of theatre in the
Young India Project (YIP) a group of social activists based in rural Andhra
Pradesh. Initially they started with conventional theatre exploring
themes like landlordism, money-lenders, exploitation, women as sex
objects, corruption, politics. It was soon felt to be too ideological and
propagandistic. In the second stage they took to folk forms like *kolattam*
(a dance with sticks) and *burrakatha* (a folk form of story-telling), forms
available to the lower castes and poorer sections. The results were
positive. However, the group felt that although the form was indigenous,
the contents were induced by the activists themselves. It was at this

juncture, in early 1982, that the group got interested in the experiments of Sircar. His workshop introduced the villagers to non-verbal communication, body movements and rhythms taken from the people performing on the same level as the audience. The villagers soon got involved in the productions in the new-found form.

Themes

If the street theatre format works well in the villages, what about themes? Can the messages, themes and plots in street theatre be presented unchanged in village theatre? Opinions vary on this issue. The problems of the villagers, some argue, are essentially different from that of the city dwellers. However, others argue that those who live in slums are villagers who come to the city looking for a living. The lack of clean drinking water, poverty, discrimination and exploitation at the hands of landlords, middlemen or power brokers are problems common to villagers and slum-dwellers alike. City dwellers also face problems like unemployment, corruption and malpractices at high places. All are prey to the national malaise of communal riots, price rise and caste conflicts. Issues like poverty, illiteracy, communal hatred, low status of women, bonded labour, child labour, degradation of spiritual and moral values and superstition are problem that confront every Indian. Plays on these themes can be staged anywhere in the country. However, if the themes are of immediate importance to a particular community the play succeeds beyond measure. For example, issues such as exploitation by landlords, caste disparities, bonded labour and superstitious beliefs are suitable for a village audience. On the other hand, exploitation by middlemen, insanitary conditions, or unemployment make more sense to slum-dwellers. Issues of national importance like communalism, the low status of women, falling social values and corruption in high places go better with an educated audience. Ultimately the best scenario would be if everyone was aware of the problems of everyone else, if an audience sees local problems in relation to the problems of the country. For example, a villager watching a play like *Toba Tegh Singh*, on the issue of communalism during the 1947 partition, realizes that members of other communities living in his neighbourhood also deserve to be respected and cared for. The differences, if any, in presenting plays in the villages and cities lie more in form than in their content.

As observed earlier, villagers do not respond well to theme analysis or other intricate methods of images building as expounded by Sircar.

They prefer a clear story line with a narrative form, a plot that moves and appeals. Hence plays with strong contents are more easily adapted to village situations than others that are highly imaginative and display stylized techniques. Adapting the story to the villagers' own dialect, idioms, phrases and images is of a great importance.

In the cities the pace of life is such that people generally wander away from the performance area without paying much attention. Hence there is no scope for large scale, long productions. In the villages, normally the plays are staged in the evening, when everything else is over. People sit down peacefully and are ready to sit on for the whole night, prepared to be entertained! Plays can be as long as the performers can carry on. The high standard of flexibility and improvisation techniques involved in street theatre make these adaptations comparatively easy. Again, in the villages it may often be necessary to sing a number of extra songs, the *sutradhar* may have to explain matters clearly to the audience. These demands require more time.

Post-performance discussions, too, are common in the villages, as normally no one walks away after a performance. Hence in between the short plays, discussions may be organized in groups, if the performers take an active interest.

Effects of Street Theatre in the Villages

There are limitations to street theatre groups extending their services to the villages. One-off performances by these groups help to widen their own popularity. At first they are welcomed with great fanfare by the villagers as they have heard of the performers. However, what is gained in grandeur is lost in depth as the performances are few and far between. The relationship with the audience remains at a superficial level. Follow-up and evaluation hardly ever take place.

Nevertheless, the visits of such groups to villages kindles in the villagers a genuine interest for such plays. When similar attempts are made by groups within the village, people take to them easily.

Part II

Social Action Groups

In the past two decades India has seen a proliferation of social action groups (SAGs), for whom theatre has become a major tool for developing the consciousness of the rural people.

Normally SAGs work with communities which have been marginalized and victimized like tribals, landless labourers, fisherfolk or rural women. The realization that the landless remain poor because they do not have the means to utilize their labour to enter into a self-sustaining process of development is what motivates the SAGs. To them development is not simply economic fulfilment and the management of 'projects', as understood by the voluntary and relief agencies in the past. Rather it involves a constant struggle towards economic and social justice. Some groups have taken to imparting relevant information, skills and knowledge that would help the people in their struggle for an egalitarian society. Others have started organizing the people with a view to forcing the government to implement existing legislation and schemes to benefit the poor and to protect the people's economic and political rights. They also work to ensure the people's participation in the decision making bodies in charge of these schemes. Issues like bonded labour, minimum wages, caste discrimination have attracted their attention.

Central to the organization of the SAGs is the notion of participation, democratic decentralization and collective management and responsibility. Participation is actually the key element. It is not the kind of participation as in the so-called democratic governments through elected representatives, rather it is a process which begins at the grass-roots level. Ideally, its success depends on the collective involvement of all the people in all aspects. It means that the entire community takes initiatives, asserting themselves, contributing their share to the analysis and planning of the various programmes. Thus participation itself becomes an educational process and an essential element in the act of conscientization. Through collective introspection and analysis of their own experiences and problems people become more aware of the dimensions of the reality and of what they can do to transform it. Periodic evaluations take place where free and forthright opinions are expressed by all to help increase awareness and form collective decisions.

As enunciated by Freire, the two dimensions of action and reflection are essential aspects of this process of development. When the entire group interacts on an equal footing and access to the resources is democratized, there can be a growing awareness. The leaders of the SAGs strongly believe that it is not their function to hand down skills or information to the people but to act as catalysts of change, involving themselves along with the people in a process of learning. One of the main areas of work is to encourage the cultural modes of expression most familiar to the people. Following the example of Freire and Boal, who insisted on people's participation at every stage of the action, these groups have used cultural activities, especially theatre, to analyse socio-economic problems.

Theatre in Social Action Groups

Although theatre may be used by any voluntary agency, here we are concerned with the use of theatre by SAGs who, ideally, have the right kind of methodology and try to use theatre in a creative way. It is estimated that about 25% of the SAGs have at least one theatre troupe, though they are not very articulate about how to use theatre for social analysis. Another 60% use theatre as a starting point or as a 'front' activity, once in a while, with improvised groups. The rest, about 15% do not have any theatre at all.

I. Organization and Structure of Theatre in SAGs

To understand SAGs' work in theatre, I have selected a few groups with whom I spent some time either as an observer or as an animateur conducting workshops and helping in their evaluations.

1. Lok Samiti (People's Union)

The Lok Samiti is an action group founded in 1974, inspired by the call of Jai Prakash Narain to students to unite for total revolution. JP, as he was known, was a Gandhian who later succeeded in uniting the opposition parties to form the Janata Party and win the elections in 1977. The leaders of the group are Satish and Girija, then engineering students in their penultimate year at the Institute of Technology, Kharagpur, West Bengal. Along with six other youngsters with similar background they came back to Bihar. Initially they raised enough funds by selling their belongings to buy a plot of land and establish a small office on the Grand Trunk Road, four miles east of Champaran, in south Bihar. The group has grown considerably in the past 14 years, deepening their own commitment to the cause and rallying together a large group of villagers around them. Funded by Gandhian and Sarvodaya charity schemes and foreign donors like Bread For the World and Oxfam they bought a 40-acre farm and set up a buffalo rearing scheme, which is used to educate the people about model farming and animal husbandry. The income, hopefully, will help Lok Samiti to support itself. Today there are 16 other branches spread around south and central Bihar. Each of these branches has a paid staff of two or three persons with an office and reaches out to as many as 20 to 30 villages. The people are tribals and low caste Hindus—both deprived and oppressed groups. Lok Samiti's activities include organizing the exploited and the poor around specific issues and building up their confidence.

Lok Samiti's central theatre group Lok Natya Manch (People's Theatre) established in 1981, has seven full- time members—all men. The leader Prabhat and two other members have had short-term training in theatre with street theatre groups in Calcutta and Delhi. All of them are fine players who have done a lot of acting and dancing. They do not belong to any traditional actor's castes. They are Harijans and have learnt the art by watching films and village dramas. They have indeed a natural flair for acting.

Like the other field workers they are paid labourers. When asked about what they thought about being paid for the performances one of them said: "This is what we do all the time. We have families and children. You expect us to starve them? They perform plays on social evils such as bonded labour, wage discrimination, landlessness, caste issues, alcoholism. Normally the group assembles for a week-long programme in one of the villages manned by a branch. They also conduct workshops for fieldworkers from their various branches at the Champaran centre and at other regional branches. The attempt to form regional and ultimately village theatre groups is on the agenda, but has not yet succeeded. There are, however, signs that each branch may have a group with scripts and workshops.

All the plays performed in the villages have been prepared earlier, either by adapting already published scripts or from self-improvised workshop materials. The problems of the villages in south Bihar are covered in a general way in these plays. The workshops are a great help in improvising plays on topical issues. Before each performance the plays are updated and adapted to suit the immediate needs and issues in the village concerned.

The plays are normally staged in that of part of the village where the lower castes live. The group camps in the village for a week. They live in one of the rooms made available to them. During the day they rehearse the play, mingle with the villagers and some even join them to work in the fields. They have about ten plays in their repertory. The plan is to stage two plays on a specific theme every evening and, on the following day to organize study circles.

The plays are not necessarily performed in the round if the villagers are keen to put up a temporary stage made up of borrowed *chaukis* (wooden beds), bamboo poles and sarees. At other times, the village square is easily transformed into a cosy show corner. For the villagers the visit of the group is like to going to a village fair. Everyone comes home early in the evening from work. Women finish cooking. The actors are fed at the house of the village *mukhya* (chieftain), to which the villagers have contributed. Children mill around the performance area. A public address system blares out film songs. This is the normal custom in any Indian village for a celebration. As night falls, three lanterns are brought onto the stage. The six actors, already in make-up, begin to sing action songs that have very powerful social messages. The people join in the singing. After about half an hour it is time for the play to begin.

The two plays for the evening are about bonded labour. The first play *Sawa Ser Gehun* is based on a very popular short story about bonded labour by the celebrated Hindi writer Premchand. After the play the actors come out to the audience to find out if they grasped the message of the play. However, children walk away and there is a general hullabaloo in the audience as they want to see more acting. The actors go on to sing two more songs and then everyone is ready for the next play. This play also, is about bonded labour, but is improvised by the group based on an actual event that happened in a village. It is about a landlord who demands that the five year old son of his bonded labourer come to his home to graze his cattle. By the time the play ends it is close to midnight and people are sleepy. The programme closes for the night. Next day, people talk about the play in the fields, by the fireside and the tea stalls.

This programme goes on for nights. And then the groups moves to another village. During the rainy season (July-August) and the extremely warm (May) and cold (January) months the group does not visit villages. At all other times they move from village to village performing plays. At times the fieldworkers in the various regional branches invite the group to perform plays on the specific issues dealt with in their programmes.

The Lok Samiti has just one group covering nearly 200 villages. Most probably, the group may never return to the same village again!

2. Social Work and Research Centre (SWRC), Tilonia

Tilonia, a desert area, is in Rajastan, a state in the north-west. SWRC was founded in 1977 by Bunker Roy, a trained social worker and human rights activist. It has now five regional branches. Besides the various activities in the villages, the centre also concentrates on training those interested in rural development. From providing technical services the centre has now developed as an agency for promoting groups of rural women, artisans, marginal farmers and members of scheduled castes to organize themselves and realize their own potential.

The communication department of SWRC comprises a group of competent rural performers who have combined the traditional art of puppetry, acting, story-telling, singing and performing with their commitment to social change. When Shankar Singh, the main inspiration on the cultural front, jointed SWRC in 1981 his main concern was the survival of these local traditions. His commitment has since developed political overtones. Other members of the troupe, Ram Lal and Chottu Ram, who were professional puppeteers, Babu Lal, a drummer and Banwa Gopal, a painter of Rajastani miniatures and a graphic designer of some standing, also got involved in the venture. The last member, Ghasi Ram, was a revenue and land officer at the village level. Being in the group helped them discover their own commitment to their fellowmen as artists and social workers.

In sharp contrast to the harshness of the desert and the equally harsh realities of the caste system and landlessness, the people of the area have generated a life-style rich in colour, music and design. Their bright apparel is not only symbolic of their determination for survival but also conceals from the unsuspecting eye of the outsider their daily struggle to make both ends meet.

Puppetry is the main tool of their theatre. In the villages where SWRC is active, the people respond to the form instantly. Historically puppetry in India is considered a low caste occupation. The traditional arena for puppeteers and their act was the courts of kings and queens; they depended on the patronage of the monarch. This was reflected in the content of the puppet programmes which glorified and justified the hierarchical order in society. As the group's brochure points out:

The puppet was born in the palace and to this day tells the tales of kings and gods. A lot of theatrical performances are controlled by religious organizations making society all the more rigid and conventional, hardening attitudes and stalling the keenness for change.

Given this historical background and the position puppetry occupies even now in Indian society, the way the group makes use of this art form is very different from what it was originally meant for. They have moved it away from palaces and from playing to amuse the upper castes, to playing in front of the landless lower castes, the poor, the Harijans. Also, instead of telling the tales of gods, the puppets now challenge the order they once glorified.

As professionals, it was only natural for the SWRC team to use puppetry, especially when plays had to be readied at short notice. However, now dialogue dramas are also part of the repretoire, to cater to the needs of everyone. They have also realized that puppetry offers only limited opportunities for audience involvement.

3. Association for the Rural Poor (ARP)

The Association for the Rural Poor in northern Tamil Nadu (1971), was the inspiration of Felix Sugirtharaj, an ex-pastor and his five companions. They were all educated, enlightened Harijan Christians and adherents of a church that was ready to work for the poor, but not willing to go all the way. It was this half-heartedness of church that forced Sugirtharaj, a doctorate holder in Development Studies from the University of Chicago, to relinquish his pastoral duties and form a group to work with the Harijans and landless peasants of Chingelpet District. Initially the group was called Action for Cultural and Political Change (ACPC). They had to choose a more innocuous name, and renamed the group the Rural Community Development Association (RCDA), during the Emergency (1975-77) when the government's crack-down on radical social groups was the order of the day. As funds from abroad encouraged social activists all over India, the RCDA's work became more decentralized. In 1980, the more motivated assistants of Sugirtharaj opened new centres at different areas of Tamil Nadu. The original group is now known as Association for the Rural Poor (ARP).

Initially the group worked only among a few villages of Chingelpet District. From 1980, ARP spread to North and South Arcot Districts. This was in addition to the numerous other villages in which the newly formed groups were involved. A number of unions for agricultural labourers, fishermen, women and other 'front' activities like orphanages, dispensaries and homes for the disabled have been established during this period of expansion and the people have cooperated with these ventures admirably. ARP's headquarters are in Madras while its training and rural centres remain at Ambakkam, a village in Andhra Pradesh four miles away from the Tamil Nadu border.

ARP's work in theatre has centred mostly around organizing the landless and Harijans, following Freire's methods of literacy and cultural action. Children, youth, women and adults were organized in various groups around specific issues. Theatre became one of the tools for bringing the people together. ARP was in fact one of the first groups in India to use theatre in such a creative fashion. Initially the plays were quite simple and followed a pattern designed by the group.

One of the popular formats initiated in 1976 was a dramatic presentation in four episodes, like a serial strung out over several weeks. This gave the audience ample time to reflect over the questions posed, before these were analysed in the next episode.

The first act concentrates on the lives of the Harijans in the village and follows up with a discussion on their problems like untouchability, unemployment, lack of drinking water and their attitude towards the landlords. Skits emerge where the landlord confronts the Harijans. This 'act' lasts for several days and is followed by an exchange of views by the audience. By observing as well as participating in these fora the villagers begin to comprehend the various facets of their problems. They bring to their own consciousness their repressed perceptions as well as an awareness of the reasons (fear, lack of self-esteem and organization) for internalizing their problems vis-a-vis the landowners and other powerful figures. The second act emphasizes the need for unity among the Harijans if they are to bring their problems before higher authorities. The third act focuses on the oppression in the village hierarchy. The landowners, merchants and local government officials are easily identifiable as the culprits. These presentation enable the Harijans to understand the structures of oppression inherent in their society far more clearly. In the final act the methods by which the corrupt and malicious state of affairs may be transformed are explained and enacted. The emphasis is often laid on the ability of the Harijans themselves to solve their problems. The remedies include: finding the most appropriate way to petition the landlord for a redressal of their grievance, making sure that negotiations are conducted on a basis of equality, seeing through the negotiations are conducted on a basis of equality, seeing through the designs of the landlords and preventing themselves from being trapped by the oppressors.

Intensive attempts were made to train village leaders. Gradually a group of 'action initiators' emerged who met in the evenings for a deeper analysis of the problems of the village and to see what concrete steps might be taken. Several of their plans were dramatized to evaluate their efficacy. Attempts were also made to encourage a distinctive Harijan culture and to show it as something different, noble and worth adopting. Here local folk forms were introduced.

ARP's format became so popular that various other action groups in the country learnt from them. The group members also attended a number of international workshops on theatre for consciousness raising. Foreign researchers like Ross Kidd, Kevin Burns and others visited them and exchanged ideas with the group. The branching out of the group in 1980 to seven other areas did not disrupt the group. They met often and later, in 1983, developed different forms of theatre under different leaders. The existing group of 24 players were divided according to their talents into four sub-groups dealing with folk theatre, historical and political theatre, problem-oriented theatre and lastly the silent theatre.

(i) Folk theatre

This group was headed by two senior animateurs Perumal and Chinnathambi and had ten members in all. They were quite knowledge-able in the folk forms of the area like *therukoothu, swamiyattom* and *kathakalakshepam.* However, their adaptations did not stop with the content but distorted the forms too, showing a disdain for the traditional folk forms.

(ii) Historical and political theatre

Headed by Jeyaraj and Prabhu, this six-member team was the most proficient. Their plays analysed the current socio-political issues in a way the people could grasp. A number of discussion sessions with the audience enlivened the proceedings.

(iii) Silent theatre

Anandan, a senior animateur was the brain behind this form. Mime, freeze, slow motion and a few more techniques evolved from street theatre were used to enable the group to express their ideas through body movements and facial expressions. But it was rather dull and not particularly appreciated in the villages.

(iv) Socially oriented theatre

This form was headed by an independent theatre activist, Gunasekharan, with experience in conventional theatre. The plays analysed social issues, same as group (ii) but the enormous expenses involved and the long preparation time were handicaps.

These groups concentrate on regular workshops for village workers and occasional seminars for other SAGs. In the workshops the animateurs reinforce the sessions with informative talks on the socio-political structure in the villages. They also organized an international seminar on Popular Theatre in 1983. These efforts have helped develop theatre as a medium of considerable importance in their social awareness work. Their plays have an earthy and realistic quality about them. Despite the poor use of folk theatre, the topics of the plays are relevant. The mode of presenting the plays has shown some improvement over the years.

The players visit the villages on foot, at times on cycles, for an evening programme. At other times, all the players are taken to the village by ARP vehicles and are picked up after the show is over

These three groups—Lok Samiti, SWRC and ARP—typify theatre activities of action groups in India. Next, one must examine the themes that are treated in these plays.

II. Theme Analysis

The SAGs are obviously involved in developing awareness among oppressed classes to issues affecting their lives. This is not to disregard other action groups which are concerned with specific issues like environment, forestry, women's rights, or minority rights. Although India is vast and the people are culturally poles apart, the basic issues of concern are the same for all the action groups. That is why plays improvised by one SAG, can be used by several other groups.

In India, where the government participates in development theatre it is necessary to distinguish between the themes and the methodology of government sponsored plays and SAG plays. Basically, themes like nation-building, civic education, health, family planning, agricultural extension, co-operative education, community development, literacy, land and agrarian reforms, resettlement, social welfare, university extension, employment creation, radio schools and media usage are dealt with in the plays of the SDD, the Department of Advertising and Publicity and the publicity divisions of state government.

But the themes dealt with in the SAG plays are often more fundamental. For instance in India, land is wealth. Therefore, the patterns of landsholding and the land ceiling acts have immense implications for the landless people. In 1985, ARP was involved in regaining land for some Harijan workers. In the area around Ambakkam a large number of Harijan labourers worked on the fields of rich Reddiars and Naidus (both higher castes). These caste landlords had appropriated for themselves or donated to temples vast plots of common land. In January 1985, through a series of plays ARP animateurs persuaded the Harijans that this land belonged as much to them as to the higher castes by showing how the upper castes had cheated them out of this land. Encouraged, over 100 Harijan families occupied nearly 500 acres and have stood firm despite threats from the police and the upper castes.

Another very revealing play, *Parivartana* (1983) by the Young India Project (YIP), Andhra Pradesh is based on an actual case. In 1974, K. Raju, a rich, high caste man sold 150 acres of forest land, belonging to the government, to a merchant in Madras after bribing the local *tehsildar* (dispenser of land-rights, appointed by the government). Later, realizing his folly, the merchant mortgaged 55 acres of the land to a bank and ran away, after giving the bank manager 5 acres as bribe. Since he was not heard of any more, Raju sold the same land to another businessman from Madras. When the elections came in 1979 Raju asserted that the Harijans had a right to this land. Naturally it was not easy for the Harijans to occupy the land. Questions were raised about the ownership of the land and the matter was taken to court. Meanwhile, Raju got away scot-free. Among other things, the plays exposed how the poor are manipulated by the power-holders and how the government turns a blind eye to such injustices.

SWRC's play *Garib Ki Maar* (1983) using the medium of puppets, is also about oppression at different levels.

Dhukal, a poor man, goes to graze his cattle on a plot of land allotted to him under a government scheme for the benefit of those living below the poverty line. Mewa a rich man, shouts at Dhukal and claims that he is the rightful owner of the land. Dhukal's argument that he pays tax on the land holds no water with Mewa. Dhukal is forced to give up his land.

Disappointed, he returns home. The Secretary of the village cooperative, from whom Dhukal had borrowed to invest in the newly allotted land, asks for repayment of the loan. Dhukal says that the has paid his dues to the previous Secretary but is unable to produce a receipt as he was not given one. The Secretary warns Dhukal of dire consequences if he does not pay up within the next few days. Next, the revenue officer comes for the land tax. Dhukal tries to tell him about his problems with Mewa but such details do not interest the officer. Dhukal must find the money or else face the court. Dukhal is totally at a loss; he must pay for a land he does not possess. His wife advises him to borrow from the money-lender as a last resort. The money- lender is only too happy to lend the money, provided Dhukal mortgages his house. The poor man has no option but to agree. On his paying the dues a second time the officer asks him to go and claim the allotted land. Dhukal goes to plough the land. Mewa comes and a fight ensues. Mewa kills Dhukal. A shepherd, Cheta sees the incident, but runs away, frightened. Villagers gather around Dhukal's body. They suspect foul play but do not want to get involved with the law. So they hasten to cremate him. The wife names Mewa as the culprit, but no one listens to her and Dhukal's body is taken away. Cheta reports the matter to the police, but is afraid to name Mewa. The constable accuses Cheta of the crime and beats him up. Eventually they agree to investigate the case in the village. The wife is questioned. On mentioning Mewa's name she is scolded for defaming a respectable man. She is accused of having conspired to kill her husband because of a lover and advised to keep quiet. Meanwhile the money-lender and his men throw her belongings out of the house her husband had mortgaged.

Adaptation of this play have been tried in other villages followed by animated discussions.

Wage discrimination, bonded labour and physical brutality form another series of themes. The landlords grow rich at the expense of the laboures whom they pay paltry wages. This theme is central to several plays. For example, in a play often staged by the Rural Development Advisory Services (RDAS), Andhra Pradesh, a real life situation is presented. A number of villagers work in a landlord's field. In the evening when wages are to be paid it is seen that there is a vast difference between the wages of the Harijans and those of the higher castes. A Harijan youth protests and is quietly told not to come to work any more. The next day when his friends are about to stage a strike, they are reminded that it is they who will ultimately suffer. When the protestors persist, the landlord's henchmen beat them up. In the end the Harijans give in and agree to work for lower wages. Although the play ends on a pessimistic note, its message is clear: in their fight against injustice, the Harijans must stand together. The play offers no easy solutions but presents the problems in a cogent and telling manner.

Another popular play in the same genre is Premchand's *Sawa Ser Gehun*. A Brahmin priest visits a poor village. A devout villager asks him to stay in his home for the night. It is generally considered auspicious to offer hospitality to a priest. Since he does not have good quality wheat in his home, he searches all over and finally finds the right sort in a rich Brahmin's house. Later, the wheat is returned in full measure. However, the Brahmin leaves it unrecorded and the villager, being illiterate, does not notice it. Years later the Brahmin demands the wheat, this time calculated at its highly inflated value, piled up in interest. Because the villager is unable to pay back the amount, the Brahmin who has by now grown avaricious and greedy, carries away all the animals and utensils from the poor man's home. The Brahmin frightens the poor man by saying that if he doesn't keep him happy the gods will punish him. The puzzled villager gives him everything he has. Not satisfied, the Brahmin demands that the poor man work in his home as a bonded labourer. He takes away his wife too and tries to molest her. In the end, when the Brahmin comes to take the brother and son, they revolt and attack him.

The story describes the condition of some of today's Indian villages very clearly. Aspects like illiteracy, bonded labour, religious traditions and their misuse by Brahmins and others in power have been woven into the fabric of this play. Wherever staged, the villagers have watched it spell-bound.

One of the popular plays in the repertory of READ, Bihar, is *Aadhunik Ramlila* (1984). The play, devised by the group, focuses on the popular religious myth of Ram and his victory over the vicious king Ravan. Woven in with this is the story of a present-day village where the misdeeds of another demon, the local landlord (played by the same actor who plays Ravan) assume diabolic proportions.

The play opens with the citizens of Janakpuri complaining of the drought—a common phenomenon in Bihar. The heavenly messenger, Narad, tells the king that if everyone, including the king, ploughs the earth with respect, rains will come. As king Janak ploughs, Sita, the would-be wife of Ram emerges from the earth. Meanwhile, Ravan the embodiment of all evils reigns supreme while Ram continues his crusade for justice. In the next scene, the landlord, resembling Ravan, brutally punishes bonded labourers. He also persuades the village social worker to hand over to him the lucrative housing projects for Harijans. As the Ram story unfolds, the landlord is elected as the local MLA. In the final confrontation Ram wins over Ravan and calls on the people to fight for justice at any cost.

While one of the two parallel themes appeals to the villagers' religious sentiments and is a depiction of the victory of righteousness over evil, the play argues that in today's scenario where exploitation and corruption are rampant, only the concerted efforts of the poor can guarantee justice. Obviously it is a theme that goes down well with the audience most of whom are deeply religious. To interpret Ram as the liberator of the masses may sound revolutionary to some. By the same token to portray Ram as an ordinary hapless human being may hurt the sensibilities of many others. Whatever the response, the fact remains that the oppressed found in the play elements which helped them identify with their hero, Ram and the group succeeded beyond doubt in introducing a social theme into an epic which often upholds retrograde values.

Caste discrimination is another major problem tackled in these plays. It is not so much a case of lower castes being segregated or denied entry to public places, as the attempt of the higher castes to concentrate all the efforts of development in their part of the village. For example, in *Aaj Yahaan* (1984) by Lok Samiti, the village council decides to apply for a new tube well. The higher castes insist that it should be dug in their courtyard which is out of bounds to the lower castes. The local school master, himself a low caste, takes up the matter and is murdered. The Harijans, in a state of panic, bow to the decision of the upper castes.

The fact that almost every play staged by these groups touches upon the caste system shows how deeply this problem is ingrained in the Indian villages. Often one hears about brutal murders of Harijans, burning down of entire Harijan villages and, at times, of cruel punishments meted out to them like cutting off their arms and feet or slicing off their eye-balls—all in retaliation for some minor acts of protest.

A strong motif for protest is derived from one of the sub-plots from the *Mahabharata*. In the epic Eklavya is a low caste young man keen on archery. He asks Drona the mighty teacher of the Pandavas to train him in the art. But he is turned away as he is of low birth. Undaunted, he practices strenuously before a mud statue of Drona in the forest and becomes a great archer. Years later when the Pandavas visit the forest on a hunting expedition with their dog, Eklavya sends an arrow into the barking dog's open mouth and pierces its tongue. When the identity of the archer is revealed, he is challenged by the Pandavas but Eklavya gets the better of them all. A humiliated Drona demands that since he learnt the art before his statue he needs to pay an offering. Eklavya is willing to pay anything. The cruel master tells him to cut off his thumb, the part of the hand that grips the arrow.

Several progressive SAGs have used this story to evoke a sense of revolt and protest in the Harijans' minds. Plays on caste conflict normally draw heavily from everyday life. An observant theatre practitioner cannot but see the numerous incidents of caste discrimination happening all around him in the villages. In fact they are so ubiquitous that the people hardly notice them. READ, Bihar, staged a play *Hum Sub Ek Hain* (1988) on various incidents of caste discrimination. In the school a teacher asks the low caste students to sit at the back. In a shop a Harijan is given tea in a mud cup. An animateur visiting a Brahmin family is offered yoghurt in a tumbler borrowed from a Harijan family. The audience, mostly Harijans, saw nothing embarrassing about these events. Only when the animateurs began to analyse the issue after the play did the villagers start realising the enormity of the injustice.

In India a poor man without education is a prey to exploitation in all its forms. In *Bali Ka Bakara* (1986) staged by Rural Development Programme (RDP), Bihar, a poor villager's goat, his only source of livelihood, is stolen. He reports the matter to the local policeman who demands Rs. 50 for his services. After some haggling the amount is reduced to Rs. 30. The villager tries hard to raise the money but without success. A money-lender offers to help him if he pays Rs. 5 per month as interest. In the end, some local leaders organize a fund raising drive. They raise as much as Rs. 90 and hand over Rs. 30 to the poor man. However, when he goes to the policeman to get his goat back, the policeman's cook tells him that the goat was eaten a month back at a feast in honour of a senior police officer to win his favour.

In the same vein, in *Murda* (1987) staged by Alok, Bihar, a beggar dies on the village road. As a sign of respect for the dead man, the villagers contribute towards the cremation. A group of youngsters use the opportunity to collect money for themselves and throw the dead body into a nearby river.

Both these plays reveal the helplessness of the poor and pose questions like, "Should this continue? Can you do something about it?" to the audience.

Another theme that exposes corrupt officials and is found in the repertory of most of the groups concerns a Block Development Officer (BDO) who informs his peers that a particular village is in urgent need of a well. He gets the money sanctioned to dig the well. However, he does not get the well dug. After a few years he is transferred and a new officer comes in. As he leafs through the files he notices that a well had been sanctioned but not dug. He informs his superiors that the well dug a few years back in the village has become insanitary due to a nearby sewage and advises closing it down for the safety of the villagers. Finally the money is granted for the closure of the well that was never dug. He, no doubt, keeps the money.

Such incidents are almost everyday happenings in the villages. By portraying them the villagers are made aware that government officials should not be blindly trusted.

III. SDD and SAG Plays

Several SAGs have staged plays on themes which have already been dealt with by the Song and Drama Division and other official media groups, such as unity, cooperation, small savings, alcoholism, communal harmony and superstition. Ideally, there should be a marked difference in the treatment of the topics. This presents quite a challenge.

SAGs try not to present a final solution to these problems in their plays. In a play on alcoholism for instance, the SDD may well go on to suggest not only the evil of alcoholism, but may present forcibly the only way of tackling the problem. SAGs in sharp contrast, explore the problem and leave the audience to seek solutions. This methodology not only respects the sensibilities of the villagers but also leaves them with the responsibility for their own well-being.

Of late some SAGs, recognizing the importance of using theatre as a tool for developing the consciousness of the people, have begun to encourage the villagers themselves to act in the plays instead of a visiting outside group. In some SAGs animateurs train the villagers to analyse issues and to improvise plays through discussion. This places the responsibility squarely on the villagers themselves. The SDD, which is a government body, presents a certain official point of view, which is thrust upon the people. The official point of view safeguards the statusquo, namely that of a divided country—roughly 15% rich, 25% rather well-off and the rest struggling to make both ends meet. Inevitably, one can hardly expect the government to advocate any revolutionary changes. In sharp contrast, the *raison d' etre* of the SAGs is to encourage reflection leading to structural changes. Hence when SDD and other allied groups advocate family planning methods, fertilizer usage in agriculture and eating healthy vegetables, SAG theatre groups ask that the poor be given equal opportunities with the rich, that social inequalities be abolished and corrupt government officials brought to justice.

The SDD plays are often conceived within government ministries in capital cities where bureaucrats prepare the scripts, with hardly any contact with the target communities. SAGs on the other hand are based in the villages—although several have their administrative centres in the cities—and to some extent have first hand knowledge of the problems of the villagers.

The SDD employs groups from outside whose adaptations to local language and folk idioms often seem ridiculous to the villagers. In SAGs, attempts have been made to unearth local talent and to utilize local language and idioms. This has helped to ensure follow-up programmes. In the case of the SDD there is only a one-off performance, at the end of which leaflets with guidelines for action are distributed.

Another crucial difference is in the concept of theatre itself. Although SAGs began like the SDD by concentraing on the final production, a few SAGs have altered the plays according to the specific requirements of the villagers. There have been cases when standard scripts were changed to make them more appropriate for the audience. In principle, some SAGs accept that it is not the production itself but the process of producing the play that enables social analysis. At times the plays keep changing as the understanding of the audience about the issue deepens.

SAGs have initiated post-performance discussions, seminars and workshops for the audience, to help them understand the dimensions of the problems. By comparison, the SDD appears to be merely selling messages to the poor.

SAG theatre practitioners are conscious that there needs to be a sharing of visions, ideologies and strategies with the people. However, often these visions and ideologies are not really compatible with the concrete situation and mind-set of the people and if the people do not comprehend, the sharing turns out to be an imposition.

IV. The Form of SAG Theatre

There are constant debates as to which theatre form is most acceptable in the villages. It has already been pointed out that street theatre activists visit the villages occasionally in some parts of India. Hence villagers are not totally unfamiliar with this form. Folk theatre and Western conventional forms have also been popular in the village.

1. Street Theatre Forms

Due to the visits of several street theatre practitioners to the villages, the villagers have come to accept a theatre without the paraphernalia of stage and sophisticated techniques, which relies more on mime, freeze, slow motion and other participative elements. Sircar claims that several activists like Poonachandra Rao (Chalanam, Andhra Pradesh), Shivasanthakumar (KEDS, Tamil Nadu), Sr. Claire (Palmera, Tamil Nadu) and Debashish Chakravarthy (Aruna Theatres, Calcutta), all of whom were his former students, have succeeded in translating the form of street theatre to village productions. In the theatre section of Comprehensive Rural Operation Service Society (CROSS) and Rural Development Advisory Service (RDAS), Rao has given over 30 workshops on the use of theatre techniques in village animation theatre. In the workshops of Dynamic Action (Kerala), a Christian SAG, street theatre techniques are taught to village cadres. In the same way the Programme for Community Organization (PCO), Trivandrum also trains their activists who work with fishermen in street theatre techniques. YIP has experimented with various forms of theatre and has found the street theatre mode the most satisfying. Ganguly, a cultural activist at the Penukonda branch, sums up:

We organized a workshop in street theatre for some cadres in 1982. Through this workshop we learnt the importance of non-verbal communication and how the body, through various movements and rhythms taken from the people's culture, can communicate non-verbally. This also helped to understand the difference between proscenium and ground level theatre. By the latter we mean at the level of the masses and in which the masses can also participate. We are slowly becoming aware of the vast potentiality of a new kind of theatre which uses only body movements and rhythms and could be learnt by anyone and performed at no cost.[8]

In several of ARP's productions the action is 'frozen' in front of the audience. One of the animateurs comments on the image—a typical village situation—and then asks the audience questions to clarify ideas. The audience finds this format particularly fascinating.

2. Folk Theatre Forms

Among number of SAG theatre groups the incorporation of folk theatre techniques has become a passion. Following the example of the SDD and the IPTA which left no stone unturned in their zeal to explore the possibilities of the folk media to popularize their ideas, SAGs too have taken to various forms of folk theatre adaptations.

Most of the plays of the Association for Community Development by Learning and Doing (A CODE LAND), a SAG based in central Tamil Nadu, concentrate on using *therukoothu* — a form similar to the South Indian classical traditions of *kathakli* and *yakshagana* to analyse social issues using the *kattiyankaran* (stage manager-cum-jester) as the representative of the people. The form is normally espoused by the lower castes and is transmitted from family to family. The Aryans had, in the 7th century, learnt and adopted the form to spread their ideologies. They excluded womenfolk from the performances as unholy and polluting. Amaldoss, the main animateur, and his team conducted research into the possibility of adpating the content of *therukoothu* to socio-political issues. The Vidiyal Natak Sabha of the SAG has identified 53 professional troupes working in the villages of South Arcot and a Therukoothu Committee has been formed. Twelve troupes have trained to enact plays on social themes in a professional way using costumes, masks, and make-up. In its original form there are gods and demons vying for power. The group follows a similar pattern. Contemporary evils like corruption, superstition, illiteracy and lack of awareness have been depicted as *asuras* (demons) and the opposite qualities of unity, cooperation, and honesty as *devas* (gods). The *kattiyankaran* adds critical observations about the corrupt powers and other evils in the village. For instance, in the *Mahabharata* episode of the stripping of Panchali the *kattiyankaran* does not want the audience to assume divine intervention in real life. He poses questions like, "Can all Panchalis wait for Lord Krishna to come to their rescue? Can Lord Krishna afford to come to the ever-increasing number of Panchalis in distress?" He calls upon the people to take up the cause of the Panchalis and not to leave it to chance or divine intervention.

The plays have been shortened from night-long performances to between 2 and 3 hours. They have also introduced women back to the plays, which they have discovered, helps the development of village women. The committee has helped organize the hitherto scattered performers to fight for their legitimate rights against the upper classes, the police and the onslaught of the mass media on their art form.

One of CODE LAND's attempts at adapting the folk form has been quite innovative. The performers have been organized to form a group which can raise its voice to get certain benefits from the government, for example, scholarships for their children and recognition of their art form.

In Maharastra, Asha Kendra, headed by Ajit Murickan, has tried to make use of the traditional *yatra* forms to conscientize the people. Normally during a *yatra*, a socio-religious festival, the people of a village gather together, irrespective of caste and class. This has the symbolic value of upholding the unity and togetherness of the village. Murickan explains:

The traditional concept of *yatra*, the feelings and emotions it evokes have deep roots in the psyche of the masses. To understand the dynamics of the social process operating at the grassroot levels one has to delve deep into the roots of consciousness which are being shaped by a complexity of ideas, values and cultural forms in terms of which people both interpret the world and direct their activities. Even the social consciousness assumes the form of religio-cultural representations and still constitutes a dominant organizing principle of social life giving it unity, coherence and a system of meaning. Therefore any restructuring of social life necessarily entails restructuring of the traditional meaning systems.[9]

In the area in which Asha Kendra is working, many women are marginalized. They have been deserted by their husbands, for not bringing enough dowry, or for not bearing sons or because the husbands, who work in cities like Bombay and Pune, have found alternative families. It is in this context that in 1986, the team organized *Sthree Yathra*, a programme to educate rural women at the time of the annual religious *yatra*. The *yatra* lasted for 15 days. It started from the rural health centre at Mathulthan village. During the day there was an exhibition of charts and posters, health camps for women and children, identification of leprosy and tuberculosis cases and the setting up a Women's Council. Traditional folk forms used in Maharastra villages such as *powada, tamasha,* story-telling, *bhajan* singing, puppetry were used as cultural forms to highlight these issues. Evening programmes, lasting for 4 to 5 hours educated the audience in a most enthralling way. The teams in attempting to rivet the attention of the villagers on their own cultural expressions made the *yatra* a forcible form of communication. Various cultural activities in the traditional forms helped the people develop self-expression, overcome fears and difficulties and nurture a sense of identity, self confidence and consciousness as a community. Throughout the programme the team attempted to channel various socio-cultural activities for mobilization and consciousness raising of the masses against the onslaught of capitalist cultural influences.

Asha Kendra has shown that by concentrating on local media they can enable the people to take control of their own lives.

KSSP, although based in Trivandrum, has been more successful in the tribal and Harijan belts of Kerala. Folk forms like *ottamthullal, kakkasinatakam, chavittunatakam* and *mappilapattu* have been used extensively to put across their message. In one of the plays, *Parasuramapuram* (1981) done in *kakkasinatakam* form there is a severe indictment of the dowry system. A man who wants to marry off his daughter consults a friend. He is advised to go to Parasuramapuram market, where grooms are on sale. Some excerpts:

The announcer: "This is Parasuramapuram market. Here we trade in prospective sons-in-law."
"You want a doctor? How about this handsome boy? Only Rs. 400,000. No, that is not too much. His father says he gave Rs. 200,000 as capitation fee alone."
"I am afraid this boy would be beyond your means. He would cost Rs. 1 million. What do you say? May be he looks like a moron but he has property worth 2 million.[10]

In several of KSSP's plays it is the form that grips the audience— a fine blend of folk music, songs and ritual dances add colour and charm. For instance in a play about dowry deaths the girl's marriage is arranged by the parents. After that she is ill-treated and killed by her husband as she has brought in only a meagre dowry. The husband is represented in the play as a demon. The story may be weak, but in presentation the form makes up for it. The use of folk songs as a means of education has caught the imagination of the people. An opening song number of KSSP, quite popular all over Kerala, is based on a famous poem by Brecht. It exhorts the oppressed, the destitutes and the illiterates to arm themselves with the powerful weapon of knowledge: "Abandon blind faith and ask questions before you accept anything" is the recurring theme in the song.[11]

In another song, there is a portrait of a doctor living in an ivory tower far from social realities. To the audience he typifies the rudimentary medical facilities in the country beyond the reach of the average person. In *mappilapattu* form the people ask him:

Hey doctor, where did you get your education?
Your pearl-studded carpets and your glittering palace?[12]
Artists like Karivallur Murali and P. Thankappan Pillai of KSSP though craftsmen by profession are genuine folk artists with a keen revolutionary sense.

In ARP, adaptations of *therukoothu* have been tried by the Folk Theatre Group. They have quite a popular play about the powers of the king and the religious authorities over the people of feudal India. A poor oppressed villager, supported by his wife and the court jester organize the villagers and succeed in overthrowing the king and the religious leaders. Everyone understands this as an analogy for a corrupt political system. However, ARP's adaptations of the *therukoothu* format, without costumes, masks and make-up came under fire from several quarters as there was hardly any respect for the form.

This Calcutta based Centre for Communication and Cultural Action (CCCA), headed by Sanjib Sarcar with a rural base in Purulia, has experimented with several forms of folk dances like *chhau, machaani, karam panta* and song forms known as *jhumur*. In Jhargram, West Bengal, Soumen Roy and Jamini Mahato have also tried to analyse social issues using these forms. Unlike other forms of folk theatres these forms did not originate as the instruments of a dominant Brahmin class. Neither were they used as instruments of oppression. Even though they were addressed to the gods, and may have tended to make the people apathetic and dependent, they were in fact always fashioned to articulate the problems of ordinary people.

Several SAGs still feel it is safer to follow the format of Western theatre, similar to theatre in the villages as referred to in the beginning of this chapter. A number of folk performances are staged from a well set up stage with curtains, light effects and canned sound. Groups like Chorus, working in rural Bengal and suburban Calcutta and Rural Development Programme (RDP), Bihar, use this form more than any other. These groups are not so much unaware of the advantages of other modes of presentation as lacking in enthusiasm to explore newer forms.

The villagers themselves have created in their minds an illusion of theatre which is stage-bound, with all the 'effects' of a West End production. Other forms of experimental theatre are looked down upon as pure educational devices. Basically what really happens is that the magic of the stage-audience separation produces for the audience a world of make-believe, like the cinema but on a smaller scale.

V. Theatre Animateurs

There are theatre activists who do not necessarily belong to any particular SAG, but have taken up the theatre as a medium for building social awareness. They have trained themselves in theatre and have also developed a keen understanding of social issues. It is their conviction as activists that inspires them to team up with SAGs to train theatre groups. In the last two decades, with the SAGs proliferating, the number of animateurs has grown. Activists like Badal Sircar, Tripurari Sharma, Poornachandra Rao, Malati Rao, Rati Barthalomew and many others, all belonging to the upper caste and class, have abandoned lucrative academic or institutional positions and taken up the plight of the rural poor. To them theatre provides by and large a simple medium for awareness building and for generating discussion and participation on issues of community concern. It will be of interest to consider the efforts of a few animateurs.

I present the example of two animateurs among the many I met. I have chosen these two, one from the north and the other from the south, as they seemed to me to have understood the concept of Popular Theatre and to possess a clear methodology.

1. Tripurari Sharma

After graduating from the National School of Drama (NSD), Delhi, in 1979 Sharma did not turn to the theatre of the elite or to cinema as would a normal NSD graduate. She joined Laksmi Krishnamoorthy's Delhi based SAG, Alarippu, a group that specialises in low cost media for development workers in rural areas. Jointly they ventured into conducting workshops for action groups involved in the struggle of the poor in north India.

Sharma realizes that there is a philosophic basis to the people's culture. She understand that the 'poor, underprivileged and uneducated' people have created and sung songs for centuries about the beauty of nature, the sorrows of life, joys of love and the trials of famine, drought and migration. The written word seems to have no meaning for them, and is equally inadequate in expressing any single collective experience. Their legacy of wisdom and knowledge about the land and a world view have passed on from generation to generation without written documentation or transliteration. It exists in memory, music and imagery passing from one generation to another as an oral tradition. Very often what emerges is a way of life that advocates survival and not change. It is a down-to-earth approach, similar to home-made remedies, that may not have detailed diagnosis and radical cures but shows an awareness of the ills and how to overcome them, based on easily available ingredients. A philosophy ingrained in their culture is the vision that has helped them to counter adversities and survive to this day.

For Sharma this understanding of the rural psyche is crucial. Hence in her workshops her main objective is to simplify the process of making plays. The team, consisting of Krishnamoorthy and another helper, meet the people on their own grounds, without indulging in too many theatre games or aerobics. The people are encouraged to talk, share their lives in a free and informal atmosphere. As they talk, stories, characters and images emerge. When the proposal to do a play on a particular event is suggested the people are instantly attracted—a sign that the team has already gained the confidence of the group.

Extended research and explorations into folk theatre is not Sharma's methods. The emphasis is on available resources. If one person can sing and another dance, their talents are always channelled into the production.

The workshops with the SAGs are designed to highlight the process of participation using group dynamics, theatre games and analysing the responses of the participants at every stage. The workshops begin with a series of exercises designed to create an atmosphere where everyone can feel free to explore their creativity and express themselves frankly. In the workshops a number of improvisations are prepared and staged in nearby villages. The responses are gathered together to formulate guidelines for developing the exercises. Normally these workshops enable the participants to conduct similar workshops back in their own villages.

Sharma also conducts longer workshops for specialized groups, selected from cultural activists of various SAGs. This type of workshop normally has several phases:

1. A month-long training programme in one place where participants

live together. Apart from body movements, script writing and acting
they also visit villages and improvise on situations they observe,
sometimes working with the villagers.
2. After their return to the parent group the participants are   required
to work in their own area. After five weeks the resource people visit
them and help them in organizing further discussions, work out
problems and experiment with certain styles of presentation. This
may last for as long as four months.
3. At the completion of the second phase the trainees meet together
once more, for about 10 days, to share their experiences and in all
probability, decide on the possibilities of a regular link-up (A
detailed report of a Sharma workshop follows in the next section.)

Looking back to ancient times when performances were part of every
day life, Sharma contends that theatre can be used to analyse social
problems like poverty, minimum wage, health, environment and
education. She suggests that in order to make plays a viable form, the social
activists need to know the people and their problems well. She warns that
plays with a powerful contents can fail if the people do not have a
sufficient role in their preparation. Making plays has to be an occasion for
enlightening the villagers as well as the social activists. The aim of the
plays is not applause and appreciation, but involvement and questioning.
What is important is not the size of the audience, but the level and quality
of participation.

Sharma is in constant touch with the NSD repertory company and
other professionals to produce conventional plays on socially relevant
themes, using her own unique improvisational style. Her production of a
play on leprosy patients for the NSD repretory is worth noting. She
developed the concept of *Kaat ki Gaadi* (1984) from ideas, images and
characters gleaned from an earlier workshop she had given to the
leprosorium workers at Purulia, West Bengal. Unlike in a conventional
production, she presented the actors with pen pictures of characters.
After some homework which included a number of field trips, research
and interviews with patients, a story line was evolved. When some of the
actors resented the hard work involved, Sharma insisted that as communicators they have a role in providing information and service to society.
According to her, true artists cannot communicate anything in which they
themselves do not believe. By performing this play Sharma succeeded in
inculcating a sense of social   responsibility into   academic-minded
professionals. Sharma's other stage plays like *Aks Paheli* (1981), *Dahej*
(1982) and *Reshmi Rumal* (1985) and the script for the much acclaimed

film *Mirchmasala* (1987) have made her a name to reckon with even in mainstream media. Sharma is also active in the street theatre movement. However, it is her work with the rural masses that needs more attention. Observing Sharma at work with the cultural team of SWRC of Rajastan at the Tara Arts auditorium in London in 1986, Oga Abah commented:

Sharma should be seen as an invigorator to the group in two different ways. She gives voice to the poor women of India who in spite of being a strong labour force in the home, in the fields and in work sites are the oppressed within the oppressed. Her membership validates the role of the women in deciding social and economic issues.

On the second level, Sharma's abandonment of the pleasures consequent on being born a Brahmin points to the injustice of the system which she has very strongly recognized and vehemently opposes. The conscientization workshops which Sharma organizes for members of scheduled castes and especially those for women are geared towards understanding and dealing with the social system under which they have no respite.[13]

After working for over a decade with SAGs Sharma believes that few action groups have really understood how powerful a means of education theatre can be. Misguided by their organizational compulsions, foreign aid and governmental manipulations several SAGs are more intent on building up their own structures, forgetting their main thrust, namely to organize the rural poor. Sharma observes:

Communication through theatre cannot bring about change because change has its own dynamics. But what it can do is focus attention on issues, keep certain events like the Bhopal gas tragedy alive in public memory and be a means to understanding certain attitudes.[14]

Referring to the Tilonia Kala Jatha organized by the cultural team of SWRC in 1988, which focused on drought and related questions of employment and environment, Sharma writes:

Through all the meetings a positive thought is emerging—people want to focus the issues of the 63 villages as one voice. They feel that isolation is weakening them. To tell hungry people that it is a long difficult march to their piece of bread is not saying very much. Yet that is the truth. During the workshop, when we had performed the plays for the first time someone remarked: "It is all very good, but there is no message." And we had involuntarily asked, "Can we possibly have a message? Can we claim to have an answer?" The question was with us throughout the *jatha*.[15]

Sharma's search for a relevant methodology continues.

2. Poornachandra Rao

An activist from his early university days, Rao has been involved in merging various street and folk theatre elements to form a suitable form of rural theatre in the southern state of Andhra Pradesh. He began his work in 1981 with RDAS, a co-ordinating body of several action groups. Initially a film enthusiast, he began using socially relevant films to initiate discussions among the rural masses. At first he was weighed down with problems of carrying around film projection equipment and coping with failing electricity supplies in the villages. However, through his contacts with the villagers he discovered the enormous acting talent and performing traditions among them and chose the medium of theatre to reach the rural poor more effectively and meaningfully. Initially, professional theatre practitioners like Sircar and Sharma were invited to conduct workshops for select groups. Learning from these experts, Rao designed a method of training groups in the villages. The many theatre games proposed by Sircar and improvisation techniques of Sharma were combined. Attempts were made to generate confidence among the local groups by employing traditional folk expressions. Contemporary themes concerning the rights of the working and peasant classes were inserted into traditional forms like *voggukatha* and *burrakatha*.

In a ten-day workshop (1982) for nearly 25 field workers, attempts were made to experiment by integrating elements of folk expression. By the end of the seventh day each of the participants, had devised a play with the assistance of other members of his group, who were all from the same SAG. The last two days were spent in revising and completing a selected script. On their return, a team of five was asked to launch a troupe.

Later it was felt that it might be hard for a person from a village, with hardly any education and on the basis of one week of theatre training, to form a theatre troupe in the village. Hence in the next stage of the workshop (1983-84), Rao and his team concentrated on field workshops — visiting the various SAGs under RDAS, spending time with the core groups of players and others like the night school teachers, field workers and some prominent villagers (men and women). This form of field training helped the process of establishing theatre in the villages. Attempts were made to follow up on the field workshops. Each group was advised to devise a complete play every two months.

There efforts did a lot to enhance the conscientization work begun by the SAGs under RDAS. Mohan Rao, a senior education co-ordinator of CROSS, a sister organization of RDAS observed:

The people are receiving the plays on caste and quarry workers' problems very well. They really move them. The caste problem has created commotions wherever staged. The plays on Harijan reservations cause some trouble. The pro-establishment Harijan leaders are using these plays to propagate against CROSS. Their contention is that CROSS is insulting Harijans by enacting such type of plays in which too much subservience on the part of the Harijan is shown.[16]

At the insistence of Rao a number of SAGs appointed co-ordinators to organize theatre teams for regular activities in the villages in 1984-85. A number of younger cadres capable of running workshops emerged in the villages. Several groups under the purview of RDAS and CROSS had by now begun active theatre work. It was noticed, however, that the activities of all these groups came to a standstill when the landlords or government officials intervened. The groups would then switch over to vague and non-controversial issues like co-operation and health care.

Since RDAS had nearly 40 groups under its sponsorship it was not possible to reach out to all of them. Regional workshops were therefore organized for 10 to 12 groups at a time. For example, in 1983-85 such workshops were organized in Rayalaseema, Telengana and Hyderabad. However, the results of workshops were not very encouraging. Rao's groups were more or less convinced that field training was the only effective means of propagating the methodology. By this time Rao had begun touring other states and regions in south India on invitation, conducting workshops for other SAGs.

During his five-year long association with RDAS, Rao began questioning Popular Theatre as practised in the SAGs. He was finding it increasingly hard to understand why a middle class catalyst like himself should dictate to the villagers on how to perform plays about their lives.

Being a member of RDAS-CROSS he had to take orders from above. Besides, it was becoming increasingly difficult to concentrate on 40 or so groups at a time. So in 1986 he quit the organization to found Chalanam— a cultural forum for the rural poor. Financially helped by a friend whose foreign—aided organization sponsored cultural activists, Rao began to concentrate his efforts on fewer groups—all radical and leftist and obviously more committed than the RDAS-CROSS amalgam of SAGs. These were the two YIP teams in Penukonda and Sri Kalahasthi, a tribal group in Srikakulam with Naxalite leanings and a Telengana group of bonded labourers in Rangareddy District.

Rao was keen to concentrate on themes that were specific to the groups. Discussions with field-workers revealed that issues like bonded labour, land-grabbing, employment generating schemes and minimum wages were the major preoccupations in the area. Rao was particularly pleased with the earnestness of the local groups which had a sound tradition in follow-up activities, and is still optimistic about the way things are moving.

In 1986, in the Macchlipattanam area, working with the fishermen who are constantly under threat from the Birla groups, Rao has built up a powerful theatre group that has been struggling against all odds to fight for their rights. The local people are well motivated and the theatre group leads from the front in identifying issues and rallying the people around them. Rao has kept away from the group after the initial workshops in order to allow it to stand on its own but is in constant touch through letters and visits from the fishermen to his Hyderabad home.

In Chittor District, a YIP theatre group animated by Rao mobilized nearly 2,000 agricultural labourers around the issue of 110 acres of land unjustly appropriated by one Obviraju Kandriga. In early 1988 sit-ins, strikes and relay hunger strikes were still going on to persuade the local authorities to act against such a blatant act of land-grabbing.

Another of Rao's successful experiments was to get the real victims of oppression to act out their experiences in the plays. Very often their oppressors would be part of the audience and would disrupt the show by shouting and stone-throwing. However, Rao believes that such confrontations do help in the eventual consciousness raising of the villagers.

In Rangareddy District one of the YIP teams conducted a theatre workshop with a group of 15 bonded labourers in 1987. They enacted a recent event of their village. A 50-year old bonded labourer enacted the role which he in fact lived in reality. The village has a group of Harijans (bonded labourers), Kurmas (middle caste) and Reddys (high caste). Since the Reddys despise the Kurmas, they patronize the Harijans. One day an ox belonging to the Kurmas got into a Reddy field. A Reddy servant broke its legs. The Harijans who were witnesses to the incident spoke up for the Kurmas. But the Reddys took their servant's word. A fierce quarrel followed. In the court the Harijans spoke out against the Reddys, who were declared guilty. But they released the servant on bail, burned down the Kurmas' fodder heap and accused the Harijans of the crime. The Kurmas thrashed the Harijans and became more isolated. The Harijans tried to convince the Kurmas but did not succeed. When the police came to inquire, the Reddys won them over to the their side. They found a poor Harijan who was in dire need of some money to marry off his daughter. They paid him some money and asked him to own up to the crime. An irate Harijan community beat up the Harijan, who revealed the whole story. The Reddys, though not punished, were fully exposed.

In the enactment of this event the Kurmas and Harijans played their real roles, while the YIP field-workers played as the Reddys. According to Rao the play did enormously well in bringing home the message of unity and co-operation among the poorer classes and warding off oppression from higher castes.

After his experiences with Popular Theatre Rao feels that specialized drama groups, standard scripts and middle class catalysts who impose their ideologies need to be totally shunned if theatre is to grow. He observes that theatre is called 'popular' and yet is made up from standard, even published scripts and rehearsed behind closed doors as in a conventional play. Besides, he feels there are SAGs that have in their service semi-trained theatre groups, whose main task is to prepare plays by day and perform by night. Rao lashes out against this practice:

> There is a vast difference between theatre for the poor and theatre by the poor. Both have their roles, but at present most action groups are content with the former. This is simply because the middle class catalysts who even get paid for their work have been given a free rein.[17]

Rao is convinced that the poor villagers have both the content (their daily experiences) and the form (the rich folk theatre tradition) to perform plays. All they need is a catalyst who is sympathetic to their cause and can guide them to use their talents creatively for social awareness work. As for Rao's role as a catalyst, his only contribution, he claims, is in promoting the idea of staging a play about their own problems instead of borrowed scripts.

VI. Workshop Design

The pattern of workshops varies according to the expertise, experience and background of the animateurs, some of whom have learned from Sircar's experiments in 'third theatre'. Others like Sharma and Bartholomew have their experiences of working with villagers. A third group of animateurs, influenced by theories of Theatre-In-Education and other Western experiments, have developed their own techniques. However, depending on the target audience the format varies considerably.

Participants at a workshop may be divided into three categories: (1) Theatre activists who are middle class educated youngsters, keen on development. (2) SAG activists and field-workers with no theatre background. Again, most of them are middle class and make up for what they lack in academic education with enthusiasm. Nearly 50% belong to this category. (3) Villagers with natural acting talent. Often a mixed bag of all three groups attend a workshop.

After studying the practices of a number of animateurs it may be said that they follow a basic pattern:

1. Developing improvisational techniques using theatre games.
2. Integrating folk elements like singing, dancing, mime and other specific forms available in the area.
3. Playmaking: The process of studying a problem and dramatizing it using, images dialogues, movement, etc.
4. Play presentation before a target audience to collect responses which are used to develop the play further.
5. Learning a number of slogans and action songs with a revolutionary content.
6. Physical exercises to develop every part of the body so that body movements can be used as effective tools of expression. These exercises are normally done everyday in the morning.

Besides these, several action groups also emphasize the need to do social analysis. Although this is the most important element, not every animateur has a clear idea about it. Examining situations they are confronted with in the villages, the participants are taught to analyse them carefully and to identify the various forces influencing a particular action. Animateurs insist on discussion after the play has been presented. To a great extent this helps deepen the analysis.

In every workshop the initial session is made up of self-introductions and sharing the expectations for the workshop. After that, in the workshop proper, some emphasize techniques and others content. For instance, Sircar's workshops have been technique-oriented while Sharma, Rao and several others have concentrated more on concrete methods of play-making. Sircar's emphasis on abstract techniques, especially in his village workshops, has often been attributed to his lack of contact with the real problems of the villages. Being city-bred, his audience has mostly been the urban middle class.

1. A General Workshop for Field-Workers

In certain workshops, the making of a play is often a prelude to analysing particular aspect of society. For example in Tripurari Sharma's workshop with 40 field-workers from all over north India at the Sucheta Kripalani Siksha Niketan, Jodhpur (1981) she developed two plays on the scarcity of water and the problem of dowry in ten days.

On the first day, after the daily chores and exercises, the sessions began with removing the tables and chairs in the hall and everyone sitting in the round, on the carpeted floor. A clear and tight time table was drawn out for the next ten days.

The initial sessions were on the origin and the power of theatre in communication. A number of games were played to lessen inhibitions and bring out the best in every one. On the second day, in a brainstorming session, the participants suggested topics like adult education, dowry, the *purdah* system, water shortage, landlords, money-lenders, low wages and superstitions as the major problems of the villagers. Sharma told them briefly about certain points that they need to keep in mind while putting together the improvisations:

  (i)   the themes should be simple;
  (ii) the issue must be easy to understand;
  (iii) each character must be clearly identifiable;
  (iv) the improvisation should be appealing and not simply didactic.

The entire team was divided into five groups. After an hour-long session in groups the improvisations were presented and discussed. Two of these— the evils of dowry and water shortage—impressed the group as a whole. It was decided to divide the entire group into two and work on these two plays separately. During the next few days, planning for various scenes in these plays continued using techniques like mime, singing, dancing and freeze. A working script was finally prepared for each of the plays. In the following sessions the processes needed for putting a play together—imagination, body movement, continuity, co-ordination with others, tone and rhythm of speech were explored.

In the next stage some research was done in the villages in order to bring home the point that Popular Theatre is almost meaningless without proper knowledge of the people and their culture. In the context of the plays to be staged questions like: "How much land does a small farmer own? What sort of a house would he live in? How much debt would he have? How much dowry would he give his daughter? When is the dowry given? In what form? How many people come in a *barat* (guests at marriage from the bridegroom's side)?" were asked to find out more about the situation. All these and more were based on knowledge gained from nearby villages. Once these aspects were gathered the plays were broken down into sequences. For example, the dowry play went this way:

1. News of elder sister's death through burning because of dowry.
2. Songs. Passage of time.
3. Discussions regarding younger sister's marriage.
4. Search for bridegroom by uncle and pundit.
5. Tea shop dialogue between prospective bridegroom and friends. Bangle seller overhears them boasting of dowry.
6. Bangle seller comes from tea-shop to centre of village, repeats conversation. Dowry has been exaggerated but bride's mother says bangle seller must have heard wrong.
7. Bride is got ready, the *barat* arrives.
8. Demand for extra dowry.
9. Bride's father pleads, falls at the feet of bridegroom's father.
10. Bride steps forward, says she does not want this marriage.
11. The *barat* is chased away.

After this the songs were set to music. The participants then began improvising the scenes, with self-made dialogues, local humour and plenty of rural charm.

In the same way the 'water' was worked out by the other group.

On the fifth day both groups performed the plays for each other. Naturally, they were a shambles. The girls still seemed to be shy and inhibited. The next day special efforts were made to make them participate fully. After more practice both plays were staged on the seventh day in a village six miles away. For most of the trainees it was their first experience of performing in public. The audience, sat through the performance with great interest. Since the dialogues were in Hindi a Rajastani interpreter was employed to translate from time to time.

Back at the centre, they practised again with more stress on character building and performed once more in another village before they disbanded. At the evaluation of the ten-day effort the participants expressed great satisfaction in words like:

- "Didn't realize how one actor can become a number of characters."
- "Miming 'things', e.g. a pump, is a wholly new experience."
- "People have begun to express themselves, especially the girls, without worrying whether they might not be making sense."
- "Only at the end realized how physical exercises and improvisations fit into the whole thing."
- "Enjoyed letting oneself go— in the acting, in the dancing."
- "Thought villagers would never understand plays, but know better now."
- "Theatre is far more effective than speeches."
- " Never before thought of the relationship between actors and audience."

For the trainees the most important part of the workshop was the process of working up to the play. The performance itself was a necessary cathartic experience. More importantly, after the performances, they gained an enormous amount of confidence. This helped the group to continue to experiment further, back in their home villages.

2. A SAG Village Workshop

In this section a personal experience of conducting a workshop for a SAG is documented. In the absence of Badal Sircar whose wife took ill, I was drawn into conducting a workshop for Rural Education and Awareness Development (READ), in north Bihar. The workshop ran for eight days, 17-25 February, 1988.

READ was started in 1970 in Bettiah by the Jesuits working in north Bihar. In 1977, when the Janata government initiated the National Adult Education Programme (NAEP), READ was one of the main patrons of the programme in Bihar. Its work extended to as many as 900 villages and about half a million people. Later, with the funds for NAEP cut off by the Congress regime which came back to power in 1979, READ's work floundered. With a little help from foreign developmental agencies located in India it initiated training workshops in rural education. In 1984 it began a drama troupe, Chetna Natya Sangh, to educate the rural masses. The team consist of 8 paid actors from different villages and castes. They meet once a week at the READ headquarters with the director, animateurs and field-workers to prepare and rehearse plays. Their plays are either written by themselves or adapted from published sources. They are accustomed to playing from a conventional stage with curtains and makeshift sceneries.

The participants in the workshop were eight actors and other field-workers. I followed a methodology that I knew in theory only. Since the participants were good actors, my immediate concern was to give them an experience of preparing plays as a means of analysing social problems. I also wanted to bring home the point that it is in preparing the plays that one is conscientized.

The group of twenty-one, all men, was divided into three smaller groups. Each group was asked to present a play on any event they were familiar with. After an hour they presented their plays. Group 1 showed the effects of illiteracy and how the poor can be cheated by religious bigotry. The second play was about the need for unity in the village to stand against the higher castes and third was on the evil of the education system in the villages. All the plays had the following in common:

1. They were staged as from a proscenium, with the audience on one side.
2. They had stereotyped characters, like the village idiot, the wise old man, the wily landlord, etc.
3. They ended with a fine solution to the problem.
4. None of them had any songs, dances, or any other local flavour.
5. As far as possible they spoke in pure Hindi.
6. The acting was good, although at times they were somewhat off the mark.

It didn't take me long to realize that these plays had been done before by the READ drama group and that they were initially adapted from popular plays they had seen. We had discussions on each of the plays and none of them had anything much to add except, 'whatever happened is right.'

My immediate reaction was to take them through the same plays and show how in the process of making a play, one can analyse society. The groups were asked to stage their plays again, with three changes:

1. Imagine that the audience is sitting around you. Talk straight to them.
2. Highlight the problem in the play clearly and do not solve it.
3. As much as possible, be realistic in the acting and speak in the local dialect.

Now, for the sake of an example, I will follow one group only. The story for the first group is about a poor villager who is told by a local Brahmin priest to pay a large sum of money to a goddess for having killed a cat by mistake. When he reaches the temple the Brahmin's henchman gets hold of the villager, asks for a bribe and collects the offering for the Brahmin priest. The group failed to decide on the central problem. They were sent back to the nearest village to meet people and ask them if such an incident could happen in real life and if so why. After a day, they came back with the startling news that nearly 95% of the people said such things do happen. The reasons varied. Some said they are frightened of priests, others said people are illiterate and ignorant. Another group contended that cats are sacred to the gods and hence an offering is a must. Still another group talked about bribery. After gathering the information, the group was asked to find links between these issues and a deeper malaise in society. A number of theatre games, role plays and improvisations were used to zero in on certain aspects. Several facets of exploitation in the village came to the fore. A lot of soul-searching helped them become aware of the various levels of oppression and how they are interlinked. Next, I asked them to put across some of their new realizations in a form which is interesting to an audience. Imaginative ways were tried out through using some colourful local imagery. Eventually, the killing of the cat became an allegory for a small human error.

On the fourth day, they had a performance, closely following the three guidelines. The other groups responded with critical comments.

In the next stage, the participants were asked to include songs, available musical instruments and simple dance movements. This they did admirably well. One of the participants, volunteered to teach a harvest dance. It was quite easy to include songs as they knew several revolutionary action songs. Gradually they got used to moving with the rhythm of the songs. The third performance looked more interesting. The dialogues included the nuances of the discussions that preceded. The characters were based on real people they knew in the villages. Further discussions followed. And they went on to make more suggestions to make the play hard hitting. I asked them, what if they opened up the last part of the play to get the audience to suggest ways of solving the problem presented. They tried this and other group members came up with a number of improvisations.

The other groups also went on to recreate their plays in the same way.

On my return I wondered whether I had got them to do what I thought was the right method of doing Popular Theatre. But is that the right method? Would the participants have done better if I hadn't instructed them? Did I ask questions in a way as to elicit the very answers I had in my mind? For a moment my mind went blank. And then I realized, if I cannot be one with them, feel from their side, I cannot teach them methodology.

3. A Workshop Festival for Villagers

Here a typical ARP workshop is documented in which a number of villages are included. The purpose of the workshop is to reach out to a cluster of villages, half-a-mile apart, that have similar problems. The ARP animateurs and field-workers reach the first village, sing a few revolutionary songs and invite the people to join in the singing, improvisations and simulation games. These are followed by co-ordinators addressing the people. They explain the purpose of the workshops and emphasize that their aim is neither political nor simply to provide entertainment. The objective is to build an effective theatre group at the villages level, so that the people themselves can use this form as a means of analysing their situations. They are told about the ravages caused by the dominant cultures like film and other media in the villages. After this, followed by a number of people from the village, the group goes to the next village singing and playing instruments. After spending some time with the villagers, the group arrives on the site with a large crowd of people. During the time spent with people in their villages, the field-workers find out more about the problems the villagers face. The performances in the open have also helped them spot talent.

In the next few days, the problems discovered will be analysed and dramatised by the field-workers. They structure the events in two or three half-hour plays in terms of content, characters and theme. The villagers who show interest in acting are given a brief training. They are also helped to rehearse their lines. After two days the plays are presented. Massive crowds turn up for the performances. Before the team leaves the area, the plays are staged in all the villages. Community singing of revolutionary songs followed by speeches by the field-workers concludes the programme in each village. In some villages, one-day workshops are held on the techniques and purpose of this form of theatre. The main purpose, however, is to introduce the local people to this form of theatre and relate it to the concrete issues of exploitation and the people's struggle for development.

VII. Post-Performance Discussions

Post-performance discussions are important in the theatre practised by the SAGs. Since the audience have no role in the production of most SAG plays, it is possible that they do not even understand the deeper implications of the play. However, not many SAGs are keen on initiating discussions after the performances. Even when this is done, it is a half-hearted affair. Some groups like ARP, Asha Kendra and CROSS have tried to find out if the audience have understood the play. The actors themselves divide the audience into different groups and invite responses from the audience. They ask questions like: "What did you understand from the play?" "Who did you identify with in the play?" "Did he do the right thing?" "Why was he trying to do what he did?" It has often been noticed that villagers have a tendency to wander off during such sessions. However, they return if requested and respond favourably. Groups like Lok Samiti and READ have tried to open up discussions on particular themes the day after the play has been staged with small family groups. This is possible with groups that operate in the style of the Lok Samiti and stay in a village for a whole week, each day performing different plays on different themes.

SAG theatre groups function in a way which makes it difficult to have proper post-performance discussions. As already mentioned the theatre activities are not well organized. Often the villagers who come to attend these plays are tired after a full day's work. These being 'special' evenings, it is not easy for them to keep awake for a post-performance discussion. The drama group visits these villages very rarely. And when they visit they perform some of the more popular plays in their repertory. Only if the plays are directly about the problems in the village and raise controversial issues, do the villagers rise to the occasion. Hence a major constraint comes from the choice of themes for the plays themselves. While general themes like corruption, exploitation and discrimination help people to understand broader issues, it is only when the plays are specific, about things happening in the village, does the audience react and have something to talk about.

There is also a tendency among villagers to treat plays mainly as a medium of entertainment. The milieu in which they live is dominated by film songs and ritual celebrations, where hardly any importance is given to theatre as a medium for analysing the community's problems. Hence when discussions are initiated the people normally respond by saying "yes, yes, we understand," to every question the animateurs ask. Unconsciously, the audience discourages any sort of discussion. They are not used to it, hence they do not take to it easily. If the animateur does not make a conscious and sustained effort, there is no discussion.

Here one must point out that not all actors in the plays are capable of conducting a proper discussion to elicit responses from the audience. These young men, though literate, are quite incapable of social analysis or controlling an unruly audience. ARP has held a number of workshops for actors to train them in social analysis. A number of their animateurs and field-workers also join in the acting and the post-performance discussions.

ARP has also experimented with involving the audience in a dialogue with the characters of the play. In the early years, when the emphasis was on re-enacting the problems, in between each sketch, the actors would discuss these problems with the audience, challenging them to do something about them. A typical session went like this:

"Do you know of similar situations?"
"Where, when, with whom? How?
"Why can't you do something about it?"
"We are poor, if we take any action we will get hurt!"
"But can't authorities or the landlords help you?"
"No, the last person who went for help got badly beaten."
"He was told first pay you debts. If we complain we will be fired and our families will starve.[18]
In another play the ARP team went on to narrate the story of a person

who ventured to confront a landlord but did not get beaten, as the landlord knew there was strong support from the community.

The strategy of ARP was to make use of comments made by the audience, from the defeatists to the more daring, to help them deal with their fear and submissiveness, to overcome some of the conflicts within the community and to press home the point that if they are really united no power can stop them. In some plays the scenes were devised in such a way that the actors and the audience worked out a real plan to be carried. out the following day. For example, in order to put pressure on the government to deepen the wells (to prevent them from drying up in the summer) they plan to march *en masse* to the Block Development Officer and, if he refuses, to go on a hunger strike outside his office.

In some plays opportunities were created for the audience to intervene in the action of the play. In a play about a bonded labourer who remains loyal to his landlord, towards the end of the play he (the labourer) taunts the audience about their lack of loyalty to the landlord. An animateur planted in the audience begins to argue back and soon everyone joins in, ridiculing him for being so submissive and not standing up to the landlord. This argument may at times go on for 10 minutes. Again, a little later, another actors asks the audience, "Your brother is being beaten up and why are you sitting here quietly? Why are you allowing this to happen?" This provokes the audience to another lively exchange. Often the audience continues the discussions or there are fierce arguments after the play is long over.

In the earlier years of ARP there were attempts at what used to be called "struggle planning" meetings within a play. For example, after introducing the notion of a corporate strike and the need to overcome fears, the actor playing the youth leader leads the audience in discussing how to organize it—the strategic time, stopping the labourers from other villages breaking up the strike, winning the support of the peoples, informing the police, surviving the anxieties, the terms of the strike, the landlord's tactics to put it down, other retaliatory measures and so on.

Similarly, KSSP also has an infrastructure through which the people are involved before, during and after a performance. Its regional units and publications invite discussions on the various issues raised.

VIII. Evaluation and Follow-up

Evaluation and follow-up action are attempts to ensure that the process of Popular Theatre is firmly rooted among the people. Through such sessions continuity is assured by reminding people of what has already been analysed. These sessions help to carry out activities planned in a systematic way. As with post-performance discussions, here too due to the scant presence of the theatre groups in the villages, not much has been done. Often through plays and *jatha* people's enthusiasm is whipped up and they are ready to cooperate but they are unable to do so and their hopes are belied and energy dissipated.

However, there are exceptions. The SAG theatre can claim a few successes, through continual follow-up programmes. After the play has been presented attempts have been made by the local field-workers, even while the theatre groups was away, to chalk out a plan of action as advised in the plays. If groups like ARP, SWRC and READ have tasted success in various campaigns, it was due to the constant pressures put on the villagers to stick to certain principles. The abolition of bonded labour in some villages of Andhra Pradesh and Tamil Nadu, the improvement in school-going attendance in Bihar and a general awareness among the villagers of the exploitative structure in the country may all be partly attributed to the efforts of these SAGs and their theatre.

In general, however, both follow-up and evaluation have been negligible and Popular Theatre has yet to be productive in many of the SAGs. Several SAGs would argue that it is not that they are unaware of the importance of follow-up, but the sheer exhaustion caused by the extent of their activities prevents them from giving more time and energy to theatre. However, if the cadres are serious about theatre they need to place it higher on their list of priorities. No media can be expected to yield results if not used well.

XI. The Effect of SAG Theatre

Assessing the effect of SAG's theatre activities is a hazardous task, not only because what has been done so far is insignificant, but also because one can never say that any particular effect in a community is due to a single cause. Theatre has contributed, but how little is a question for further research.

In fact, while looking at the theatre activities of various SAGs, I intended to study the effects of theatre exposure in one particular village over a prolonged period of time. However, in all the areas I visited there was hardly any place where systematic theatre programmes were organized with a proper follow-up lasting for at least three years. Most of the SAGs return to a village any time they can, sometimes, after a year, with new plays, for fear that people may say, "We have seen this one before." The difficulty is that because every SAG works with over a hundred villages and theatre groups are too few, awareness building through theatre has never been done in a systematic way. Moreover in several groups theatre has merely remained on the periphery.

It is important to record the ripples that this form of theatre has caused in different parts of the country. This includes the effect on the field-workers of SAGs, the upper castes, the government powers and finally on the people themselves. Much of this information was gathered from a particular group of villagers who had been exposed to a number of plays by an action group.

1. On the Field-workers and Actors

Most of the animateurs and cadres who man the action groups have hardly any background in theatre. They have heard that in various countries and other action groups, theatre has been used to educate the masses. Hence when a workshop on theatre is announced for a SAG, they join in with the selected members from the villages. These selected people are mostly talented actors. The function of the cadre is to see that the social education incorporated into the plays is accurate and not misleading. However, their presence can often be harmful as they tend to enforce their viewpoint on the group as a whole

Psychologically, they consider themselves privileged, being better educated and, moreover, paid workers of the SAG. With this superior background they find it hard to operate smoothly within the context of a theatre workshop, in which a democratic form is essential. But if they can help others reflect and reach a decision, their presence as catalyst is more than justified. In workshops conducted by better equipped animateurs, the cadres have shaped up very well. Many of them have become better organizers, especially in collaborating with the preparation of plays to be staged in the villages. Experience has shown that several activists have become more democratic and respectful in their approach to the masses due to exposure to Popular Theatre

As for the actors themselves, obviously performing in a play is not

merely an act that enhances their confidence, but the fulfilment of a dream
as they are able to articulate before the audience what they truly believe
in. Efforts are made to understand and relive the characters and
ideologies they portray on stage. Thus youngsters who join as actors see
things more clearly and become more socially conscious. In the process
of making the play, they go through a learning experience, analysing the
issues involved, studying characters and scrutinizing situations.

2. Upper Caste and Government Reactions

Most of the SAGs work with the lower castes who live in segregated
parts of the villages. Obviously these are the poorer, dirtier and less
attractive parts of the village. The plays are normally performed in the
courtyards of lower caste homes. The upper castes quickly hear of a theatre
group's arrival. Their children flock to see the plays. The men and youth
stand apart and watch the performance although they are drawn towards
it. Often they may ask the SAGs to ignore the low castes and come to their
part of the village. However, when the play turns out to be an indirect
attack on the upper castes, their land- grabbing patterns and other
exploitative measures they react violently. Often the electricity supply is
cut off and stones thrown at the actors and the crowd. Several groups have
been chased away by heavies in the landlords' pay. Hardly anyone will
have a man-to-man confrontation with the animateurs of the SAGs. For the
landlords know only too well that what the SAGs are trying to put across
is factual. Hence they use strong-arm tactics.

The local government officials are often in league with the landed
gentry and the exploiters. They too try to frighten away the SAGs. And the
SAGs have to play it safe. For if the local government officials do not give
them a good report, the SAG quota of foreign contributions may be
discontinued. This has happened with several groups. Kurien, director of
READ, Bihar, describes their plight:

> We can hardly do anything in this part of the villages. For we are
> in the bad books of the local CO. Our FCRC has been confiscated,
> since we tried to expose the laws of the jungle they follow. And
> without depending on foreign money we have not learnt to run
> SAGs successfully.[19]

Local government officials penalise SAGs that do not toe their line.
A number of SAGs, short of their financial support and stalled by legal

action have ceased to be active. Very often SAGs are reported to be disrupting the peace, spreading violence, and are accused of being CIA agents with foreign connections. So the SAGs have to be particularly careful not to offend local politicians. Their non-cooperative attitude towards political parties is also held against them. In such situations theatre can have explosive repercussions. Consequently, plays on milder topics of social re-construction become routine.

3. Effects on the People

To study the effect of Popular Theatre I spent sometime interviewing people in a few villages of Bihar who had been exposed to various plays. Madwaha is such a village, close to the READ training centre with a population of about 1600. Among these about 700 (85 families) are low castes who live a hand-to-mouth existence. None have any land or income except from odd jobs. The people work periodically in the fields of the higher castes for a meagre wage. Bonded labour was once prevalent, but has since been abolished through the efforts of READ. Only about 10% can read and write. Among the children about 20% attend schools, others help their parents in the fields or by grazing cattle. The children are often married off when they are around fifteen. The READ team has consistently tried to persuade the villagers to concentrate on issues like cleanliness, sending their children to school, attending the evening adult literacy classes, abolishing child marriages, becoming more sensitive to the exploitative measures taken by the higher castes and landowners, becoming more united in their fight against corruption and to press for their demands for communal benefits from the government. READ's plays with such themes have been staged over and over again in this village. However, the villagers have hardly any interest in fighting their oppressors. Fatalists as they are, their only concern is survival. They know that if they fight the oppressors they will die of starvation. Nevertheless the random survey revealed some changes in their thinking.

Everyone had appreciated the story in *Aadhunik Ramlila* and felt that the play presented today's problems realistically, but when it came to the question of whether people could come together to oppose an exploitative situation no one answered for some time. Then a middle aged man spoke up: " We appreciate the work done by READ and the drama troupe. They have made it very clear to us that exploitation is mainly due to our own lack of education and unity. However, if anyone of us raises our voice against the higher castes they will dismiss us from their fields and someone else will get our work. And then we will starve". Clearly awareness has been raised, but no concrete plan of action has been worked out.

General hygiene has improved. The children look cleaner. The tube-well and the surrounding area is kept dry and clean at all times. The pond, where everyone, including the animals, bathe and wash clothes could not be cleaner. In the village proper, a number of places where marsh developed in the rainy season have been reclaimed.

There are youngsters who resist early marriage. However in the case of girls the parents are still adamant that they need to have their first marriage ceremony when they are around 12. They go to their husbands only when they are around18. For many sociological reasons this was found to be extremely hard to change.

School attendance has risen from 12% in 1979 to 20%. Among the youth there is a growing understanding about the problems in the village. A number of them have shown a keen interest in doing plays with similar themes although READ had not yet been able to initiate a stable group.

Issues like minimum wages, legal tangles, exploitation by money-lenders and local political and government leaders have been analysed through many of the plays and the villagers today feel the need to turn to someone for guidance in these matters. But with regard to action for change initiated by the people themselves, hardly anything has yet been done. This is due to the sparseness of the activists and the approach itself which needs to be corrected.

Notes

1. These reports are based on my field work in several villages of Bihar.
2. Bartholomew, Rati, "Samudaya's Jatha: Karnataka", *How*, Jan-Feb. 1983, Delhi.
3. Singh, Gurcharan, "Can Punjab be Saved through Gurcharan's Plays?", *Eve's Weekly*, April 1987, Bombay.
4. Premchand was probably the most socially conscious Hindi writer during the independence struggle. His novels and short stories have been widely translated.
5. Interview with Sircar on 5/12/87 in Calcutta.
6. Interview with Sharma on 23/11/87 in Delhi.
7. Rao, Poornachandra P.V., *To the Rural Masses through Street Play*, Cultural Forum, RDAS, Secunderabad, 1985.
8. Young India Project, *How*, op. cit., (no. 2).

9. Murickan, Ajit, "Cultural Action for Creating Integral Awareness," Maharastra, 1988.
10. Quoted by Radhika Menon, "Science Goes to the Streets," *Times of India*, 23/4/84.
11. This was adapted from Brecht's poem "To the Students of Workers and Peasants Faculty" in *Bertolt Brecht: Poems 1913-1956* (eds.) Willett, John and Manheim, Ralph, with the assistance of Erich Fried, Eyre Methuen, 1976, p. 450.
12. Adapted from "A worker's speech to a Doctor", op. cit., p. 292.
13. Abah, S. Oga "Group Media for Development Communication: The Example of Ram Ram," *Group Media Journal*, Munich, March, 1987.
14. Interview on 24/11/87.
15. Sharma, Tripurari, "A Desert Drama," *Hindustan Times*, 10/1/88, Delhi.
16. Rao, Mohan, quoted in Rao, op. cit., p. 22.
17. Rao, Poornachandra P.V., "In Search of an Alternative Theatre of Illiterate Masses," in *Sampreshan*, National Council of Development Communication, Varanasi, 1986.
18. Sugirtharaj, Felix N. "The Role of People's Theatre in Rural Development and People's Movement." *Dialogue*, an occasional publication, Madras, April, 1986.
19. Interview with K. Kurien on 12.11.87 in Bettiah.

Chapter VI

A Critique of and a Methodology for Popular Theatre

Part I

A Critique of Popular Theatre

A study of Popular Theatre in India through its street and SAG theatre groups leads one inevitably to ask questions about its effectiveness such as:

1. Are activist groups, at present fragmented and weakened by crises of ideology, ethos and legitimacy, capable of using Popular Theatre as a tool for social awareness?
2. Does Popular Theatre, spread among thousands of small communities, contribute in any significant way to the development of a stable, people-controlled network that can ultimately influence government policy on a long-term basis?
3. As a result of efforts to raise the social and political consciousness of the poorer and oppressed classes, what kind of cultural changes are taking place? Can long-term behavioural changes be expected from the work of the Popular Theatre?
4. To what extent can Popular Theatre be a true continuation of community performance traditions at the local level?
5. Can activists and animateurs belonging to the middle class provide genuine leadership among the rural masses?

Evidently, there are no clear answers on these issues, but the questions are relevant to the development of Popular Theatre in India.

I. Street Theatre

From chapter IV it is clear that street theatre has much room for improvement. However, before we examine its constraints and limitations it is important briefly to highlight some of its positive aspects in comparison to the SAG theatre.

To begin with, those involved in street theatre have been trained in theatre communication. In several cities they are break-aways from established conventional theatre groups. Badal Sircar's Shatabdi, Samudaya and Janam have professional experience. Consequently their theatrecraft, discipline and commitment to theatre are beyond question. There have been conscious attempts by several street theatre groups to improve the quality of their productions. Workshops by Badal Sircar, Tripurari Sharma and a number of visiting experimental theatre practitioners from the West like Schechner, Barba, Brook and others have helped them sharpen their use of imagery, movement and adaptations of folk forms.

Commitment to political causes is quite high among the members of street theatre groups. Most of them are in it not for any personal gain, but for the love of theatre and, more importantly, to promote socio-political causes. Financial advantages can be ruled out as these groups always perform in the open, free of charge. They often have to share the minor expenses among themselves. Incidentally groups which have survived for a number of years have been able to rely on a nucleus of stable, middle class employees. Groups like Janam, Nishant, Chitra, Shatabdi, Amritsar School, Jan Sanskriti Manch, IPTA (Patna) prove the point.

These groups come alive when an important issue of social and political concern emerges. They attempt to provide an alternative explanation and a different point of view from government controlled media. For example, in the wake of the Bhopal gas tragedy, while the official media were content with providing statistics on the extent of damage, it was the street theatre groups who focused the attention of the people on the wider aspects of exploitation by multinationals and the continuing horrors of the tragedy. In the same way, during the Deorala Sati incident several street theatre groups zeroed in on the brutal treatment of women in Indian society. Thus while the media look at social problems as technical matters requiring technical solutions, street theatre has tried to delve deeper to examine their root causes.

Constraints and Limitations

It has been mentioned that sincerity and commitment are two essentials in street theatre. These basic elements are missing in some groups. This probably accounts for the disappearance of some groups. Already some of the groups mentioned in this analysis may have ceased to exist! What causes this untimely end? Is it governmental pressure, dearth of talent, non-acceptance by the people, personal problems or loss of interest in the ideology they once believed in? Any of these may be a sufficient reason. Samudaya, the movement that threatened to create a cultural revolution in the whole of Karnataka, has lost its enterprising founders. Krishnasamy, one of the brains behind the movement observes:

When we started in 1975 it was the need of the time. Now that youngsters have taken to it, we have left. Several things have contributed to the decline of Samudaya. There came a point when I felt there was no forward growth, everything seemed static–structure, development and all. No new plays were forthcoming, organization was breaking up, follow-up was poorer. And today I ask myself, can we urbanites really create awareness in people's mind? Why should I feel superior?[1]

The insistence of some groups on topical events alone could be another reason for the decline of street theatre. Some groups who have performed in the past are inactive and waiting for an occasion that is dramatic enough to begin again. A play on a topical event becomes irrelevant after some time, and they need to be on the look out for newer themes. There are issues in plenty, but the groups fail to rise to the challenges. Creating a new play means a lot of intense group work to devise something new and different in technique and theme. Very often the 'new' creations are repeats of old plays.

The youthful exuberance that drives people to street theatre does not sustain them for long. Like everything youthful, it gradually fades away if the idealistic urge is not sustained by political motivation.

Some are led away by the lure of the conventional stage, cinema and television. There are some who use the medium of street theatre as a stepping stone to mainstream media or try to enter the media with false pretences. As Islam observes:

Some ex-activists under the spell of government powers put forward the argument that the rulers want us to remain in the gutters and do not allow us access to TV, radio, literary and academic circles, etc. Therefore we must get into these institutions to defeat the conspiracies of the rulers and abandon 'gutter theatre'.[2]

The lure of glamour and fame certainly affects the middle class performers of street theatre.

Several street theatre groups have been criticized for not living up to what they advocate in their plays. People are sensitive to how the performers live their lives outside the theatre atmosphere. There have been cases when the performers themselves have been dishonest, a prey to bribery, uncooperative with their own group or unwilling to challenge unjust situations in their midst.

Several groups have strong political party support and some, indeed, are floated by the parties. Support from political parties has its disadvantages; it was perhaps one of the major reasons for the break-up of IPTA. Reminiscing over the decline of IPTA, Niranjan Sen, General Secretary of IPTA (1945-54), commented:

The artists and party workers had gone in two different directions. The demand of the party had become too much for the artists. They had to part company.[3]

Toeing party lines can mean that theatre activists are cut off from people and their lives. Studying the relationship between the Communist party and theatre in China, Liu remarked:

The politicising of theatre means that it is no longer a people's art, but rather a party's art. It now belongs solely to the ruling class, the Communist Party.... To insist that such media carry policies and nothing but policies is to sever the media totally from the masses.[4]

Lack of Follow-up

Performances on topical events, especially in the place where the actual event took place, help the people become aware of the seriousness of the problem. However, one-off performances on routine or perennial issues may not produce much result. A performance may be said to be completed at the end of a play, but that is when the real work begins. Contacts thus established need to be strengthened through occasional feedback and evaluation.

Needless to say, any programme, to be effective, needs to be planned and executed for a considerable span of time in a specific place with a definite audience in mind. A theme may be explored in its entirety through a series of plays, with the audience becoming involved in post-performance discussions and proposing a plan of action to be carried out to improve the situation under analysis. There has not yet been a case of a group doing a survey to find out its effectiveness with the audience. A number of groups perform in many places on a variety of topics, by invitation or on their own initiative, which reduces them to the level of peripatetic radical entertainers. This makes proper follow-up impossible. There are some groups that believe that their task is simply to pass on a message without bothering about the outcome. This is escapist and leads to a light treatment of themes and to suggesting unrealistic goals or solutions. This is why street theatre is often criticised as too abrasive, agitational, emotional and without much substance

The Limitations in the Form

The nature of street plays does not allow time for study and research, or for finding popular responses to various issues. Often the group's analysis prevails over the community's interest. Due to brevity and emphasis on theme rather than plot, characterization is poor, which makes the plays seem shallow. Plays created in the form of mosaics, with fragments of life, rather than clear-cut stories, fall in this category. Characters are mostly black and white. Politicians, landlords, police and industrialists are always shown as wrong doers, who get away with anything, whereas the poor always suffer. Choudhary, the Secretary of Anarya observes:

> a labourer or a peasant for instance tends to be idealized, for within the
> context of the play, he is the oppressed. But they are not all in reality
> non-communal, non-racist, all good. You are romanticizing them and
> that is regressive.[5]

A number of plays rely on plots drawn from films, which makes them popular but less credible. This film influence can be noticed in the burlesque nature of humour, which at times becomes slapstick.

The adaptations of folk elements can look pathetic. Lack of proper study of these forms is often evident. Dutt condemns this arbitrary use as tomfoolery:

Our theatre has all along suffered from chronic constipation of imagination. The recent use of folk elements, tales, songs is all geared to comedy and sounds more like parodies of the original.[6]

Several groups depend on published sources for scripts. To some extent this helps inspiration, but the groups can become addicted to borrowing better scripts from other groups and eventually neglect their own originality and ability to improvise. Besides, the result resembles conventional theatre where the words of the playwright are followed closely. Moreover, preparing written scripts for a mass audience goes against the very idea of street theatre. It is important that the groups speak to a specific audience on issues directly concerning that audience.

Repetition and imitation has become the bane of street theatre all over India. Untroubled by copyright laws, groups borrow or steal plots and themes from each other. Cliche-ridden images and situations like the three monkeys, the magician's act, or the irreverent singing of patriotic songs have made many a street play redundant.[7]

The acting is not always of high quality. To be a convincing performer when surrounded on all sides by the audience is more difficult than performing on a stage with the help of lighting, an amplifying system and spatial separation from the audience. In street plays there is more emphasis on words, making them unduly verbose. At times loud sloganeering and lengthy speeches have drowned the emotional impact of the plot. Excessive borrowings from Sircar's techniques have made a few productions overly complicated. Groups relying more on improvisation seem to suffer from a lack of sufficient action and mime in their perform- ances. Although Indian theatre is essentially visual[8], street theatre, due to its limited resources, has remained verbal. Plays have become drab with total absence of colour, costumes and simple props. However, if carefully planned, even performative skills like juggling, stilt-walking, clowning, tumbling and acrobatics can be beautifully integrated. Not many groups realize that these simple things not only add visual emphasis, but can bring out other levels of meaning. An emphasis on the symbolic use of props needs to be developed

Some Recommendations

After four decades of relentless struggle against the odds, street theatre has yet to become a people's movement. Their growth if any, has been occasional and spasmodic, with their survival depending mostly on the enthusiasm of activists. If a group folds up hardly a tear is shed and no one ever misses it. That it is a communication medium capable of enlightening the ordinary masses is shown by the attack to which it is subjected by the police and bureaucracy. Street theatre has the capacity to withstand these onslaughts if it is truly in the hands of the people. But the way to becoming a people's movement is clearly slow and tedious.

Politicizing the movement—quite different from accepting the patronage of a political party—is necessary for growth. This can happen only if there is a growing commitment among the practitioners leading to more consistent and conscious efforts to build it up as a people's movement. Professional training as well as the ability to analyse socio-political issues need to be developed, so that participation in a play is understood as a socio-cultural activity, rather than play-acting for entertainment. Theatre groups need to conduct workshops for minority groups helping them to understand how play-making can be a proper method of analysing and studying their problems. In this way a people's movement may begin. Groups need to cut down on imitating better equipped groups, and concentrate on developing the art of acting, the creative use of space, colour and other aspects of performing on the streets.

The larger persistent problem of integrating folk elements needs to be studied critically. What is essential is that street theatre evolves an indigenous form, integrating traditional ways and modern experimental forms of expression with plenty of vitality and dynamism, so that a new identity is created while preserving the traditional culture. Integrating local forms of visual and aural expressions, subtle symbols, local imageries, myths and stories help each group to develop indigenous modes.

A number of group—political groups, social activists, health workers—with no theatre background have taken to street theatre forms primarily to spread their ideologies. This is indeed a healthy sign, for theatre needs to spread its wings and include many types of themes and messages. Street theatre need not content itself with protest and propaganda themes and crude rhetoric. The content does not have to be agit prop: bombarding people with statistics is a disservice to the people and to theatre. There can certainly be struggle and violence, but also high emotion with humour and celebration and, most of all, dreams presented in a sensual way with dance and music, energy and rhythm. Ultimately it should become a looking glass in which the audience can see themselves and should include their whole life. Street theatre should become

... a presentation that talks to a community of people and expresses what they as community all know, but no one is saying: thoughts, images, observations and discoveries that are not printed in newspapers or made into movies; truth that may be shocking and honesty that is vulgar to the aesthete.[9]

It is also essential that groups are affiliated to each-other and work with a common sense of purpose. This does not only mean sharing each other's scripts; it should also lead to planning the overall themes to be analysed in a particular area over a period of time. This is hard in the present Indian context, where several groups are controlled by party and other group interests. Even co-ordination of groups within a state may be difficult. However, more workshops, meetings, seminars and *jatha* can surely be organized to pool together resources and to spread the movement.

In conclusion, it may be said that street theatre has tremendous potential to become an alternative to the giant media set up in the country, provided it is properly planned and realized. Today several groups feel that television can be a severe threat to street theatre. Some groups have given up performances on evenings when feature films and other popular programmes are televised. However, when television has become commonplace, people, if made aware of the severe media control and vested interests of the government and industrialists, will be more receptive to street theatre. Meanwhile much remains to be done to make street theatre a vibrant and a truly participative medium of the people.

In the near future in India, TV and films may replace conventional theatre, but street theatre, if its potential is fully explored, will continue to play an important role by providing wholesome entertainment and by acting as a tool for social education and consciousness raising among the illiterate masses.

II. The Strengths and Weaknesses of SAG Theatre

The Strengths

A major advantage of SAG theatre groups over street theatre groups in the cities is the possibility of post-performance discussions and follow-up action. The SAGs can be sure that when they return to a certain village they will confront the same people and the same situations. Even if the theatre groups can do no more than perform plays, the local field-workers or the SAG animateurs from the central headquarters can surely undertake some form of follow-up action. Theatre may be used as a means for graded study and analysis of social issues.

Another strength is the interest shown by villagers in exploring more serious themes in their plays. Inspired by the SAG theatres, socio-political themes have mushroomed in village plays. Religious and patriotic plays have given way to plays dealing with the suffering masses carrying on their fight against their oppressors.

The Weaknesses

As previously mentioned, voluntary agencies have travelled a long way from the days of charity and welfare schemes. There has been a visible shift to development issues and conscientization. Their ideal has moved from social work to education and agitation to awareness building and mobilization and now to organization through identification with the poor. The tools they use have changed from Gandhian idealism to Marxian rhetoric and to Freirian participatory methods. Now they use theatre. For how long this trend will continue is an open question. Already two prominent theatre movements—IPTA (1941-1956) and Samudaya, Bangalore (1971-78)—have disintegrated due to ideological conflicts. This does not augur well for the future of theatre in SAGs.

It must be admitted that in several groups theatre is not used either to help the people explore their socio-political problems or to enhance their participation in social re-construction. Several groups consider it purely an entertainment medium useful in gathering people together for a bigger meeting or, at best, as a starting point for a discussion. This is taking theatre too lightly. But it is hard to take theatre seriously, for the reality of village life is intense and villagers have to work hard every day to make both ends meet. If they do not work they do not eat. Hence it is hard for them to find time for workshops or study sessions. Many are not interested in theatre ; the harp and fiddle can wait, let us get on with matters of significance, that is the attitude.

In the villages there are often warring factions. If the catalysts make contact with one group, others will keep away. Besides some people are apathetic to Popular Theatre, as they have had similar experiences with the SDD. So they may shun any new ventures that try to 'educate' them.

The drawbacks of SAGs mentioned earlier affect the theatre groups as well. The attempts of SAGs to create parallel structures of development, often ignoring or in opposition to government plans, may not take them very far.

Problems in Theme Analysis

One cannot deny that SAG theatre has attempted to highlight the immediate issues the people face. They have inherited the protest element from street theatre but often do not sufficiently analyse the issues raised. This aspect will be further examined.

1. Local issues of immediate importance to the people are not their concerns

SAG theatres have largely failed to present plays improvising on events in their village. Plays based on borrowed scripts and general themes of oppression are fine but improvising plays on local events can be more effective. It helps the audience to identify with the characters and concentrate on the issues. Opposition is sure to follow, but when people power is challenged it can gain a sharp edge. Thus not only the production of the play, but also the after-effects can help unite the oppressed.

2. The micro to macro movement is missing

There is a tendency among action groups to build up plays based on factual events in their own village or on borrowed scripts that portray exploitation of some sort. The play is staged and analysed. But hardly any attempt is made to relate the events in the play to the national and international oppression of the poor. It is important for the people to understand how an isolated event in the village is linked to the overall theme of oppression in the country and across the world. Hence after a play is staged it is necessary to draw parallels with events happening in other villages, districts and states. This can be done more easily in the case of scripts borrowed from outside, for they have already been proved to be expressions of the experiences of other groups. Without this macro approach there is hardly any possibility for the movement to acquire a mass character.

3. Weak analysis of issues raised

This is the most important criticism levelled against SAG plays. It has often been noticed that the issues raised in the plays are not sufficiently understood by the villagers. On the face of it an issue may seem immediate but it often has deep roots which are not fully explored. Typical examples are plays about situations of oppression. The person responsible for the oppression is convicted and instant justice is meted out. A landlord or a money-lender is found guilty. Hardly any attempt is made to find out why the villains are what they are. A deeper analysis will lead to identifying the oppressive system working in the country. The historical, economic and political factors underlying a particular situation need to be explored. This is how the poor come to know that the real causes of poverty and underdevelopment are not the ignorance and weaknesses or the wickedness of the rich but the structural relationships which keep them powerless and exploited. They can come to realize that the real problems are not lack of proper drinking water, illiteracy, superstitions, large families and malnutrition, but exploitation, victimization, injustice and corruption. The former are only symptoms of the real problems. Understanding in this manner is close to the Freirian model.

Another drawback is not attempting to find the link between various problems. For example, alcoholism and malnutrition result from exploitative working conditions. Often SAG plays treat them separately and prescribe solutions. Such problems are not analysed in relation to their society. The 'change of heart' response is an escapist solution which by-passes the oppressive situation.

Again some SAG plays have a tendency to treat problems as caused by the backward behaviour of the people themselves. The economic and social relationships are not considered; 'blaming the victim' only make them more insecure and fatalistic.

4. Lack of proper understanding of the people

Several animateurs live outside the village in semi-urban communities. Hence they do not have sufficient understanding of the mind-set of the villagers. Often they develop superficial opinions about the fatalistic and non-co-operative attitudes of the people. In the absence of sufficient familiarity with the rhythm of life in the villages these outside catalysts can end up analysing village issues in a superficial manner. Several of the lower caste communities suffer from an absence of self-worth and are denied even human dignity. For centuries, under the magic spell of the caste system, people have been subjugated by having it drilled into them that they are the scum of the earth and that as human beings they are worthless. This has had a tremendous effect on their personal lives. Due to this, low caste villagers may not easily respond to outsiders. They may find it very hard when the catalysts expect trust and responses from them.

Kizhakekala and Vadassery, studying the myths and stories prevalent among the Harijan communities in the Dharaut village of Gaya District, Bihar, have commented that the community suffered from the effects of a fall from grace and degradation. A closer analysis showed that this was due neither to their inherent incapacity or a self-inflicted wound. The ancestors of this group had been deceived and their trust in others abused. A number of stories revealed that the Harijans were reduced to a demeaning status because of the services they had generously rendered.[10]

Plays which show Harijans in high positions, holding responsible jobs, confronting unjust authorities or in the company of people in high positions like local government officials give the audience a sense of worth and dignity. This sort of gradual building up of their confidence is essential to their development.

5. Lack of positive outlook in themes

This is not the same as indulging in mere educative themes like cleanliness, health care and use of fertilizers. SAG theatres have been too preoccupied with themes of oppression. Plots have begun to sound like cliches, with stock situations, standard wit and 'black and white' characterization. An agit-prop style of revolutionary treatment has been their forte. The presentation of too many desperate situations can only help to emasculate revolutionary potential and strengthen fatalistic attitudes. Apathy and disregard towards Popular Theatre begin to develop. There are those who say, "Oh! you people always talk about the same thing," and walk away. Creative and innovative efforts at re-working the village structures and a promise of better days could perhaps enliven the spirit of the people. Not many realize that theatre is a celebration, a festival and a means to reflect different aspects of the colourful lives of the people. The medium could be used to explore the qualities in their lives: their cultures, their fears, anxieties and dreams. Such forms of celebratory theatre help to develop people's power and self-esteem.

Weaknesses in the Treatment

1. The ' complete' presentation

Even in a fictional narrative, it is natural for a people weaned on ˙a culture of dependency to seek solutions, rather than critical analysis. Hence several SAGs present polished, well-finished plays performed by roving groups. These present one view only, that of the outsider. In the final count, such efforts do not help raise consciousness. Structured primarily as a performance they are presented at night, on stage, under disciplined conditions. People are questioned down and are advised to watch silently. The performance proceeds in a manner similar to the conventional theatre. Some groups encourage question and answer session at the end of the play which helps only to extract confirmation of what has been communicated. Although the villagers might not agree at all with some of the solutions, because they are presented by the 'all-knowing' activists, the disagreement is left unexpressed.

2. Process of play making not only fully utilized

If play in SAGs are primarily meant to educate, their very preparation should surely hold tremendous promise. But sadly, no group has yet realized that the process of play making is the crucial time for analysing social issues and building social awareness. Improvisation, which is the vital part of this play-making, is taken lightly. It is a fact that several action groups prepare their plays from completed and even published scripts in isolation, behind closed doors, away from the people, very much like conventional theatre.

3. Lack of people participation

It must be stated emphatically that the very essence of Popular Theatre is the full involvement of the people in every aspect of play production. But unfortunately not many SAG activists have understood the essence of audience participation. In fact, several activists who live away from the people do not feel at home with them and ride roughshod over their sensibilities by trying to hammer down a few home truths. This is very similar to the capitalist model of communication which treats the public as mere consumers of information, reinforces the notion of passivity and legitimizes the 'culture of silence'. Thus they perpetuate the 'top down' format. In SAG theatres the programme are planned by the 'staff', themes to be dramatized are chosen by the animateurs and the scripting is done by the field-workers. This is not very different from the SDD troupes that plan and organize everything with no participation by the villagers. Several SAGs own transport, possess electricity supply, a PA system and stage facilities—all of which have been made essentials for their theatre. Hence theatre is not allowed to take root in the village as it travels with the SAG troupes.

4. Lack of action orientation and follow -up

It is true that in several SAGs after an initial workshop and some activities, the catalysts have stopped visiting those villages. An important function of Popular Theatre is to examine the indifference among people and explore why they are not keen on taking action to change their lives. This is where activists will have to make participation an important goal. Gradually activists will have to realize that long years of oppression and exploitation have dampened the villagers' enthusiasm for anything. They have seen the SDD cadre dictate to them. The resultant passivity, suspicion and fear need to be taken as challenges. The effort of SAG theatre in such instances of apathy should be to create an atmosphere conducive to sharing and dialogue.

5. Lack of cultural continuity

SAG theatre cannot claim to have touched the issues that are crucial to the people. A culture which represents a society's awareness of its values, aims, visions and dreams can, no doubt, provide an important incentive for development. If Popular Theatre can concentrate on the villagers' identity as a group seeking justice and equality, then it could rightly be said to be a true reflection of their culture.

There are different opinions in SAGs as regards the use of folk forms. While some groups present plays in folk forms others select only a few folk elements. From the tradition of folk theatre it is evident that in most places it was performed by specialized groups. Years of training alone make a good folk performer. Although the ordinary people respond to these instantly, they have hardly any experience and so find it difficult to perform. Establishing a folk theatre group has often ended up in vulgarising the form.

Few SAGs realize that not every form can be adapted and that each has its own historical background and significance. Many well meaning social activists have tried to adapt even elements of religious rituals. For example, as part of a social awareness play, a group of people suffering from an epidemic is advised by the goddess to turn to the doctors. The villagers satisfied that it was the goddess herself who spoke, go to the doctors. D'Abreo condemns this superstitious element found in the SAGs' productions. He cites a pertinent example. The young Farmers Club in a village in Tamil Nadu wanted to erect a shed for their association in the temple premises but the trustees of the temple were strongly opposed to this. At one of the temple festivals a SAG got a dancer to perform. During the dance he lay down on thorns, burnt himself and performed other strange acts causing himself pain. The people were tremendously impressed by his performance even though they knew him to be a common drunkard. They believed he was possessed by the spirit. In a trance he said: "Annan (a local god) has come and said that the farmers are my people and those who do not let them build their shed will be punished." What the SAG did not realise was that the temple trustees could get the same man to say the opposite at a better price![11]

Bordanev, condemns the use of folk media for disseminating development messages:

> Development thinkers' obsession with goal achievement and not with human growth may take up these folk media as another set of instruments for changing people's way of thinking, feeling and behaving. And this is not the purpose and function of the traditional media. I am afraid, as soon as the people realize that their folk arts are being used for subliminal propaganda they will let them die [12]

This observation is valid not only in the case of using folk theatre for disseminating development messages, but also of using it for any purpose other than letting it play its role in society. Folk theatres always echoed the needs of the people and it should continue so. Adaptations of its contents, if validated by this criterion, can be justified and deemed ennobling. It would have been better if development communicators had convinced the folk performers of the meaningfulness of the intended message, and given them the freedom to present it in a manner the performers considered suitable.

Not many groups concentrate on using the simple ordinary resources of the people. The people may not be proficient in folk theatre, but there will be some who are good in story-telling, singing, dancing and so on.

These abilities have not yet been explored sufficiently. If the local people have not been involved in the preparation of the plays then these resources will remain unused.

Theatre can be a powerful cultural expression as it has the potential to actively involve a wide range of physical, emotional and imaginative capacities. It can bring together many facets of cultural creativity: socio-political, religious, ritual, myth and story-telling, dance, music, satire, mimicry, role-playing and the festive celebrations of a community. If the catalysts make it a point to explore these inherent capabilities they will surely contribute to education through cultural action.

Conclusion

Popular theatre needs to grow qualitatively and numerically. More committed groups need to come to the fore which means more animateurs and more performers. A centrally organized way of approaching crucial problems in the country needs to be explored and developed. SAG theatre can be politicised as is the case with street theatre, only if it is spread widely and has massive grassroots support.

As for SAGs depending on foreign aid, the theatre groups need to become financially more independent. Only then can they express their views unimpeded by outside forces. The people, moreover, need to feel that it is their own group and need to support it whole-heartedly. Until and unless the desire for change and development comes from the people, all efforts of the SAGs are futile. Hence the role of the animateurs is to concentrate on engaging people's interest and participation, and empowering the people and making them feel responsible and confident of changing their lives. For this initial work some foreign aid may be necessary, but when the people have been empowered they need to continue their struggle by themselves despite all constraints. Their concerted effort can help them organize against the government middle-men who care little for their well-being. In this struggle Popular Theatre can help build up the confidence and strength of the people.

Table Showing the Relative Differences Between Various Forms of Theatre

Factors	Folk Theatre	Street Theatre	Present SAG Theatre	Suggested SAG Theatre
1. Content	Religious, romantic and some social protest.	General and current themes of socio-political unrest, protest.	General themes of oppression, development issues.	Problems specific to a community, themes to celebrate life, macro approach to problems.
2. Mode of production	Erected stages, or in the round. Nightlong. Open air.	Open air, road sides, street corners, very short finished productions.	Erected stages in village courtyards, finished plays.	Free stages, incomplete plays, people invited to complete, completed in real life.
3. Theatrecraft	Learned from elders, vibrant and spontaneous.	Some professional, well trained and imaginative.	Little training, but lots of natural flair.	Not necessarily high quality but will train in local resources. Capable of drawing in local talents.
4. Method of improvisation	Oral tradition, no scripts, learned from others.	Creates its own or borrows from other groups.	Improvised by activists from popular plays or borrowed.	Improvised by the people with assistance from animators, and later by the people themselves.

5. Consciousness raising	Traditional values, mostly retrograde.	Solutions presented to problems, the performers are partially conscientized, NOT the audience.	Fails to reach root problems. Each issue seen independently.	Should lead to analysis of social structure, people enabled to do social analysis.
6. Audience participation	In performance, adding to the festivities.	Little in performance, hardly any in the preparation.	Very little as a whole.	Total control by the people from planning to follow-up action.
7. Cultural continuity	Truly part of the people's (retorgrade) culture.	Concerns of the people are dramatized. The form is a mixture of Western, folk and classical.	General concerns, not local enough. Adapting, resurrecting and borrowing folk forms.	Concentration on local issues, people's concerns. Use all available media in the area.
8. Post performance discussion (PPD), follow-up, action plan	Year round repetitions, Little effect on development issues.	No PPD, evaluation or follow-up.	Some groups have a bit, but as a whole, negligible.	Continuous action-reflection-action, after the animateurs leave. Structural changes to challenge the status quo development.

Part II

A Methodology for Popular Theatre in India

As we have said earlier, a theatre in which as many members of the community as possible participate and are encouraged to carry out in reality the inspiration of the play, is the ultimate form of Popular Theatre. The rather obscure and amorphous process of promoting theatre by SAG activists in several Indian villages has been outlined. Evidently, Popular Theatre, as practised by the SAGs has the largest scope for improvement and increased effectiveness, for the SAGs are committed to the all-round development of the less privileged. However, their theatre is least developed. Still, since they operate within the SAG network there is ample scope for co-ordination, evaluations and follow-up action. If the activists can live and work with the villagers, who show a great natural flair, talent and enthusiasm for theatre, a well-guided programme can develop among them.

The poorer sections can find their cultural identity through the development of a people's theatre in which their talents, tastes and needs are brought together. Their own myths, stories, dreams, visions need to be dramatized in their own art forms. This form of theatre makes them more confident and proud of their own culture and identity. This ultimately helps them become conscious of their roles in re-shaping their society. When such a theatre is built upon the performative tradition of the Indian villages which includes story-telling, dance, music, mime and masquerades, it provides the continuity so essential for establishing one's cultural identity.

Evidently this requires two forms of theatre among the SAGs. For convenience sake I call them 'Learning Plays' and 'Festival or Celebrational Plays'. Both these aim at the same thing, but the emphasis in their methodologies varies. Learning plays are directed at smaller groups of opinion leaders and others who command the obedience of the village. Here theatre is used as a tool to analyse and understand social issues in depth. This is similar to Boal's 'theatre without audience'. Celebrational plays are meant for larger crowds, where plays about the history and current situation in the village are enacted in a celebrational manner with a powerful story. These are considered in detail below.

I. Devising Learning Plays

1. The structure of the theatre group

Since each SAG works with a number of villages, there needs to be one main animateur, who has sufficient knowledge of theatre and its uses in education and development. Under him/her there should be a number of regional animateurs whom he/she has trained. Each of these animateurs plays the catalyst's role for at least five to six villages. Their function is to initiate and supervise theatre action in each of the villages under their jurisdiction. Each village needs a theatre group with a leader, a secretary (reporter) and a treasurer. The group must have at least ten members. Everyone in the village may be invited—even insistently—to participate in the plays, as actors, 'writers' and observers.

It is the duty of the main animateur to hold workshops for would-be regional animateurs and prepare them to face the task ahead. These workshops, normally held at the SAG headquarters, may last for as long as a month, with the SAG animateurs and director contributing their share in developing the participants' ability to do social analysis. In this programme, exposure to village realities, devising plays based on these realities and staging them before select audience need to be included. At least three workshops should be held in a year. Another three short, week-long, follow-up workshops also need to be included in a year. Those who have attended the one-month programme may be included in this to re-animate themselves.

Even though educated women like Tripurari Sharma and Rati Bartholomew have been efficient animateurs, it is often hard to find women to be regional animateurs or even to take part in the plays in the villages. Given the Indian situation where village women are kept inside the homes, it is not advisable for a drama group to tackle this issue immediately. Nothing can be misunderstood in villages more than young men and women working together in groups. Nevertheless, efforts must be made to include women in the process.

After a few teams of regional animateurs have been trained, it is up to them to organize separate workshops for each of the villages under them. For each workshop, the main animateur (if possible) and 4 to 5 other regional animateurs may be deployed. The basic format for conducting a workshop in a village is made up of 8 stages, though the duration of this workshop should be left to the villagers and the animateurs. The purpose is to develop a process of doing theatre, not to propagate a rigid methodology. The workshop must be held at a time when the villagers are free from work. An open space in the village is ideal for the programme.

The 8 stages are:

1. Group Building
2. Community Research and Problem Identification
3. Analysing the Problem
4. Improvisation and Scenario Making
5. Community Performances
6. Post-Performance Discussion
7. Organizing Action
8. Follow-Up Action, including Studying Constraints.[13]

This methodology is akin to the participatory research approach suggested by Byram and Kidd, the main elements of which are:

1. The problem being researched originates in the community itself and is defined, analysed and solved by the community.
2. The final goal of research is the radical transformation of social reality and the improvement of the lives of the people involved. The main beneficiary of the research is the community.
3. It should involve the full participation of the whole community in the research process, including the powerless, the poor and the oppressed.
4. It should set out to create a greater awareness in people of their own resources and mobilize them for self-reliance.
5. The researcher must become a committed participant with the learner in the process of research.[14]

The ultimate aim is not merely to enable the poor to discuss their problems, but to become aware and to seek solutions that lead to structural changes. Hence this *modus operandi* need not be followed in strict order, but may be changed according to the needs of the people. Each of the 8 stages will now be examined more closely.

1. Group Building

Except for one regional animateur who belongs to the village, all the others are strangers although they come from nearby villages. By their education, upbringing and youthful tastes they will be different from the villagers. They probably feel superior to the villagers and expect to be accepted as such unqestioningly. They may come to the village with the idea of educating and uplifting the poor and underprivileged. The villagers may therefore feel estranged from the animateurs.

There are also any number of natural adversaries for the animateurs, like party cadres, government development officers, government's SDD sponsors and other vested interest groups who have been exploiting the villagers for years. The villagers themselves have seen several types of cultural and political activists come and go under the pretext of development. Most of these groups have trampled underfoot the traditional values and sentiments of the villagers. As a result the animateurs may find the villagers watching them suspiciously and giving nothing more than the traditional hospitality accorded to strangers. Hence the animateurs will have to prove that they are different.

Obviously, these animateurs should find it much easier to establish contact with the villagers than would a group of college or (social work training) school students. If the SAG has already established a name, there will be hardly any problem. But this is not normally the case. The SAG may be totally unknown or notorious. The local representative among the animateurs can be of great help. If he commands the respect of the villagers, contacts are easily made. The village leader, or the section leader in the case of a particular caste group, needs to be contacted. Often the village leader may not co-operate as he is on the side of the government leadership. The animateurs could visit the village informally in the company of the representatives, introduce themselves, join chats, games and even entertainments. Initially efforts must be made to let the people know that they do not represent the government, for already the people have seen how the latter operate. Conversely, if the people perceive the animateurs as government agents they may try to win their favour, hoping to get some benefits. The basic problems of contact can be surmounted if the village leaders are identified and an amicable relationship is established. The animateurs will soon discover that the local leaders are not all on talking terms, that there are animosities among them. Hence earnest attempts have to be made to iron out these differences.

The next problem is to establish a close, working relationship. Once the contact has been made, group building is not done through group dynamics games as in urban centres. The people may be alienated by such efforts. Meetings may be called and the purpose of the workshop clarified. In such meetings performances by way of singing, dancing, role-playing may be introduced, which are very close to the villagers' traditions. Singing, dancing and celebrating together also help the animateurs discover the performative talents latent in the villagers. A potential theatre group may already be visualized at this stage.

The attitudes of the animateurs in these initial days are crucial. The villagers observe them carefully. Living and sharing with the people in everything is vital. Dressing like the villagers, speaking their dialect, sitting on the floor with them, going into their houses for chats and eating food in the way the villagers eat can be of great help. Accepting the villagers' culture in every detail enhances the success of the workshop. All these attempts at identifying with the people show that the outsiders have tremendous respect for the people's culture and, consequently, the villagers come to feel at one with the animateurs and the animateurs 'belong' to the village.

2. Community Research and Problem Identification

Community research is done mainly through informal conversations. Here the animateurs need to move around with the villagers to the tea shops, to the fields and on outings to nearby towns. They also need to share with the villagers their own experiences of rural life. This helps the villagers open up about themselves, to speak about their worries and anxieties. The similarities in their experiences help develop affinities and strengthen relationships. The animateurs will no longer be treated as strangers but as friends who really care.

The interpersonal and informal approach reveals more than formal questionnaire methods. It not only provides vital information, but also develops relationships and confidence, qualities so necessary for working together. The people are quite familiar with the questionnaire method adopted by researchers who study them, or government functionaries who impose taxes or other new measures unacceptable to them. Another weakness in the questionnaire method is the prior assumption of several facts gathered from other communities. Hence a 'specific to this village' approach is lacking. In the method of personal contacts there is respect for the people and first-hand information about vital issues.

As the villagers and animateurs discuss the problems of the village, the latter may notice the fatalistic manner in which everything is accepted in a village. It is for the animateurs to keep calm and understand that this is an outcome of centuries old oppression by the holders of power. At this stage it is not advisable that the animateurs start correcting or questioning the villagers on these issues.

Gradually the villagers will come out with problems like poverty, low wages, religious and caste disparities, exploitation of all sorts by the powerful. Listening to specific issues patiently and with care will help the villagers trust the animateur genuinely. After a few days have been spent in this way, it might be advisable to call another meeting to put together whatever has been gleaned. The problems may then be listed according to priority and studied at length.

3. Analysing the Problems

In the third stage a deeper analysis of the problems is presented. Here again small informal group sessions are more useful than a long, large assembly. It is inappropriate for the animateurs to analyse the information by themselves. Any information gathered needs to be of importance in the lives of the people. Hence it is vital that everyone should realize why such and such a problem is of greater importance to them. This is where the micro to macro approach comes in, to help people see the connections between their problems and the world order. The animateurs have to be cautious not to analyse issues themselves and give their own slant to the situation for this would be detrimental to the whole process.

Freire has used the term 'dialogue' to signify the system of debate and participation that needs to be followed. In the dialogue system the people have an equal or greater share in leading discussions and deciding issues. Evidently, the people know the problems better for they live with them. The animateur's role is to ask questions that help analyse the issues from various critical perspectives. Questions such as, 'Why does the problems exist? 'How does the problem manifest itself in a given situation?' 'Is there a basic pattern in which it recurs? 'Is this problem related to any other?' 'How many people are affected by the problem'? 'Does it affect only the poorer sections?' 'Why doesn't it affect other groups?' can help the villagers understand the situation better. These inquiries help the people realize that the problem is man-made and that it can be changed with commitment and human effort.

The discussions and analysis cannot proceed usefully without being specific and action-oriented. Hence it is always advisable to use role-play. For example, a sample case gathered from the discussions, the roles of bonded labour may be played by villagers. The animateurs must keep silent and ask the people to take roles. When the problem is acted out the complexities become evident to the gathering. A number of questions may be asked, 'What really happened'? 'Has the event been pictured realistically?' 'Have there been any serious drawbacks or omissions?' 'Who is responsible for bonded labour as seen in the play?' 'How is it related to other problems?' How does it link to the world order?' 'How did bonded labour originate in the first place?' 'What is the thought behind such a system?' 'Who profits by it?' Such questions make the problems sharper. After the villagers have witnessed a scene, it becomes easier for them to reflect and deepen their understanding with the help of such questions.

If anyone strongly disagrees with the representation he may be asked to represent the play in the way he thinks is right. The others may be allowed to intervene, correct, supplement, or change the event.

During this third stage selected number of problems are studied in detail. It is important for the animateurs to intervene and explain to the group how the problems being considered are paradigmatic of the global scene of exploitation. This is helped by case studies from other villages, districts, states and countries.

In the case of a problem like caste discrimination a detailed analysis may be made of the caste system, including its history and development. It should be made clear why the practice continues and how the upper castes stand to gain from it. Several cases of discrimination may be outlined and the general trend determined.

Once the workshop is in progress, at least three problems can be chosen to be dramatized. The group may be divided into three, with two animateurs helping to run each group. Thus three plays can be devised separately in the following days. A loose time table may also be planned in order to ensure the full participation of the entire community

4. Improvisation and Scenario Making

At this stage, each of the three groups works separately on a different issue. It is advisable to have nearly 15 people in each of the groups including men, women, and children. As for the story to be dramatized, it is always better to stick to an event that has happened in the village.

In the beginning the animateurs may ask for volunteers to conduct the sessions. Someone may accept, but if not, one may be appointed in consultation with village elders. The two animateurs should always be with the groups, seeing that they proceed in a purposeful manner. They need to make sure that everyone has a say, is heard, understood and questioned.

It is not enough to present a play through dialogues and movements. The people have enormous reserves of artistic talent. These need to be unearthed and used to their full potential. Singing, dancing, story-telling, games come naturally to them. They may know melodious and catchy tunes. They may have very interesting stories about themselves. Less common abilities like acrobatics and clowning can be utilized to make the plays more interesting.

Although the folk theatre prevalent among the villagers may have retrograde themes, their forms can be adapted to suit modern themes. Examples of these have been given in chapter III. Folk forms are used solely for the purpose of developing a people's culture. In a situation where all the messages of the dominant media are irrelevant to the people, going back to the people's media is itself a sign of emphatic protest.

At another level, is also an attempt at discovering the cultural identity of a community. For one thing, everyone in the community participates in traditional art forms like group singing, story-telling, games, dancing, festivals, masquerades. They are deeply involved, both as performers and as audience. When the community begins to find relevant and educative values in their own cultural format, it creates a sense of dignity and pride. This mind-set is an asset for developing Popular Theatre for awareness building. From this viewpoint, although it is a cultural event it has political dimensions. Gradually, the villagers' cultural background energizes them to find their own identity in society.

Having considered this aspect, a few methods of improvisation and scenario making are presented.

Method 1

The first task is to devise a workable plot from a chosen event. For example, a plot about natural calamities like floods and drought may be treated this way. It would be necessary to note down short and co-ordinated scenes which may be woven together to make the final scenario. The scenes based on a real event as proposed by the group members may finally run like this.

1. A Harijan village is threatened by floods. We concentrate on a poor
    family of father, mother, five children. People drop in and express
    their anxiety for floods can devastate the year's crops. Several people
    make comments, some humorous, some tragic. One man says that
    the floods are due to god's anger. It is the god's tears flowing down
    in abundance at the people's evil doings! They decide to make a
    special offering to the deity. All these matters may be brought out in
    one scene which may include a number of sequences. It is left to
    the discretion of the group to invent ways of developing the scene in
    an appropriate way. The dialogue needs to be clear and the type of
    characters definitely portrayed, without making them stereotypes.

2. It is two months later and people are once again threatened, this time
    by drought. A similar scene as the first may be built up
    highlighting various aspects like lack of drinking water, animals
    dying of thirst, children getting skin diseases. Here again the
    solution is recourse to the gods.

3. This is when a rich farmer may be introduced who offers to help the
    poor by getting government aid. With the help of his son he draws up
    a scheme to prevent floods. They manage to get a large sum from
    the government's flood relief funds, bribe the local Block Develop-
    ment Officer and use the money to buy a car. This is when one of the
    poor boys, a classmate of the richman's son, enters the scene asking
    the villagers some simple questions: "Why is it that we alone have
    to suffer?" "Why is it that during the floods and drought, the rich
    people are not affected?" "How do they manage?"

    Such questions may bring to the fore some important facts. The rich
get the government to build tube wells for them so that they, not the poor,
have clean water throughout the year. The government has sanctioned,
through the flood relief fund, sufficient money to build embankments
along the river bed. There is also a scheme and funds allotted for
diverting the rivers. However, the money has been appropriated by the
middlemen and the rich have not allowed the river to be diverted as its
present course helps to water their animals.

    The sequences may be developed according to the imagination of the
group members. At every stage, anyone is free to suggest improvements.

    'Hot seating' could be a useful tool at this stage for developing
character sketches. This process helps the actor to deepen his own

understanding of the part and explain to others how he visualizes himself. Others ask him a number of questions about the role he is to play. Using his own imagination and observation, his understanding of that character may be pursued as he tries to answer questions like—'Who is he? 'Why is he interested in the village?' 'What is his relationship with others in the village?' 'Is he honest?' 'What about his temper?'

In the next stage, after the characters have been explored in some depth, a kind of audition is necessary to find out who can play each of the parts best. The characters are listed. Anyone who would like to play a particular character is asked to improvise a sequence with another volunteer. After a number of trials, those who best portray the roles are chosen after everyone's opinion has been taken.

Next, the sequence is played in order. The group is allowed to intervene, to supplement with dialogue and other details to make the scene realistic. Each sequence may be revised as and when new ideas emerge. The entire story is run through in this manner during the next three or four days. In the process, the 15 or so participants have gained a much deeper insight into the problem they were studying. They have analysed why the problem exists in society, who gains from it and how it needs to be tackled. They have proposed a solution, probably escapist, but, nonetheless, a solution, which can be criticised in group sessions later. This criticism may help them further raise their consciousness. As a matter of fact the process has helped them reflect deeply about issues that are vital to their lives.

Method 2

Another series of improvisations are based on Boal's theories. As already stated in chapter II, his approach, i.e., simultaneous dramaturgy, forum and image theatre, invites the participants to try out various solutions to a given problem.

When *simultaneous dramaturgy* is tried out in a village suggestions normally flow from every corner as the villagers are quick to realise the limitations of any one solution. They will continue looking for a more appropriate solution, examining the problem from different perspectives. In the process, the villagers study the problem by themselves. When it is enacted before them they can tell whether it is realistic or not.

Forum theatre sharpens the ability of the villagers to see hidden structures surrounding their problems. It also deepens the issues, opens up new and unseen areas related to what is being discussed. Thus it becomes an apt method for analysing and studying problems. With this background, let me give a concrete example.

Panjam, a hard working garrulous young Harijan is forthright in his opinions and often quarrels with the people in the village, especially his beautiful wife whom he accuses of flirting with other men. He is a thorn in the flesh of many of the higher caste men. One day his wife's body is found in a nearby abandoned well. A high caste man accuses Panjam of murdering her. The Harijans know that the wife was raped and killed by a high caste man. However, as the law is on the side of the upper castes, Panjam is arrested.

At this juncture the story may be stopped. The villagers may be asked to carry on improvising. Some possible suggestions that may emerge:

1. Save Panjam—but how?
2. It was alright to get rid of Panjam. He was a menace, even for the Harijans. Defeatist?
3. Help Panjam escape from jail and kill the high caste man who caused all this. But, violence only breeds violence.
4. Get Panjam to kill the police. What about further consequence? Is it realistic?
5. Appeal to higher authorities. But do the Harijans really know how to do this? Is there a higher authority that cares for justice?
6. Organize a few rallies to conscientize people in town about the injustice.

As each of these suggestions are performed, the audience judges whether they are realistic or otherwise. They also notice other connected issues, such as the higher castes' fear of lower caste unity, how they exploit the ignorance of the poor, how difficult it is for the poor to get the law on their side and, most important of all the realisation that if the lower castes stand together and demand their rights, their power can be considerable.

By contributing their share to the presentation of the play, the audience eventually realises how each one of them is capable of contributing to useful changes in their society through collective action. This gives them the confidence and stimulation necessary to intervene in the real context from which the play's content was originally drawn.

Image theatre can become an exercise in carrying out change in transforming society. Various aspects of oppression, exploitation, shortages, failures may be represented through images theatre which makes thought visible to the participants. Language, which is at times inadequate in expressing ones innermost feelings, is given a rest and the visual senses take charge. Each of the concepts is given concrete, rather than linguistic expression. For example, if a revolution is to be signified, its form, and how and when it happened, is clearly depicted through the images, whereas in language they may not be specified in the word 'revolution'.

These theories of Boal reassert certain facts that need to be considered. In forum and image theatre the actor/spectator practices a real act even though he does it in a fictional manner. For example, while he rehearses throwing a bomb on the stage he is in fact rehearsing the way a real bomb is thrown. While he acts as a strike organizer he is learning the rudiments of the act of organizing a strike in real life. In effect these forms evoke in the actor/spectator a desire to practise in reality the act he has rehearsed in the theatre. Acting the role creates an uneasy sense of inadequacy which seeks fulfilment through real action.

Boal's unfinished theatre is totally different from the conventional spectacle theatre where, in order to provide entertainment, a fixed ending is provided according to middle class concepts. In the 'unfinished theatre' the people are invited to experiment and rehearse, to try out different ways of combating a problem. In the process they deepen their understanding of the problem and provide solutions that are more congenial to them. The solutions are not presented as final, rather as part of a response to the problem.

An another level, Boal also stresses the fact that great artistic talents are latent in ordinary villagers. There is a belief that academics and scholars alone can have any understanding or appreciation of the arts. They are obviously more exposed to the wider world but the depth of their experience or their understanding of a particular event may not equal that of the villager subjected to everyday exploitation. Art and poetry emerge from such depths of experiences.

Method 3

In the world of the upper classes today television serials have an important place. In a similar manner a serial theatre may be developed among the villagers, too. Serialising a story in several consecutive weeks can help in education. Each week a new group may be asked to continue the story. The purpose is to give the audience more time to decide on the next step through discussions, study and research. This method can be used in conjunction with village workshops. In a few days a play may be improvised, each day completing a scene and posing new problems for the next day. The audience think about these, discuss among themselves and even consult those who know more about the issues involved.

5. Community Performances

It has been said often that the primary aim of Popular Theatre is not to put on a performance—that is the role of professional companies or amateur troupes—but to animate or activate groups. Here theatre is not the well polished play of a professional folk troupe presenting a particular world view. Rather, it is the play-in-the making, performed by the popular classes and providing an ever deeper analysis of their situation, the possibilities of action and the implications of each course of action. If this be the case, what is the place of community performances? From the above section it is clear that in our workshops the villagers are working in three separate groups. None of the methodologies proposed, except the first improvisation, require a final performance, for these take place almost simultaneously with the improvisation.

However, in the case of the first improvisation, where a play is devised gradually, a final performance may take place. The ultimate aim of the final performance is to share with the rest of the community, especially the other two groups, the lessons learnt while improvising the play. It is also an occasion for the group to gather together once again and display the richness of their folk arts, their own talents and their new found confidence. This final performance gives the actors an enhanced confidence and encouragement to continue in this form of play-making. Most important of all, it is an opportunity to open up the issues for wider debate, analysis and action and a post-performance discussion. Other members of the community who were not involved in the improvisation have an opportunity to participate. They can make contributions and reject or support the argument of the play.

It would be ideal if the play ends with a strong challenge to the audience or presents the central question without answering it. This definitely leads to post-performance discussions, which is the next stage. For example, in the Eklavya story from the *Mahabharata* the play may be stopped when the scheming *guru* demands that Eklavya give up his thumb as a gift to him. The audience would be agitated. The team of performers could then ask them what would happen if the event were to take place to-day.

In this way the group is able to re-tell the myth of *Mahabharata* in a way that awakens the consciousness of the people to present-day caste disparities.

If the play is powerful and enlightening and the performers can reach the level of acting skills required, it may be staged as a celebrational play.

6. Post-performance Discussion

Post-performance discussion (PPD) may be conducted in three freshly formed groups, so that each group has a good representation from each of the plays. Newcomers may be introduced to the group for discussions. However, it is best to limit the group size to 20.

The play is by no means an end in itself. Its ultimate purpose is to present a dialectical view of the situation and not a well-rehearsed solution. Before any follow-up action can be taken, there is a gap to be filled and that is where PPD comes in when every issue raised in the play is analysed, debated and a consensus reached to the satisfaction of all. The views offered in the play naturally open up discussions between the players and the villagers. It is in this process of dialogue and discussion that clarifications are sought and alternative suggestions made. This gradually leads to a deeper knowledge or understanding of the people's habits, fears and frustrations. A series of questions that may help organize PPD may run like this:

"Has anyone experienced something like this in their life, or seen or heard of it?"
"Do you agree with what happened in the play?"
"In a similar situation (place yourself in the protagonist's position) what would you do?"
"What can we as a community do about it, here and now?"

Speaking of the PPD, Tar Ahura observed:

The post production dialogues must seek to reach down to the bottom of frustrations and oppressions experienced by the villagers. If follow-up action is to come through this dialogue then it must seek to rationally align individual sufferings and frustrations to one another. This helps to unite them in a common action since they now realize that they are not alone in their predicament. This realization helps to give the community purpose and action. Thus the thing that was started in the drama becomes consolidated and crystallised into action through post performance dialogue. This dialogue tries to open up possibilities of creating a new culture—a culture of challenge as opposed to the culture of silence which has often been used for the intimidation of the seemingly helpless masses.[15]

PPD can also provide the micro-macro link which helps the people to understand the dynamics of oppression nationally and worldwide. Finally and most important of all, it is during these discussions that an organizational base for follow-up action is formed.

PPD may take as long as two days for each of the three plays. These sessions have to be well moderated to get the best out of them. The villagers should take the role of moderators while the animateurs stay behind and watch.

7. Organizing Action

Ultimately the play must lead to action for change. The purpose of PPD is not merely to understand issues but also to plan a concrete method of action. It is also the stage when the animateurs hand over total control to the people, for eventually it is the people who need to work out their own problems. The animateurs can remain in the background. The entire responsibility of continuing action needs to rest on the people themselves. The enthusiasm at the PPD can be very high. However, when it comes to the nitty-gritty of taking steps to counter a situation volunteers may not step forward.

For instance, after a play on caste repression , concrete suggestions may be made to counter it, such as:

1. Bring the accused to book.
2. Organize a demonstration in the village to protest against the action.
3. Counter the abuse of repression by violence, that is, beat up the culprit.
4. Educate the Harijan groups so that such abuses are not taken lying down.
5. Put up banners and posters denouncing the event and the caste system in general, all over the village.
6. Inform the police or higher authorities.

Once all the suggestions are listed the impossible ones can be eliminated. After that steps are taken to carry out the feasible ones. Volunteers may be asked to take up the responsibility of putting some of the suggestions into practice. After the assignments are made, a time limit may be set for certain actions. This is necessary in order to underline the immediacy and importance of the actions concerned. The overall supervision of the assigned tasks may be done by the regional animateur who belongs to the village. However, it is always done in conjunction with the newly formed drama group and the SAG headquarters.

A theatre group needs to be formed at the last stage. It is essential that members of this group be voluntarily elected. Their primary duty is to carry on the process of improvising plays on current and topical issues in the village. They need to involve as many people as possible in these productions. The format of the plays needs to be similar to the workshop designs already set. However, they may occasionally stage a full length play on the village's problems.

8. Follow-Up Action

After the workshops has ended, the euphoria and enthusiasm fade away. If the organization is sound the animateurs can rest assured that the newly formed drama group will succeed. If not, follow-up action may be further encouraged through more short workshops, and animation activities. Often in the follow-up workshops the participants will talk about the difficulties they are facing. For example, one of the persons who has agreed to organize night schools in order to educate the villagers against the caste system might inform the group that he has failed since no one turns up for evening classes. The group may study the situation carefully and suggest steps such as holding classes with a team in an informal way, trying to meet the people in places where they normally assemble. The methodology for teaching too may be made more visual, example-based and drawing more from the local culture. Efforts may be made as a group in these directions. Every suggestion may be role played for further enlightenment. These workshops may also help in sharpening further skills in play acting. The people may be given opportunities to run the workshops, organize group meetings. Some of the follow-up action may be for developing more theatre skills by using locally available media.

The newly formed drama group would need to plan its programmes concretely. For its own survival the members need to devise at least two to three plays a year, based on the relevant problems in the village. The major thrust of the group should be to see that the problems in the village inform and shape their plays. It is of great value if village theatre teams exchange performances with other villages. Occasionally, it could be helpful to organize theatre festivals and competitions at the SAG level.

Financially, the group needs to have sufficient money for its own production. Occasional trips and participation in seminars would require money. All these may be collected either through donations or 'gate-money' for special productions. It is important to submit an annual report to the SAG headquarters.

Periodic evaluation of the work of the group in the presence of a few regional animateurs is necessary for the group's growth. Sincere self-examination coupled with earnest attempts at improving the standard of the group to its desired goal can be mutually beneficial to the villagers, the drama group and the animateurs. The use of role play and improvisations in these sessions can be helpful.

In conclusion, since this form of theatre is people oriented, it can take on the form of a community celebration. The fact that the stories presented are of immediate concern to the audience and have easily identifiable characters, makes them all the more popular. Everyone gains something by participating in it. It is, indeed, a people's theatre where cultural action is geared to awareness building.

II. Festival or Celebration Plays

Celebration plays are discussed below with respect to three areas— content, preparation methodology and the form of presentation.

1. Content

A truly Popular Theatre is one which reflects the villagers' lives, their historical experiences, their cultural, social, political, and economic realities and expresses the needs of the majority of the villagers. It needs to be cumulative, progressive and dynamic in both content and methodology. The religious, political and social history of the people provide examples of courage and hard work that have challenged exploitative situations, re-established cultural identities and breathed new life into oppressed communities. Event in the lives of great men and women like Gandhi, Tilak, Rani Laxmi Bai, Amebdkar, Shivaji, Bhave, Indira

Gandhi, can be dramatized to great effect. Historical events too lend themselves as material for adaptation into plays just as anniversaries and jubilees can be occasions to dramatize the contribution to community growth of an institution or person.

The present-day world situation and the socio-political and economic events in the country can be explained through parables and story-telling forms to celebrate the importance of the events.

Popular Theatre may also be developed from the festivals that are often celebrated in the villages. In an average village, about thirty or so festivals are held in a year. These are occasions when the myths, dances and stories are handed down to succeeding generations. Some of these festivals are important and concern the villagers in a special way. Festivals like, *Chatth* (annual cleansing festival for women), *Raksha Bandhan* (brother-sister relations), *Deepavali* (festival of lights), *Saraswati Pooja* (festival of the goddess of learning) have a deep meaning which, very often is not fully known even to those who celebrate them. The real meaning behind these festivals can be dramatized in the form of theatre.

2. Methodology of Preparation

The preparation needs to be organized in such a way that the entire community is able to participate. The improvisations should be preceded by research into the event. For example, in recreating the story of Amebdkar, emphasizing his indictment of the evils of the caste system could be a worthwhile attempt. The villagers will have to study his life, the socio-political situation at the time, the state of the lower castes, the role of catalysts in his work. As these elements are researched and fused together with the help of animateurs, a clear pattern of presentation may emerge. The important thing is that every one in the village has a part in preparing the play, so that it can truly be called Popular Theatre. In the workshop preceding the production, improvisations of specific move-ments to dramatize village life patterns, social relationships and folk life may be tried in symbols and images, dialogues, choreography, music, poetry and sound effects that are genuinely rural in order to make the production part of the community. The creation of costumes, masks and make-up using objects easily found in the villages like branches of trees, hay, paddy leaves, vegetable dyes—all this adds to their sense of involvement and they are able to relate more meaningfully to the stories in the play.

3. The form

Whatever be the form, the value of devising the play with the community is paramount. If the community devises a play about their lives, and presents it on a stage, in the round or on a street corner, that is fine. But the process of preparing the play is the main thing.

However, to achieve better results, two formats may be attempted: community theatre and the multi-media theatre approach.

A. Community Theatre

Community theatre involves as many people as possible—ideally a cast of hundreds—helped by a small group of professionals. The feeling that a community has been confronted with a slice of their own past and that in the process it may have learned something vital about the turbulent present, is the essence of such performances. To a great extent, the format resembles the indigenous festival, pageant and carnival popular in rural cultures. *Ramlila* of Ramnager is probably one of the best examples of celebrational community theatre, notwithstanding its retrograde content. Some of its elements may be conveniently extended to community theatre anywhere in India. For instance, months before the opening of the 30-day festival theatre till its unfolding, everyone in the community has a part to play in the production. It is staged in the open and spreads out to various parts of the city. In the same way other forms like *Seraikella chhau, bhootha kola, patayani* offer total involvement by the people in the preparation and production of the play. Weeks before the festival the youth are involved in cleaning the streets and the temple, decorating the chariots. All this creates a mood, and gets everyone fully involved. In such a festive atmosphere relationship are built and renewed, community feelings are deepened and important messages are exchanged. Another important aspect of such a festival theatre is the fusing of aesthetic and social behaviour. According to David Edgar,

> the point of a carnival is that it is an event of sufficient size and space to encompass both the most high aesthetic behaviour, and the most untutored communal enthusiasm, not community or art alone, but the two together.[16]

This fusion between the quest for the artistic sensibilities and developmental content is paradigmatic of the two great traditions of 20th century radical theatre: the surreal, the symbolic and the absurd on the one hand and the polemical, didactic and Brechtian on the other. No theatre can wholly ignore either, but in community theatre these can be effectively fused.

In devising a play according to this format there are several elements to be borne in mind. Careful planning is needed to include artistic taste and powerful content and also aspects of audience participation. The emphasis need not be on presenting a full-fledged story. For example, over a number of days, events from the life of a veteran of the freedom movement may be enacted. Thus one night a public address in an open air ground may be enacted. The response of various kinds of people— members of the upper castes, government officials, both British and Indian and soldiers—could be shown. The whole background to the address may be built up with gate-guards, volunteers, leaders of the political parties, representatives from other villages and soldiers patrolling the area. The entire mass of the village could be part of the audience, eventually culminating in a powerful show of unity with emotional outbursts which, of course, the soldiers and guards are there to contain.

The area may be decorated with traditional festoons, umbrellas, and plantain leaves. Masquerades, way-side circuses and other side-show characteristic of the community can add charm and create a carnival atmosphere. Sales and exhibitions of indigenous goods, and other festival attractions may be added. The whole community needs to be well prepared for the event, giving as much as time as possible to ensure the smooth running of the programme. Briefly, the entire programme becomes a community celebration, well planned and executed, which is also an educational experience.

Similar efforts may be made through studying other festivals and myths popular in the village. The role of the elders in supplying oral material may be cardinal. A community theatre workers from Telford noted:

Personal experiences expanded through groups work into an entertaining and socially relevant show can, when performed locally, touch the consciousness of the community and air subjects of concern in a way more effective and memorable than can be done through discussions.[17]

In the same way the political, social and economic history of a country, village or institution can be re-enacted by the villagers after thorough research. These can be appropriate lessons in learning about themselves.

B. The Multimedia Approach

This, too may be done in the same manner but the emphasis is on using the available media. Wherever advanced media like cinerama, holograms, video are available these may be effectively fused together. Alternatively, indigenous media may be utilized carefully to tell a story powerfully. In villages, media like puppetry, story-board, shadow puppets, songs and dance, live acting, mime, shadow play, sound effects, live story-telling etc. may be blended together with a cast of hundreds to narrate a powerful story. Here again, careful planning of details is necessary. It is through making the people responsible for each item that many are able to participate.

Adapting to any form is legitimate if the stress is on supporting effective communication through community participation. A large variety of colourful costumes, make-up, masks and sets may be utilized, but these should not alienate members of the community. It is important that the central theme does not get lost in the midst of grandiose formats.

Ultimately, the people need to control the theatrical process. Thus, as Kidd says.

> the ultimate aim is to place a high priority on organization and collective action by the oppressed, *learning and developing confidence through organization together and taking economic and political action.* Their central goal is the development of people's organization run and controlled by the people themselves.[18]

Postscript

The Development of the Animateur Concept

It is important to realize that recent upsurge in Popular Theatre has been brought about by middle class animateurs. The nationalist movements of Gandhiji, Tilak, Bhave's Bhoodan or the Jharkhand movement may be said to have led the way. If the middle class animateurs have succeeded in capturing the imagination of the masses it is because they have managed to integrate themselves with them and have concentrated on issues that are close to the masses. It looks almost certain that the future of Popular Theatre depends on the continuing and well researched inputs of the animateurs.

However, in India such animateurs are rare. More often they are a dangerous species. Caricaturing the middle class, Dutt observed:

this class is inherently opposed to revolution. For in his world he is respected and does not have to bother about the absence of material or intellectual satisfaction. He suffers from an acute sense of para-noia; an anti-people, anti-proletarian and pretentious standpoint domi-nates his works of art. He is anti-feminist and opposed to change. India's bourgeoisie are arrogant, superstitious thieves who prostrate themselves before the monkey god before going out to rob the workers. Art made to the bourgeoisie's order is trash.[19]

If this is the background, it is irrational to expect the middle classes to produce conscientious animateurs who can help the poorer classes to develop. Their tendency is to teach a few new skills and techniques and leave the area. They think and behave in a certain pattern due to their upbringing. They know only too well that animating the masses is like setting fire to a forest in the dry season and they are frightened of getting burned. In India now, there is only a small minority of academics, activists and artists who have renounced the glories of the elite life to side with the poor. The examples of Sircar, Sharma, Bartholomew and Rao have been given earlier. Nevertheless, the success of Popular Theatre will depend on whether or not the middle class animateurs prove themselves capable of identifying with the masses.

The role of the animateurs is mainly to listen to people and give form to what they say, to try to reconcile the ideas expressed by the various members of the group. They need to do this work with people, never alone.

Qualities Required of Animateurs

Normally the main animateur needs to have an academic education, and even training, from a drama school. In India such people normally yearn after main stream cinema. The regional animateurs may be youngsters who have given up studies, but have a keen interest in theatre. They may be unemployed and wayward with a more than passing interest in films, fashions and city culture. Their exuberance can be gradually

transformed into social awareness and the desire to do something for
their own village.

It may be said that animateurs, besides, being excellent community
builders need to combine the capabilities of a theatre activist (high quality
of efficacious theatre), the ideologue (a socialist's quest for an egalitarian
society) and the developmental worker (one who knows how to use
drama as a tool for conscientization). They also must have a high level of
sensitivity to the feelings of the people in the village. Their sense of
balance and judgment may be called upon in cases of antagonism,
jealousy, stress and clashes in the group. It is of vital importance for them
to act impartially in a reassuring and comforting way so that the dialogical
process can go on unhampered. It is up to them to help develop a collective
standpoint on the issues without giving in to pressure groups, political
parties or the superiority feelings of some members. They need to be keen
judges of the people's interest.

Ultimately, they need to impart all their talents and capabilities to
the people. They have to look for the moment when this transfer can be
made successfully and at this point allow themselves to be fully integrated
with the general will.

Notes

1. Interview with C.G. Krishnasamy. Although without the charisma of the
   founders—Krishnasamy and Prasanna—Samudaya is still active in a small
   way in the villages.
2. Islam, Shamshul, "Theatre vs. the State," *Padgham*, Bombay, 1987.
3. Interview with Niranjan Sen on 12/3/87.
4. Liu, Alan P., *The Use of Traditional Media for Modernization in
   Communist China,* MIT Press, Cambridge, Mass., 1965, p. 87.
5. Mukerjea, Sarbani, in Charu Sahane, "All the Street Is A Stage," *Indian
   Express,* 12/2/86.
6. Dutt, Utpal, *Towards a Revolutionary Theatre,* Calcutta, 1982, p. 132.
7. These are images from Indian mythology and history but, due to overuse
   they have become hackneyed,.
8. In fact the Sanskrit word for drama is *drishya kavya,* meaning visual poetry.
   The generic word for drama is *rupak* meaning 'that which has a visual form'.
9. Davis, R.G., "The San Fancisco Mime Troupe: The First Ten Years," in Tony
   Coult and Baz Kershaw, *Engineers of the Imagination,* The Welfare State
   Manual, Methuen 1983, p. 33.
10. Kizhakekala, K., and Vadassery, J., *The Chamars: Their Beliefs and Prac-
    tices,* St. Xaviers, Patna, 1985, p. 4.
11. D'Abreo, D., *Giving Voice to the People,* manuscript, 1988.

12. Diaz, Bordanev J., as quoted in John Lent, "Increasing Importance of Folk Media in Third World Nations," *Vidura*, Delhi, October 1981.
13. These eight steps have been suggested by groups in Africa, Asia and South America.
14. Kidd, Ross and Byram, Martin, *Participatory Research Project*, Working Paper no. 5, ICAS, Canada, 1980.
15. Ahura, Tar, "Popular Theatre and Popular Development Strategies," in (ed) H. Ndumbe Eyoh; *Hammocks to Bridges, An Experience in Theatre for Development*, Cameroon, 1985, p. 179.
16. Edgar, David, "All Aboard the 'A' Train and Join the Carnival" in *Guardian*, February 1986.
17. Telford Community Theatre brochure, 1985.
18. Kidd, Ross, "Popular Theatre and Non-Formal Education in the Third World: Five Strands of Experience," *International Review of Education*, vol. 30, UNESCO Institute of Education, Hamburg, 1984.
19. Dutt, Utpal, op. cit., p. 132.

Select Bibliography

Abah, O.S,. "Popular Theatre as a Strategy for Education and Development: The Example of Some African Countries," unpublished Ph.D diss., University of Leeds, 1987.

—————"Group Media in Development Communication: The Example of Ram Ram," *Group Media Journal,* March 1987.

Abrams, Tevia, "Tamasha, People's Theatre of Maharastra State," unpublished Ph.D. diss., Michigan State University, 1974.

Amalan, Vima,*A People's Theatre for Community Development in Tamil Nadu,* Sathangai, Madurai, 1987.

AMPO, "Theatre as Struggle: Asian People's Drama," special issue of *AMPO,* 11 (2-3), 1979.

Anbarasan, R.S. (ed.), *People's Movements: A Perspective,* Association for the Rural Poor, Madras, 1982.

Appavoo, J.T., *Folklore for Change,* T.T.S., Madurai, India, 1986.

Asian Action, "Asian Rural Drama," no. 7, 1977.

Atta, K., Beko F., and Russel, R., *Cultural Groups in Action*, Ghana Africa Bureau, German Adult Edn. Assn., 1978.

Awasthy, G.C.,*Broadcasting in India*, Allied Publishers, Bombay, 1965.

Awasthy, Suresh, *Drama, the Gift of Gods: Culture, Performance and Communication in India,* Tokyo, 1983.

Bandyopadhyay, S., "Caste Lost and Caste Regained—Some Aspects of a Sociology of Empirical Research in Village India," in Srinivas M., *Dimensions of Social Change in India,* Indian Council of Social Research, New Delhi, 1978.

Bappa, Salihu, "The Maska Project in Nigeria: Popular Theatre for Adult Education, Community Action and Social Change," *Convergence*, Canada, 14/2, 1981.

Barker, Clive, *Theatre Games: A New Approach to Drama Training*, Methuen, 1977.

Barnow, E. & Krishnaswamy, S., *Indian Film*, Columbia University Press, 1963.

Bartholomew, Rati, "People's Theatre in India", a special issue of *How*, vol. 6, New Delhi, 1983.

Basham, A.L., *A Cultural History of India*, Clarendon Press, Oxford, 1975.

Benegal, Som, *A Panorama of Theatre in India*, Indian Council for Cultural Relations, New Delhi, 1967.

Bernstein, H., "Modernization Theory and the Sociological Theory of Development" *Journal of Development Studies*, 1971.

Beteille, A., "Elites, Status Groups and Caste in Modern India," in Mason P. (ed), *India and Ceylon: Unity and Diversity*, Institute of Race Relations, OUP, London, 1967.

Bharucha, Rustom, *Rehearsals of Revolution, The Political Theatre of Bengal*, The University of Hawaii Press, Honolulu, 1983.

Bhat, G.K., *The Vidhushaka*, New Order Book Co., Ahmedabad, 1959.

Bhattacharya, Malini, "The IPTA in Bengal," *Journal of Arts and Ideas*, Delhi, January 1983.

Bhattacharya, Ashutosh, *Chhau Dances of Purulia*, Rabindra Bharati University Press, Calcutta, 1972.

Biek, Janet, *Hausa Theatre in Niger: A Contemporary Oral Art*, Garland Publishing Inc., New York, 1987.

Biswas, Kalpana, *Political Theatre in Bengal, The Indian People's Theatre Association*, Calcutta, unpublished manuscript, 1982.

Boal, Augusto, *Theatre of the Oppressed*, Pluto Press, London, 1978.

Bowers, Faubion, *Theatre in the East: A Survey of Asian Dance and Drama*, Thomas Nelson and Sons Ltd., London, 1956.

Brandon, J.R., *Theatre in South East Asia*, Harvard University Press, Mass., 1967.

————The Performing Arts in Asia, UNESCO, 1969.

Brandon, Su, *Artists and People*, Routledge and Kegan Paul, London, 1981.

Brecht, Bertolt, *Brecht on Theatre: The Development of an Aesthetic*, (trs.), John Willet, Methuen, London, 1964.

Brook, Peter, *Empty Space*, Hart-Davis MacGibbon, 1977.

——————*A Theatrical Casebook*, complied by David Williams, Methuen, 1988.

Brustein, Robert, *Theatre of Revolt*, Methuen London, 1965.

Burns, Elizabeth, *Theatricality*, Longmans, 1972.

Burns, Kevin, "Theatre for Education and Change: The Catalyst Theatre," *Media in Education and Development*, London, 17/3, 1983 and 18/2, 1984.

Byram, Martin, Moitze F. and Boeren A., "The Report of the Workshop on Theatre for Integrated Development," unpublished report, University of Swaziland, 1981.

Byrski, M.C., *Classical and Folk Dances of India*, Popular Prakashan, Bombay, 1963.

—————— *Concept of Ancient Indian Theatre*, New Delhi, 1974.

Campell, F., "The Practical Reality of Development Communications," *Intermedia*, 12/2, 1984.

Carter, A.F., "Neo-Marxist Approaches of Development and Underdevelopment," *Journal of Contemporary Asia*, 7/1/, 1977.

Chambers, Colin, *Alternative Theatre in Britain*, Methuen, 1979.

Chambulakazi, E. and Mlama, P., "Popular Theatre and Rural Development in Tanzania." paper prepared for a workshop in Bangladesh, University of Dar-es-Salaam, 1982.

Chifunyise, S. et al (eds.), "Theatre for Development: The Chalimbana Workshop," International Theatre Institute, Lusaka, 1980.

Clark, Brian, *Group Theatre*, Pitman, London, 1972.

Clark, Ebun, *Hubert Ogunde: The Making of Nigerian Theatre*, OUP, 1979.

Coggin, P.A., *The Uses of Drama*, Thames and Hudson, London, 1956.

Coult, Tony and Kershaw, Baz, *Engineers of the Imagination: A Welfare State Manual*, Eyre Methuen, London, 1983.

Cuba Review, "Transforming Theatre," no. 4, 1977.

Cultural Collective (South India) Reports, October 1987 & February 1988.

Dall, Frank, "Theatre for Development," *Educational Broadcasting International*, London, December 1980.

Dastoor, Meher, "Between the Acts," *Illustrated Weekly of India*, Bombay, March 23, 1986.

David, E.R. George, *Three Ritual Dramas of India*, Chadwyck Healy, Cambridge, 1986.

Davies, Cecil, W. *Theatre for the People: The Story of the Volksbuhne, German Theatre of the People*, Manchester University, Press, 1977.

Deak, Frantisek, "The Agitprop and Circus Plays of Vladimir Mayakovsky," *TDR*, 17(1), 1973.

Desai, Sudha, R., *Bhavai*, New Order Books, Ahmedabad, 1972.

Dialogue, An occasional bulletin, Madras, 3/1, 1986.

Diaz, Bordanev Juan, "The Need to Respect the Function of the Folk Media," *Instructional Technology Report*, 12/4, 1979.

——————— "Latin American Initiatives in New Approaches to Rural Communication," *Educational Broadcasting International*, 13/4, 1980.

Dissanayake, W., "New Wine in Old Bottles: Can Folk Media Convey Modern Messages?" *Journal of Communication*, 27/2, 1977.

Dorson, R.M., *Folklore to Folklife: An Introduction*, University of Chicago, 1972.

Dutt, Utpal, *Towards a Revolutionary Theatre*, M.C. Sirkar & Co., Calcutta, 1982.

Epskamp, C., "Development Oriented Theatre in Nicaragua Libre," occasional paper, The Hague Centre for the Study of Education in Developing Countries, 1981.

——————— "Training Popular Theatre Trainers: A Case Study of Nigeria," paper presented to the 7th International Conference of Professors in Theatre Research, NUFFIC/CESO, The Hague, 1982.

——————— "Fools for Development, Paper at Arizona State University, 1982.

Epstein, T.S., *Economic Development and Social Change in S. India*, Manchester University Press, 1962.

Erven, Eugene Van, "Beyond the Shadows of Wayang: Liberation Theatre in Indonesia," *New Theatre Quarterly, Cambridge,* 17/5, 1989.

Eyoh, H.N., Amvela, E.Z., Butaka, B., Mbangwana, P., *Hammocks to Bridges: An Experience in Theatre for Development,* BET and Ltd., Yaounde, Cameroon, 1986.

Etherton, Michael, *The Development of African Theatre,* Hutchinson University Library for Africa, London, 1982.

——————"African Theatre and Political Action," King Alfred College, Winchester, 1987.

Fajardo, Brenda, "The Philippine Education Theatre Association," Sonolux Information, 1983.

Fanon, F., *The Wretched of the Earth,* Penguin, Hammondsworth, 1973.

Fernandez, Walter (ed.), *Social Activists and People's Movements,* Indian Social Institute, Delhi, 1985.

——————(ed.), *Voluntary Action and Government Control,* No. 29 in the Monograph Series, ISI, Delhi, 1986.

Finnegan, Ruth, *Oral Tradition in Africa,* Oxford Library of African Literature, 1970.

Foley, K., *Drama for Development: Sundanese Wayang Golek Purwa— An Indonesian Study,* East West Culture Learning Centre Report, 6/1, 1979.

Foster, George, *Traditional Cultures and the Impact of Technological Change,* Harper and Row, New York, 1962.

Freire, Paulo, *Pedagogy of the Oppressed,* Penguin, 1972.

——————*Education for Critical Consciousness,* Penguin, 1972.

——————*Cultural Action for Freedom,* Penguin, 1972.

——————*Education, the Practice of Freedom,* Writers and Readers Publishing Co-operative, London, 1974.

——————*Pedagogy in Process: Letters to Guinea Bissau,* The Seabury Press, New York, 1978.

——————*The Politics of Education: Culture, Power, Liberation,* Macmillan, 1985.

French, Joan, "Organizing Women through Drama in Rural Jamaica," *Ideas and Action,* FAO, Rome, no. 168, 1984.

Gargi, Balwant, *Theatre in India*, Theatre Arts Books, New York, 1966.

——————*Folk Theatre in India*, University of Washington Press, Seattle, 1966.

Gaspar, Karl, *The History of the Growth and Development of Creative Dramatics in Mindanao-Sulu*, Creative Dramatics Training Manual, Davao, Philippines, 1982.

Gheddo, Pierro, *Why is the Third World Poor?*, Orbis Books, New York, 1973.

Ghosh, Manmohan, *Natyasastra*, Asiatic Society of Bengal, Calcutta, 1958.

Gooch, Steve, *Altogether Now*, Methuen, 1984.

Goodlad, J.S.R., *Sociology of Popular Drama*, Heinemann, London, 1971.

Goonatilake, Sussantha, *Crippled Minds: An Exploration into Colonial Culture*, Vikas, N. Delhi, 1982.

Goldstein, Malcolm, *The Political Stage*, OUP, New York, 1974.

Gowda, Anniah, (eds.) *Indian Drama*, seminar papers, University of Bangalore, 1971.

Grace, F.A. and Larkin, Gary, "The Characteristics of Traditional Drama," *Yale Theatre* 8/1, 1976.

—————— *Drama in Development: Its Integration in Non-Formal Education*, Institute of International Studies in Education, Michigan State University, 1982.

Grotowski, Jerzy, *Towards a Poor Theatre*, Eyre Methuen, London, 1975.

Guha Thakurta, P., *Bengali Drama*, Kegan Paul, Trench Tribner and Co., London, 1930.

Hansen, K., "Indian Folk Tradition and Modern Theatre," *Asian Folklore Studies*, 42/1, 1983.

Harrap, J. and Huerta, J., "The Agitprop Pilgrimage of Valdez and El Teatro Campesino", *Theatre Quarterly*, no. 5, 1975.

Hawley, J.S., *At Play with Krishna*, Princeton University Press, 1981.

Hein, Marwin, *The Miracle Plays of Mathura*, Yale University Press, 1972.

Hiro, Dilip, *Inside India Today*, Routledge Kegan Paul, London, 1976.

—————— "The Untouchables of India," CAFOD, London, 1978.

Hodgson, J.R. (ed.), *The Uses of Drama*, Eyre Methuen, London, 1972.

—————— and Richards Ernest, *Improvisation*, Eyre Methuen, London, 1966.

Howard, Roger, "People's Theatre in China Since 1907," *Theatre Quarterly*, 1/4, 1971.

Ideas and Action, FAO, Rome:

> NGOs: no. 165.

> Social Action: nos. 148 & 161.

> Cultural Media: no. 152.

> India: no. 142.

Idoye, E.P., *Popular Theatre and Politics in Zambia: A Case Study of Chikwakwa Theatre*, unpublished diss., Florida State University, 1982.

IEC Newsletter No. 20, On the Use of Indian Folk Theatre for Development, East West Centre, Hawaii, 1975.

Indian Institute of Mass Communication, *Communication and the Traditional Media*, New Delhi, 1981.

Information Centre on Instructional Technology, "Folk Media in Development" Special issue of *Instructional Technology Report* no. 12, Clearing House for Development Communication, Washington, 1975.

Innes, Christopher, *Erwain Piscator's Political Theatre*, Cambridge University Press, 1977.

—————— Holy Theatre : Ritual and the Avant Garde, Cambridge University, 1981.

Itzin, Catherine, *Stages in the Revolution*, Eyre Methuen, London, 1982.

Jackson, Tony, *Teaching Through Theatre*, Manchester University Press, 1980.

Jagran, *Theatre of the Oppressed*, a brochure of the organization, Delhi, 1986.

Jagori, *Nukkad Nukkad Aangan Aangan*, collection of street plays on women's issues with introduction, N. Delhi, 1988.

Jain, L.C., *Grass Without Roots: Rural Development under Government Auspices*, Sage Publications, 1985.

Jan Natya, Quarterly journal on political theatre in India, IPTA (revived), Delhi, May 1987. (4 issues).

Japanese National Commission for UNESCO, *Proceedings of the International Symposium on the Theatre in the East and the West,* Tokyo, 1963.

Jellicoe, Ann, *Community Plays: How to Put Them on,* Eyre Methuen, London, 1987.

Jeyifo, 'Biodun, *The Yoruba Popular Travelling Theatre of Nigeria,* A Nigeria Magazine Publication, Lagos, 1984.

John, J., "A Critique of Action Groups," *Marxist Reveiw,* August 1982.

Johnson, Liz and O'Neil, Cecily, *Dorothy Heathcote: Collected Works on Education and Drama,* Hutchinson, London, 1984.

Jones, C. and Betty, J., *Kathakali: An Introduction to the Dance Drama of Kerala,* University of San Francisco, 1970.

Kamlongera, C.F., *Theatre for Development in Africa with Case Studies from Malawi and Zambia,* German Foundation for International Development, Bonn, 1988.

Kanellos, Nicolas, "Chicano Theatre in the 70s", *Yale Theatre,* no. 1, 1980.

Kapur, Anuradha, *Ramlila of Ramnagar,* unpublished Ph.D diss. Leeds University, 1982.

Kasome, Kabwe, "Theatre and Development" paper presented at the international workshop on *Communication for Social Development,* University of Zambia, 1974.

Kavanagh, R.M., *Theatre and Cultural Struggle in S. Africa,* Zed Books, London, 1985.

Keith, A.B., *The Sanskrit Drama in its Origin, Development Theory and Practice,* London, 1962.

Kerr, David, "Didactic Theatre in Africa," Harward University, Review 51 (1), 1981.

————"Performers, Audiences, and the Aesthetics of Transformation: Theatre and Health Innovation in Malawi," *New Theatre Quarterly,* Cambridge University Press, 1988.

Kidd, Ross, "Liberation and Domestication: Popular Theatre and Non-Formal Education in Africa," *Educational Broadcasting International,* London, March 1979.

——————— "Indigenous Performers Take Back their Show", Report of Popular Workshop, Ontario, 1982.

——————— "Folk Media, Popular Theatre and Conflicting Strategies for Development in the Third World," 1982.

——————— "Popular Theatre and Popular Struggle in Kenya: The Story of Kamiriithu," *Race and Class*, 24/3, 1983.

——————— " A Testimony from Nicaragua: An Interview with Nidia Bustos, the Co-ordinartor of Mecate, the Nicaraguan Farm Worker's Movement," *Studies in Latin American Popular Culture*, vol. 2, 1983.

——————— "Didactic Theatre", *Media in Education and Development*, March 1983.

——————— "Popular Theatre and Non-Formal Education in the Third World: Five Strands of Experience," *International Review of Education*, vol. 30, UNESCO Inst. of Education, Hamburg, 1984.

——————— and Kumar K., "Co-Opting Freire—A Critical Analysis of Pseudo-Freirian Adult Education," *The Economic and Political Weekly*, January, 1981.

——————— and Rashid Mamunnur, "Theatre by the People, for the People, and of the People: Peoples Theatre and Landless Organizing in Bangladesh," *Social Action*, 34/2, ISI, N. Delhi, 1984.

——————— and Byram Martin, "De-Mystifying Pseudo-Freirian Non-Formal Education," *Canadian Journal of Developing Studies*, 3(2), 1983.

——————— and Colletta Nat (eds), *Traditions for Development: Indigenous Structures and Folk Media in Development*, German Foundation for International Development, Bonn, 1982.

Kirby, E.T., *UR-Drama—The Origins of Theatre*, New York University Press, 1975.

Konow, Stan, *The Indian Drama*, (trans) Ghosal, S.N., Calcutta, 1969.

Kraai, Z. et al., "Popular Theatre and Participatory Research," no. 12, Popular Theatre Committee, University of Botswana, 1979.

Krishnan, Prabha, "Catalyst Theatre," *Indian Journal of Youth Affairs*, New Delhi, March 1980.

Labad, Lutgard, "Towards a Curriculum for a People's Theatre," *Sonolux Information*, Munich, No. 6, 1982.

Laedza Batnani, a handbook, University of Botswana, 1977.

Lambert, Pru, *Popular Theatre as Conscientization: An Effective Approach to Non-Formal and Social Education for Rural Development*, M.A. diss., Reading University, 1981.

Lee, Philip (ed), *Communication for All: The Church and the New World Information and Communication Order*, World Association of Christian Communication, London, 1984.

Leis, R.A., "Popular Theatre and Development in Latin America," *Educational Broadcasting International*, March 1979.

Lent, John A., "Grassroots Renaissance: Folk Media in the Third World," *Media Asia*, 1982.

Lerner, D., *The Passing of a Traditional Society*, Free Press, New York, 1958.

Levi, Sylvian, *Le Theatre Indien*, (trans.) Narain Mukherjea, Writer's Workshop, Calcutta, 1978.

Loveland, C.A., *Communication in India: Mass Media and Cultural Media*, unpublished Ph.D. diss., Duke University, 1975.

Luzuriarga, Gerardo, *Popular Theatre for Social Change in Latin America*, University of California, 1978.

Mackie, Robert (ed), *Literacy and Revolution*, a critique of Freire, Pluto Ideas in Progress, London, 1985.

Mahoney, H.R., *The Malaysian Information Department's Rural Communication Programme*, unpublished paper, School of Communication and Theatre, Temple University, Philadelphia, 1979.

Malik, M., *Traditional Forms of Communication and the Mass Media in India*, no. 13 of the 'Communication and Society' series of UNESCO, Paris, 1983.

Masani, M., *Broadcasting and the People*, National Book Trust, New Delhi, 1976.

Mathur, J.C., *Drama in Rural India*, Asia Publishing House, London, 1964.

McBride, Sean; *Many Voices, One World*, Kogan Page, London; unpublished, New York; UNESCO, Paris; WACC, London, 1980.

McGrath, J., "Theory and Practice of Political Theatre," *Theatre Quarterly*, 9/1979.

————— A Good Night Out: Popular Theatre, Audience, Class, Form, Eyre Methuen, London, 1985.

Media Development, XXXV/3 World Association of Christian Churches (WACC), London, 1988.

Michalsky, Y., "The 'Active Spectator' Takes the Floor: An Interview with Augusto Boal", Theatre Yale, 12/1, 1980.

Mies, M., "A Peasant's Movement in Maharastra—Its Development and Perspectives", Journal of Contemporary Asia, 6/2, 1976.

Moffat, M., Untouchable Community in South India, Princeton University Press, 1979.

Mukherjea, Sushil Kumar, The Story of the Calcutta Theatre 1953-1980, Calcutta, 1982.

Mukhopadhyaya, D., Lesser Known Forms of Performing Arts in India, Minimax, New Delhi, 1976.

Murdock, G. "Radical Drama, Radical Theatre" Media, Culture and Society, 2/1980.

Mwansa, Dickson, "Third World Canadian Popular Theatre Exchange," Ideas and Action, FAO, Rome, no. 146, 1982.

————— and Kidd R., "We Will Turn the Whole World Upside Down," a Report on the Third World Canada Popular Theatre Exchange: Thunder Bay Workshop on Community Animation Theatre, 1985.

Myrdal, Gunnar, Asian Drama: An Inquiry into the Poverty of Nations, vols. I, II, III, Pantheon, New York, 1968.

Namboodiripad, EMS, "Culture as an Element of Superstructure," from Kurien K.M., (op cit.) 1975.

Neog, Maheswar, Shanakardeva and His Times, Gauhati, 1975.

Nettlesford, R.M., Cultural Action and Social Change: The Case of Jamaica, Institute of Jamaica, Kingston, 1979.

Nijera Kori, Annual Report, Dhaka, 1987.

Obafemi, Olu, "Political Perspectives in Popular Theatre in Nigeria," Theatre Research International, 7/3, London, 1982.

Ogunba, Oyin and Trela, Ahiola (eds), Theatre in Africa, Ibadan University Press, 1978.

Ogunbiyi, Yemi (ed), Drama and Theatre in Nigeria: A Critical Source Book, Nigeria Magazine Publication, Lagos, 1981.

O'Hanlon, R., "Maratha History as Polemic: Low Caste Ideology and Political Debate in Late 19th Century Western India," *Modern Asian Studies*, 171, 1983.

Omvedt, G., "The Sathyashodhak Samaj and Peasant Agitation," *Economic and Political Weekly*, Bombay, 844, 1973.

—————"Jyotirao Phule and the Ideology of Social Revolution in India," *The Economic and Political Weekly*, 1974.

—————"India, the IMF and Imperialism Today," *Journal of Contemporary Asia*, 12/2, 1982.

—————"Non-Brahmins and Nationalists in Pune," *Economic and Political Weekly*, Annual Number, 9/1984.

Pandey, Shashi, "Role of Voluntary Action in India", *South Asia Bulletin*, 4/2, 1984.

Pani, Narinder, *Staging a Change*, A Samudaya Publication, Bangalore, 1979.

Pani, Rajni, "A Maiden on the Street: An Experience of Street Theatre," Jyoti Niwas College, Bangalore, 1983.

Parmar, Shyam, *Traditional Folk Media in India*, Geka Books, New Delhi, 1975.

Peacock, J.L., *Rites of Modernization: Indonesian Proletarian Drama*, University of Chicago Press, 1969.

Piscator, Erwin, *Political Theatre*, Avon Publishers of Brad, Camelot, Discus Books, 1963.

Popular Theatre Workshop Handouts, Koitta, 1982 and Madras, 1986.

Pradhan Sudhi, *Marxist Cultural Movements: Chronicles and Movements*, vols. I and II are on IPTA. National Book Agency, Calcutta, 1979.

Pronko, L.C., *Theatre East and West*, University California, Press, 1967.

Proshika, "Popular Theatre and Organizing in Bangladesh," Annual Report of Proshika Theatre Unit, Dhaka, 1980.

Publications Division (Government of India), *Indian Drama*, Ministry of Information and Broadcasting, New Delhi, 1956.

Raghav, Bellary, *The South Indian Stage and other Lectures*, Hyderabad, 1976.

Raghavan, M.D., *Folk Plays and Dances of Kerala*, Trichur, 1947.

Raha, Kironmoy, *Bengali Theatre*, National Book Trust, New Delhi, 1978.

Rangacharaya, Adya, *The Indian Theatre*, National Book Trust, New Delhi, 1971.

Ranganath, H.K., *Using Folk Entertainment to Promote National Development*, UNESCO, 1980.

Rao, M.S.A., "Themes in the Ideology of Peasant Movements," in Malik S.C., *Dissent, Protest and Reform in Indian Civilization*, Indian Institute of Advanced Studies, Simla, 1977.

Rao, Pooranchandra, *To the Rural Masses Through Street Play*, Cultural Forum, RDAS, Secunderabad, 1982.

——————"In Search of an Alternative Theatre of Rural Masses," *Sampreshan*, National Council of Development Communication, Varanasi, 1986.

Rao, Y.V.L., *Communication and Development*, University of Minnesota Press, Minneapolis, 1966.

Rea, Kenneth, "Theatre in India, the Old and the New," 3 parts, *Theatre Quarterly*, 8 (32), 1974.

Red Letters, Augusto Boal and His Work, London, 1985.

Report of the Delhi Rural Broadcasting Scheme—1944-45 (War Series L/I/1/967), India Office Library, London.

Richmond, Farley, "The Social Role of Theatre in India," *Sangeet Natak*, New Delhi, 25/1972.

——————"The Political Role of Theatre in India," *Educational Theatre Journal*. 25/3, 1975.

Rogers, E.M., *Modernization Among Peasants: The Impact of Communication*, Holt, Reinhart and Winston, New York, 1969.

——————'Communication and Development: The Passing of Dominant Paradigm," *Communication Research* (C) 3, 1976.

——————and Shoemaker E.F., *Communication of Innovation A Cross-Cultural Approach*, Free Press, New York, 1971.

Roose-Evans, James, *Experimental Theatre from Stanislavsky to Peter Brook*, Routledge and Kegan Paul, London, 1973.

Roy, M., "Developing Media in Developing Countries: A Historical Review of Policies", *Gazette*, 24/1978.

Ryan, G.T., *Stage Left: Canadian Workers' Theatre*, 1929-40. Simon and Pierre, Toronto, 1985.

Samar, D.L., "Rashdhari Khyal", *Sangeet Natak*, New Delhi, 1981.

Samuel, R., MacColl, E. and Cosgrove, S., *Theatres of the Left: Workers Theatre Movements in Britain and America*, Routledge and Kegan Paul, London, 1985.

Sarcar, Sanjib (ed), *Popular Theatre—People's Theatre*, three articles on Popular Theatre, Centre for Communication and Culture, Calcutta, 1985.

Schramm, W., *Mass Media and National Development*, Stanford University Press, California, 1964..

————and Ruggels, "How Mass Media Systems Grow," in Lerner and Schramm (eds), *Communication and Change in Developing Countries*, University of Hawaii, 1967.

————and Lerner D., *Communication and Change in the Developing Countries Ten Years After*, East West Centre, Hawaii, 1976.

Schechner, Richard, *Environmental Theatre*, Hawthorn, New York, 1972.

————*Performative Circumstances from the Avant Garde to Ramlila*, Seagull Books, Calcutta, 1983.

————*Between Theatre and Anthropology*, University of Pensylvania, PA, 1985.

Sedley, Marian, *Theatre as Revolutionary Activity: The Escambray in Cuba, The Second Decade,* (eds), John and Peter Griffiths, Writers and Readers Co-operative, London, 1979.

Sethi, H., "Alternative Development Strategies: A Look at Some Micro Experiments," *Economic and Political Weekly*, Special Number, 13/1978.

————"The Immoral Other: Debate Between Party and Non-Party Groups," *The Economic and Political Weekly*, March 2, 1985.

Shank, Theodore, *American Alternative Theatre*, Macmillan, London, 1982.

Shankarapillai, G., *Theatre of the Earth is Never Dead*, University of Calicut, 1986.

Sharma, Tripurari, Report of a Workshop held at Gandhi Memorial Leprosy Foundation, Purulia, 1984.

—————Report of a Workshop with the National School of Drama (NSD) Repertory Company, 1984.

—————"Drama as a Medium of Change" in *People's Action*, New Delhi, July 1987.

—————and Krishnamoorti, Lakshmi, "Diary of a Theatre Workshop," Sucheta Kriplani Siksha Niketan, Jodhpur, 1984.

Shekhar, Indu, *Sanskrit Drama: Its Origins and Decline*, E.T. Brill, Leiden, 1960.

Sinha, Arbind K., *Mass Media and Rural Development*, Concept Publications., New Delhi, 1985.

Singer, M., *When a Great Tradition Modernizes*, Pall Mall Press, London, 1975.

Singh, C.P., *Bharatiya Natya Parampara* (Hindi) in *Nagari Pracarini Patrika*, Benares, 1958.

Singh, Gurcharan, "Theatre as a Mode of Communication," paper presented at a Seminar on *Communication and Society*, Nehru Memorial Museum and CENDIT, New Delhi, July 1987.

Singh, Sukumar, "Popular Theatres and Development," Mass Education, Calcutta, 1979.

Sircar, Badal, *Third Theatre*, Naba Granth Kutir, Calcutta, 1973.

—————*Changing Language of Theatre*, New Delhi, 1982.

—————*Three Plays : Bhoma, Procession, Stale News*, Seagull, Calcutta, 1984.

Smith, Anthony D., *The Geopolitics of Information : How Western Culture Dominates the World*, Faber and Faber, London, 1980.

Southern, Richard, *The Seven Ages of Theatre*, Faber and Faber, London, 1973.

Srampickal, Jacob, *Understanding Communication Media*, Asian Trading Corporation, Bangalore, 1982.

—————and White, Robert, *Communication Research Trends*, CSCC, London, IX/1 and 2, 1988.

Spellman, J.W., "Development Through Indigenous Resources," Lecture at Indian Culture Development Centre, Madras, 1982.

Srivastav, Sahabla, *Folk Culture and Oral Tradition*, Abinav Publications, New Delhi, 1978.

Stourac, Richard and McCreery, Katherine, *Theatre as Weapon: Workers' Theatre in Britain, Germany and USSR 1917-1934* Routledge and Kegan Paul, London, 1986.

Szanto, George, *Theatre and Propaganda,* University of Texas Press, 1978.

Tapper, B.E., "An Enactment of Perfect Morality: The Meaning and Social Context of a South Indian Ritual Drama" in Mayer A.C. (ed.), *Culture and Morality,* OUP, New Delhi, 1981.

The Drama Review, New York.

——————Indigenous Theatre: T. 64 (1975).

——————Indian Theatre: T. 50 (1971), T. 82 (1979).

——————Popular Entertainment, Performance and Avant Garde, T. 61 (1974).

——————Theatre and Therapy T. 69 (1976).

——————Political and Development Theatre L.T. 66(1975), T. 73 (1977).

—————— Performance Theory T. 82 (1979).

The Rural Poor, Association for the Rural Poor, Madras, three irregular issues, 1983-86.

Thomas, P.N., *Communication and Development in India,* unpublished diss., University of Leicester, 1987.

Third World Popular Theatre Newsletter, edited and published irregularly by various activists from different centres. Four issues have appeared from founding year (1978).

Turner, Victor, *Drama Fields and Metaphors: Symbolic Action in Society,* Cornel University Press, New York, 1974.

——————*From Ritual to Theatre: The Human Seriousness of Play,* Performing Arts, Journal Publications, New York, 1982.

Upadhyaya, A.K., "Class Struggle in Rural Maharastra," *Journal of Peasant Studies,* 7, 2, 179-80.

Usmaini, Renate, Second Stage: *The Alternative Theatre Movement in Canada,* University of British Columbia Press, Vancouver, 1983.

Varadpande, M.L., *Traditions of Indian Theatre,* Abhinav Publications, New Delhi, 1978.

Varma, K.M., *Natya Nritta Nriyta,* Orient Longmans, Calcutta, 1937.

Vatsyayan, Kapila, *Traditional Indian Theatre: Multiple Streams,* National Book Trust, New Delhi, 1980.

Venkatramani, H. "Silencing Protest," *India Today,* October, 31, 1984.

Wa Thiong'o, Ngugi, *Decolonizing the Mind,* James Curry, London, 1981.

———————— "Women in Cultural Work: Kamirithu People's Theatre in Kenya," *Current Development Dialogue,* Geneva, 14/2, 1983.

Weber, B.N. and Heinen, H. (eds.), *Bertolt Brecht: Political Theory and Literary Practice,* University of Georgia Press, 1980.

Wells, Henry W., *The Classical Drama of India,* Asia Publishing House, London, 1963.

White, Robert, "Communication: Popular Language of Liberation," *Media Development,* WACC, London, 3/27, 1980.

Winnicott, D.W., *Playing and Reality,* Tavistock Publications, London, 1971.

Wolf, Janet, *The Social Production of Art,* Macmillan, London, 1981.

Yajnik, R.K., *The Indian Theatre,* George Allen and Unwin, London, 1933.

Zarilli, P.B., *The Kathakali Complex : Actor, Performance and Structure,* New Delhi, 1984.

Index